Praise for the Nauti series

"The Nauti series is one that absolutely no one should miss. The characters are brilliant, sexy, and real, while the high-octane action and soul-gripping plots have you on the edge of your seat. I loved it!"
—Fresh Fiction

"Completely blown away by this surprising story. I could not put [it] down . . . and before I knew it, I had read this entire novel in one sitting . . . A smoldering hot tale of secret passion and erotic deceptions."
—Romance Junkies

"Wild and thrilling."
—The Romance Studio

"The sex scenes are, as always with Leigh's books, absolutely sizzling."
—Errant Dreams Reviews

"Heated romantic suspense."
—*Midwest Book Review*

continued . . .

More praise for

Lora Leigh

and her novels

"Leigh draws readers into her stories and takes them on a sensual roller coaster."　　　　　　　—Love Romances & More

"Will have you glued to the edge of your seat."
　　　　　　　　　　　　　　　—Fallen Angel Reviews

"Blistering sexuality and eroticism . . . Bursting with passion and drama . . . Enthralls and excites from beginning to end."
　　　　　　　　　　　　　　　—Romance Reviews Today

"A scorcher with sex scenes that blister the pages."
　　　　　　　　　　　　　　　—A Romance Review

"A perfect blend of sexual tension and suspense."
　　　　　　　　　　　　　　　—Sensual Romance Reviews

"Hot sex, snappy dialogue, and kick-butt action add up to outstanding entertainment."　　　—*RT Book Reviews* (Top Pick)

"The writing of Lora Leigh continues to amaze me . . . Electrically charged, erotic, and just a sinfully good read!"
　　　　　　　　　　　　　　　—Joyfully Reviewed

"Wow! . . . The lovemaking is scorching."
　　　　　　　　　　　　　　　—Just Erotic Romance Reviews

Nauti Angel

Lora Leigh

BERKLEY SENSATION
NEW YORK

BERKLEY SENSATION
Published by Berkley
An imprint of Penguin Random House LLC
375 Hudson Street, New York, New York 10014

Copyright © 2017 by Lora Leigh

Library of Congress Cataloging-in-Publication Data

Names: Leigh, Lora, author.
Title: Nauti angel / Lora Leigh.
Other titles: Naughty Angel
Description: First edition. I New York : Berkley Sensation, 2017. I Series: Nauti girls ; 4
Identifiers: LCCN 2017028072 (print) I LCCN 2017030160 (ebook) I
ISBN 9780399583865 (ebook) I ISBN 9780399583858 (trade)
Subjects: I BISAC: FICTION / Romance / Contemporary. I FICTION / Romance / Suspense.
I FICTION / Contemporary Women. I GSAFD: Love stories.
Classification: LCC PS3612.E357 (ebook) I LCC PS3612.E357 N35 2017 (print) I
DDC 813/.6—dc23
LC record available at https://lccn.loc.gov/2017028072

First Edition: November 2017

Printed in the United States of America
. 1 3 5 7 9 10 8 6 4 2

Cover photos: couple © Claudio Marinesco; lake © Leventina; sky © Anthony Heflin
Cover design by Rita Frangie

Nauti Angel

PROLOGUE

Iraq

Twenty years ago

She was only three years old. She wasn't supposed to be outside alone without her momma or daddy, or her aunt. Beth knew that. As she stumbled along the dark, deserted street, she knew she was going to get in trouble. Her momma promised to take away all of her cartoons if she ever wandered off alone.

But her daddy hadn't woken up after he closed his eyes, just like Jenny. They were so still and white, and she knew they were gone forever like Momma told her Grandma and Grandpa were gone forever.

The place where she was waiting for Momma was so scary now. It was just big rocks and pipes and it was so hard to breathe in the small space where she'd awakened.

She needed her momma.

She was just a little girl. She wasn't supposed to be by herself, especially in this place where she didn't understand what people were saying and the sound of cries and angry voices seemed to echo around her.

The houses didn't look like the ones at home either. They were little and rough-looking. The road was dirty and uneven and there weren't any cars moving on it. She hadn't even seen anyone. She hadn't heard a single sound that made sense.

Where was her momma?

Her arm hurt, and her pretty white dress was so dirty. It was hard to walk. Every step she took made her leg hurt worse and she'd lost one of her little white sandals.

She still had Binny, though.

The big teddy bear her momma had put the straps on so he would be easier to carry rode right on her back like he was supposed to. And she knew her momma's favorite knife was still in the pocket sewn into Binny's belly.

The knife would keep her safe. It had always kept her momma safe; now it would keep her safe.

Stopping in the middle of the street she stared around the night again, wondering why everything was so strange.

Everything was dirty. The houses had boards on the windows and there were no lights inside. And she'd yelled for her momma so many times her throat hurt, but no one had answered.

"I don' know where to go, Binny," she whispered, sniffing back her tears. "I want Momma."

Pushing the hair back from her face she wished she hadn't lost the bow that had kept it out of her eyes. It was hard to keep pushing her hair back, and she was so tired. She just wanted to lie down. She just wanted everything to stop hurting.

She wanted her momma.

As she looked around, she suddenly stilled, blinking at the dark shape that edged from an alley, watching her curiously.

The dog was big. Probably bigger than any dog she'd ever seen. Black and brown, its dark eyes watching her quietly for long moments before he eased closer, sniffing at her.

"Don't bite me," she whispered, so tired she didn't have the strength to run away from him as he tilted his head and made a snuffling dog sound.

He was so big she could probably ride on his back if she wasn't so tired. As it was, all she could do was shudder when he came closer, sniffed at her hair, then her face. His nose was wet and cold when he nudged her arm, pushing her toward the alley he'd stepped from as he whined at her.

She wanted to find her momma, not play with a dog that was too big for her to run away from.

She tried to push him away, but he gripped her dress in his big white teeth, whined again, and tugged at her harder.

Maybe he knew where her momma was. Maybe her momma had sent him after her.

The dog whined again, pulling her into the dark, narrow road as the sound of voices could be heard in the distance. They sounded angry, and Beth couldn't understand them. They frightened her as bad as the dark did.

The dog whined again and pulled at her dress more firmly, almost making her fall.

"I'm coming, you big dog," she muttered, feeling a little angry herself and so scared.

Where was her momma? Why hadn't she wanted to come get her?

She forced herself to follow the dog's urging, putting one foot in front of the other even though it hurt so bad and her head was feeling funny again.

The dog kept walking and walking and making her walk with him. When she just wanted to sit down, he growled at her. The sound was a warning and she was so scared he would bite her if she didn't keep walking.

Down one narrow street then another until she felt so confused, so tired.

Head down, following the dog's nudges and tugs at her dress, she concentrated on just walking, just moving. The dog wouldn't let her do anything else.

"Brute, what do you have here?"

The man's low, comforting voice had her freezing, fear causing a sob to escape her throat. Hope making her shudder because she could understand what he was saying.

Beth stopped, still trembling as she forced herself to look up. And up.

The dog rubbed against the big man's leg, whining in happiness as the man knelt down to her, and still he was very tall. But she understood him.

"I want my momma," she whispered, tears falling from her eyes even though she tried not to cry. "Please, I want my momma. . . ."

Then, just like at the hotel, everything went completely, silently black.

J. T. Calloway caught the tiny, delicate girl before she hit the ground, shock tearing through him in that single second before he straightened and ducked into the doorway of the hut where he and his family had taken shelter, the overgrown war dog he'd trained himself as a pup, Brutus, following silently behind him. He'd have to remember to get the Rottweiler a steak as reward for what he'd brought back with him. Waiting in the hut were the two men that fought with him, their small force covert and highly lethal. And for the moment, they were stuck in the chaos that was Iraq, unable to fly out for several more hours.

"J.T.?" His wife, Mara, rushed to him, her expression concerned as she caught sight of his small burden. "Oh my God. J.T.?"

There was no mistaking the little girl's blond hair, her bloodstained face, or the fact that her arm was broken.

"She's been beaten." Mara's voice was flat as J.T. laid the little girl on the cot in the corner of the room. "This world is full of monsters."

"She's a blond child in a war-torn city," he snorted, moving to put water on the small propane burner they hadn't yet packed before turning to the two men now standing on alert at the doorway. "I'm surprised she managed to escape whoever had her."

"Small group coming this way. Iraqi, chattering about that damned hotel," one of the men muttered as they stood next to the wood barrier, their automatic rifles held ready.

That damned hotel.

It had exploded earlier that day, the rubble creating a mess several blocks over. Thankfully, it seemed to be deserted at the time.

"The water, J.T.," Mara demanded. "And I need you over here. She's in bad shape."

He hadn't completed his medical degree, but his education still served him, even fifteen years after dropping out of college.

"Did she say anything?" his wife demanded as J.T. placed the metal pan of steaming water next to her.

"'I want my momma,'" he answered her. "That was all she said."

"Poor little angel," she whispered, brushing the bloody, tangled hair back from the child's face as J.T. did a quick examination.

Her arm was definitely broken, but her leg was likely fractured, too. How the child had actually walked was beyond him.

The damage to her tiny body was horrifying.

"We can't leave her here." The distress in Mara's voice was more a demand. A statement of intent.

"We're not leaving her," he promised. "We'll take her out with us. I have enough contacts here. I'll hear if anyone's searching for a missing American girl."

That didn't mean he'd tell Mara if he learned one was actually missing.

"Wake Tracker and Chance and finish packing," he told her as he quickly began placing a splint on the kid's arm. "I'll make sure she can make the flight, then we'll pull out. I don't want anyone to see her when we leave. We'll figure out who she is later."

Mara didn't question him, didn't object. She jumped to her feet instead and rushed to get the boys ready to leave. The girl would have to be ready to travel, J.T. decided. They couldn't stay here any longer; their mission was over. And if he wanted to keep the child Brutus had found wandering in the streets, then no one could know she'd ever been there.

Whoever had so carelessly lost her would just have to do without her, because she was his and Mara's now.

She was their Angel.

ONE

Somerset, Kentucky

Twenty years later

"Angel. Angel, you're here!" Bliss Mackay jumped up from the large towel she was lying on and ran to the young woman making her way along the grassy bank from the marina store.

She carried a pizza box and a cooler full of drinks toward Bliss and the teenagers. Beyond Angel, through the large glass window of the store, Bliss could see her parents, Chaya and Natches, watching. And Bliss could see the frown on her mother's face and the confusion on her father's.

Behind her, her cousins Annie, Laken, and Erin stood up from their own towels, all of them hurrying to meet the young woman at the wooden picnic table beneath the shade of a large dogwood tree.

"I have arrived," Angel agreed, the smile that lit up her face much different than the one she always gave the adults.

It wasn't the pizza that caused Bliss and her cousins to greet

Angel so enthusiastically, though. It was Angel herself. She liked
to talk about girly stuff, even though she wasn't the least bit girly.
But she could talk about fixing cars and motorcycles and show
the girls how to protect themselves and fend off the sometimes
too-excited boys that decided they wanted more than just a kiss.

She knew cool stuff. Like what a desert wind felt like, or the
scent of a jungle and how the smell of the different blooms
would only tease and make a person want to smell it more. She
had been places and seen things Bliss only dreamed of going and
seeing.

As Angel placed the food and drinks on the table and turned
to them, Bliss threw her arms around her in a tight hug, knowing the pizza must mean Angel would be leaving, if not today
then the next morning. And she couldn't help but hold on tighter
for a moment as she made herself hold back all the things she
wanted to say.

"I'm going to miss you so much," Angel whispered a second
before she pulled back. She hugged the other girls and said the
same thing.

Even though she said the same thing to her cousins, Bliss
knew Angel meant the words more for her than the others. She
knew it and couldn't say anything because she was never certain
why. It was just a truth that was there, like she and Angel were
best friends all their lives, despite their eight-year age difference.

"I'm starting to hate pizza," the youngest girl, Erin, sighed
as they all sat at the table. "It always means you're going to
leave."

"Yeah, we hate it when you leave, Angel," Annie, older than
Bliss by a few weeks, agreed as she glanced away for a moment.

"It won't be for long," Angel promised, but Bliss saw the sadness in her eyes. "I'll be back."

That didn't mean they'd get to see her. Bliss had overheard her mother telling her father how she didn't trust Angel. She thought Angel was hiding too many secrets.

She might be, Bliss thought at the time, but her mom didn't have to know everything about everyone. Sometimes people liked to keep their secrets.

Bliss was silent as she ate a slice of the pizza and sipped at the iced tea Angel had brought.

"Angel, you should talk to Dad and get hired on with the police," Erin stated as they finished their pizza. "I heard Sam Bryce telling Dad he should ask you about it."

Bliss saw Angel's surprise before she gave a roll of her eyes.

"Sam probably just wants to flirt with her." Annie giggled. "She told Aunt Zoey that Angel was hot."

"Good God," Angel muttered, frowning a little as she brushed back the front of her hair in the same way Bliss often saw her mom do when she was really nervous. "That woman scares even me."

Bliss laughed at the comment. Sam was really attractive, and Bliss had overheard several of Aunt Zoey's friends talking about how "tempting" she could be.

Bliss had overheard another conversation, too. One where her mom had told Erin's dad, the chief of police, that someone needed to find out what Angel was hiding.

There was no way Uncle Alex would hire Angel, even if she wanted to work there.

"I'd get arrested if I tried to work with Sam Bryce," Angel assured them all. "I'd end up shooting her just because she can be so irritating."

It was a friendly threat, but one that assured Bliss that Angel had no intentions of working on the police force.

"Sam's fun," Laken assured her. "She told Dad to suck her dick the other day and made him blush all the way to the roots of his hair. Mom was laughing so hard I thought she was going to bust a gut or something."

They were all laughing then. They had all heard the comment, watched Uncle Dawg rub at the back of his neck, mutter something about damned smart-assed women, then stalk away. Even Bliss's mom and dad had laughed at it.

The conversation flowed around the table until several girls from school drew her cousins' attention and they excused themselves to go talk to them. Bliss stayed, staring down at the pizza she hadn't finished and wishing it didn't hurt so bad to tell Angel good-bye.

"Everything okay, Bliss?" Angel asked her, her voice softer and echoing with something Bliss just didn't understand.

"You're going to go fight again," Bliss muttered, shooting Angel an accusing look. "That's what you do, isn't it? You get paid to fight other people's wars."

Angel looked confused, hurt. "I didn't lie to you, Bliss. I get paid to rescue people. Sometimes those people are caught in other people's wars, but it's not the war I'm fighting."

Bliss clenched her teeth for a moment, feeling angry, sad, and fed up with how angry her mother always stayed with Angel.

"Why don't you just tell my mom whatever it is she wants to know so she'll stop being so worried about us being friends?" she demanded. "I don't make friends easy, Angel. I don't want to lose one."

That was her fear. That one day, Angel just wouldn't come back because Bliss's mom would forbid it.

Surprise flashed in Angel's eyes, the blue contacts she wore giving her gaze an oddly shattered appearance. Her mom was right; Angel hid too much of herself and who she was, even for Bliss's comfort.

"Telling your momma my secrets wouldn't do anything to help the situation, Bliss." Angel looked away and brushed back the front of her hair again, even though it hadn't yet fallen around her eyes.

Breathing out hard Angel drew the knife from the sheath at her belt and began cutting up the empty pizza box so it would fit easily in the mouth of the trash can.

It was the knife that silenced Bliss's protests.

All she could do was stare at it, her entire world centering on that knife. The bone handle, weathered with age and the many hands it had passed through. Silver capped the bone, untarnished and gleaming from the constant handling and careful polishing. It was the blade that had her heart racing in her chest, had her wanting to scream, to deny, to demand explanations.

Because as Angel paused, holding the knife against the cardboard, the inscription on the blade jumped out and seared her brain:

Godspeed

It was right there, a little darker in the grooves, easy to read, impossible to deny.

"My momma told me once that sometimes it was her job to worry and my job to let her do it." The words beat Bliss's brain when Angel uttered them.

"Sometimes, it's just my job to worry, Bliss, and your job to let me do it." Her mother's lips curved with a hint of sadness. "And every day I just pray that if I worry enough, I won't lose you, like I lost Beth. . . ."

Oh God.

A cold chill swept over her, almost causing her to shudder. It was even worse than the one she'd felt the other day when she'd seen her friend Bran getting yelled at by someone in another language, so angrily.

Angel was still talking. The knife was moving, but she couldn't take her eyes off it. Because she'd seen it before in pictures. She'd heard about it, been told the history of it, and she was certain it was the same knife her mother had given to her first daughter, Beth, before her mother had to leave Beth to go to Iraq so long ago.

The way Angel brushed her hair back when she was nervous . . . Bliss remembered the tears that fell from her mom's eyes when she told her about how Beth did that so much that she'd bought bows to pin back her hair.

The way Angel sometimes moved when an unfamiliar sound caught her attention . . .

The same way Bliss's mom moved when the same thing happened . . .

Angel always wore contacts, kept her hair colored. She was always angry whenever Mom would ask her about her parents. . . .

The scars Angel had on the back of one hand, so fine they were almost invisible. When Bliss asked about them, Angel told her she'd gotten them when she was three and her father and sister had been killed. . . .

Oh God, she didn't know what to do, didn't know what to say.

How was she supposed to keep this to herself?

"Bliss, are you okay?" Angel asked, pulling the knife back, pushing it into the sheath at her belt. "You aren't saying anything."

Concern filled Angel's voice.

Bliss could only shake her head. "You're my best friend," she whispered. "You should talk to Mom. . . ." She was screaming inside, so scared she was wrong, so certain she was right.

"We don't have anything to talk about, Bliss," Angel said then, but Bliss saw all the pain, and even anger, that filled her gaze. "My secrets aren't her business. But they don't endanger you. I'd never allow that."

"Bliss!" The sound of her mom's voice had Bliss jerking around to see her mother bearing down on them, her expression holding that "all business" look she could get. "Your father needs your help."

Bliss jumped to her feet and ran to her mother. She knew her mom, knew how she could get, how protective she was. She caught up with her before she could step to the grass, where Angel would hear what was said even if Bliss whispered.

"Mom." She stopped in front of her mother, seeing it now, how much Angel looked like her mother. The contacts and hair color fooled people. They stared at her eyes, not her face, Bliss realized. "If you really, really love me, Mom, you won't be mean to her. Please, Mom. Please. Not this time."

Her mother stared down at her then, her expression softening even as her lips thinned.

"Your dad needs help in the store, Bliss, before Uncle Rowdy and Aunt Kelly get here." Her voice lowered. "Tell your friend good-bye now and we'll both go help him."

A reprieve. It was just a reprieve and Bliss knew it, but it might give her time to figure this out, time to keep her mother from making a horrible mistake.

Turning, she saw Angel had risen, and she was staring back at Bliss's mother with that same determined expression, but in

Angel's eyes Bliss saw the need and the anger. And she had no idea what to do.

Moving back to the picnic table and drawing Angel's attention once again, she saw the pain, the hope, and the fears that filled her eyes now more clearly than she ever had before.

"Don't leave," Bliss demanded, certain that if Angel left then she'd lose her nerve for sure.

"I'll be back, Bliss." She glanced over her shoulder, her expression flickering with regret.

Bliss knew Angel wouldn't be back soon, though, and there was no way to hold her there.

"I love you, Angel," she said, knowing now why she loved the other woman, but the shock, the fear that lit Angel's eyes broke her heart. "You're my best friend. Always. And I love you."

She threw her arms around Angel in a tight, fierce hug. She couldn't let her leave without telling her. Not now. Not now that she knew.

Angel returned the hug and in it, Bliss was terribly afraid she felt good-bye. If Angel left, she might never come back. . . .

Trudging back to her mother, Bliss avoided her eyes, but she couldn't avoid the truth. The truth that somehow, for some reason, someone had told her mother a terrible lie. The lie that her first daughter was dead. Because Beth Dane wasn't dead, she was Angel.

TWO

Parking the motorcycle in front of the marina less than twenty-four hours later, Angel forced herself to dismount slowly and wait as her foster brothers, Tracker and Chance, did the same.

It was nearly impossible when panic was searing her insides. The news that Bliss had nearly been abducted had shaken her to her core. Another hour and she would have been on the plane heading for Rio, away from the teenager. Away from her sister.

Bliss could have been taken, dead before Angel could get back to her.

Releasing her helmet and pulling it off, she looked around, matching the appearance of mild concern exhibited by her foster brothers, holding back her fear. It was the greatest test of her patience and training as she pushed back the instinctive need to run, to race, to hurry, and to make certain Bliss and her mother were safe.

Tracker led the way to the marina's store, then to the office where the Mackay family had gathered. Angel stepped inside, her gaze locking on Natches and Chaya Mackay where they stood across the room with their daughter, Bliss.

Anger and suspicion immediately flared in Chaya's already-hard expression and cold brown eyes as her husband merely stared back curiously, though his emerald gaze was flat.

Merciless. A Marine sniper's eyes.

"Angel!" a voice shrieked, still filled with adrenaline. The teenager that called out to her drew her gaze from the couple. It was Rowdy's daughter, Annie, who saw her first and announced her presence. "I thought you were leaving."

Bliss swung away from her parents at Annie's cry, her emerald green eyes widening with relief as she followed Annie and rushed to her.

"We were on our way to the plane when I heard the report that Bliss was in trouble, so I thought I'd come check on you first." As she spoke, Annie, Laken, Bliss, and Erin were throwing their arms around her in one of those group hugs they'd perfected and Angel so enjoyed.

Touching their hair in a ghostly caress, she felt a surge of such overwhelming relief it was weakening. She fought, but knew she failed to hide her emotions, to hide the fear she'd felt until the moment she saw Bliss was indeed safe.

"How can we help?" she heard Tracker asking behind her.

"I don't know if I can afford you and your group, Tracker," Rowdy, the second eldest cousin, the one known as the most logical, answered wryly.

"There's no charge, Mr. Mackay," Angel stated without turning.

She'd pay Tracker's and Chance's parts herself if she had to.

Her money just sat in the bank anyway, rarely used. They didn't stop long enough to really buy much.

"Tell him, Tracker," she commanded her foster brother.

Behind her, Tracker started to assure Rowdy there'd be no charge. Lifting her gaze again Angel found herself meeting Chaya's suspicious one. Chaya was a DHS interrogator and an expert knife thrower, and she seemed to see right through her.

"Can you tell us what happened?" Angel kept her voice soft, as unthreatening as possible. She wanted to know who did this and why.

"A man in a ski mask grabbed Bliss and tried to pull her into a van," Rowdy explained. "Luckily her cousins were close by and managed to delay the abduction long enough for me to hear their cries. When the kidnappers saw me, they ran. But that's all we've got."

That was all they had. No reason why. No way to identify who had made the attempt or why.

"I'm so glad you're safe!" Angel said to Bliss. Then to her parents, she said, "I assume you'll be keeping the girls together?" Angel couldn't bear to be separated from Bliss again as she had been in the past weeks. Not now that Bliss was in danger. "If you do, I'd like to spend some time with them."

If she was there and Bliss was endangered again, then she'd be able to help. The wound she'd taken on her thigh at the beginning of the week, during the two-day quick-rescue operation they'd been involved in, notwithstanding. She'd make certain no one took Bliss, that she wasn't hurt, that nightmares didn't come alive in her young life as they had in her own.

"Angel," Tracker warned her quietly, so quietly she probably only heard it herself, a reminder that she was passing that invisible boundary the Mackays had placed between Bliss and Angel a year and a half ago when she'd helped the family in another matter. They'd been relegated to acquaintances and nothing more.

But she wasn't just an acquaintance, Angel cried out silently. She was more, so much more. . . .

"Zoey." Rowdy's voice hardened. "Why don't you and your sisters take the girls to the front of the store? Get them some drinks and snacks?"

Angel forced herself to show no reaction.

No regret. No pain.

Just as Tracker had been warning her, she'd pressed too close, too fast. But they would hide Bliss from her. She knew they would. She'd never know until it was too late if the teenager was abducted, or worse.

She would worry herself to death.

She could see the distaste in Chaya's expression now and had to force herself not to scream out in pain at the sight of it.

Distaste? As though Angel were somehow dirty, or carried an offensive scent that couldn't be tolerated.

The women escorted the girls from the room, the door closing quietly behind them and leaving her, Tracker, and Chance to bear the weight of the suspicion in the Mackay families' gazes. And it was a weight that settled against her already-ravaged soul. Nearly a dozen Mackays focused their attention on her.

"Why are you so concerned about our children?" The attack came from Chaya.

And it was indeed an attack, one filled with suspicion and determined denial of Angel's request.

She'd thought her heart couldn't be broken further until this woman ground the remaining shreds with her dislike.

There, she admitted it.

Chaya Mackay didn't just distrust her, she actually disliked her. The pain that resonated through her was shocking, weakening her knees and the shields around her emotions. For a second, she actually wished that damned traitor Duke were there, so that he could see why she was so certain Chaya Mackay wouldn't give a damn if he sent her all the intel he'd gathered on Angel.

What did this woman see in her, Angel wondered, that was so bad that she was disgusted by it?

That aching pain she always carried exploded inside her.

Her mother had loved her once, when she was a little girl. When Angel had been the child Chaya Dane had called her sweet little mini-me. Before Chaya had gone to Iraq, before she'd met the sniper Natches Mackay.

"I apologize," Angel expressed politely, pushing it back, determined that no one see how bad it hurt. "On second thought, I'm certain you have this covered. . . ."

Too little, too late.

Anger flared in Chaya's expression and that dislike intensified to the point that Angel had to force herself not to cry out in pain.

I'm sorry, Momma, she whispered silently. *So sorry . . .*

"You have insisted on placing yourself in a position to gain our daughters' trust and affection and I want to know why." Chaya pointed a finger at her accusingly. "Because I know women like you and I know it's not for the sake of those kids out there." That finger stabbed toward the door, but Angel barely acknowledged it.

Women like you, her mother sneered, her tone so filled with disgust that the mental and emotional recoil Angel felt stole her breath for a moment.

Women like her . . . ?

"Chaya, that's a little harsh," Christa, Dawg Mackay's wife, protested firmly but Angel barely acknowledged it. And Chaya sure as hell didn't.

Angel could only stare back at her mother, the proof that she had disappointed her, disgusted her, causing her stomach to churn sickeningly.

"Women like me?" Angel spoke without intending to. "What kind of woman do you assume I am, Mrs. Mackay?"

She'd tried so hard, she thought in confusion, tried to remember all the lessons her mother had taught her when she was just a baby. To be polite. To be a lady. And she had failed. She had failed so bad.

"My damned name is Chaya," her mother snapped disdainfully, that sneer in her voice, her expression, ravaging Angel's heart, causing her stomach to heave from the pain. "You've been here off and on for a year and a half now, and for some reason we end up seeing you often whenever you're in town. You're no child nor an employee, so you stop the Mrs. bullshit right now."

Angel simply stared back at her, hating herself, hating whatever she'd done to make her mother hate her, hating that she'd allowed herself to care and the realization that she had no idea what she'd done wrong.

"What kind of woman do you think I am?" Angel asked her again.

"Chaya." It was Rowdy who stepped forward to keep Chaya from revealing whatever she saw in Angel. "We're all upset. . . ."

Rage flashed in her mother's face, fear glinting in her gaze.

"Someone just attempted to abduct my daughter—" Her voice broke, her pain ripping inside Angel, tightening her throat with unshed tears. "And I want to know why a grown woman is trying to ingratiate herself into four teenagers' lives." The look that flashed across her mother's face was the only warning Angel had. "A mercenary. She sells herself to the highest bidder with those two." Chaya's hand flipped to Tracker and Chance as silent, ragged wails nearly choked Angel and became trapped in her throat.

Silent. Always silent . . . Oh God, it hurt. It hurt so bad.

"A killer," her mother continued. "What makes you think my daughter is any of your concern?" The sneer wasn't hidden, not on her face nor in her voice.

"Fuck," Chance cursed, shocked, behind her. "Let's go. Now."

She couldn't go. She couldn't move.

Agony was rupturing inside her, tearing her apart, shredding dreams, needs, and a lifetime of so much hope. She was being laid bare, sliced open. She'd tried, she'd tried so hard to be polite, to be good. . . .

"As I said"—she forced herself to speak—"I obviously stepped out of line in my concern." She felt dazed with the pain, so off-balance she couldn't quite make sense of it. "I didn't consider my words."

"And what is your concern?" The fury . . . Her mother was so angry and the pain tearing through Angel was brutal.

"Easy, Chay." Her husband's arms wrapped protectively around Chaya, his green eyes watching Angel. Suspicion filling them. She focused on the way he held her mother and she suddenly wished Duke were there. That his warmth surrounded her and he could see what she'd tried to tell him. This woman would be horrified to learn Angel was the daughter she believed to be dead. The daughter she hadn't wanted.

"Don't any of you pretend you haven't asked yourself why she's so interested in our children." Chaya's gaze went around the room, demanding they see the killer she saw in Angel.

That was what she saw, Angel knew, just trying to breathe. Her mother saw a ruthless killer, not the little girl she'd thrown away so long ago.

"Rowdy. Natches." Tracker stepped in front of her, Chance moving protectively behind her. "We'll be going now. If you need our assistance, please don't hesitate to call the service. They'll get a message to us."

Angel wanted to howl in denial. No, she couldn't leave yet. Her mother was so angry with her. . . .

"This is the wrong time to leave, Tracker," Dawg told him as Angel stared at her foster brother's back. "The question's easy enough."

"The question shouldn't have been asked," Chance snapped, his ruined voice furious. "We were here when your family needed us, without charge or question. We could have refused the contract on your sister Lyrica instead of trying to find out what the hell was going on and we could have gone on with our lives. No one the wiser."

"And I want to know why you didn't." Pain filled Chaya's voice, and torment. "Three mercenaries? By the very definition of the word you don't work for free. What do you intend to demand later? What does she want?" That finger pointed back at Angel accusingly.

Someone had tried to take the daughter she'd raised, the sweet, polite little lady Angel wasn't. "Tell me, Grog." Chaya used his codename, the pseudonym Chance was known by. "Tracker?"

All her mother wanted was answers? The truth? What would she do with the truth? Angel wondered. It wasn't as though her rejection of her could be worse. And maybe, maybe her mother would at least let her be a part of her sister's life if Angel told her. She could live with Chaya not liking her, as long as Bliss was safe.

She could live with that, couldn't she? God knew she wouldn't be able to live, though, if anything happened to either of them and she could have stopped it.

The tension in the room thickened to the point that it was nearly visible in the air itself. Smothering, it had adrenaline leaking into her system, preparing her, pumping her instincts to fight or flight, and she couldn't seem to make herself do either.

"Rowdy, we're walking out of here. We came to help and it was obviously a mistake." Tracker tried again to find a graceful way out of the confrontation Angel could feel brewing in the air.

"Chaya has a point, Tracker," Rowdy argued. "We've all been asking ourselves 'why' since you showed up. If you walk out of here without answering that question, it's just going to make all of us nosy. You know what happens when Mackays get nosy."

"Don't turn this into a war," Tracker warned him, and Angel knew well the lengths both Tracker and Chance would go to protect her. "Wrong move."

"If it becomes a war, then you'll start it. I'd hate it, we all would. But if Mackays were suddenly in your business without so much as an introduction, then you'd be asking the same questions." Rowdy's tone, despite its softness, resonated with danger.

Angel couldn't allow this and she knew it. Tracker had warned her so many times and she'd refused to listen. This was her fault and she would not allow her foster brothers to pay for her mistake.

Besides, a war with these men would only draw Duke into it and she didn't think she could bear the choice he'd make when faced with the need to do so.

"I don't need your protection, Tracker." Stepping from behind him, she faced the Mackay family again, steeling herself to hold the pain inside no matter how bad it became, no matter how cruel her mother's words became.

"I wasn't trying to protect you," he assured her, though she knew he was lying. "I merely wanted to get back on the road."

She was aware of Rowdy watching her closely. Too closely.

He didn't trust her either; none of them did. They didn't like her and they never would. Not that she had expected them to.

How much worse could they strike at her?

Turning, she faced Chaya Mackay once again, knowing she'd run out of time.

"Why do you think I give a damn about your kid?" she asked, resigned to the fact that the sliver of hope that had lived inside her for so long was dying. "You're not a stupid woman," she continued, staring her mother directly in the eye now, refusing to hide anything any longer. "Why do you think I care?"

The anger that vibrated in the air around her mother only rose, her tension level increasing.

Behind Natches, Dawg Mackay stepped closer.

"Come on, kids, let's play nice on the playground," he chided them, and Angel and Chaya faced off.

A mother's fury and a daughter's determination.

"You're not answering me, Mrs. Mackay," she pointed out, that bleak, hollow pain that raged inside her making her voice huskier.

Chaya's lip lifted in another sneer. "Girl, you're testing my patience." Disdain filled her voice and her expression. "And you don't want to do that."

No, she didn't want to do that, but there was no doubt she would.

Poor Momma, she thought painfully. She shouldn't have to suffer a child she didn't like.

"Bliss is my sister." She made herself say the words, emotion nearly overwhelming her as hope rushed through her in waves, when she'd believed she had no hope left inside her.

"Whoa, fuck me . . ." Dawg jumped back from her even as her mother turned quickly to stare at Natches in shock.

She thought Angel belonged to Natches?

Angel would have laughed if everything inside her didn't seem to freeze at the knowledge.

Natches did laugh, though, his amusement genuine.

"Good try, sweetheart," he drawled. "I was a bastard, but I was a careful one."

Chaya turned back slowly, moving farther away from Angel, her eyes narrowing on her.

"You're not my father," she agreed. Now wouldn't that suck? "Too bad, though. I think you're a hell of a one."

Behind her, Tracker shifted closer as Chaya's expression immediately turned icy cold. Dangerous.

"Then how is Bliss your sister?" Natches demanded, the compliment not even registering. "Kid, you need to take this act somewhere else. Fast."

Angel didn't answer. She stared back at her mother silently, willing her to say something, to welcome her, acknowledge her. Anything.

See me, she wanted to scream. *Please, Momma. Please.*

"That's not possible." Natches's voice lowered, became harsher, colder as he seemed to realize who Angel claimed as a parent. "Chaya has no other children."

And Chaya wasn't speaking. Her gaze kept moving over her face, but she didn't speak.

"Is Bliss your only child, Mrs. Mackay?" Angel could feel the fear beginning to build.

Once she'd followed Tracker and Chance into a category five hurricane and that hadn't been as frightening as the fear congealing in her belly at the knowledge that her mother was silently yet very firmly rejecting her.

Angel swallowed against the lump in her throat. She'd thought nothing could hurt so bad as having her mother call her a killer, as knowing she didn't want the child that had so loved her. Seeing the proof of it hurt worse, though.

"Stop this!" Natches ordered her with grating fury as his expression hardened into lines of savage mercilessness. "Get her the fuck out of here, Tracker, before I kill her myself!"

Before he killed her . . . Yeah, he could be protective like that, she'd heard.

She felt Tracker's hand on her arm, his fingers firm.

"Angel, let's go," he whispered gently as she fought to accept this reality.

But she'd known. She had known this woman wouldn't care.

"Bliss—" she whispered.

"Is none of your concern." Natches's voice was hard and cold. "Don't keep pushing this. Don't keep pushing me."

"Angel." Tracker said her name again as Natches shifted subtly behind his wife, the mask of a killer hardening in his face as a small almost-cry whispered from Chaya's lips.

He was becoming more dangerous by the second. She could sense it, feel it.

Her breathing hitched just enough to warn her she might be losing control of the emotions she kept so tightly reined.

She'd tried, hadn't she?

And she'd failed.

"I'm so sorry I've upset you and your family," she forced herself to whisper even as she shattered on the inside, and shattered, and shattered. "I promise I won't bother you anymore." Turning her head, she looked up at Tracker, saw the pain he felt for her and the anger he felt because of her. "I'm ready. I guess we're heading out after all."

"Thank God. Fuckers," Chance snarled beneath his breath as Tracker wrapped his arm around her and swept her from the marina. "Assholes. I guess I'll just have to pray for the lot of ya." The sarcastic statement was more of an insult than they could imagine.

"Can you ride?" Tracker's voice wasn't pleasant. It was guttural, grating.

"I'm fine, Tracker," she promised as they stopped next to her cycle. "I'm tough, remember?"

Taking her helmet she pulled it on, secured the strap, and mounted her cycle as Tracker and Chance followed suit. Within seconds they were riding away and far too quickly they were on the road, the marina not even in her rearview mirror any longer.

Dry-eyed, her throat tight and raw, she felt as though she were on autopilot, outside herself and unable to find her way back.

She hadn't expected rejection.

She hadn't expected that complete icy, silent denial of her identity.

Chaya hadn't even asked for DNA. Angel had expected that much at least. She was even prepared for it.

"Angel, we can wait a day or so to leave," Tracker said through the communicator's link, his voice gentle.

"No. I'm fine," she lied. "And the plane's waiting. It's time for you and Chance to leave."

"Dammit, Angel!" he began to protest.

"The job in Rio won't wait," she reminded him. "It's not like I can do much there anyway. I'm just going to hang around, watch, and make certain she's safe. That's all."

Silence met her promise, but she knew he and Chance couldn't afford to cancel the Rio job this late. The fee was extraordinarily high and they were known for not canceling out, for always getting the job done. And she really did know how to hide. He'd taught her how.

"You'll call if you need us?" he finally questioned her, his voice harsh. "Promise me, Angel."

"The very second, if you're needed," she promised. "Come on, Tracker, I won't risk her safety by not calling. You know that."

She'd do whatever she had to when it came to protecting her baby sister, to ensuring Bliss never knew the nightmares Angel lived with. It was all she had to give the girl who would never know how much her sister loved her.

"I'll have our contact rent you a room, and I'll send your gear back from the plane," he finally promised. "Don't try to take that family on alone."

"I'm not going to try to take them on, period," she assured him, blinking past her tears and concentrating on keeping the cycle at a reasonable speed. "I told you. I'm going to hide and watch. That's it."

"Hide and watch," he repeated, though she wasn't entirely certain he believed her.

She wasn't entirely certain she believed it herself.

"I've got this, Tracker, I promise." She kept her voice easy, confident. "Get the Rio job done and come back and pick me up. You know the Mackays. They'll have Bliss's would-be kidnappers buried within a week. But I know me. I'll worry. . . ."

She'd drive herself insane. The nightmares would kill her.

"Stay safe, Angel," Chance ordered, the dark raspiness of his voice assuring her of his concern, his affection. "Don't make us have to bury you. I promise, I'd consider every Mackay I come across an enemy if that happened."

"Really, Chance?" She would have laughed at that comment if she could have found any laughter inside her.

"Really, little sister," he promised. "All shit aside. Really."

Through the window, Bliss saw Angel's face as she left and felt fear explode in her chest at the complete devastation she glimpsed in her sister's expression.

Breaking away from her cousins, she headed back to the office as her mother suddenly shot out the door and all but ran to the store entrance just in time to watch Angel, Tracker, and Grog ride away.

What happened? What had her mom done to make Angel leave? Angel would have never, ever left, knowing Bliss was in trouble. She knew Angel wouldn't do that. Angel loved her. And Angel was tough, she knew how to fight, how to shoot, and how to use that very distinctive knife she carried at her hip.

"Mom?" She stared at her mother's face as she turned to her. It was almost white, her brown eyes filled with . . . something. Something that assured Bliss her mother had done something she never should have done.

She'd made Angel leave.

"What did you do? Why did she leave?" Confusion overwhelmed her.

Her mother shook her head.

Bliss clenched her fists furiously. "Why did you make her leave, Mom? She's my friend."

"Pick better friends," her mother cried, tears glittering in her eyes as she swung away, leaving Bliss to stare at her back.

Pick better friends?

She backed away from her mother, feeling her cousins come around her, drawing her away to the other side of the store. But all she could hear was that anger in her mother's voice.

Pick better friends?

Angel wasn't just her friend. . . .

THREE

Natches Mackay waited, not quite patiently, in his home office that night. Through the window he stood next to, he could see his cousins, as close to him as brothers, in the room behind him.

Dawg was pacing, his impatience more volatile than his or their other cousin's.

Rowdy was the one who kept drawing his gaze, though, as he stood in front of the floor-to-ceiling shelves, directly in front of the picture of Chaya and the child she'd lost all those years ago.

Everyone claimed Bliss was a female replica of Natches. Black hair, green eyes, the Mackay features softened and finely sculpted into what was rapidly becoming an exquisite beauty. If that were true, then Beth Dane had been her mother's mini-me, just as Chaya had called her.

Even at three her resemblance to her mother was incredible

and promised to become even more so. Features Natches could close his eyes and see a hint of in Angel Calloway's face.

A child that DNA tests had proven dead, yet she lived. And she'd lived for twenty years without the mother who had grieved for her every second of that time.

He knew the two men he was watching. A lifetime spent with them had ensured it. And because of them and Rowdy's father, Ray, he'd survived a childhood that should have seen him dead. And because he knew them so well he knew they were restraining themselves, restraining whatever was on their minds.

"The two of you are too quiet," he said, turning to them as they waited for the lesser-known cousin who had called earlier. "Just say it and get it the hell over with."

The two men turned to him, but it was each other they looked to first. Dawg shook his shaggy black head, that tiny hint of silver at the sides giving him a more distinguished look than Natches had expected before it showed up.

"I believe her." It was Rowdy who spoke up, his somber, sea-green gaze piercing as he stared back thoughtfully. "The minute she said she was Bliss's sister, I knew what was bothering me about her since I met her, and when she left the marina, she looked broken, Natches. Whether she's Beth Dane or not, she believes she is."

Dawg blew out a hard, deep breath, drawing Natches's attention to the regret that creased his face.

"Christa's said all along that Angel was too much like Chaya, and that was why Chaya was having problems with her." He propped his hands on his hips for a moment, hanging his head before lifting it again and giving Natches a regret-filled look. "I'd never believe she was your kid, but yeah." He rubbed at the back of his neck. "I believe she's Chaya's. It was in those eyes, contacts and all, she was beggin' Chaya to see her. To accept her."

Natches wanted it to be a lie. He fully admitted that. To know her daughter had lived the horrendously dangerous life they knew Angel had lived would kill Chaya. It would kill him if he was facing Bliss twenty years later, knowing he'd lived a life that included love and laughter while she'd suffered. Chaya would feel the same, and it would break both of them.

"Bliss is brokenhearted." Rowdy's words had Natches's heart tightening. "She told Annie she didn't think she would ever forgive her mother if anything happened to Angel now. Told her she felt like Angel was as close to her as a sister."

Pain struck at his heart and tore to his soul. God help him. God help Chaya.

And if he called Bliss from her bedroom to question her about it, Chaya would follow. She wouldn't let Bliss out of her sight. She was presently curled in the large, oversize chair in Bliss's bedroom. The two hadn't spoken since they'd left the marina. Which was odd for Bliss. She usually went into a Mackay meltdown when she was angry. But she was eerily silent now, refusing to discuss Angel or the attempted kidnapping. And Chaya refused to leave her alone.

"Timothy's going crazy," Dawg said then, worried for the former DHS special agent who had been with Chaya in Iraq when Beth had supposedly died. "One of my contacts from DHS said he arrived about two hours ago and demanded all of Army Intelligence's records as well as DHS's from that operation. He's in meltdown."

Timothy's lab had run the DNA and verified the child's body as Beth's.

"We're all in meltdown," Natches said heavily as the silent alarm on the watch he wore vibrated, indicating a vehicle had passed over the motion detector set in the driveway leading to the house. "And I have a feeling it's about to get worse."

Because he knew the man arriving.

Duke Mackay had been investigating Angel Calloway for about five years. When Natches noticed the young woman showing up at the lake or at events that Bliss attended, he'd become curious about her. Tracker and Chance hadn't even blipped on his radar until eighteen months ago.

Just out of Army Intelligence, Duke and his brother, Ethan, had taken the job of tracking Angel down and learning why she'd taken such an interest in the preteen. At first, Duke had reported that Angel's presence in Somerset must be a coincidence, that a young mercenary, a sister to the commander she followed, couldn't have any true interest in Bliss.

But Duke had decided to stay with the team for a while, and Natches had let the information and the young woman slip to the back of his mind. Until Tracker, Angel, and Chance had shown up a year and a half ago, out of the blue, to protect Dawg's sister, Lyrica, while Duke had been involved in another job Natches had sent him to.

He didn't believe in coincidence, he thought as he opened the door leading into the kitchen for his younger cousin and stared into the mossy green eyes of the man who had spent all of his adult life away from his home. A man he knew had his own demons and haunted past.

"Office?" Duke nodded his head toward the opened doorway across the kitchen. "I'd like to talk to you and the cousins alone first."

First.

Duke's features, reminiscent of Dawg's at the same age, were sharply hewn, brooding, and touched with the same sun-bronzed stroke of Native American ancestry. Raised by distant relatives in Montana from the time he was fifteen until he joined the Army at eighteen, he wasn't a man many were comfortable around.

He was a man Natches could understand and respect, though. And the fact that Duke wanted privacy first had the tension already radiating through him building instantly.

"Come on," he breathed out roughly, turning and heading for the office. "Let's get it over with."

Natches had known grief in his life. More than anyone could imagine, but as he stood silently next to his desk with Rowdy, Dawg, and their younger Mackay cousin, Duke, he knew this was the nightmare he never could have imagined before today.

He'd thought the past and its monsters had been vanquished when his father, Dayle Mackay, died in prison. Now, he realized, the nightmares he'd known as a boy were never going to be forgotten.

And as much as he wanted to, he couldn't vanquish the monsters that were going to rise up to torment the wife he loved more than he loved anything else in his life. And now Chaya's nightmares were only going to be added to as well. Nightmares of the life her daughter Beth had lived for the past twenty years.

Duke showed him a photograph of Beth and another little girl almost identical to her but younger, with Chaya's first husband, Craig Dane. He explained that the other girl was Jenny Dane, the child Chaya's sister had had with Chaya's husband. The Canadian birth certificate verified the parents. Jo-Ellen was murdered when the girls were taken from her, and she had never told anyone about her baby.

Jo-Ellen hadn't possessed many friends, worked from home in Canada, and hadn't told those she did know that Jenny belonged to her. She'd hidden the pregnancy and the birth, presumably to keep Chaya from knowing how she and Craig had betrayed her. Then, somehow, Craig got both girls to Iraq and they were all in the hotel when it was bombed.

A mercenary named J. T. Calloway found a little blond-haired girl wandering the streets of Baghdad and had assumed she'd been beaten. There was no report of a missing American child, so he'd kept her, given her his family name to hide her, just in case she was in danger, and raised her as his own.

He'd raised her amid the blood and death he, his wife, and two sons lived within. A child taught from the age of three that survival meant kill or be killed. Homeschooling lessons included hand-to-hand combat training and how to use a knife, a gun, or fingernails to disable an enemy.

She'd nearly been raped at age six by an enemy combatant, forced to kill at age fifteen, and taken her first bullet at age sixteen. And her eyes weren't a shattered blue, intense violet, or brilliant green as listed in differing reports on her, but a soft gray ringed by a darker blue.

And when she smiled, she looked like her mother.

She looked like Chaya.

That resemblance had been what Natches hadn't been able to put his finger on since he met her. That "something" that just bothered the hell out of him.

Halfway through the pages of notes, reports, photos, and proof of a hell a child had lived, he couldn't take any more.

He stomped away from the pages spread out on the table, his

arms crossing over his chest to hold back the pain ravaging his soul.

This would kill Chaya, especially after the confrontation with Angel. His wife, who had nightmares every year on her first daughter's birthday, who still bought a present and wrapped it for that daughter every Christmas, who couldn't let go of her belongings for fear the grief would tear her apart.

He wiped one hand over the side of his face. God, he had no idea how to begin figuring out how to handle this one.

Fuck, as though there was a way to deal with this? He couldn't even make himself believe it and the proof was right there, spread out on the damned table.

Natches rubbed his neck, trying to ease the tension threatening to snap his spine. He'd known not to let her walk out of that marina, but Chaya's grief had been strangling him at the time.

"I knew something wasn't right," he admitted, hated it, cursed himself for ignoring it. "Especially with Chaya. She knew Angel was hiding something, since the first day they met, she knew. That was what pissed her off so much about the girl."

And Chaya had fully admitted her anger at Angel was out of proportion. As a mercenary, Angel had no choice but to hide her real name, her family, her private life.

Mercenaries made enemies.

That knowledge would only make Chaya more furious.

A child, she'd ranted after first meeting the girl. Angel was still just a baby at twenty-three, and her parents let her live such a life? Selling herself, her loyalty, to the highest bidder when she should be in college, dating, figuring out what she wanted in life. Not figuring out how to avoid the bullets whizzing around her or the best way to kill a man.

Subconsciously, Chaya had known as well. She'd sensed it,

felt it, and had known Angel was hiding that truth from her. Delivering that truth in the same hour Chaya had nearly lost her second child had just been poor fucking timing for all of them.

"What are you going to do?" Rowdy asked, his voice low as all eyes watched him.

Natches turned back to them, grief building, burning in his soul.

"I have to tell her." He breathed out heavily. "What choice do I have?"

"She'll want to go straight to Angel, to question her, to claim her," Duke inserted, his face, his voice, as hard as Natches remembered his own being at one time. "I know this woman, Natches. In the time I've been working with her, investigating her, Ethan and I have fought with her and her brothers, gotten to know them to some small extent. She won't come to Chaya easily. Not after this afternoon."

"She won't have a choice," he snapped. "I won't accept anything else."

"And she'll shoot you the finger as she's flying into the sunset," Duke snorted, his vivid green eyes filled with knowing mockery. "She's not like anyone you've known, Natches, and trying to order her to do anything will only piss her off."

Natches could feel the fury beginning to build, to burn through his senses. Chaya wouldn't be able to live with that. It would kill her.

"You say you know her," Rowdy stated, the calm tone of his voice pulling Natches's attention. "What do you suggest, Duke?"

Rowdy was watching the younger Mackay closely, almost knowingly. That look on his face had Natches paying more attention to him as well.

"She told you she was there today because of Bliss. She tried to tell Chaya who she was, because she wanted to protect Bliss. Angel lost a sister in that hotel bombing and I know she's still haunted with nightmares from it. The only way you'll be able to get to her is with Bliss."

Natches's eyes narrowed on the other man. There was something almost angry, definitely territorial whenever he spoke of Angel.

"Pull her in," Natches decided quickly. "You know her. . . ."

The derisive snort Duke made had him pausing.

"Natches, you don't understand, that woman is a powder keg waiting to explode over any man working with her, besides Tracker and Chance. She doesn't take orders worth shit, goes her own way, and nine times out of ten ends up with a bullet buried in her somewhere that's all but guaranteed to kill her. It's been all Ethan could do to keep her ass alive since joining that team. . . . And they threw us the hell out eight months ago when Tracker somehow figured out we are Mackays."

It wouldn't have been that damned hard to figure out, Natches knew; not once Tracker had worked with him, Rowdy, and Dawg a year and a half ago.

"She obviously trusts you enough to allow you to fight with her," Natches snapped. "Don't give me fucking excuses, Duke. Make it happen."

"Make it happen?" Duke repeated, his large body, reminiscent of Dawg's at the same age, tensing until his shoulders appeared broader and more imposing. "I'm no Marine and you're not my fucking commander, Captain Mackay."

Natches smiled. A slow, easy smile that lacked any humor whatsoever. "Think Memmie Mary will see it the same way?"

Memmie Mary was the iron will of the Mackay family on the other side of the mountain, just as Natches's uncle, Rowdy's father, Ray, was on their side of the mountain.

Duke's eyes narrowed on him. "That's low, even for you."

"Not nearly as low as I'd go, Duke," Natches promised him. "I won't see Chaya destroyed any further than this is going to do already if Angel disappears. And I have a feeling, as much as Chaya and I both will hate it, you're likely the only one with enough influence, where that stubborn-assed daughter of hers is concerned, to keep her here."

As the final sentence left his mouth he saw the looks on Duke's, Dawg's, and Rowdy's faces as their gazes jerked to the door behind him, and he knew with a sense of fatalistic regret that he no longer had to worry how to tell his wife.

He turned to her slowly, watched what little color she had in her face leech away as she stared back at him in horror.

"Duke. Find her. Now," Natches ordered his cousin.

"We'll go sit with Bliss." Rowdy and Dawg moved to the door on the other side of the room that entered into the kitchen, with Duke following them.

Natches didn't bother to watch them leave. He didn't take his eyes off Chaya, nor did he try to hold her back as she glanced at his desk, saw the papers and files spread out over it, and began moving toward it slowly.

"You sent Duke to investigate her," she said, her voice hollow as she neared the desk. "You didn't tell me."

"I actually sent him out five years ago," he told her, staying close to her, knowing the blow this would deliver to the twenty-year-old wound in her soul. "He didn't tell me what he'd found until tonight, though. . . ."

Natches's words faded away when Chaya lifted a picture from the various papers and photographs on the desk.

She could feel herself screaming. Silent, agonized screams that she didn't have the breath to actually push from her chest.

The little girl, her dark blond hair tangled and dirty, a little white bow barely hanging at the ends of the soft waves that ended at her shoulders. A matching white dress, torn, filthy, and stained with blood.

A single white sandal on her bloody, dirt-caked foot.

Red arrows pointed to her broken leg, her fractured arm.

She looked like a tiny, broken doll lying on the rough cot, unconscious, so pale she could have been dead.

Chaya heard the small, keening cry that left her lips. She knew that child. Knew her with every fiber of her heart and soul and knew the mistake she'd made when she faced the young woman that child had grown into.

Angel.

"What did I do?" The sound of her own voice was a shock to her, whispering from lips that trembled with the violent emotions surging through her. "What did I do to my baby . . . ?"

She was only barely aware of Natches's arms going around her, holding her on her feet when she would have sunk to the floor.

There were other pictures. Pictures taken each year at about the same time, others taken with each new injury, each broken bone, and each gunshot or knife wound. And there were many of them.

There was a notation made of a near rape, an abduction by

one of the men holding another child who the family had been sent to rescue, and a detailed report of the collapse of a small hospital in Uzbekistan five years ago that resulted in hysteria and further injuries when Angel had been trapped in the basement.

Twenty years of training, near fatal wounds, and a life devoid of her mother's love.

Included with the pictures was a birth certificate for another child. Jennifer Ellen Dane. Chaya read the parents' names: her ex-husband and her sister. Her sister had had a child? With Craig? Beth's half sister.

Chaya knew she was fighting to breathe, to throttle the screams echoing in her head, to find reality in the midst of the nightmare converging on her.

"My baby . . ." Strangled, filled with horror, the knowledge of what she had done to her daughter that afternoon sliced jagged, ever-deepening wounds into her soul. "Oh God . . . Oh God . . ."

What had she done?

"I know women like you. . . ." Her accusation had shattered the cool, remote look on Angel's face.

"A mercenary . . . a killer . . ." Her words had caused the younger woman to pale.

"Bliss is my sister. . . ." The desperation in Angel's voice had caused Chaya to freeze.

She had fought to deny Angel's claim. She'd stared at the girl, fighting to see past the vulnerable hunger that reached out to her to the deception she'd seen in the girl every other time Angel had stared back at her.

"Is Bliss your only child, Mrs. Mackay?" Angel had whispered, and Chaya had been unable to answer her.

Sobs broke from her chest, agony ruptured inside her and caused her to tighten violently in her husband's arms, to fight to be free of him. She had to get away from this; she couldn't accept this. . . .

Oh God, she had found happiness all these years while her daughter had suffered. . . .

She tried to scream for her baby, to scream out to God for mercy, but all she could do was collapse against the bands of steel wrapped around her as Natches turned her to him, held her to his heart.

Memories ravaged her soul. Her baby from birth. Her first smile, the first time she said "ma." Her laughter. How she formed words early, walked early, then as she watched her mother practicing with the knife she'd trained most of her life to use, Beth began to try to mimic it.

At three. Three years old and she would try to turn, to thrust and parry, then laugh as she landed on her rear, her pretty gray-blue eyes alight with laughter.

The teddy bear Binny . . .

Beth's sobs when Chaya had been forced to leave her with Jo-Ellen.

The knowledge that Jo-Ellen's daughter had died, and Chaya had never known Beth had a sister.

And she hadn't known her baby was still alive. . . .

How could she have not known?

How could she have allowed her baby to suffer?

"Who held her?" she whispered brokenly, staring up at her husband, her fingers clawing at his shirt, grief ripping her apart. "Who held my baby?"

Sitting in the dimly lit hotel room Tracker had arranged for her, Angel peeled back the bandage on the knife wound she'd gotten the day before returning to Somerset. The long, deep gash in her leg was over a week old and still showing no signs of healing. It was actually all she could do to keep it from slipping into an infection.

Had Tracker or Chance known the condition of the wound, they would have sent her straight to home base rather than flying away and leaving her there in Somerset.

Applying an antibiotic salve to the inflamed skin barely held together by the stitches Tracker had sewn so carefully, she covered it again with a waterproof bandage, secured the edges, then took another dose of the antibiotics she kept in her pack.

She was almost out of the powerful pills, though. That, along with the inflamed edges of the wound, the growing sensitivity in her leg, and her tiredness, assured her she was going to have problems very soon. And the doctor Tracker had arranged to be on call for the team the year before would surely report back to him if she called.

Lying on the bed, simply too damned drained to dress after her shower, she threw her arm over her eyes and bit back the emotions threatening to swamp her.

She could call Duke. She'd even pulled up his number on her sat phone earlier. He and Ethan were close, she knew. Duke had sent her a message the day before asking her to contact him. But it wasn't the first such message he'd sent her in the past eight months after Tracker learned who he was. It was the first one she considered replying to, though.

They fought like children sometimes, but if Duke knew she needed him or his medic brother, then he wouldn't refuse to come to her.

Calling Duke would create a whole set of problems she wasn't certain she wanted to deal with, though. Her response to him had been particularly strong the last time she'd seen him. Her body became hypersensitive whenever he was around and all she wanted to do was taste those totally kissable lips.

No matter how mad he was at her at the time. No matter how mad she was at him now.

She was insane. That knowledge had a sigh escaping her lips as she settled more comfortably on her bed. He was something else, someone else, she couldn't allow herself to have.

The bastard.

Lying fucking Mackay.

Reece Duquaine was actually Reece Duquaine Mackay. A former Army Intelligence investigator rumored to be working for his cousins, Rowdy, Dawg, and Natches Mackay. Tracker had learned too late that she was the important investigation they'd had him working on—for, like, five fucking years.

And even though they hadn't heard of him before he arrived in Uzbekistan with his brother, Ethan, the summer she turned eighteen, the fact that they'd been there, that they'd helped save her at the time, had overridden the normal hesitancy in trusting them.

Background checks on Reece and Ethan Duquaine had come back squeaky-clean, though. Army, a few years in military intelligence for Duke, training as a field surgeon for Ethan. It was a chance encounter, a drunk on a military base, and Tracker's suspicions—or so her foster brother claimed—that finally led to the truth.

The black hair and green eyes should have given him away, but hell, she knew plenty of black-haired, green-eyed men. It wasn't as though they were scarce.

The brilliance of Duke's dark, mossy green eyes was different, though. That tall, broad body and the tight, lean muscles. She almost grinned at the memory of him. He was tough, hard, not exactly handsome, more rough-hewn. And though he didn't so much look like the Mackays now, she knew he resembled Dawg Mackay when the older man had been the same age.

But he was still a Mackay, she reminded herself. Dangerous to her and her secrets at the time and even more dangerous now that Natches Mackay wanted her head on a platter.

Hell, she was actually surprised Duke hadn't tracked her down yet. No doubt he was in town. Come to think of it, he was likely most definitely in town. He was probably trying to help Natches find her at that moment.

A wave of desolation threatened to overtake her at that thought.

Her mother hated her, the man she lusted after on a daily basis had been betraying her for five years, and the sister she only wanted to be friends with would be kept from her now.

The ties she was starving for were moving further and further out of her reach.

Not that she wasn't aware that what she wanted so desperately was unrealistic. Her mother hadn't wanted her twenty years ago, why would she change her mind now? When Angel's birth father, Craig Dane, had called, demanding Chaya come for Beth and Jenny when he learned he couldn't use them to secure his trip to wherever he was going, Chaya had refused. She was too busy with her new lover to bother with the child she'd had with another man. The child who had idolized her, had been so certain her mother would come for her and her newly discovered sister, Jenny.

And Angel had promised . . . she had promised Jenny. As the younger child cried for the mother whose arms she'd been torn from, Angel had been certain her mother would rescue them.

Everything would be okay, she had sworn to her sister; her momma would find them.

But her momma hadn't found them. She hadn't cared.

Her mother had a new lover, a new life to live, and that life hadn't included the baby whose heart was broken that day.

And now, it didn't include the woman that child had become. But it wasn't the mother that concerned her as much as her baby sister, Bliss. Another sister in danger, another sister that could be taken from her.

The vibration of the sat phone on the table next to her bed had her reaching over to retrieve it, her arm lowering from her eyes as she brought it up to read the message.

Duke requests a call. Do I need to return? Tracker's message had her lips snarling.

Coward. Duke couldn't just message her, he'd gone through Tracker instead. And Tracker had liked Duke just enough that he hadn't killed him for being a Mackay. But this demand was a surprise.

Only if you want my head served up to his cousin, she messaged back.

Call Duke. Now. Regardless. She frowned at the message.

The wording was more a warning.

Do as he said or he was returning. Questions would likely piss him off and have him turning the plane around no matter the importance of the job he was flying to.

Fine. I want roses on my grave. Put lilies on it and I haunt you. Because calling Duke was going to ensure Natches found her.

Don't piss me off or I'll have you cremated when the time comes.

His response had her cursing. The words so vile she was

certain they would cause him to give her one of those disgusted male looks of disappointment.

Stop cursing me. The next call I get from him, I'm turning around. Then I'll call the parents.

Call J.T. and Mara?

They were more soldiers than parents and therein lay the problem. They claimed Angel as theirs, so they'd damned sure head to Kentucky if they thought she needed them. Them as well as the extended family.

"Bastard. Fucking whoreson," she muttered, then pulled up her contact list and hit Duke's number.

"Where are you?" The demand was made instantly.

"Evidently where you couldn't find me before this call," she snapped. "You bastard-Natches-Mackay wannabe." It was the worst insult she could come up with. "Calling my brother and pushing his buttons. I'm going to shoot your ass."

What information had he found on her? Had he already given it to Natches and Chaya? Or was he calling her first?

"Someone hit the safe house an hour ago," he stated without responding to the threat. "Bliss wasn't there, but they were looking for her." A second attempt in less than twenty-four hours meant someone was damned serious.

Angel checked the clock. It was nearly two in the morning. The perfect time to hit a safe house and catch the inhabitants off guard.

"Is she safe?" she asked, pushing back anger, pain, everything but protecting her sister.

"For now," he assured her. "But I'm not a stupid man, Angel. And I didn't spend five years proving who you were to discount who you've become and how damned good you are at it. Now, are you going to help me protect your sister, or are you going to keep hiding?"

Proving who she was . . . He knew. He'd proven it.

She had to blink back the moisture that filled her eyes, force back the hurt that threatened to break free.

He was a Mackay and he knew who she had been, as he stated; that meant every other Mackay living would know as well. Or did they already know?

"You told her?" she asked, referring to her mother, her heart aching, breaking further because she knew it wouldn't matter to Chaya Mackay.

"I gave Natches proof, something you should have tried," he informed her, the snap in his tone assuring her he had an issue with her where her delivery was concerned. "But I waited. Remember that, Angel. I gave you a chance before I gave him the proof."

He could kiss her ass with his chances as far as she was concerned.

"I gave her the benefit of the doubt by not jerking Bliss out of the game to begin with," she shot back instead. "I've been on this call long enough that I'm sure you've traced it. I'll be waiting."

She disconnected the call and messaged Tracker again.

Taken care of. I won't forget. She wouldn't forget that his demand was putting her in Natches's and Chaya's sights and the damage that resulted would lay on his head.

She stared at the phone far longer than it should have taken him to message back. Just as she placed the phone on the table to get up and get dressed, his final message came through.

It's time to stop running. I love you, little sister.

She stared at the message for long, intense moments. Not

even his parents had ever told her they loved her. From the beginning it had been Tracker who comforted her, called her "little sister," and fought to protect her rather than simply training her.

Godspeed, she typed in reply.

She wouldn't stay angry with him, and both of them knew it. No matter the outcome, no matter the cost, she wouldn't blame him. Because she was the only person Tracker had given those words to, and she knew it.

She was, in his eyes, his baby sister, just as Bliss was her sister in truth. And those ties were ones she'd never allow to be broken, because God knew, no one else allowed them.

FOUR

The safe house that the assailants believed Bliss was being protected in was located just within the Somerset city limits on a quiet residential street. Or, it had been quiet until gunfire had filled the night, awakening neighbors and terrifying the children that had never experienced such shocking violence.

Thankfully, Bliss wasn't actually there. Chaya had taken her to the neighboring county, where several lesser known, but no less hardened, cousins had gathered to ensure her protection.

Leaning forward to get a better look Angel tried to ignore the man sitting next to her and concentrated on what was going on instead. Police cruisers, both city as well as state, lined the street as officers moved around the small two-story house. Windows were shattered, the front door riddled with bullet holes, and the fact that violence had touched this previously quiet street was readily apparent.

Alex Jansen, the chief of police, stood on the once well-manicured front lawn nodding at the female detective who stood next to him, pointing something out. Next to the detective, the sheriff listened, his expression brooding and angry.

Detective Samantha Bryce was dressed in her customary jeans and T-shirt, a low-profile white ball cap on her head, a mass of dark brown curls hanging from the back of it to the middle of her back. Sneakers covered her feet; a holstered handgun was secured on her belt.

The sheriff was no more a typically dressed sheriff than the detective. Shane Mayes, son of a former sheriff, wore jeans as well, boots, and a white shirt with the sleeves rolled back along his strong forearms, rather than the typical uniform.

Alex Jansen was Bliss's uncle through his marriage to Natches's sister, Janey, and Erin's father. Shane Mayes and Samantha Bryce were close friends of the family.

Moving to them were three undercover DHS operatives and one very pissed-off assistant director of DHS, Chatham Bromleah Doogan. The assistant director was engaged to Dawg's youngest sister while two of the others had married his older sisters, Eve and Piper.

The family ties were starting to get a little tangled amid the Mackays, Angel thought with a spurt of humor, and with that group involved she had no idea what Duke thought they could do there.

"Why are we here?" she asked him quietly as he parked the Jeep behind a black pickup in a neighbor's yard. "Looks like Mackay family members have this pretty well covered."

Duke glanced at her before turning his attention back to the scene. "There's a lot of people here." He nodded to the crowd.

"And there are two dead bodies inside. I figure whoever came in gunning for her might be curious."

Oh, she had no doubt they'd be curious, but she wasn't so certain they'd hang around and risk being seen just hours after hitting the house.

"Why go in shooting? They tried to abduct her earlier, not kill her," she pointed out.

"And that didn't work," he reminded her, his gaze still narrowed on the crowd. "Maybe they weren't taking chances this time, or maybe they thought to get anyone protecting her out of the way before snatching her. Whatever they were here for, they figured out the hard way that this house was a setup. I want to ID the bodies and I want to see who's here, who's watching, and see if I can't get a lead on who's so determined to get one little fifteen-year-old kid."

As he spoke, he was quickly snapping pictures with the small camera he'd pulled from the glove box. And if his movements were any indication, he wasn't missing much where the milling crowd was concerned.

"You're just here for pictures?" She slid him a doubtful look. "Wouldn't you learn more if one of us was actually in the crowd? And what's on the security cameras?"

"The cameras showed four black-clad, black-masked figures, and a van parked across the street but no plates. So they weren't of much help. We have the crowd covered, though," he assured her. "There's no less than four friendlies making their way among those gathered out there and hearing what there is to be heard. And I'd rather just sit back for the moment and see what Jansen and the others find first."

A waste of time, in other words.

"I could be sleeping." She sat back in her seat, ignoring him as he scowled at her. "I didn't come out with you to sightsee."

And she was damned tired. It had been a hell of a day and all she wanted to do was escape it.

"You're the one that always demands recon," he pointed out, staring at the people milling around in the street.

It was three o'clock in the morning, for Christ's sake. Hadn't they figured out that the excitement was over for the night?

"I don't demand recon when I haven't slept for twenty-four hours and I'm running on caffeine rather than a good night's rest." She was running on aspirin, caffeine, and ragged emotions was more like it. "Even I have my limits."

She sipped at the coffee she held in her hand, aware that she was defeating the purpose by drinking it.

"You're admitting to limits," he murmured. "You surprise me."

She just bet she did.

"This is pointless." She brushed at the fringe of bangs that escaped the clip she'd hastily anchored her hair in. "What's going on in that house isn't going to help us until they identify the dead. Unless something useful was actually recorded by the security cams." She took another sip of coffee.

Her eyes narrowed on the crowd, assessing the bodies, the expressions, the small groups that huddled together and those standing alone. Not that many were standing alone.

Two of the four standing back and watching were definite Mackay associates; she'd seen them with one or another of the cousins several times in the past year or so. The other two she remembered seeing recently fishing at the lake.

"Those two." She nodded to where they stood some distance apart. "Did you snap their picture?"

"I did, but they're turned this way more now." He snapped several more shots. "You recognize them?"

"I've seen them at the lake, just as I've seen the majority of everyone else that's milling around here rather than going back to bed," she snorted. "I saw them hanging around at the fishing hole near an old cabin a few miles from the marina. But since they're not known to me as Mackay associates, let's check them out. I'd rather be safe than sorry."

She continued to stare around, watching the crowd silently, the way groups shifted, grew then dissipated. Even the four loners drifted into the smaller groups a few times, but there was nothing that really snagged her attention.

"Why did you wait so long to tell Chaya and Natches who you are?" The question was asked casually, as though it were something commonplace to ask.

It had her staring blindly into the small crowd, though, tension building through her body as she fought the need to confide in him.

"Why? Need more information to give your cousin and his wife?" Her lips curled derisively. "I think you probably had enough to give them."

He should have. He'd fought alongside her and her brothers, he'd met their parents, and he'd even vacationed with them in Bermuda.

"I had enough to ensure the truth was backed up," he admitted. "Something you should have done. Instead, you threw the information at her as though it were a grenade ready to explode."

She turned her head, staring through the window at her side and, hopefully, hiding her expression. "It was what she wanted. It was what she demanded."

And she'd never imagined she'd be turned away. At the very

least she was certain someone would demand DNA. Question her, maybe. Give her the smallest benefit of the doubt. Ask for proof. Ask her why she hadn't come forward sooner maybe. She hadn't expected a complete denial, though perhaps she should have.

"Or was it what you demanded?" The question had anger flaring inside her. "Why didn't you tell her sooner, Angel? Years ago?"

Because she'd known, she had already known her mother didn't want her. That wound was still too deep, too agonizing to allow anyone to delve into it.

"This isn't a conversation I want to have with you." It wasn't a conversation she wanted to have with anyone. "It was a mistake and I should have kept my mouth shut. . . ." She snapped her fingers and turned toward him with mocking innocence. "Oh yeah, that's right. You just handed over the information, right? I should have just waited for you. Funny that, considering how well you hid the fact that you were a Mackay from me."

Turning his head, he just stared at her, the deep, bright depth of his green eyes gleaming back at her.

"You shouldn't have ditched me when you found out who I was." His expression, shadowed by the night and the interior of the vehicle, gave away little as to what he was thinking. Or what he was feeling. If he was feeling anything. "I didn't take you for a coward."

"Yeah, I should have just gone to my knees and thanked you for finding me," she drawled with heavy mockery, the insult stinging more than she would have liked. "But I guess I just didn't consider myself lost, now did I?" She gave a little wave of her hand. "But you Mackays, just so certain you know every damned thing, right?"

Silence met her words.

Turning back to stare out the windshield as he rested his arm on the steering wheel, Duke seemed to be glaring out at the scene.

"You've known who your mother is for a while, haven't you, Angel?" he asked softly. "Well before I showed up in Uzbekistan."

Angel clenched her teeth; the memory of being trapped, held beneath that steel beam as the weight of the debris above it tried to crush the life from her, was just an added nightmare in her life.

She was going to die there. That certainty had filled her, a knowledge she hadn't been able to escape from. And she'd begged Tracker, made him swear to watch out for Bliss for her.

That was the moment Duke and his brother had arrived. When no one else outside the bombed hospital would enter for fear of collapse, Duke had rushed inside. There was no panic, nothing but sheer confidence as his brother, Ethan, moved to her to assess her condition, and Duke moved to Tracker and Chance as they fought to hold the weight from her body.

And somehow, through some miracle, Duke had managed to find the one place where that beam could be lifted just enough for Ethan to drag her free of it.

"I knew." There was no point in denying it. "I've known since I was fifteen years old. There's very little of my time in Iraq that I don't remember now."

"You were only three." The question in his tone was unmistakable. How could she remember what had happened when she was only three?

"I remember my first birthday party," she said softly, the memory, though not as clear as others, there all the same. "The faces of the children that attended, the clown that scared the hell out of me. I remember Chaya dancing in the backyard with the knife she kept on her. I remember when she pushed that knife

into a pocket she'd made in the teddy bear I loved." She blinked
back the emotions the memories always brought. "I'm a little
fuzzy on what happened after the world shattered around me,
but according to Tracker's father, I had a concussion and several
broken bones, so I'm going to excuse myself for not remembering that time clearly."

She'd existed in ignorant bliss for twelve years after the hotel
explosion, though. She was Angel, Tracker and Chance were her
brothers, and she had to train, and learn how to survive. That
had been her world. Until the day Brutus, J.T.'s huge war dog,
had died from old age.

She remembered the horror, the abject certainty that without
Brutus, she would die. She'd sobbed until she fell into an exhausted slumber, and when she'd awakened, she knew who she
was, where she came from, the mother that had betrayed her.
And the sister that had died in her arms.

She could feel Duke, waiting silently, certain he'd gain more
information for the family he was apparently so damned loyal to.

Not that she could blame him, really. The Mackays were
good people for the most part, especially the three older cousins,
Dawg, Rowdy, and Natches. They were more often than not
referred to as brothers rather than cousins.

Hell, she was as jealous as she could be of the father her half
sister, Bliss, had been born to. Natches loved his daughter, protected her, would die for her, but even more, he'd kill for her. But
he'd never use her to save himself as her own had done. And
after watching Bliss's mother, Chaya, Angel suspected the same
of her. Which only bred the anger inside her because Chaya
hadn't felt that same loyalty for her first child, or for the niece
who had died waiting for her.

"You're going to have to talk about this eventually," Duke

warned her when she didn't say anything more. "If not to me, then to Natches and Chaya."

That was something she hadn't even done with Tracker, no matter how often he encouraged her to, or how deeply she trusted him.

"I don't have to talk to anyone about this," she stated coolly despite the burning emotions searing her. "And calling Tracker won't change my mind. If he wants to fly back here because I refuse to discuss this with you then it's his choice. I won't be blackmailed further."

"What do you think is going to happen when you refuse to give Natches answers?" Was that amusement in his voice?

She turned her head, narrowing her eyes on him as their gazes met, and she detected a gleam of humor.

"Natches isn't the boss of me," she enunciated clearly, teeth clenched at the very thought of it. "No more than you or Tracker are."

He chuckled at that, a dark, warning sound that had her fists clenching at her thighs.

"Honey, when Natches can't get his answers from you, then he'll track down Tracker and Chance. If they don't have those answers, then he'll go for J.T. and Mara. Is that what you want?" The gentle if foreboding question was no more than another warning and she was growing sick of them. Going to J.T. and Mara would be about as productive as asking Tracker, Chance, or even Duke. Because they didn't know. Angel had never told anyone about the phone call her father had made to Chaya. Except Bliss.

"Take me back to the hotel, Duke," she demanded. "There's nothing to see here and this conversation isn't going anywhere. . . ."

"Natches wants you at the house," he interrupted her, his

tone hardening. "You revealed yourself to Chaya because you wanted to protect Bliss. And I know you're probably one of the best protection agents I've ever met. Well, you've been contracted for the job. Call Tracker if you want to argue the decision."

The Jeep started with a powerful rumble as Angel stared back at him in shock, her heart clenching then beginning a hard, sluggish beat. Jerking it into gear he reversed smoothly before pushing it into first and heading away from the decoy safe house.

"That's not going to work." She had to force the words past her lips. "And taking me to their home isn't going to work. Take me back to the hotel."

She couldn't face Chaya, not tonight, not with so little time after her mother's denial of her. She would have begged Chaya to allow her to help protect Bliss if the other woman hadn't become so determined to know why.

Why? Why?

The demands and the insults had bit into her like a dagger, twisting and turning in an already brutalized wound.

There was a part of her, she readily acknowledged, that was still three and feeling the horror of her mother's refusal to come for her and Jenny. To know that her mother was too busy with a man she'd just met hadn't made sense at the time. Her mother would never choose anyone over her, definitely not a man.

But she'd done just that.

By the time the memories had returned Angel was old enough to understand, to have seen the things some women would do for a man. She'd seen women leave their children with family, with strangers, and she'd even realized that some women would kill their children to have the man they wanted. Loyalty to a child, to their own flesh and blood first, wasn't something a lot of people understood in the world she'd been raised in. But as a child, as a three-year-old, it had been intrinsic to her life.

"Tracker officially accepted the contract just after he contacted you. Are you refusing the job?" The question was delivered with a smooth, masterful stroke as he glanced at her, his brow lifting, his brooding expression revealed by the Jeep's interior lights. "Cancellation goes through the service, not Tracker," he reminded her. "So far the team has a clean slate where black marks are concerned. Want to bet Natches will be pissed enough to inform the service that Tracker can't control his people now?"

As if she wasn't aware of the drawbacks of listing through the anonymous service that secured the jobs the team agreed to. Without a hell of a good excuse, there was no way to cancel out any black mark Natches or Chaya used for Angel's denial of the job.

She just hadn't considered the fact that they would do so.

"This is a personal matter. . . ." she tried to argue.

"Won't matter, Angel," he assured her as he made the turn onto the main highway leading back to the hotel. "If you don't show up to the house before dawn, the listed time of arrival, then don't think Natches won't lose his fucking temper. He's already had to watch Chaya completely break down when he showed her the file I arrived with. If he has to watch her hurt further because you're refusing to come to them, he won't care how he hurts Tracker professionally. He'll do it, even if he has to regret it later."

She turned her head again, watching as the Jeep passed the heart of the business center, the lights lowered, shops closed. Sometimes, she wondered at the life that passed by her as she drove through the cities and towns she'd been in over her life. What she was missing, what she might have known, if only . . .

"You'd think Tracker would realize that she's hurt me enough without giving her carte blanche to further it," she finally said, the words slipping free before she could stop them. "She didn't want me when I was three and she doesn't want me now." She turned back to him, eyeing him with icy fury. "And I don't appreciate you or Natches Mackay forcing me on her. So, don't expect me to pretend that I do."

The Jeep swerved as he twisted the wheel, pulled it into the parking lot of a grocery store, and jerked the vehicle to a stop.

"And what makes you think I'm trying to force anything from you or her?" he demanded, anger ringing in his voice as he pulled the parking brake and turned to her. "Damn you, Angel. You make me crazy!"

Before she could anticipate his next move or prepare herself for it he gripped the back of her head in one hand, his fingers threading through her hair, holding her still, and his lips covered hers.

Shock held her still, but it wasn't shock that had her lips parting for the hungry lick of his tongue, and it wasn't shock that had her fingers suddenly gripping his shoulders as she found herself lost in a pleasure she couldn't have expected.

Where had this come from? Why?

His fingers tightened in her hair; the ones gripping her hip slid higher, pressing beneath the suddenly swollen, sensitive curve of her breast. She was too warm, too excited now. It wasn't anger surging thick and hot through her bloodstream, but need, pleasure. . . .

A hunger she'd never experienced before and now had no idea how to combat. She became lost in it instead. The sensations, lightning and fire, her stomach tightening, her sex aching, her clit swelling so abruptly and with such demand that she had no idea how to counter it or how to stop it.

She responded to it instead.

The touch, the warmth, the hunger of his kiss; it had lived in her fantasies since she was rescued from the bombed hospital five years ago. From the moment she saw him, saw that hint of a smile at his lips and became lost in his gaze, she'd hungered for this.

And now that she had it, her heart ached, because she knew there was no way in hell she could ever claim the heart she'd dreamed of as well.

As quickly as his lips had covered hers, Angel found herself free long seconds later. Silently staring up at him as he continued to hold her, her gaze locked to his, her lips parted as she fought to drag in enough breath to think sensibly.

"You make me crazy," he muttered, releasing her far more slowly than he'd dragged her to him. "Absolutely fucking crazy."

Hadn't he already said that?

Rather than pointing that out she remained still and silent as he pushed the Jeep into gear and pulled out of the parking lot. She was certain if she tried to speak, her voice would tremble. The emotion she fought so hard to contain would slip free. That was the effect on her. It didn't matter how hard she tried to remain aloof from him, her emotions sabotaged her every time.

It was nearly four in the morning when they reached the hotel. She was over twenty-four hours without sleep and her ass was seriously dragging, not to mention her common sense where Duke was concerned.

Approaching her hotel room door, aware of Duke coming in behind her, she did a quick check, though the sliver of folded paper she'd inserted between the door and the frame was exactly where she'd placed it earlier.

There were no guests or surprises inside, just the tempting mattress and silence of the room and the knowledge that facing Natches and Chaya by dawn was a really bad idea.

"Call Natches, Duke," she breathed out wearily, knowing she was in no shape for such an emotional event. "I need to sleep first, then I'll be there. If you wanted me there at dawn, then you shouldn't have taken me into town instead."

She would lodge a protest with the listing service if a Mackay decided to be prick enough to complain. And Tracker would just have to deal with it in the event that they were charged a fee for the protest.

"They'll let you sleep there, Angel," he scoffed behind her.

"You don't want me to face her right now!" She turned on him, the words tearing past her clenched teeth as her patience level dipped lower.

He was closer than she'd known, only inches from her. So close that he gripped her arms as the sudden turn left her wobbling, the wound at her thigh protesting the move with painful force.

"Dammit." She pulled from him, breathing out with a harsh sigh and unclipping her hair as her head actually began to ache. "My patience is nonexistent. If I have to deal with her, I won't be nice. Don't you understand that?"

She knew the person she was and she knew what pain and exhaustion did to her. She became a bitch. A vulgar-mouthed, take-no-prisoners, hurt-them-as-she-hurt bitch. And that wasn't the person she was now. It wasn't the person she had been for years.

She was aware of Duke watching her closely now. Did he remember the vicious, always-angry person she had been when he'd first joined the team? That had actually been the nice her at the time.

Moving away from him she would have stomped to the bed if she thought her leg could handle it. Stepping to the side of the mattress she sat down next to the bedside table. There, her trusty bottle of aspirin waited. Uncapping the bottle she shook three into her palm then reached for the bottle of whiskey tucked between the bed and table, and washed down the pills.

Replacing the bottle she pushed her fingers through her hair and lifted her head, staring back at him as he stood a few feet away, his arms crossed over his chest as he stared down at her suspiciously.

"You can pick me up at noon," she told him, trying to sound reasonable as she rose to her feet and tried to project an air of demand rather than weakness. "I'll be ready to go then."

A mocking snort met the attempted compromise.

"You'll be gone, likely flying out to skin Tracker for agreeing to the job." His smile was knowing. "I don't think so, baby."

"I promise, Duke," she assured. "I'll be here."

And she didn't break her promises any more than he and Tracker would.

"I'll give you to noon, but I'm staying with you," he announced, moving to her slowly as Angel felt her breath beginning to shorten. "That way, I'm not awake all morning worrying about it."

Sleep with him?

"That's not a good idea. . . ."

"You've slept with me before, Angel," he reminded her, his voice pure, silky seduction. "Go on, get ready for bed." He nodded to the bathroom.

Sitting down on the chair next to the table he pulled off the first boot, then the second.

Yeah, she'd slept next to him, fully dressed, a time or two. But never like this.

"I don't need a babysitter," she ground out between her teeth.

"Too bad." He grinned. "You want to sleep? We'll sleep and then leave together."

Her lips thinned, eyes narrowing as she shot him a look of promised retribution before turning and going to the bathroom. He was so damned stubborn, so bossy. The man was a freak when it came to demanding.

And sleeping with him was a very bad idea. And yet, she knew she would do just that.

She hurriedly brushed her teeth, removed her jeans and shirt, leaving her clad only in the boy shorts and tank top she wore beneath them. Something he'd seen her in plenty of times, she reminded herself. She changed the bandage on her leg at the unsightly dark stain of blood beneath it, and hoped a few hours' sleep would help the healing process.

When she was finished, she left the bathroom, went straight to the bed, and climbed beneath the blankets. She didn't even pause at the sight of him already propped against the pillow as he typed a message into his phone.

"No later than noon," he warned her, turning his head to stare at her, his green eyes darker, the latent sensuality on his face causing her breathing to shorten once again.

"Fine. Turn out the light so I can sleep." She felt like she was suddenly strangling on the heat and desire flooding her body.

She knew this was a very bad idea.

The light went out; the powerful body next to her was close enough that she could feel his warmth. That she didn't feel so alone.

And she was tired.

So very tired.

FIVE

She was tough, she'd told Tracker before he'd left her in Somerset the day before. She didn't need his help. She didn't need protection.

When she'd risen from bed she'd ignored Duke, showered, changed the bandage on her leg again, and dressed in a pair of dun-colored mission pants, matching T-shirt, and the well-worn ankle boots she used while on a job.

She strapped the knife Chaya had given her so long ago to her thigh. The small Glock she carried was holstered and clipped in the small of her back and hidden by the loose fit of the T-shirt.

It didn't take long to collect the few items that weren't already stored in the duffel bag she carried while Duke showered. Within an hour after waking she picked up the bag and followed Duke from the room to the Jeep.

It was just another job.

She'd done this so many times she could handle it in her sleep, she told herself as Duke drove away from the hotel.

She would stay at the clients' home, protect their daughter, and when the threat was taken care of, she'd go to another job.

That simple, that easy.

She stared out at the sun-drenched scenery as Duke drove through the town's busy business center and into the more rural area leading to Natches Mackay's lakeside home.

She fought the emotions roiling inside her. Years of anger, pain and betrayal, hopes, dreams, and nightmares.

"Momma was supposed to come get us." She assured the little girl who lay so still and silent, her face and pretty dress covered with a heavy layer of dust and so much blood.

She patted Jenny's face, sobbing, her own tears making it hard to see, the fear and the pain that Momma wasn't coming clawing at her chest. "Momma was supposed to come. . . ."

"You okay?" Duke's voice pulled her back from the destructive memory. "You're too quiet."

"I'm fine," she forced herself to answer him, just as she forced herself to stay in the Jeep, to breathe, to keep from screaming out in rage.

Inside, the emotions threatened to break through the carefully built defenses she'd erected over the years. She'd gone to war since she was a child, fought, protected, been forced to kill, and never had she felt so off balance as she did now.

Never had she been so aware of the fact that she had spent far too little time doing anything other than going to war.

It had simply been her life. Kill or be killed. Protect or die. That was J.T. and Mara's motto. Protect or die. It was the motto she'd been raised with right along with Tracker and Chance.

"You're too quiet." Once again Duke interrupted her thoughts, pulling her back from that place where she could hide from the implications of what was coming just a little while longer.

"I'm working," she stated, concentrating on the road rather than the scenery, refusing to track the remaining distance to their destination.

"You're lying." The accusation wasn't unexpected.

"Leave me alone, Duke."

"I was fifteen when I met Chaya the first time. Did you know that?" There was a heaviness to his voice, an edge that she didn't understand.

"What does that have to do with anything?" She needed to hide just a little while longer, and he wouldn't let her.

"The first time I ever saw her was the day she arrived with a dozen DHS agents and dragged my parents from our home in handcuffs. It was the same time I learned they were part of Freedom League, and working closely with Natches's father, Dayle." The statement wasn't filled with anger, fury, or betrayal. It was a statement of fact.

Chaya had been the agent involved in uncovering Dayle Mackay and the remaining Freedom League members as the traitors they were, Angel remembered.

"My parents were Trent and Marie Mackay. Trent Mackay was responsible for the command that sent that missile slamming into the hotel in Iraq. He's the reason she believed her daughter was dead."

Angel turned to him slowly, seeing the two-fisted grip he had on the steering wheel, the savage expression on his face.

She watched his jaw work as his teeth clenched and she knew the toll this confession was likely taking on his pride.

"I already knew who sent that missile to the hotel," she told him, ignoring the surprise in his look. "J.T. and Mara realized who I really was because the news of the arrests in Kentucky had been a hell of a sensation at the time. Then they pulled in everything they could on Chaya. But I was only nine at the time, so they didn't tell me what they learned. I didn't remember anything about Iraq until I was fifteen, and then I started asking questions. Once Tracker told me *you* were a Mackay, it didn't take long to piece together your real identity."

The look he shot her was so shocked and filled with offended male pride it almost caused her to be amused. Unfortunately, even offended Mackay pride didn't have the power to affect the sheer terror building inside her.

"I've known since about two seconds after Tracker told me you're a Mackay," she stated. "But you're not to blame for his crimes any more than Natches is to blame for his father's crimes. Or I'm to blame for Craig's."

Duke let that sink in for a moment. "Did your brother tell you that Ethan and I stayed with her and Natches for a while after the arrests?" he asked her when he turned his gaze back to the road.

She could only shrug. "Is it important?" She couldn't imagine why it would be. "If I don't blame you for your father's crimes, then I won't blame you for being forced to spend time with Chaya."

He grunted at the comment.

Not that she was completely fair-minded, Angel admitted. There had been a week or two that the knowledge that Duke's father, Trent, had been the cause of Jenny's death had sliced at her like a particularly sharp dagger.

The knowledge had dug inside her, infuriated her, until she remembered the man that helped rescue her in Uzbekistan. The same man that nearly lost his mind a year later when a knife had been pushed in her back, piercing her lung; and a year after that, she'd been hit by a pickup driven by one of the men that had kidnapped a preteen in France. Last year, she swore she remembered hearing him pray when she'd taken a bullet in her side—that one had nearly killed her.

Ethan had to work hard to fix her that time. He operated on her right there in the same shack where they'd busted two terrorists holding a young couple they'd kidnapped while on honeymoon. Tracker and Duke both had yelled at her later. They always yelled at her later for not being careful, for being reckless, for being at the wrong place at the wrong time.

She'd spent a week in that shack with only short periods of lucidity that included listening to not just Duke and Tracker yelling at her, but Chance and Ethan as well.

"Ethan and I weren't forced to stay with Chaya and Natches," Duke objected, shooting her a cryptic look. "They took us in. The rest of the family was still under investigation. Chaya wouldn't let social services take us, though. She looked at us and told the agent in charge that she wouldn't allow another child to suffer, just because hers had been taken from her. When my uncle arrived from Montana and convinced my father's parents to let him take custody of us, Chaya and Natches actually suggested letting us stay with them. Ethan and I needed to leave, though. Needed distance, despite Chaya's objections."

Angel wanted to roll her eyes at the point he was obviously trying to make, but that would take at least a measure of levity. And that was something she just didn't have and couldn't fake right now.

"I really don't want to hear about her," Angel told him, her tone carefully bland. "Not now. Not later. I'll protect her daughter with my own life if need be, but I want nothing beyond that, and I won't give anything beyond that."

She couldn't. She simply didn't have the emotional fortitude to bear the pain it would bring.

The way it was, her heart clenched as ridiculous hope threatened to awaken inside her when Duke turned onto the one-lane, gravel road. She breathed in deep, reminded herself of the many difficult jobs she'd been on. She'd survived those, she could survive this.

"Will Bliss be there?" she asked, more to keep herself from exploding inside.

"She's with family outside the county at the moment. I think two Navy SEALs, two rangers, and two DHS agents can keep up with her until Natches and Chaya get back to her."

She nodded. What he wasn't saying was the fact that Seth and Saul August, distant cousins from Texas and hardened Navy SEALs, had arrived in the county just hours after the attempted abduction then disappeared. They were no doubt watching over her along with the others.

"How's she handling it?" Angel felt as though she were strangling on her own fears as they drew closer to Natches and Chaya's home.

"She's scared." Duke shot her a worried look as he made the second turn onto yet another gravel road. "Confused. But she's a lot like you, Angel. She's doing her best to learn how to help those around her protect her. I know Natches is both proud as hell and terrified of the strength he's seeing in her."

She nodded at that.

Bliss looked like a feminine version of her father, all the savage male lines blurred and softened to an exquisite beauty even at fifteen. She was like Natches inside as well, Angel always thought, no one else. She was strong, determined. What no one ever mentioned about Bliss, though, was the fact that a personal challenge was like a drug to the girl. When she won, it was a high for her.

The final turn was made, and Angel knew the twenty-year reprieve was over. She would once again face her mother as a daughter. But she wasn't three any longer, she reminded herself. Chaya couldn't quell anything she had to say or any decision she made with no more than a look. It was a privilege the other woman had thrown away the day she refused to come after her daughter.

As the house came into view, she felt it.

First, she felt the sights coming from two directions, the knowledge she was being tracked by a sniper. It was an unmistakable feeling, but in this case, she didn't feel the sensation when a finger lay on the trigger. She was being watched, nothing more. But she also felt a veil slam down over her emotions.

She'd survived because of that shield that held back fear, mercy, even pain whenever she faced combat. Training, J.T. called it. The mind's knowledge that the heart had no place there, that emotions would only weaken her, defeat her.

A mile later Duke turned onto the paved road that led to the house. Heavy evergreen vines and shrubs bordered the road on the side the house sat on. Growing tall and appearing impenetrable, the thick, thorny vines of the wisteria twisted and grew within the shrubs, and she knew the smaller, thickly growing vines were a trap just waiting for the unwary.

There were three ways past the natural border that grew nearly eight feet tall. The break at the front of the house when the gates across the driveway were open, another on the lake side of the house, and one that led into the mountains at the back of the house. All three were gated and armed with motion detectors as well as security cameras.

Natches Mackay was not known for his trusting nature.

"Angel, this is going to be okay."

She turned to him, staring at him, seeing him, and hearing him as she felt herself shutting down inside.

"Of course it is," she agreed. "It's just another job, Duke. Nothing more."

The front door opened and the couple stepped out.

Tall, black-haired, still handsome and powerful, Natches Mackay wrapped his arm around his wife's back, holding her beside him as he whispered something to her.

His wife didn't reply. She stared at the Jeep.

Angel slid from the vehicle, saw the flash of distaste in her mother's expression before it was carefully controlled, and reminded herself—it was just another job.

She'd faced other women that looked at her and saw a killer rather than an agent. A woman that was beneath them because she didn't wear silk blouses and linen slacks, makeup, or pretty jewelry.

There was a flash of pain as Chaya's gaze dropped to the knife Angel wore, though. But Angel had expected that as well. The knife had been given to her because she wouldn't stop crying before Chaya took her to the woman who was to keep her while Chaya was out of the country. It was given to her to shut her up, she guessed. Nothing more.

Keeping her head held high, her chin up, her shoulders straight, she walked at Duke's side, aware of the look Natches obviously shared with him but refusing to attempt to decipher it.

"I'm glad to see you made it." Natches nodded to her as they stopped at the single step to the cement porch.

Angel merely nodded in return. What did he expect her to say? She'd more or less been forced to show up.

"Come in. I put coffee on when you turned into the drive,"

Chaya invited, turning from them and leading the way to the house. "I'm sure you have questions."

"I'll need to know how much time I have before your daughter arrives back at the house. And I'd like a chance to walk through the property, ascertain its strengths and weaknesses for myself, then we can discuss any concerns I might have over coffee if you like." It was just another job.

So why did it feel as though she was breaking apart behind that shield she was hiding behind? And why did the memory of her own screams when she was only three haunt her?

Duke caught Natches's concerned look as he and Chaya turned back to them slowly. Restraining himself was never easy for the other man, Duke knew. He would have been more prone to drag Angel into a hard embrace as he welcomed her to his and Chaya's home. Chaya would have beat him to it. The need to drag Angel to her, to hold her daughter was like a hunger burning in her eyes.

Until Angel had stepped from the Jeep, her military correct shield in place, her "soldier" face more than just an appearance.

He'd felt her shut down. The second that door had slammed shut on her emotions, he'd felt it. Just as he'd felt it every time it happened after he'd joined Tracker's team five years ago. This wasn't the woman Duke knew. It was the woman she'd been at one time, but in the past few years, she'd softened until the hardened edge only showed itself minutes before going into danger.

The problem was, Angel wasn't merciful, she wasn't nice when she stepped into the soldier role. And neither she nor Chaya needed more pain at the moment.

"Very well." Chaya surprised him when she gave a sharp nod, but Duke caught the edge of her tone. "Would you like a brief rundown of the house or would you prefer to go through each room on your own first?"

Angel turned to her slowly, her blue-ringed gray eyes flat and hard.

"A brief rundown would be preferred, then I'd like some time to go through on my own," she replied, the ice in her voice nearly causing Duke to wince.

He'd give anything to warn her first about the one room he was sure she had no idea existed.

"Natches, would you like to show Angel around?" Chaya requested as she laid her fingers against his arm. "I'll take Duke to the kitchen for coffee and a slice of Ms. Tully's buttercream cake. I know how he likes that."

Angel showed no reaction, no preference either way.

"I can do that." Natches kissed her cheek gently, the tenderness, the obvious love he felt for her apparent in the gesture. "We'll be right back."

"Come along, Duke, you can tell me how Memmie Mary's doing," Chaya stated, turning her back and moving for the kitchen. "We rarely see the cousins these days. . . ."

Angel turned to Natches, watching the gentleness in his expression slowly evaporate as his gaze flickered with disapproval.

That look almost pierced the distance she placed between her and the situation. For some reason, his disappointment threatened to matter.

"I don't have a conflict with you, Natches, and I have no intentions of doing or saying anything that will hurt Bliss's mother unless she strikes first," she assured him, watching the disappointment ease, though his expression remained somber. "I'm here to do a job, just as I offered. Nothing more, and nothing less."

She'd protect her sister or die trying.

Before she could evade him, his arms were suddenly around her, her face smashed into his chest.

"Welcome home, girl," he whispered, his voice thick, obviously sincere. "You won't let her welcome you, but you can't stop me."

Angel jerked back, the shield cracking, pain surging through it, slapping at her, threatening to steal her objectivity, her training.

"Thank you for the gesture." It took everything she'd learned, every iota of strength she had found over the years to stare back at him as though she wasn't being flooded with a lifetime of grief and pain. "I'd like that tour of the house now, if you don't mind."

Duke saw the hunger, the pain, and the need as Natches jerked Chaya's daughter into a quick embrace before Angel pulled back.

He saw Angel's face when she pulled back, though.

Now Natches was showing her to the office that opened into the living room as well as the kitchen on one side. There was a door that led to a small patio outside as well.

"He'll show her the downstairs first," Chaya whispered, wrapping her arms around her breasts as she turned back to him. "He'll take her upstairs last."

Duke rubbed at the back of his neck. "He could wait. . . ."

The look he called Angel's "soldier" face flashed across Chaya's expression now. "No. If we're going to come to a place where we can talk and hear each other then she needs to see it."

"I hate to point this out," he reminded her. "But right or wrong, she faced you with that chance and she was told to leave, Chaya. Shocking her now might not be a good idea."

"Shocking her now is all I have left," she whispered. "But I'll give you the option of joining them. I don't think I can bear it."

Natches took Angel through the house, room by room. The office, then the kitchen, where Duke was enjoying a slice of Ms. Tully's luscious cake and coffee, then through the other side of the kitchen to a hall. There they turned to the left and entered the guest suite.

She and Duke would unfortunately have to share the suite, he informed her as they walked through a small kitchenette. Then he showed her into the sitting area and pointed out that the couch let out into a surprisingly comfortable bed.

The bedroom had a king bed, covered with an obviously old white bedspread that kissed the floor on each side. Soft, cream-colored carpeting, heavy wood shutters over the windows that folded back to open the room to the sunlight, and light oak furniture. An attached bathroom with both a walk-in shower as well as a garden tub. And a door to the patio off the kitchenette.

Leaving the guest suite they moved farther down the hall. Bliss's room was next, with a full-sized canopied bed, antique furniture, and a padded white rocking chair.

Angel stared at the chair as Natches pointed out the teenager's bathroom. The soft pink cushions were well-worn, the paint a little faded here and there, but it was sturdy and comfortable.

Especially to a three-year-old who liked reading her two-words-to-a-page storybooks.

Hop. Hop. She struggled with the word then did like her momma taught her and made the sounds of the word. Hop, boy.

"Angel?" Natches paused beside her. "The safe room's next."

She turned, followed him, ignoring the need to sit in that chair for just a moment.

He showed her the safe room, though she knew she'd have to

make him explain it to her again before Bliss came home, because she barely saw it. The same with his and Chaya's bedroom, then back into the living room.

She stared around, looking at the pictures in the room, seeing so many, but none of Chaya's first child.

"There's only one room upstairs," he told her as Duke joined them at the stairway leading to the upper room. "It's never used. Are you sure you need to see it?"

She nodded, still seeing that rocker, remembering the room it had sat in first. The room in the house Chaya had sold.

"Very well." He seemed to make some silent decision, then led the way up the wide stairwell. "Bathroom." He opened the door on the left of the landing. "Bedroom."

She stepped into the bedroom then froze.

She couldn't breathe.

She stared around the room, refusing to speak, barely able to hold back the screams of rage.

The twin bed she'd once slept on, the quilt she'd so loved still covering it. The big chair sitting beside the gas fireplace where Chaya had taught her to read. The white dresser, chest, and child-sized vanity littered with ribbons and bows and the brush she'd used to brush her hair.

On the bench at the bottom of the bed and in front of it were several small stacks of gaily wrapped presents. Who bought presents for a child that they believed was dead?

On the walls were white shelves, lined with her dolls.

Lying on the bed was the doll she'd slept with and hugged to her as a child. The large rag doll had been her favorite besides the teddy bear she called Binny. She didn't realize she'd walked to the bed, reached out, and almost touched the doll.

Cora. She'd named the doll Cora and she told her "good night" every night before she went to sleep. Cora lived in her bed; she didn't travel with the child as Binny had, but had waited patiently to hold back any bad dreams she might have while she slept.

The real nightmares didn't come in dreams, though, she thought. Life itself could be the real nightmare.

Duke moved to Angel, his chest aching as he blocked her expression from Natches just in time to allow her to keep the agony that crossed her face hidden. His cousin didn't need to see it. Dammit, he hadn't needed to see it.

She swallowed tightly as she caught sight of him in her periphery. Her body stiffened and she turned from the bed, her gaze meeting his for only a second. What he saw there had his jaw clenching in fury.

"I'm finished." She walked past him, moving with that precise, loose-limbed walk she used when she knew danger was close. "We can discuss the layout after I walk the grounds."

Angel felt threatened. She was off balance and she was hurting and all that training over the years was the only thing that kept her from breaking.

He followed her, aware of Natches closing the door softly behind him as Angel went down the stairs, not even pausing on her way to the front door when her mother stepped to the foyer.

She was escaping. Running away until she could handle whatever emotions were threatening to escape all that careful control.

Chaya might be right, she might have needed to see the room, but Duke still disagreed with the lack of warning she'd been given.

"Did you know about it?" she demanded, her voice rougher, her control shakier as he caught up with her in the front yard, moving beside her as she strode along the rock walkway that wove through the multitude of flower beds.

"The bedroom?" He breathed out roughly. "I knew," he answered at her sharp nod. "But would you have believed me if I told you? Or accepted it?"

She paused, breathing in deep, and Duke saw the faintest tremble at her lips.

Damn Natches and Chaya.

Damn him.

He should have gone to Natches a year ago, the second he had the proof he'd been looking for, the pictures he'd found in an envelope in the back of one of the albums Mara Calloway had brought with her to the vacation house they'd invited Duke and Ethan to.

The pictures of the nearly broken child, the same child in the pictures Duke had seen in Natches and Chaya's home when he was younger. Though in those pictures, the child had smiled, laughed, and looked out at the world with curious, bright eyes.

"It's just a job," she said then, her voice low, her shoulders straightening as she turned and stared at him coolly. "It's just a job."

Duke nodded slowly. "If that's what it takes to help you sleep at night, then I'll go with that. For now."

Because he knew better. Both of them knew better. But he knew she wasn't quite ready to accept it yet.

SIX

The house was beautiful, as were the grounds, and it was obvious Natches and Chaya loved their home, Angel admitted silently as she and Duke retreated to the guest suite several hours later to settle in.

And their daughter.

Through the entire house the one thing that had really drawn her attention was the pictures. Framed, sitting on end tables and the mantel in the living room, hanging on the walls along the hall were dozens of pictures of Bliss growing up. Family portraits and spur-of-the-moment shots, yet there wasn't a single picture of Chaya's first child. Not alone, nor with her mother.

Not that Angel pointed that out.

She noticed it, felt the loss in her soul, but she remained silent.

Dropping her pack onto the overlarge chair next to the patio doors, she set the duffel bag beside it and stared at the cushioned furniture and shaded bistro table, ignoring Chaya, Natches, and Duke.

"Bliss will be home later tonight," Chaya stated, pulling Angel's attention back to her as she noticed the additional tension in the other woman's voice.

Natches stood behind his wife, his hand at her hip, his gaze locked on Angel, the emerald color of his eyes predatory and wild with the fury he was holding back. Chaya stood with her hands clasped in front of her nervously, obviously worried.

"Is she okay?" Angel directed the question to Natches.

"She's safe." The snap in Chaya's tone drew Angel's gaze back to her. "Bliss doesn't know who you are yet. I don't want to tell her."

Chaya continued speaking, Angel continued staring at her, but something was crashing through her soul. It swirled inside her with a dark, vicious pain she had no idea how to process.

How could it hurt more? How could anything inside her be left to shatter? Her heart simply couldn't break any further, could it?

Bliss was dealing with too much right now. Fear and pain filled Chaya's voice, her expression. She didn't want the teenager to lose focus, to be distracted from remaining safe. She didn't want her daughter to have to process another shock until the time was right.

Is there a right time? Angel wondered in disbelief.

She nodded when appropriate. She made herself breathe, made herself live through the additional, unexpected blow. Though she knew she should have expected it.

"Angel . . ." Chaya whispered when she finished, her arms lifting as though pleading for Angel to understand.

"Not a problem." She pushed the words past her lips. "That's for the best, of course. There's no reason for her to be further upset when this is over and it's time for me to leave."

Chaya's arms lowered slowly and she turned to her husband, his expression hardening savagely as he stared at Duke.

As though Duke could do something, fix something. They were obviously expecting more from her and she had no idea what more they could expect.

"We'll let you settle in," Natches said, his voice grating. "Breakfast is usually at seven." His gaze sliced back to her. "I expect you to be there, Angel. We don't miss family meals in this house. That means breakfast at seven, the evening meal at five, and if you want lunch, make yourself at home in the pantry."

He drew his wife from the suite then and closed the door behind them.

"She must have learned to cook," she said softly, remembering Chaya's habit of burning most of the meals she attempted when Angel was younger.

Propping one hand on her hip she narrowed her eyes on the door. They didn't miss family meals. He expected her to be there. As though she were three again.

"As though they consider me family." Bitterness threatened to overwhelm her.

"Being a bitch isn't going to help the situation, Angel," Duke accused her, causing her to turn and glare back at him. There was no anger in his expression, but she could see the disappointment there.

"What the fucking hell do you and Natches want from me?" she snarled, the emotions tearing through her finally boiling over. "God damn the two of you. Son-of-a-bitch Mackay misfits. You're a fucking plague with no hope of a cure. Leave me alone already or get the hell away from me!

"'We don't miss family meals in this house,'" Angel mocked Natches's order. "Who the fuck does he believe he is? My father?" She sneered, but it was the pain that added the insulting tone. "Not hardly. And when did that woman learn to cook without trying to burn the kitchen down at the same time? She couldn't have cooked when I was three if her very life depended on it. And you." She pointed at him then, her gray eyes like thunder clouds rolling over the mountains. "Being a bitch, am I?" She sniffed at the accusation. "I have yet to be a bitch. I was actually putting myself out to be fucking nice."

His brow arched at the statement, lips quirking in challenge as he watched her flush with anger.

"Sorry, sweetheart, that's where you're wrong," he informed her. "For the situation and the emotions ripping at both of you? She was doing her best to hold back the need to grab you and hold you while you were doing your best to keep her as far from you as possible."

The bitter, jeering laugh that passed her lips was painful to hear, Duke acknowledged.

"Dying to hold me, was she?" She snorted, that sneer curling her lips causing his hands to touch her, his heart aching to take away the pain. "I guess that's why she couldn't possibly tell Bliss who I am. Right? Because she just loves me so much, doesn't she, Duke?"

The emotions raging through Angel didn't need a gentle touch, though. She was looking for a fight instead. How many times had he watched her burn like this until she became lost, completely alone in the fury consuming her? It never failed that she'd end up in a fistfight with someone when she was like this. If he, Ethan, Tracker, or Chance didn't manage to stop her.

"She's dying to hold you," he assured her. "And all you

wanted to do was draw blood. You're not that person, baby, to deliberately hurt an innocent person."

He was pushing her and he knew it. Pushing the anger and the pain, but until she acknowledged the fact that she felt it, she'd never get past it.

"Innocent? You think you know so much, don't you?" She flipped her hand toward him dismissively. "All your fucking research and your big file on my life. You don't know a damned thing. You're so called facts? Those aren't facts, those are other people's ignorance of the situation, nothing more."

His brow arched at the deliberately goading statement.

"Did you see the file?" he asked knowingly.

She hadn't, and part of that was his fault, he admitted.

"I lived it," she exploded, pointing at him accusingly. "Every second of the last twenty years I lived the life that . . . woman," she spat, "left me to live. I don't need to read your fucking file. I was there!"

"You were three, not an adult," he reminded her, frowning back at her, his gaze harsh. "Just because you remember the event doesn't mean you understood it. Or that you remember it correctly."

Her eyes narrowed, her fists clenched at her side.

"Don't presume to pretend you know anything about my memories, because I assure you, you don't," she snapped furiously.

A fine tremor raced through her, the emotions she kept so carefully contained inside her tearing her apart.

"Because you refuse to discuss it," he told her calmly, shrugging at the accusation. "Because you tell no one, Angel. You keep it all inside you and draw your own conclusions, just as you did when your mother tried to explain to you about Bliss."

"Bliss's mother," she burst out, that finger pointing out again, her voice hoarse. "Not mine."

"Your mother, Angel." His expression hardened, his arms going over his chest in that dominant pose strong men seemed to like so well. "You share a mother with your sister. Chaya is your mother as well, whether you want to accept it or not."

The hell she was. Angel didn't have a mother. She hadn't had a mother for twenty years and she didn't need one now.

"Not my mother," she rasped, enraged now. "My mother would have come to get me, no matter what. She would not have let my sister die in my arms because she couldn't drag her ass away from Natches Mackay. . . ."

And there it was, the answer he'd searched for, the reason Angel had refused to inform her mother she was still alive. The reason why the fury was threatening to engulf her now.

"Chaya was in the hospital when you were at that hotel, Angel," he told her carefully, watching her, wondering just how much she knew about her mother's last days in Iraq. "She'd been grabbed in Iraq and tortured for hours when Natches found her. She was lucky to be alive."

She inhaled raggedly, teeth clenching, a tremor shaking her body as she fought to bring herself back under control, to force the shield back in place.

"It doesn't matter where she was," she all but whispered. "She left me and Jenny and we paid for it. Jenny paid with her life." She shook her head slowly. "I won't lose Bliss as well."

Her fingers curled over the knife still strapped at her thigh, something she did often when she was upset, Duke knew. As though it comforted her in some way. The knife her mother had left with her, and how many times had it saved her life over the years?

"And you think refusing to discuss any of this is going to help you protect Bliss?" he asked her, watching as she paced to the doors of the private patio before turning back to him.

"It won't hurt." The shrug was careless, as though it didn't matter, but he knew better.

She was so incredibly stubborn it amazed him. It was that stubbornness that had assured her survival over the years, though. Her determination to do what had to be done to not just live but help protect the family that raised her, no matter the personal cost to her tender heart. Or the risk to her life.

"Keep thinking that," he told her knowingly. "And let me know how it works out for you."

Angel hated that look of smug male superiority that settled on Duke's face. Arrogant, superior. It never failed to irritate the hell out of her.

"It works out fine for me," she assured him with a curl of her lip. "And it will work out fine for her as well. Trust me, that woman has no desire to acknowledge who I am. Your information and her husband's Mackay sense of responsibility are the only reasons I'm here. Not because of any motherly love."

"Really?" His arms went over his chest again. "And the bedroom? How does that tie into your opinion of her feelings for you, Angel? If she didn't love her child, why keep that bedroom so pristine?"

"Guilt." What else could it be? Her heart ached at the thought, though, because as she'd stood in that room she felt a crack in the shields she'd built over the years and found hope she was certain she'd eradicated once she'd realized who she was and remembered those final days before her life exploded around her.

What mother that loved her child refused to come for her? Angel couldn't imagine ever leaving her baby in such a way.

"If you knew Chaya, you'd know that wasn't true," Duke disagreed, frowning back at her reprovingly.

"Well, I don't know her," she agreed, giving into the mockery that refused to lie silent. "I won't take the blame for that, though. It lies squarely on her shoulders. Now, if you'll excuse me, I have work to do."

She was striding for the door as she spoke, intent on escaping the room and the argument brewing between them. The potential for that argument had been there since he'd shown up the night before.

And it wasn't antagonism toward Chaya that fueled it. It was the physical attraction, the memory of that kiss, and her knowledge that giving into it had the potential to hurt far more than ignoring it.

She never allowed herself to be distracted on a job. Distractions were dangerous, and she knew it.

She didn't make it past him. In one swift move Duke caught her, pulled her to him, and lifted her so her back was against the wall, his hard thighs parting hers as he pushed her head back and his lips covered hers.

It happened so fast there wasn't a chance to protest. There was no way to know what he intended; there was only the wild, burning heat of his kiss and the pleasure exploding through her senses. It caught her off guard. It ripped through any control she'd fooled herself into believing she had, and any shield she might have thought could protect her emotions or her senses.

The onslaught of sensations was destructive, mesmerizing. His lips were knowing, experienced, moving over her mouth as his tongue licked sensually against hers.

One hand cupped the side of her neck, his thumb beneath her

jaw, as though to hold her in position; the other cupped her rear, his fingers caressing, stroking through the thin material of the pants she wore.

She didn't know what to do, how to fight it. Her body stole that control, it reveled in the caresses, in the dominance of the kiss, and some inner sex kitten she didn't know she possessed rolled her hips against his, stroking the too-sensitive flesh between her thighs against the hard wedge of his erection as it pressed against her.

The layers of clothing between them weren't enough to protect her from the shift of his hips, the slow thrusts against her sex that had her clit swelling, sensitizing. Her world narrowed to the man that held her, the kiss and his touch and the arcing forks of pleasure tearing through her body then striking at her womb.

She ached. She needed.

Oh God, she needed . . .

Touch. Duke's touch. The forceful dominance, the male lust that consumed her and called her own forward to meet it, challenge it.

She was insane and she was helpless against it, had no idea how to combat it. And when his hand moved from her rear to her hip, where he slid beneath the material of her T-shirt to find bare skin, she completely lost the rest of her breath.

It wasn't that he'd never touched her before; it was that he'd never really touched her before. The calloused roughened rasp of his fingers and hand slid up her side, then to the band of her plain cotton bra, where his fingers slid beneath, lifted the material, and found her pebble-hard, painfully sensitive nipple.

She cried out into his kiss. A sound that shocked her with the hungry need that filled it just as the involuntary arch of her body pushed her breast into his hand.

The sensations were chaotic; the feel of his fingers gripping the hard tip, tugging at it, tightening around it sent sharp explosions of sensations straight to her vagina. Her clit throbbed, ached, and she couldn't help but wonder how his fingers would feel there as well, stroking, exciting the little bud.

A gasp left her parted lips as Duke suddenly pulled back, breaking the kiss. Not that he gave her a moment to think or to find her common sense. Instead, his head lowered as he jerked her T-shirt above her breasts and his lips covered the tight, distended peak of her nipple.

"Oh my God, Duke. . . ." She latched her hands onto his hair, buried deep, and gripped the thick strands, certain she meant to pull his mouth from her.

Wet heat surrounded the tip, sensitizing it further, opening a pathway straight to her clit as the pull and tug of his mouth sent sharp bursts of heat to torment the flesh between her thighs.

"Oh sweet baby Jesus. Really!" The sharp, male disgust that suddenly punctuated the air had Duke jerking back even as he quickly pulled her shirt back over her exposed breast.

Natches stood at the entrance to the sitting and sleeping area, his back to them, hands on his hips, his head lowered to stare at the floor.

Angel felt her face flame with mortification.

"Moron!" She slapped at Duke's shoulders with both hands, struggling to extricate herself from his hold and regain her footing.

This was horrible.

Dear God.

"Doesn't anyone know how to knock on a damned door?" Duke muttered, releasing her as she struggled to straighten her clothes and cool the heat burning in her face.

She couldn't believe this. And no doubt bigshot Mackay would go tell his wife, wouldn't he?

"I knocked!" Natches turned back to them, his green eyes brilliant with outrage as he stared from her to Duke then finally settled on glaring at Duke. "I even called when I entered."

"The fact no one answered should have been your first clue," Duke snapped.

"Yeah, to get my damned rifle," Natches retorted, his tone grating. "She"—his finger stabbed in her direction—"is a Mackay daughter. For God's sake, Duke!"

"I'm a what?" She was the one outraged now. "The hell I am. Get a grip, Natches."

"The same as," he snarled. "The same as my daughter."

Angel stepped back, nearly reeling as her eyes widened.

"For God's sake!" She blinked back at the older man, then blinked again.

He was serious.

"If he tries to slap my ass in a convent, I'm going to shoot him myself," she muttered to Duke. "I need to find reality for a minute. Get rid of his ass while I'm gone."

Turning, she looked around desperately and settled on the bathroom. Ignoring the twinge in her leg she stomped to the door, stepped inside, and slammed it furiously.

A Mackay daughter? Give her a fucking break.

She ignored the ache in her chest, the envy, and the times she'd wondered what it would be like to have a father . . . a real father like her sister had.

She didn't need a father, she told herself furiously as she stepped to the sink and turned on the cold water. She was a grown woman, a mercenary. A killer. It was too late for a father. . . .

The second the bathroom door slammed, Duke turned back to Natches and his head exploded.

When he was able to shake the stars from his gaze and make sense of what happened he found himself flat on his ass staring up at Natches in shock.

"You just hit me," he accused his cousin, rather amazed that it had happened. As well as at the force behind it. "Son of a bitch."

Jumping to his feet, he made certain to put plenty of room between him and the other man as Natches rubbed his knuckles with his other hand, satisfaction filling his face.

"I should have shot you," Natches grunted, his voice irate. "What the hell were you thinking?"

His brow lifted and he watched Natches's lips compress furiously and stepped back another step. He wasn't letting that crazy bastard anywhere near him right now.

"Natches, you hit me again, and I'm hitting back," he promised. "You know how Chaya gets when that pretty face of yours gets all bruised up."

He made a mental note to make damned certain he locked the door from now on.

The look Natches shot him was one rife with outraged anger. Hell, it wasn't like he was Angel's father or anything.

"Listen to me, you little prick," Natches growled with no small amount of anger. "That girl is my daughter now—the same as—and I won't have you disrespecting her in her mother's home. You got me?" He stabbed a finger at him.

"You're insane, man." Duke stared at him, damned confused now. "Why the hell did you put us in here together then?" He couldn't help the amazed laugh that slipped past his lips. "I'm no monk and you should be smart enough to know it."

Natches's shoulders shifted beneath the light denim short-sleeved shirt he wore, his expression creasing with disapproval.

"That was Chaya's decision, not mine," he snapped. "I bet she'll change her mind now."

Duke couldn't help but laugh despite the promise of violence that flashed in Natches's gaze.

"I bet she won't," he disagreed. "Unlike you, your wife realizes Angel's a woman, not a child. What are you going to do when Bliss grows up?"

"Shut the fuck up!" Natches snarled as he took a step closer. "I sure won't let her around some deviant like you. No matter how old she is."

Duke laughed. He couldn't help it. It was simply that damned funny.

"Natches, do you forget the wild-assed shit you, Rowdy, and Dawg used to get up to?" He couldn't believe it. Mr. Ménage was calling him a deviant. "And you think you can actually—"

"Say it and I'll kill you." The promise was entirely too serious.

Hell. And if he wasn't mistaken, Natches was a little pale.

He laughed again, though this time, he did try to smother it.

"Fine, I'll let Chaya tell you all about it in a few hours." Amusement filled the promise. "Now what the hell do you want?"

Natches pushed his fingers through his hair and breathed out heavily.

"Chaya called Janey. She's sending dinner over," he growled.

"It'll be here in about an hour." He shook his head again. "Son of a bitch, there's just some things a man should never have to walk in on. . . ."

Swinging around he walked slowly from the sitting area, shaking his head and mumbling about convents.

Poor Natches.

He and Chaya should have had a boy. . . .

SEVEN

Breakfast wasn't exactly what Angel expected when she and Duke stepped into the kitchen the next morning, but at least everything she remembered about Chaya hadn't changed after all. The woman still couldn't cook worth a damn.

The smell of burned bacon attested to that fact.

"Mom, Dad said he'd do it when he came back in," Bliss reminded her mother patiently as Angel came to a stop and watched curiously.

She remembered a time when she had watched warily as Chaya attempted to cook. She was a hazard around the stove.

"Bliss, I'm begging you . . ." The frazzled, raw edge to Chaya's tone wasn't at all like her normal cool, calm tone. She actually sounded as though she were on the verge of tears.

"Mom, the bacon doesn't matter." Standing next to her mother, her eyes on the plate of well-blackened bacon, Bliss was confused and uncertain in the face of her mother's emotional response. "Angel won't care."

"Well, I care." Husky, torn, Chaya's tone had a fist squeezing around Angel's heart.

And it still pissed her off that she couldn't boil water without burning it, it seemed.

"Can I help?" It was as though even the air itself stilled in the room for long, silent moments.

Bliss's and Chaya's gazes jerked from the plate of bacon to Angel. Chaya's in regret while excitement and pleasure bloomed in Bliss's.

"Angel. Oh my God. You're here!" A little squeal and Bliss ran across the room, her arms going around Angel in a quick, tight hug.

"Hey, imp." Angel didn't bother to hide her affection for her sister, but she saw the way Chaya turned away and hurriedly dumped the bacon she'd burned in the trash.

"I'll have Natches run out for breakfast. . . ." she began as Bliss stepped back and Angel turned her attention to the other woman.

"Not necessary," Angel assured as she joined her at the kitchen island.

Chaya gripped the handle of the skillet and turned, placing it in the sink, keeping her back to the room as she began washing it.

"He won't mind in the least," Chaya continued. "He's used to it."

It sounded as though those were tears in her voice. Chaya crying because she couldn't cook? She should have already been over that little fact of life.

Moving silently, Angel selected another skillet from the rack hanging over the stove, turned on a burner, and placed the pan on the flame, then took the plate of unfried bacon Bliss pushed across the counter to her.

"Bliss, get Angel a cup of coffee," Chaya ordered, obviously fighting to control her breathing and whatever emotions had her near tears.

"Yes, Mom." Giving Angel a concerned look, Bliss moved to the coffeepot and the cups set out, ready to be filled.

Layering bacon into the skillet Angel remained silent, her head down, aware that Chaya turned back to her, watching her.

"I can't believe Natches let you have a gas stove," she muttered, still not glancing in her mother's direction. "Or that he actually allows you to use it. He's obviously brave as hell. Not to mention optimistic."

Silence met her statement, but Angel hadn't expected anything else.

"Coffee with plenty of sugar and cream." Bliss placed the coffee next to the stove top.

Turning to her sister she quietly asked for the ingredients she needed to finish the meal and ignored her mother.

"I can do my own cooking." The words sounded forced past Chaya's lips.

Angel shot her mother a mockingly doubtful look before muttering, "Since when?"

Chaya drew in a slow, careful breath, her nostrils flaring as her brown eyes lit with a combatant glare.

"Where are your baking flats?" Angel asked her, ignoring the assurance of culinary ability and her anger.

Evidently, Chaya was still trying to fool herself in that particular area.

"Cookie sheets?" Chaya snapped. "They are not baking flats."

"Same difference." Angel shrugged. "Just point me in the right direction."

"To your left." Natches spoke from the doorway leading to the living area. "Pots and extra pans to the left. Cooking utensils in the drawers to your right, dish towels and oven mitts in the drawers to your left."

"Leave the bacon alone," she warned her mother as Bliss began placing the ingredients she asked for on the counter next to her. "Natches, get her coffee and get her out of my way."

Chaya's breathing was choppy and a brief, covert glance at the other woman caught the trembling of her lips.

Dammit, if Chaya began crying . . .

"Come on, babe," Natches urged his wife as he stepped to her. "Let's see if she really knows what she's doing or if she's just trying to impress us."

Thankfully, Chaya allowed him to draw her away from the stove.

Angel had mastered the ability to follow recipes before she was ten and seemed to have a knack for it. She loved cooking. Or more to the point, she loved eating something edible, and with J.T. and Mara, you ate MREs, or you learned how to cook yourself.

Angel had learned to cook.

It didn't take Natches long to lead his wife, along with her coffee, to the table, where Duke was taking a seat. Within minutes the two men were discussing the property and its security as Chaya continued to watch Angel.

Angel ignored the steady regard. She'd learned how to do that as well over the years. The team often worked with others, mostly men, and they didn't care a damned bit to sit and stare. She'd learned to deal with it, but she had to admit, ignoring Chaya wasn't as easy.

Bliss stood at the counter, still excited to see Angel and delighted that her "friend" knew how to cook. She was a willing gopher to gather ingredients and a distraction Angel desperately needed.

In less than an hour, Angel had breakfast on the table and everyone was busy eating. Bliss wasn't in the least afraid to call out her mother's inability to cook, but she said Dad could fix a mean steak and hamburger.

Once breakfast was over, Angel waved Chaya back to her chair when she rose to clean up, but firmly asked Bliss for her help. She knew Chaya rarely had her youngest daughter accept household responsibilities, something Tracker's mother had never done. Mara couldn't cook either, but once she'd seen that Angel could, she'd made certain there was someone to teach her. And not just on a nice stove but a campfire and a fireplace as well.

As she and Bliss cleaned, Natches and Chaya outlined the weaknesses and strengths in security around the property, as well as the security training of Harley Matthews and Natches's adopted son, Declan, until the kitchen was finished and Chaya sent her daughter to the living room.

"Dawg, Rowdy, Graham, and Dawg's brothers-in-law will be here later this evening," Natches informed them as Angel poured herself a fresh cup of coffee before carrying the pot to the table to refill the other cups. "They've been working on the search for the men that hit the house. They haven't located them yet, but what they did manage to find was a black gear bag hidden behind some shrubbery at the back of the house." Natches shot his daughter a worried look where she sat in the living room in front of the television. "The only information we found in it was a picture of Bliss and Angel. There was a red X drawn on Angel's forehead with the message on the back that Angel would have to be dealt with." He shook his head as he gripped his wife's hand. "Whatever's going on, whatever they want, you're the one they consider a threat," he told Angel quietly. "Do you have any idea what it could be?"

"There's no way anyone could know who I am," she assured him. "And I rather doubt Duke told anyone." She shot Duke a narrow-eyed look.

"Not me," he snorted. "It was all I could do in the course of five years to prove it myself."

"How long have you known for certain?" Chaya asked, her voice carefully modulated, reflecting very little emotion.

"Now is the wrong time to worry about that," Angel suggested.

"Like hell," Chaya hissed, her brown eyes narrowing back at her as her expression tightened angrily. "He could have told us long before now, couldn't he? How many additional years did I lose with you?"

No one could say her mother didn't have sheer nerve.

"None, because I could have told you long before your dutiful husband sent him nosing into my life," Angel pointed out, then widened her eyes in false surprise. "Oh wait, I did try to tell you. You didn't believe me."

Chaya's nostrils flared, her lips parting.

"Enough." Duke and Natches seemed to speak at the same time.

Natches drew in a heavy, patience-gathering breath as he shot his wife a silencing look.

"I suspected for several years, Chaya," Duke answered her as Angel rolled her eyes in disgust. "Proof was another matter. I didn't have much evidence. Nothing concrete that I would have brought to you and Natches until the past year, and I had to verify it first. And I still had no idea why no one knew about Jo-Ellen's child."

"The birth took place in Canada," Natches said, still keeping his eye on Bliss. "Jo lived and worked in Canada, and they'd sort of lost touch."

"How?" Angel couldn't stop the question. "How do you lose touch with your sister? One you were raised with? I've known about Bliss since I was fifteen years old and I've been checking on her and making certain she was safe since I learned she existed."

She couldn't understand that, couldn't make herself accept it. Chaya and Jo-Ellen's parents had died years before Chaya had married. They had only had each other.

Chaya pushed her fingers through her hair, a momentary flash of grief shadowing her expression before she seemed to push it aside. When her eyes met Angel's, there was regret there, sadness.

"I was taken into Army Intelligence for training the first week I joined ROTC at sixteen, because of an aptitude I showed in questioning others." Chaya's voice seemed to shake. "Jo was four years older, already in college. . . ." She looked away for a moment then shook her head. "We were just never close. You and Bliss are closer now than Jo and I ever were."

And that still wasn't something she understood. She was eight years older than Bliss, but she could never betray the trust her sister was slowly giving her.

"I hadn't seen Jo for years when I invited her to my wedding," she continued. "She returned immediately afterward to Canada, where she was working. According to what Timothy learned, the affair with your father began not long after our honeymoon. I didn't see her often, but I wanted to be a part of her life." There was so much sincerity in her voice, her eyes. "We talked on the phone every few weeks. She knew everything about Beth, but I had no idea about her child."

"According to what I found, the police report of the murder scene mentioned toys and child's clothing, but all this time everyone assumed they were Beth's," Duke interjected.

"I thought she had bought Beth . . . I mean, Angel . . . additional clothes and toys to make her feel less insecure. . . . You were scared. . . ."

Scared? It hadn't been just fear that had her sobbing for her mother.

"I hated her," Angel snapped in reply. "Until the moment I met Jenny, all I did was cry. And Aunt Jo hated me just as much." She inhaled roughly, her hand clenching on the cooling cup of coffee in front of her. "I don't want to discuss this. We can discuss here and now and Bliss's protection, the weather, recipes or soap operas, or why you should never be allowed around a stove. I don't give a damn. But the past is off limits."

Chaya rolled her eyes as her lips compressed in anger at the reference to the stove.

"And if the past is the reason why Bliss is in danger?" Natches asked, his eyes burning a dark emerald green. "What then?"

"I'll do whatever I have to," she answered him coldly. "I'm proving that now, aren't I? I'm here."

What more did they want? She could be out in the field searching for the men intent on hurting her sister. Instead she was here,

"For Bliss." Chaya stared back at her, anger swirling in her eyes as though Angel should feel something more at this late date when Chaya obviously hadn't.

"Just for Bliss," Angel lied. And she knew it was a lie. "Now are we going to discuss her protection? If not, you'll have to excuse me, I have things to do."

She glared back at Chaya, so torn, so angry and filled with resentment, she could barely hold it in. And at the same time, all she wanted to do was ask why.

Why didn't her mother come get her and Jenny that day?

Why did she have to let her die?

There were no answers to her questions, but Natches did seem to have a plan of sorts when it came to protecting Bliss.

It was simple enough. They'd keep Bliss in the house, hidden as much as possible while the Mackays and the two SEALs, Seth and Saul August, protected the house and searched for the would-be abductors.

A search that had so far proved fruitless, she knew. Other than a picture of her with a red X across her face, they had nothing. The fact that the pack had been left behind was telling. Someone was trying to warn them of something, though she wasn't certain what, or why.

Angel made no objections to the plan until they made their way to the safe room between the master bedroom and Bliss's bedroom.

"The code in is simple enough," Natches explained, showing her the four sequential numbers on the keypad. Pushing enter, the shelf and hidden steel door gave a sibilant little hiss. Natches pushed it open and stepped inside the room. Wide steel steps led to the sunken room. A landline, table, full bed, television, and easy chair were placed in the steel-lined room.

"There are several hidden caverns about half a mile from here," Natches revealed. "Water and air can flow freely through the pipes I laid personally. Electric and cable come from underground lines I laid from the work shed outside, along with internet and landline. Once inside, Bliss knows the only way to secure the door from the inside is the pressure plate beside it." He pointed out the metal plate. "The door closes on its own and secures. And God help the man that thinks he'll squeeze through. The hydraulics on that door would cut a body in half. There will be no squeezing past. Once inside, Bliss can't reopen the door herself. An alarm is sent to the police, fire department, DHS, and every family member in the county once the door locks. Dawg, Rowdy, Alex, and Doogan each have a code to unlock it. It takes two of those codes to release the door. One of Dawg's and Rowdy's, one of Alex's and Doogan's. And that's something even Bliss doesn't know."

Still, it was risky to leave his daughter's ability to get out of the room hinging on the lives of four men who could be killed before ever reaching her.

"Plan A through Z," Duke murmured.

"Backup in every direction," Natches agreed. "That way Bliss can't open the door herself if she believes her parents are being threatened. And she knows our safety is dependent on her being here. There's an entrance to the room from the hall, our room, and Bliss's, and each door works the same."

Clever, Angel thought, impressed. The safe room would have cost more than the house, pool, and lakeside property combined.

"Angel, you'll join Bliss if there's a problem," Natches stated as though it were a foregone conclusion. "If they get as far as the house, then Chaya, Declan, and Harley can't afford to be distracted by you. Duke will have the hall, the rest of us will spread out and begin hunting. Are we clear?"

Angel stepped from the safe room, her gaze meeting Duke's perfectly bland expression. Of course he was smart enough to know that wasn't going to happen. She'd promised to try to play nice, though.

"Do you keep Trudy in that room?" she asked with all apparent sincere innocence.

"Trudy? My rifle?" He gave a short laugh. "She's my best weapon."

"Shut up," Chaya hissed, but Angel only smiled complacently as the warning came too late.

"I didn't train you or train with you," Natches informed her as his wife's warning connected with his brain. His arms crossed over his chest in a classic Mackay-dominant pose as he looked down his nose at her. "You'll be a distraction."

"Is that what I'll be?" She lifted her brow with mocking innocence before turning to the other woman. "I bet you have fun with him." She flicked Chaya a tight smile.

"More than you know," she breathed out, resignation filling her tone as her husband shot her a wicked grin.

Angel gave Duke a warning look. The kid gloves were about to be ripped from her hands. And he just gave her that damned blank look.

"Now that we have that settled . . ." Natches stated as silence filled the hall.

"You deal with him." She glared back at Duke. "Because we both know exactly what *I'm* going to do. Right?"

She could feel the burn of sheer offended pride as Natches

stared at her as though she were Bliss's age and unable to protect herself.

Twenty years of fighting, surviving, living in hell sometimes since she was three, and this was the respect it gained her with this man?

"And I bet *you* have *fun* with her," Natches growled back at Duke. "While you're having fun, convince her."

She laughed at him; she simply couldn't help it as Chaya slammed her fist into her husband's shoulder with a muttered, "Enough."

"Think he'd say that to Bliss's lover in a few more years?" From the corner of her eyes, she saw Chaya's look of horror and quick shake of her head.

"Thirty more years," Natches suddenly snarled with all apparent seriousness. "Bliss will not take a lover until she's forty-five."

She laughed again, a sincerely amused laugh, something only Duke had managed to draw free of her. This man was fucking insane, it was just that simple. He'd hit Duke for what he'd seen in the suite the day before. Duke's eye was still bruised, not that he'd actually admitted Natches had hit him.

"He's serious," she told Duke. "He means that, doesn't he? Forty-five? Have you forgotten she's your daughter as well? And haven't we all heard about the infamous Nauti Boys?" She wagged her brows and couldn't help the laughter bubbling from inside her.

Duke's expression was strained but mirth gleamed in his eyes.

"We'll discuss this later." Chaya's warning look only dared her to push.

"She's a girl," he snapped as though it made all the difference.

"So?" As though that made a difference. She propped her

hand on the hilt of her knife and arched her brow. "So, she'll be forty-five before she takes a lover, huh?"

She grinned back at the scowl he shot her.

"Forty-five," he snapped.

"Your doctor needs to change your meds," she assured him, barely holding back more laughter. "They're obviously making you delusional. And your daughter is a Mackay. I wouldn't forget that, if I were you. You have about as much of a chance that she'll be a virgin at forty-five as you do of getting me in that safe room."

Did he just pale? Duke definitely winced. Chaya was shaking her head desperately, worry filling her eyes.

"You're hilarious." She shook her head, nearly laughing again.

Turning, she headed back to the suite, shooting him another laughing look. She couldn't help but giggle at the bafflement in his expression and Chaya's resigned concern as she watched him. Duke just shook his head at her, but his lips were quirked with amusement.

Entering the suite, she closed the door behind her, another laugh escaping her.

"That man's insane," she said, shaking her head. "Absolutely insane."

As the door closed, Natches shot his wife a glare. "You owe me a hundred bucks. Pay up."

Her lips twitched and he glared at her harder.

Now dammit, she wasn't supposed to laugh at him, too.

"Don't you do it, Chay. . . . Don't even—" He tried to warn her.

Her laughter escaped, and he swore it sounded just like the impudent, too-stubborn little wretch that caused it.

"Just give me my damned money," he growled. "I made her laugh for you. You weren't supposed to laugh with her, dammit."

But she was laughing, and the sound lightened his heart, even if it was at his expense.

He could only shake his head as she leaned into his chest and he wrapped his arms around her, his lips twitching as he met Duke's amused gaze.

"I'll pay the hundred," Duke promised, almost grinning. "I'll be damned if it wasn't worth it." He chuckled. "Well worth it."

Natches tipped two fingers to his forehead in acknowledgment before kissing the top of his wife's head.

He was just good, he told himself, rather proud. Damned good.

But she was wrong. Bliss would be forty-five, maybe older.

He'd make sure of it.

EIGHT

The levity of that evening was forgotten by the time Natches's two cousins and various family members and children showed up. As the house began to fill, Angel completely understood why Chaya ordered in a stack of pizzas from Janey's restaurant.

Not that Mackay's Fine Dining did pizza as a rule, Natches informed her. But Janey's chef Desmond made some damned good pizza and the circumstances were excuse enough for the chef to come in early and fix them himself.

And the pizzas were damned good. Almost as good as hers, she admitted as she sat at the desk in her suite, ate, and watched the security cameras Natches had set up on the three adjustable monitors he and Duke had installed at the desk.

The cameras gave her an escape from the children, cousins, in-laws, and outlaws, as Chaya called them, that filled the house.

There were so many people packed into the kitchen that Bliss and her three teenage cousins had taken the smaller children and two pizzas downstairs to the basement playroom. Still, the number of adults and competing opinions were too much for Angel.

Finishing the pizza she lifted the whiskey she'd poured herself before sitting down and sipped at it, her gaze moving to the monitor that displayed the basement as well as a view to one of the hidden night-vision cameras mounted on the other side of the backyard and trained toward the yard's entrance. She would have expected the camera to be mounted in the yard instead, until Natches explained how easily the wildlife set it off whenever he'd placed it there.

It worked as it was and with the small joystick sitting in front of her she could choose the camera view and turn the camera somewhat if she needed to.

At the moment the girls downstairs held her attention.

Bliss was sitting with Annie, Laken, and Erin, talking as the younger children dozed or watched the cartoon currently playing on the large flat-screen television. Her sister kept her attention on the children, just as the other girls did, but their comfort and easy camaraderie as they talked was readily apparent.

Bliss's hair was pulled to the top of her head, clipped in place, though several long, loose curls had escaped to hang down her back.

She looked worried, Angel noticed. And a little scared sometimes. Her cousins were clearly concerned, and she knew from what Rowdy, Dawg, and Natches's sister, Janey, had said, the other girls hadn't slept well the night before.

"Nightmares," Janey had sighed.

Pulling her good leg up to prop her foot on the seat of the chair, Angel rubbed at the other leg; the muscle that had taken that knife was aching like a son of a bitch. She had already showered, changed the bandage, and taken her aspirin and antibiotics, but she knew she'd run out of medication before the deep wound was actually better.

For now, it wasn't infected, just irritated. She'd cleaned it again, then bore the agony of dousing it with alcohol. A last-ditch effort before she'd be forced to have Duke contact his brother, Ethan.

She grinned at the thought of Ethan. He'd pretend fixing her was becoming a job again, probably call her Frankenstein's Bride because of the scars she carried—and there were a lot of them.

The last bullet she'd taken had nearly taken her life. She remembered that place where she'd slipped into after losing more blood than her body could tolerate. She'd stayed there too long, she thought, frowning, and the dreams she'd had while she was there hadn't been comfortable.

The fact that she'd had them again several times in the last week was worrisome as well.

Scanning the other camera views she sipped at the whiskey again. There was a time when she would have simply drunk from the bottle and not worried about the job if she drank too much. A time when Tracker and Chance had railed at her, worried about her, and watched her with increasing concern. A time when she'd cussed worse than a sailor, fought like a demon, and stayed well away from polite society whenever they weren't on a job.

A time when she'd often wondered if she had a tomorrow to look forward to.

Then she'd become trapped in that hospital. She'd screamed for her momma. . . .

Tipping the glass to her lips she finished the drink, slapped the glass to the table, and rose quickly from the chair. She didn't allow herself to think about that, not anymore. It wasn't productive and it only led to heartache.

Stepping to the couch she stretched out on the surprisingly comfortable cushions and stared up at the ceiling for long moments. Her eyes were just drifting closed when she heard the door to the suite open, the momentary murmur of conversation, then silence once again as Duke entered.

He paused at the side of the couch, muttered something she didn't catch, then continued on to the bathroom as she let herself slip into sleep. He was there; she could let down her guard enough to rest, knowing he'd be awake for a few more hours at least. By then, she'd be awake. She always was. She rarely slept more than four hours without dreaming, so she'd learned to awaken herself before that point.

Duke sat in the recliner in the sitting room and dozed. He wasn't about to sleep in that big-assed bed while Angel slept on the couch. Somehow, the thought of it just seemed wrong.

He'd been certain she'd be awake when he came into the suite, and he'd had every intention of convincing her to share the bed with him, despite Natches's orders to the contrary. He had made certain he'd locked the door when he entered, though. The last thing he wanted was Natches walking in on something that might get Duke killed.

He palmed the heavy erection beneath the light cotton pants he wore whenever he wasn't actually in the bed.

He'd been so damned hard since that kiss yesterday that the jeans he wore had become torturous. Didn't matter what Angel did, all he had to do was look at her and his dick throbbed harder, became more demanding.

He could have blamed the sexual hunger on simply being a Mackay—they were highly sexed and sometimes far too dominant in that sexuality. Combined with it was the fact that when they found that woman who managed to steal their sanity, they were incredibly faithful to them.

For all the merciless evil that filled his parents, they had loved each other. They had loved their sons.

Duke remembered his father's firm guidance, the way he taught Duke and Ethan to work on a car or a tractor, to plant, and to nurture. Their mother had laughed and spoiled them. She soothed them when they were sick and helped them with homework. Their parents had attended their ballgames, had raised them without once abusing them.

And all the while they'd been hiding a monster inside them. A monster had lurked in his father that was capable of coding in the command that sent a drone's missile slamming into a hotel, knowing it would kill two children. Two tiny, defenseless little girls. They probably hadn't cared. Craig had become a liability when he contacted Dayle Mackay at the time and threatened to tell everything he knew if someone didn't help him escape.

The fact that Angel had survived amazed Duke. The fact that she'd escaped without an all-out manhunt ordered by the Freedom League confused him. Why would Trent Mackay have allowed one of those little girls to roam around alive? He would have had to have known there were two children with Chaya's ex-husband, not just one.

Or had Craig hidden Jenny from his traitorous friends just as her mother had hidden the child from her sister?

Those were the questions that were thrown out during the hours he'd spent in the crowded kitchen with Natches and the rest of the family. All but Dawg's sisters were agents or members of law enforcement and all of them had their own opinions, their own questions as they hashed out what little evidence they had managed to pull in.

Not that there was much. The fact that Angel's picture had been found with a notation that she'd have to be taken care of first bothered him, though. If they didn't know she was Bliss's sister, then why would she matter? Just because she knew the family wasn't enough reason. The fact that she was part of a highly trained extraction/rescue team wasn't enough because Tracker and Chance weren't with her. And only her picture had been found.

Rubbing his hands over his face Duke blew out a hard, deep breath.

He was going to have to discuss it with her and he hated the thought of it. If she knew she'd brought danger to Bliss, it would kill her. Telling her meant risking her leaving. She'd call Tracker and Chance in a New York minute to protect Bliss and she'd be gone.

Hell, he was surprised she hadn't already called them.

As he watched her, she shifted in her sleep, kicked the blanket from her legs restlessly, and he nearly groaned in torment. Those damned boy shorts and tank tops. They shouldn't be called sexy by any stretch of the imagination. But on Angel, they were fucking damned erotic.

One arm lifted to curve behind her head, raising those perfect breasts and causing sweat to pop out on his forehead.

Maybe sitting here watching her wasn't such a great idea. He had the hard-on from hell demanding they ride, and there Angel was—sleeping.

Amusement curled at his lips and he leaned his head back, forcing himself to stare up at the ceiling rather than at the woman. The view wasn't as good, but it was damned sure safer. . . .

The moan that whispered from her lips had his gaze jerking back to her. That wasn't a sound that denoted a pleasant dream.

The sound came again, and he knew what was coming if he didn't wake her. The question was, where the hell had she hidden that knife she always slept with?

He wasn't a foolish man and he'd already had that damned blade at his throat once before when he tried to wake her.

"No . . ." she whispered, shaking her head. "Please . . ."

Hell no.

He moved quickly from the chair and before she could reach for that damned knife he had her wrists between his fingers, pulling them to her as her eyes flared open and she tried to ram her head into his.

"Hold up, dammit," he hissed, pulling back just in time to keep his mouth from being bloodied. "You were dreaming, Angel. It was just a dream."

He pulled her to his chest, careful to keep her wrists restrained, holding her close to him as she shook whatever nightmare tormented her away.

"I'm good." Settled against his chest, no longer struggling now as she let herself calm after the dream. "How long did I sleep?"

She didn't move when he released her wrists but lay against him, allowing him to comfort her as he wrapped his arms around her and stroked her back gently.

"A few hours." She hadn't slept much, but then, Angel rarely slept for long periods because of her nightmares.

She'd conditioned herself to wake after four hours, Tracker

had told him. The only time she slept so deeply she couldn't wake herself was when recovering after a serious wound. And he knew the nightmares always came then. Hell, he was usually the one with her.

"Come on." Rising, he picked her up in his arms and strode the short distance to the bed. "I can't sleep in this damned bed while you're on the couch, and I'll be damned if I'm sleeping on a hard couch when a soft bed is just a few feet away."

She didn't argue when he laid her in the middle of the blankets he'd turned down earlier. It would be hell sleeping next to her, but better to suffer the arousal than sitting in that damned recliner staring at her all night.

"And you think this is a good idea?" The amusement in her voice had him grinning.

"I locked the door," he assured her. "The bastard comes through it and I'm shooting him."

Her soft laugh only made his erection harder, if that were possible. Hell, he didn't think he'd ever been so damned hard in his life.

"Chaya needs to get him on serious meds before Bliss gets much older. Or a leash." She turned to him as she settled against the pillow, watching as he slid into the bed and turned to her enough to flip the sheet over his hips, careful to keep his erection from making a tent.

"It wouldn't help," he assured her ruefully. "There's not enough Valium in the world to make Natches forget his sexual past. He lives in mortal fear of some pervert corrupting his baby girl now."

Soft laughter drifted through the room.

He rarely got to hear her laughter, and he realized that moments like this, in the dark, while they talked alone, were probably the only times he'd heard it.

While on missions, surrounded by danger, standing watch together, or when she got cold and he'd tease her into sharing his blanket for a few minutes to warm herself so she could sleep.

For five years he'd fought beside her, tried to protect her, and squelched his fears each time she was wounded. And he realized, he'd lived for moments like this.

"She thinks she's in love," Angel sighed in the dark. "Fifteen going on thirty."

The edge of sadness in her voice had him staring at her intently through the darkness that filled the room.

"My cousins say the same things about their girls," he agreed, remembering well Janey bemoaning the fact that Erin was growing up too fast.

"Why did he hit you?" she asked, throwing him off for a moment.

"Why do you think he hit me?" He laughed. "He caught me with the young woman he claims as a daughter now, all but fucking her against the wall. He was pissed and now he's scared I'll break your heart."

She didn't say anything, but he could see enough of her expression to see the confusion in it, just as he could see the conflict she had in accepting his explanation.

"Two days ago, he threatened to kill me," she pointed out. "Yesterday he's hitting you for touching me. Does that make sense to you?"

Unfortunately, it did.

"It's a Mackay thing." He chuckled, bunching his pillow beneath his head as he fought the need to touch her again. "Two days ago, he was in the middle of a nightmare, just as you were, honey." Reaching out he brushed the hair back from the side of her face, his fingers lingering for a moment to caress the soft skin. "He only knew what Chaya knew. The DNA testing they'd done came back as a positive match as Craig's child. No one knew Jennifer existed. Everyone thought you were dead, but there you were, claiming Bliss, but not Chaya."

She was silent, and he ached for her.

"Did you stay with the team to prove who I was for Natches?" she asked him then, a hint of vulnerability in her tone. "Why didn't you tell him?"

He was quiet for a moment, watching her closely, trying to remind himself that he couldn't blame her for believing that. Yet he couldn't hold back a flare of anger.

"If that was the only reason I was there, Angel, then you would have had Natches and every Mackay he could pull in surrounding your ass no matter where you went," he growled. "I didn't know who you were when I first showed up. It was when you were recovering from being buried beneath that hospital that I began to suspect. But I could have found the truth far quicker by leaving and backtracking your life. So no, that wasn't why I stayed."

Silence filled the room as he watched her, the tension gathering, questions raging between them until she finally asked the one question she never should have asked.

"Then why did you stay?"

He came over her, aware of her rolling to her back, staring up at him, not in surprise, but in interest and hunger.

"Because of this," he said. "I stayed because of this."

NINE

And she couldn't escape him, Angel knew, couldn't escape the need that only grew with each breath.

"It's a bad idea," she said as his head lowered, his lips almost brushing hers. "You know it is."

"Trust me, baby," he whispered. "We got this."

His lips covered hers and he stole her mind with his kiss. Angel didn't protest. She didn't want to protest.

God, how she had ached for his presence after she'd left the marina. Ached for his warmth, for the sound of his voice.

As his lips moved over hers, his kisses rough, hungry, he pushed the blankets from her, his hands touching, stroking. He released her long enough to strip her tank top from her, only to bend to the tight peak of her nipple and suck it into his mouth.

"Oh . . ." The expulsion of breath came as a delirium of pleasure cascaded through her, shaking her body and her senses.

Her lips parted, hands lifting until they lay against his sides, feeling the strength and the warmth of him against her.

She had to do something, she thought, or he was going to quickly realize just how inexperienced she was. She didn't want that. He was soothing that horrifying darkness inside her and filling her with pleasure. She didn't want to just take. She wanted to give as well.

She let her palms caress up his sides, then his back. Powerful muscles flexed beneath the tough skin, tensing against her touch. Curling her fingers she wanted nothing more than to rake her fingers down his back and test the strength and power of it.

"Softest hands," he said softly, the fingers at her hip just rubbing gently. "But don't be scared to use your nails, darlin'. It's all good, I promise."

It was like his eyes smiled, encouraging her, teasing her gently, just before his lips slanted over hers and his tongue pushed inside her mouth.

Her fingers curled, nails pressing into his tough hide in reflex as pleasure enveloped her body. The hand at her hip stroked from her hip to her breast. Cupping the sensitive mound, his thumb stroked over the aching tip, sending streaks of pleasure straight to her vagina.

An involuntary gasp escaped Angel's lips as her hips arched and her hands gripped his back. Her nails pricked then scraped over his upper back as her head tossed against the mattress. Through each kiss, each incredible plateau of pleasure he eased the boy shorts from her hips and down her legs until she could kick them off.

Until she was naked. Until there were no clothes between his touch and her flesh, between sensation and pleasure.

Those experienced, drugging kisses moved from her lips to

her jawline, kissing and tasting her, nipping gently before moving along her neck, over her collarbone, spreading a heated pleasure that began building, spreading rapidly through her senses. Waves of it were washing over her, stealing thought, stealing hesitation, and filling her with a rapidly building need for more.

This was incredible.

Hungry, heated lips stroked over the mound of her breast, brushed over her nipple.

Arching into the sizzling flash of sensation, her senses suddenly overloaded, overheated. The moist heat of his mouth surrounded the engorged tip, drawing firmly with deep, hungry pulls.

Forcing her eyes open Angel stared down at him, aware of his gaze locked on her. His cheeks hollowed, lust and pleasure filling his expression, a ruddy hint of color flushing his features.

As she watched, feeling him sucking her nipple, his tongue flicking against the tip, rasping over it, Angel felt herself sinking deeper into the chaotic storm building through her body and overtaking her senses.

"Don't stop," she whispered as the suction eased, his lips releasing the tortured point.

"I don't intend to stop," he assured her, his voice a deep, dark growl of male pleasure.

Moving to the opposite peak his lips covered the sensitive bundle of nerve endings, tormenting it, pleasuring it as he had the other. As he sucked at her hungrily his hand stroked down her side, her hip. Caressing, exciting her flesh, his hand eased between her thighs.

Calloused fingertips slid through the heavy moisture gathered along the narrow slit, easing through the aching flesh to find the swollen bud of her clit. There, he circled the throbbing flesh, rasped around it, over it.

She couldn't think. She could barely breathe.

As his fingers played, stroked, rubbed, Angel lost all sense of place and time. Her fingers buried in his hair, clenched, desperate to hold on as the hot press of his lips moved lower.

"Damn, you go to my head faster than liquor," he groaned, easing between her thighs, spreading them wider as a mewling cry escaped her lips. "I have to see if this pretty pussy tastes as sweet as I've always imagined, spilling with your juices." His fingers eased back, his lips brushing against the bare mound.

His head lowered. . . .

"Oh my God!" Her back arched, her shocked cry more a breathless gasp as she dug her feet into the mattress, her hips lifting, her need for more the only thought, the only reality she could comprehend.

His tongue slid slowly through the folds of flesh, licking and stroking, his rumbled groan of pleasure a delicious vibration against her aching clit.

All her nerve endings were clamoring to get closer to him, throbbing just below her skin, demanding the exquisite caresses and kisses now tormenting her aching sex.

"I knew you'd be just as sweet and hot here, too," he groaned, his fingers parting the plump inner lips, opening her further to his touch. "So sweet and juicy and I think I'm gonna be damned greedy."

She was addictive and Duke knew he was hooked. Hell, she'd owned parts of him for years, she might as well own the rest of him.

Parting the flushed, bare folds of her pussy, he licked, stroked, tasted the liquid need that spilled from her. When he was certain he couldn't wait much longer to take her, Duke eased from the sweetest taste in the world, his lips and tongue finding the hard bud of her clit as his fingers slid to the entrance of her pussy.

She wasn't as experienced as many of his past lovers. Her responses were less practiced, her ability to hold back any part of herself nonexistent. When his fingers rimmed the narrow opening and he eased just the tip of one inside, he felt sweat pop out on his brow.

She was tight. So damned tight that the second fingertip had a ragged cry spilling from her lips.

This wasn't possible.

It couldn't be possible.

Easing his fingers deeper, screwing them in small half circles, he worked them steadily inside her, easing deeper inside the snug grip until he met the fragile resistance of an innocence he couldn't have suspected.

Hell.

He should let her go.

He should get up, walk away, leave her to give that sweet gift to someone she loved. Someone who knew how to give all of himself to her.

As though she'd heard his thought he felt her go quiet beneath him, her breathing ragged and choppy. The whimper, a barely-there sound rife with an inner pain that had nothing to do with his touch.

"Sweet as candy," he whispered, nuzzling his lips against the still-engorged kernel of her clit, determined to draw her back into the pleasure he'd allowed her to slip from.

Lifting his head he stared up at her, flashing her a quick grin.

"I knew you'd be this good, this sweet." Gently, he parted the fingers possessing her, scissoring inside the snug grip clenched around them.

Her breath caught, heat flushing her face once again, the stormy depths of her eyes filled with need and haunting shadows.

"I can't think," she whispered, staring down at him uncertainly as her hips shifted, her body slowly growing accustomed to the feel of his fingers stretching her, rubbing against the silken flesh as her juices began filling the channel once again.

"You don't have to think, Angel. All you have to do is let us feel good together," he promised and lowered his head, his tongue finding her swollen little clit again.

A virgin.

Damn, a first for him. And he had a feeling she was going to blow his mind.

He didn't know.

She'd been certain he'd figured it out, that he'd somehow felt that barrier as his fingers pressed inside her. But he hadn't stopped, his fingers hadn't retreated, they were still there.

She lifted to him, closer, feeling the hungry licks and firm draws of his mouth build that storm inside her again. Waves of pleasure rushed through her, drugging her senses and building in intensity.

"Duke, that feels so good," she whispered breathlessly, feeling his fingers moving inside of her, stretching her deliciously.

Moving in and out, scissoring with slow stretching motions that only inflamed her clit further.

It was incredible. It was pulling her into a wicked, carnal maelstrom she hadn't known existed. She'd never known pleasure could completely burn through her senses like this.

"Duke," she cried out, shocked, helpless beneath his touch and the pleasure racing through her.

"That's it, baby." The roughened sound of his voice, his fingers moving inside her were sending pulsing waves of sensation building, gathering.

The quick flicks of his tongue over and around the aching knot of nerves he was tormenting were killing her with pleasure. The tension gathering in it, clenching her flesh around his fingers and stealing her breath. She could sense the edge nearing, feel the explosion coming.

She'd never felt this while masturbating. She'd never touched the ecstasy she could feel beginning to overtake her.

Then it was gone.

Her eyes jerked open, a protest on her lips that died quickly when her gaze met the lust burning in his as he rolled a condom quickly over the heavy erection jutting from between his thighs.

She was panting for breath, the need for more—his touch, his kiss, his possession was like a wildfire laying waste to her senses.

"Look how pretty," he groaned, coming over her as he guided the sheathed erection between her thighs, the flared crest parting her folds, throbbing against the entrance of her sex.

Angel looked; she was helpless against that need. Staring down her body, seeing the thick, blunt intruder spreading her folds, glistening with her juices, held her dazed senses captive.

Bending her knees further, her heels digging into the mattress, she tilted her hips, whimpering as the thick crest throbbed imperatively at the entrance, teasing her with the promised invasion.

"Hold on to me, baby," he ordered gently, his hand covering hers as it fisted in the sheets beneath them. "Let me feel you wrapping around my body as you're wrapped around my senses."

Hold him?

No one had ever wanted her to hold them before, had ever

asked her to wrap around them. In that moment, she realized
how the lack of that had created the barrenness that had filled
her before he touched her.

Forcing herself to unfist her fingers, she lifted them, caressing
up his arms, stretching beneath him, lifting closer to him, and
feeling the broad head of his cock pressing inside her, parting
her flesh with an unfamiliar pinching, pleasure-pain.

"So snug," he whispered as she watched her flesh give way to
the flared head of his erection, the crest disappearing inside her.

"Duke!" She struggled not to cry out, and failed.

This was just the blunt head filling her and her body was
struggling to stretch for him, clenching and rippling around the
intruder.

Her nails bit into his shoulders, heat fractured her senses,
eroticism held her captive.

"That's it, darlin'," he groaned, the sound of his voice drawing her gaze from the impaling shaft to his heavy-lidded expression. "Damn, baby, that's so good. Do you feel it? Sucking me
inside you like the tightest little mouth."

It was, she realized. The clenching internal movements were
involuntary, each one causing her breathing to hitch as his cock
eased inside her.

Angel tried to hold back the desperate mewls that escaped her
throat, tried to stop the deep, rippling spasms that tugged his erection deeper inside her, filling her, stretching her, agony and ecstasy. She had no defenses against the sensations tearing through
her body, causing her to buck against him, to drive him deeper.

"Do you like that, sweetheart?" he whispered, lowering his
lips to her ear, his voice strained as he worked the hard flesh
inside her. "Should I stop?"

Stop?

Angel shook her head desperately. She needed more. Needed more than the teasing increments he was giving her.

"Please." The room was too hot.

She was too hot.

Fire and ice licked over her body, her cries intensifying as the flood of sensations rose, drowning her in such sharp, brutal pleasure that she wondered how she could possibly survive it.

"Please what, sweetheart?" he crooned, his voice growing thicker, his body tightening between her thighs. "Please stop? Or please give you more?"

She was on fire. Every cell in her body was burning, needing. "Please, Duke, please . . ."

His powerful body tensed further, thighs bunched.

Angel's breath caught as he eased his hips back, nearly pulling free of her only to thrust forward, hard, fast.

His lips covered hers, swallowing her scream and each one that came after as he began pumping inside her, his cock sinking deeper, stretching her further with hard thrusts.

Oh God, she needed this, needed him. Her knees lifted to clasp his hips, opening herself further to him, feeling the next powerful thrust bury him fully inside her, his cock throbbing, pulsing within the tight grip her body had on him.

Angel went wild beneath him.

There was no experience to dictate how she moved, and Duke groaned in reaction as her hips lifted, writhed. Her knees tightened at his hips, her head arching back, tearing her lips from his, gasping for air.

"That's it, baby," he urged her, the dark rasp a sound of pure male hunger. "Work that sweet pussy on my cock. Keep sucking me in. Fuck yes . . ." he hissed as she felt herself beginning to unravel.

She was shuddering, tremors attacking her body as his thrusts increased, driving his erection to the hilt with each inward plunge. The guttural sound of his voice at her ear, his lips brushing the lobe, his body caressing hers, stroking against her as the intensity of the sensations built with each thrust inside her.

Angel was lost in the driving sensations, in the intensity of the pleasure-pain of each stretching, filling stroke of his cock as he fucked her with increasingly forceful thrusts.

She couldn't survive it.

She could feel the spiraling sensations beginning to tighten through her body. She fought to breathe, to find a center, something to hold on to to keep herself, her senses somehow grounded.

"Hold on to me, baby," he groaned, suddenly seeming to surround her, his larger, powerful body sheltering. "I have you. Just hold on to me."

Hold on to him.

He'd led her this far, filled her senses with the most incredible pleasure and now he was giving her his strength to survive the coming explosion.

"Duke!" She cried his name, her arms and legs tightening around him, the quickening thrusts between her thighs increasing the sensations, increasing that storm building in her senses. "I don't know how!" she gasped, the lightning arcs of white-hot pleasure building in her clit, in the sensitive channel he was possessing.

She was being consumed.

The storm building in her senses was converging, the tension increasing, pulling her deeper inside the unfamiliar bands of physical sensation as they mixed with all the emotional needs that rose with it.

She couldn't control it.

She couldn't survive it.

"That's it, love," he encouraged her as she lost her hold on reality. "Let me have you, darlin'. . . . Give it to me, baby. Come for me. . . . I'll hold you. . . ."

He would hold her.

He was holding her.

The sensations whipping through her, pleasure and pain, brilliant arcs of overwhelming ecstasy exploded inside her. And exploded, and exploded . . .

Angel lost herself as the converging sensations clashed in a white-hot orgasm that stole her breath and her reason. But he was there to hold her in place, even as he gave himself to his own pleasure, his own release. Still, he held on to her as she unraveled completely in a physical release she refused to admit had somehow changed her.

TEN

Angel could feel herself unraveling from the inside out and she knew if she didn't get a handle on it she'd end up regretting it. Slipping from the bed as Duke dressed she hurried to the bathroom, locking the door behind her. Leaning back against the door, she closed her eyes and drew in a hard breath.

Oh Lord, what had she done?

She'd just so complicated this entire situation for herself and she knew it. She'd created problems she had no idea how to solve. And she had no idea how to deal with what she'd done the night before. That wasn't like her. She normally accepted whatever decisions she made spur of the moment, even dumb ones. She accepted them and figured out how to make it work. But she couldn't figure out how to make this work or how to avoid the broken heart she knew was coming.

And she didn't need new scars on her heart.

She hadn't wanted more scars, but they were coming anyway, and she knew it.

They were coming, and she had a terrible feeling that the scar Duke left when this was over would have far more impact than even she suspected.

Breathing in deep, she wiped her hands over her face, straightened from the door, and headed for the shower. She didn't have time to stand around here and try to figure out something she had no idea how to deal with.

Right now, Bliss needed her. When her sister was safe, when the danger to her was over, then she could deal with the future scars she was allowing to be placed on her heart.

Freshly showered, the wound on her thigh cleaned and bandaged, Angel quickly dressed and stepped back into the bedroom. Where Duke was waiting for her, it seemed.

Dressed in jeans and a tan T-shirt, a short-sleeved shirt covering it and hiding the weapon holstered at his side, he was watching the cameras as he finished eating whatever he'd had in his hand.

"The family showed up this morning. Mercedes, Christa, and Kelly are in the kitchen fixing breakfast. It should be ready soon," he told her.

She pressed her lips together tightly.

"He should just send an invitation to whoever's after Bliss," she snapped. "Do you think they aren't watching Dawg, Rowdy, and this damned house for her?" Propping one hand on her hip she glared at him furiously. "Does Natches not think they're watching? That they're not aware of all the activity at this place? They know she's here."

"And there's no way to keep them from suspecting," he told her calmly. "But they can't be sure and there's a pretty little DHS agent that could pass for Bliss's twin that's made several brief, but notable appearances as she makes her way from one county to another surrounding this one."

She narrowed her eyes at him. "Natches didn't say anything about this before."

"I just found out myself this morning." As he turned from the monitors a grimace pulled at his expression. "Natches is determined that the abductors not know where Bliss is. That's why she's kept in the house, why the shades stay closed, and why Harley, Declan, and the August twins are kept so carefully hidden."

"Why didn't he give us this information when I first arrived?" How was she supposed to protect Bliss if she didn't have all the information involved?

"Timothy Cranston just told Natches and Chaya about it last night, from what I understand." Crossing his arms over his chest he leaned against the desk, his gaze moving over her warmly.

Heat flooded her body, an involuntary and confusing reaction. He was making her do things, feel things she didn't know how to deal with.

"So, Timothy arranged it?" she probed, wishing he would just finish it already.

His lips quirked with a hint of a smile. "Timothy's bad for things like that," he said, as though it were acceptable that the former DHS agent would take such matters into his own hands. "Natches knew he was putting something together, he just wasn't certain what. They've worked together for a long time, Angel."

"Over twenty years. Nearly twenty-five. He was Army Intelligence first, FBI, then DHS. He was Chaya's agent in charge in that time." She knew the former agent's history and Cranston's close association with the Mackays. She'd made it her business to know.

Duke nodded at that information. "He's been in D.C. trying to figure out what happened when the hotel exploded. Chaya and her husband both were with Army Intelligence. He's checking to be certain the attempted abduction doesn't have anything to do with that."

She nodded, realizing she was breathing a little easier. For one terrifying moment she'd been afraid she was wrong about Natches and that he was allowing the abductors to realize where Bliss was to draw them out.

She couldn't have stood that, to be so wrong about him.

"It might not work, the agent that looks like Bliss," she stated, considering all the angles. "They won't be as trusting after realizing the safe house was a setup."

"Natches is aware of that," he assured her, resigned to the fact that the plan had its flaws. "His options are limited, though, and he's not willing to allow Bliss to be used as bait. No matter how fiercely she's arguing for it."

Concern darkened his expression for a moment.

"I'll talk to her." Her sister would have to see the error of doing such a thing.

"Give me that kiss you're trying to avoid so I can get my ass outside and do my part," he demanded, ignoring her surprise. "I'm not leaving without it."

A kiss?

"You were kissed last night," she told him, suddenly nervous and uncertain. Why the hell did he want a kiss?

He strode to her quickly, slid his hand behind her neck, and before she could stop him, lowered his head to cover her lips with his. And drag her into that sensual, heated vortex of arousal that she had no defenses against.

And just as quickly, he released her.

"Be good today, and be nice to Chaya. Natches is becoming upset because you keep ignoring her." The demand was made as he strode from the room and left the suite by way of the patio doors in the kitchenette.

She didn't have a chance to argue, and she wondered if she would have known how to argue if she'd had the chance.

Be nice to Chaya.

Hell, she thought she was being nice. She was staying the hell away from her; that was as nice as she knew how to be right now.

Shaking her head at the demand, she left the suite. Rather than following Duke, she used the house entrance instead and turned into the kitchen, where Chaya and the other cousins' wives as well as Mercedes, Dawg's stepmother, had gathered.

"Angel, good morning to you." Mercedes was the first to see her.

Her smile was warm, welcoming, just as the others' were as they repeated the greeting.

"Did you sleep well?" Chaya asked from where she stood on the other side of the stove, where she'd been watching Christa slowly simmering something in a skillet.

"You can't teach her how to cook, Christa." Angel paused next to the counter, looked from the stove to Chaya. "But she can definitely teach you how to burn the kitchen down without trying."

"Let me try." Christa laughed, obviously well aware of the fact that Chaya couldn't cook.

The look Chaya shot her was a warning. "Be nice," she warned Angel, her voice low.

Ah, the tales she could tell, Angel thought, almost amused at the wariness in Chaya's expression.

"I'm always nice," she assured the woman she'd once called her mother. "Notice, I'm not saying anything. I'm leaving."

Tipping her fingers to her forehead in salute, she turned and left the house. There, she'd spoken to her. Duke and Natches could stop bitching at her now.

She made her way outside, around the grounds, and checked the position of the men Natches had hidden in the forests around the house. She could feel the scopes of their weapons on her as they watched her make her way along the natural, heavily vined border fence that grew around the yard surrounding the house.

There were two SEALs, Seth and Saul August; Natches's sniper protégé Harley Matthews; and Natches's adopted son, Declan Mackay, keeping watch on the property surrounding the house. If anyone made it past those four, as well as the two Mackay cousins "from the other side of the mountain," as Natches phrased it, and him and Duke, then they were all in trouble.

Four other Mackay cousins were still canvassing the county searching for the attempted abductors with Rowdy and Dawg leading the two teams after dropping their wives and daughters at Natches's.

The teenagers were in the basement with their video games, television, and various entertainments; Chaya, Christa, and Kelly were at the kitchen table with their coffee and mother discussions; and Angel was doing everything she could to avoid all of them.

Especially Chaya.

God, it hurt being here with her mother, facing the past and the wounded parts of her heart that she'd never been able to fully heal.

And she had to deal with Duke as well after last night.

That man was driving her insane. If ever one had been created for the sole purpose of both irritating and arousing a woman to the point of no return, then it was Duke. And for five years he'd made it his sole purpose in life to drive her crazy.

And no doubt before Bliss's abductors were found, she'd be certifiably insane.

Making her rounds of the yards, ensuring there were no anomalies and everything was the same as it had been the evening before, she made her way back to the house.

Rather than going in through the kitchen entrance, she used the sliding doors into the suite instead. She'd done her good deed for the day that morning and she was fresh out of additional ones at the moment.

Shaking her head at the thought, Angel moved to the desk and the laptop connected to the three monitors. She pulled up the traffic cam program she'd installed the night before and typed in the command to access the city's camera system. She and Tracker had been working on the program for years, perfecting it, ensuring it couldn't be tracked or traced.

Within minutes she had the program searching for the blue van that one of the marina's security cameras had recorded the day Bliss was nearly taken. If they were smart the men that attempted to grab the teenager had already gotten rid of the vehicle. Sometimes, though, intelligence wasn't always the deciding factor. Simple oversight had been the cause of many a criminal's apprehension.

Now that the tracking program was running, she was left with the option of pacing the suite or joining Chaya and her mommy-friends in the kitchen.

She was certain she preferred staring at the walls for a few hours instead. She remembered the looks Dawg's and Rowdy's wives had given her, those pity-filled looks mothers gave orphaned, refugee children, and she didn't think she could stand that for an extended period.

Watching the laptop screen shifting between different camera views as it searched for the blue van, she wondered how many other citizens or Mackay family members were doing the same thing.

She grinned at the thought. No doubt someone was, but they didn't have her and Tracker's program to work with.

Still, it wouldn't work fast.

"Hiding?" Amused and knowing, Duke's drawl had her turning to the door, her eyes narrowing on him.

"Working," she assured him. Yeah, she was going to admit to hiding. Was he insane?

She watched as he strolled into the bedroom, all hot, hard, and sexy in jeans and a T-shirt, something she'd rarely seen him in when he worked with the team. The black mission pants and protective shirts were always their best gear and almost a requirement in some areas where the terrain was rougher.

Today, worn denim and white cotton were paired with well-worn leather boots and a wide leather belt. Lean, hard-bodied, a bad boy image that would make any woman swoon, he sauntered into the bedroom. Green eyes gleamed with amusement as he watched her, making her body heat with arousal. Damn him. He should at least have to put some effort into turning her on so fast.

"Working, huh?" he murmured, knowing damned good and well she was escaping, too. "Chaya, Christa, and Kelly were wondering where you disappeared to. I think they were hoping to talk to you for a while."

She gave a little roll of her eyes before rising from the desk and shooting him a quelling glance.

"Don't involve yourself in me and Chaya, Duke," she warned him as his arms went over his chest in a classic male-dominance stance. "We're going to disagree if you try, and we'll just end up angry with each other."

His brow arched just enough to piss her off, because she knew what that meant. He really didn't care if he pissed her off.

"And you think you can get to know your mother. . . ."

"I told you not to call her that." Her hand slammed to her hip as it cocked to the side and she glared back at him furiously.

"Stop ignoring her, Angel," he all but ordered.

He was ordering her? As though she were a child to be directed?

"I spoke to her this morning," she objected. "I was nice."

"You reminded her she couldn't cook," he argued. "That's not talking to her, Angel, and you know it."

What the hell did he expect from her?

"You go spend time with her if it means so damned much to you, because I'm sick to death of you pushing her down my throat and vice versa. The door swings both ways, Duke." Chaya was making no more of an effort to get to know Angel than perhaps Angel was making to get to know her, she knew. At least she had tried, though, Angel assured herself.

"One of you is going to have to give in." Irritation flashed in his eyes.

"Who's the mother? Who's the child?" she asked sweetly. "Isn't she supposed to be the adult in the situation?" Okay, so it was damned childish of her to act that way, but she was sick of being forced to defend her right to be angry.

She had every right to feel betrayed.

She *had been* betrayed.

"And when it begins affecting your ability to protect Bliss?" he asked softly, drawing closer to her. "What will you do then?"

Was it affecting her to that point?

At present, Bliss and her cousins were in the basement. She knew they were still in the basement; she knew the men guarding the property were in place. Was there something she should be doing that she wasn't? Or something she'd missed?

"I'll have to reassess the situation then." She frowned, wondering what he was getting at.

"You're not sleeping well, you're beginning to look pale, and that bothers me. Whatever's keeping you awake at night is going to begin affecting your ability to do the job." He moved to her, his hand reaching out to touch her cheek, to brush back the hair that had fallen from the braid to her forehead.

Angel pulled back from him and shot him a glare.

"Nothing is affecting my ability to do my job," she informed him. "I'd know if it were. And Chaya Mackay sure as hell isn't affecting it. And you were the one that kept me awake all night. Now if that's all you wanted"—she extended her hand toward the door in an angry gesture that he could leave now—"I have things to do."

The amusement flashed back in his expression.

"Are you trying to dismiss me, Angel?" The vein of laughter in his voice was infuriating. "Have you ever known that to work?"

"A two-by-four wouldn't work with you," she muttered, turning her back on him to return to the laptop.

She should have known better. Turning one's back on Duke was never a good idea.

Before she could counter him, he gripped her arm, swung her around to him, and secured her to him with the other arm, his head lowered, taking advantage of the gasp that parted her lips.

Angel froze.

Pleasure exploded through her brain. Just that fast, just that effectively, he stole her ability to fight, to challenge him, to think, by covering her lips with his and parting them with the heated stroke of his tongue.

He wasn't asking permission to kiss her. He wasn't being in the least polite about it, and that fact alone should have enraged her. But this was Duke. His kiss, his touch, the easy possession of her senses was something her body was beginning to crave.

It was something she was beginning to crave.

Her fingers fisted in the material of the shirt covering his wide chest, her body melted against him, and her senses began to riot with sensation. And all he was doing was kissing her. His lips moving over hers, sipping at them, little nips and hot licks of his tongue. And she was mesmerized.

She should be trying to kick his ass; instead, she was trying to sink inside his skin, to get as close as possible.

Just as quickly as he grabbed her to him, he released her. Again. They were both breathing hard, and Angel swore she was on the verge of swaying.

"What was that for?" she all but panted, staring up at him surprised and a little confused that he'd released her so quickly.

In the past days, grabbing her for a kiss had meant far more than just a kiss.

"For distracting me," he muttered, shooting her a brooding look.

For distracting him?

The man was crazy. That was all there was to it. And before long he was going to make her crazy. Or crazier.

She had to admit the situation as it stood wasn't doing much for her sanity. Being in Chaya's life was never what she expected, and she sure hadn't imagined being in her home.

The fact that Duke and Natches had forced Chaya to acknowledge her was a pain in her side, too, and she admitted it. The woman shouldn't have had to be forced to accept Angel; she should have known, shouldn't she? When Angel stood before her, silently begging her, every hope and dream she'd ever had of her mother pouring through her, shouldn't she have recognized her daughter?

"For distracting you?" she asked him carefully.

"Natches caught me outside and tore my ass because you're ignoring Chaya." There was the faintest look of disappointment in his expression. "You should give her a chance, Angel."

"Should I really?" The sarcasm in her tone really wasn't deliberate. "And is this what you think or what Natches Mackay told you to think?"

"I think it was a mutual decision." The grin that quirked his lips was going to get him kicked.

Confidence oozed from him in waves and dominant male power was so much a part of him that it tended to completely irk her feminine independence.

"You and Natches can shove your mutuality," she informed him, walking past him into the sitting area then to the kitchenette and coffee maker.

There was a time when she would have told him in exacting and explicit detail exactly what she thought of his and Natches's mutual decision. A time when the filth she spewed from her mouth would have made a sailor wince.

Now the words refused to pass her lips, the memory of the times when they had nearly causing her to cringe.

She hadn't been a nice person then. She wasn't exactly a nice person now, but at least she'd managed to clean her language up for the most part.

"What do you think you're going to do when all this is over?" he asked as he followed her. "Ride off into the sunset and continue on your merry way?"

Popping a pod into the coffee maker and closing it in, she slid a cup beneath the spout and waited.

"Think ignoring me is going to change the question?" Just because his tone was lower didn't change the determination in it.

He wanted his answers and she knew him. He'd get them even if it meant pissing her off to the point that she exploded and threw the answers at him.

"When it's over, I'll leave." There was no point in lying, and for some reason he always knew whenever she tried. "There's no reason for me to stay here."

Chaya would prefer she leave, she knew that. No matter what Duke thought, the other woman was uncomfortable with her in the house. She was uncomfortable with her around Bliss. There was no place here for Angel Calloway, just as there had been no place in Chaya's life for the child Beth Dane.

"What about Bliss? Don't you think it'll hurt her?" The question was one that haunted her. It had haunted her even before she'd made the decision not to return when she'd been preparing to leave.

"At first," she agreed. "At first she might be hurt. She's young, though, and she doesn't know the truth. As long as she doesn't know, she'll be fine."

Chaya had made the right decision in keeping the truth from Bliss. This way, when Angel left, Bliss wouldn't feel deserted. Friends could come and go, but sisters should be forever. Right?

"And you think it's just going to happen, just like that?" Curious, as smooth as honey, his tone wasn't in the least confrontational.

Angel could feel her irritation growing with his, despite the cooler tone.

"It's going to happen just like that," she assured him as she removed the cup and placed it on the counter to spoon sugar and dry creamer into it.

Dessert. Duke had once told her she didn't drink coffee, she drank coffee-flavored dessert. She stared into the lightened liquid, the steam rolling off it, and tried to tell herself it really was going to be just that easy. She would make certain it was just that easy.

"You want me to tell you what's going to happen?" The knowing tone of his voice had her turning to him slowly.

Leaning against the wall, his thumbs hooked in the front of his belt, he watched her with a brooding intensity she didn't know how to counter.

"Not particularly." She was certain it would only piss her off.

A grin tipped his lips as he lowered his head and shook it as though in disappointment.

Damn him. She knew she was going to hate whatever was getting ready to come out of his mouth.

"If you actually manage to get out of the county, you'll find your ass covered by a Mackay twenty-four-seven. If I don't make certain of it, Natches will. And I'm betting the second Chaya realizes that you think you're leaving, she'll make certain you rethink that little decision."

And wasn't he so confident?

Angel smirked, just as confident that leaving wouldn't blip Chaya's little radar.

"Keep believing that." Lifting the coffee, she sipped at the heated brew and assured herself again that she had nothing to worry about as she stared back at him. "While you're at it, see if you can't get your pseudo-daddy Natches to find someone to make a grocery run for me. I prefer fresh vegetables over canned, and if I'm going to be feeding those August twins, and Harley, and Declan every day, then we need red meat. I'll make sure you have the list. If you'll excuse me, I need to run those gossiping women out of the kitchen so I can put a stew on."

She'd rather deal with Chaya, Christa, and Kelly than with Duke in this mood. She could tell by the expression on his face that he was getting ready to really start pissing her off.

A smug grin formed at his lips as he straightened from his slouched stance against the wall and took the few steps needed to where she stood in front of the counter.

He towered over her, but not in a way that made her feel threatened or in the least intimidated. She felt . . . secure.

Damn him.

She hated the way her body responded to him, her senses coming alive in ways they never had before.

Placing his hands on each side of her, he leaned over her, his head lowering until his lips were less than an inch from hers.

"Once a Mackay puts claim to you, baby, you're marked."

The kiss stopped any argument she might have had. Another of those soul-searing, rock-her-to-her-soul kisses that left her brains scrambled and her common sense nonexistent.

When he released her, he didn't wait around for her to find her bearings once again. No doubt, he knew better. Instead, he was out the patio doors leading to the pool, that cocky male swagger holding her attention until he closed the door behind him.

And she was able to breathe enough to clear her head and wonder just who in the hell he thought had marked her.

No Mackay owned her.

Did he?

ELEVEN

She should have left town with Tracker and Chance, Angel told herself the next afternoon when she stepped into the kitchen through the back door and came to a slow stop, eyes narrowing on the man who sat at the kitchen table.

He looked like the leprechaun he'd once been called, though she'd heard Mercedes Mackay had actually managed to tidy his once-scruffy appearance. Timothy Cranston was a legend in certain circles, and another of those men Tracker had avoided over the years. Intelligent, a natural manipulator, and an expert gamesman, he had run his little corner of military intelligence and then DHS like each mission was a personal chess game.

He sat at the table alone, a file in front of him, his expression bland despite the gleam of amusement in his brown eyes.

Angel looked around the room slowly before letting her gaze meet his once more.

"Bliss and her parents are currently in the basement with

Duke," he told her, his tone cool, unaffected. "There seems to be a glitch with one of the security monitors that they're going over."

She gave a little roll of her eyes. "I wonder who glitched the monitor," she muttered, closing the door behind her before moving to the counter, never taking her eyes from him.

He smiled back at her with a hint of the glee it seemed he was known for.

She'd expected him to make an appearance, though she hadn't expected to face him without Duke present, she realized.

"You can let them know you're back if you like." He nodded to the hall that led to the basement door. "I'm sure all of them would be properly horrified to realize you're here alone with me."

She was properly horrified herself.

"Do I need a chaperone?" she asked him instead, one hand resting on the hilt of her knife as she faced him.

Satisfaction gleamed in his eyes.

This sucked, but dammit, she should have expected it. Timothy Cranston wouldn't have let her presence there pass without interrogating her himself.

He sat back in his chair and regarded her silently. This man who had trained her mother in military intelligence, had ordered her to Iraq then pulled her into DHS with him, didn't trust her and he damned sure wouldn't take anyone's word on her identity.

"It was my department that did the DNA tests on little Jenny." He surprised her with the flash of regret and pain in his voice. "I'm sorry for that. I dropped the ball when I didn't keep Chaya's sister in my periphery. I used to be sharper than that."

She remained silent, uncertain of what he expected from her. Hell, she didn't know what to expect of herself at the moment. She was wary of this little man, his reputation and his influence over Chaya. He could convince the other woman to send her away, to refuse to let her protect Bliss. Angel knew she couldn't bear that.

"Nothing to say?" he asked then, his head tilting quizzically as he watched her.

"About what? How sharp you used to be? I imagine you had to blink sometime." She shrugged, trying to restrain the smart-ass she knew she could be.

He stared back at her somberly. "It was the wrong time to blink."

Angel glanced away from the sense of despair that flashed across his expression. It might have been the wrong time to blink, she thought, but the man was human, wasn't he? Despite the stories she'd heard about him, she rather doubted he was some-how paranormal.

"Well, it was lovely to meet you." She forced a smile to her lips and took a step toward the hall. "If you'll excuse me . . ."

"Are you here to somehow make Chaya pay for a past she wasn't responsible for?" His question stopped her cold. "Because if you are, then we're simply not going to get along, girl. . . ."

"Don't call me 'girl'!" She turned on him, glaring, fighting against the emotions and the anger she was trying so desperately to keep contained.

Didn't they understand? She didn't want to hurt Chaya; she didn't want to see Bliss hurt. She just wanted to keep another sister from dying, to keep from losing someone else she loved.

A frown creased his brow as those penetrating brown eyes stared back at her, seeing too much, she feared, and perhaps not enough.

"And don't look at me like I'm a bug under a damned micro-scope either," she demanded, fists clenching at her sides. "I don't need your approval of me and I damned sure don't need you judging me. I'm here to make certain Bliss is safe. No more. No less."

Make Chaya pay for the past? She didn't want to make Chaya pay for anything. She'd wanted her mother to come for her and Jenny. She'd wanted to go home and be safe again. When she'd lost all hope of that, she'd just wanted to forget. And that was exactly what she'd done for far too many years. She'd just forgotten.

"And what about your mother?" he demanded.

"What about her?" She wished to hell everyone would stop with the "her mother" crap. She was tired of hearing it, tired of having it thrown in her face as though the past were somehow her fault. "What the hell is your problem anyway and how am I suddenly any of your business? Mister, you need to get a damned life and stay out of others' business."

Men like him should be locked up somewhere.

"You refuse to acknowledge her," he accused her then. "You're breaking her heart."

"Oh God, give me a motherf—" She bit off the word, breathed in deep, and tried again. "Just stop, okay? This is none of your business. I'm none of your business. Once this is over, I'll be gone. . . ."

He laughed at that.

Angel clamped her lips closed, her breathing harsh as she fought the cauldron of emotions she didn't want to let free.

Like Pandora's box, once that door was opened, it would never close again, she feared.

"You really think you'll just disappear on her, and the Mackays will give you a cheerful wave good-bye?" The smile on his face was frighteningly knowing. "Girl, Duke will be the least of your problems if you try that one. Natches will surround you with so much protection you won't be able to breathe without smelling a Mackay invading your personal space."

Yeah, she was ready to put her faith in that one. Natches was a true family man, she'd give him that, but she wasn't his daughter; she was just the grown-up child his wife hadn't wanted. Once he realized that, he'd let her go easily enough.

It would hurt when Duke walked away, though, she knew that. When he wasn't in her bed, wasn't touching her, holding her . . . That one would cut deep. Deeper than she'd imagined until the night before.

"I don't have time for this." She tried again to extricate herself from the confrontation she could feel rising inside her. "And you don't want me to make time for it. Because as intimidating as I'm sure you can be, mister, I can be a pure bitch on speed if you piss me off enough. And neither one of us needs that, right? We sure as hell don't need Bliss or anyone else walking in on it, now do we? I for one would prefer not to take that chance."

And she didn't want to let the bitch out to play; she really didn't. She'd put that person behind her years ago. That scared, broken young woman who couldn't accept her past or find a future to look forward to. The drinking, cursing, and fights hadn't quelled the fury; they had only made it worse.

"Yeah, you weren't a nice person when you were younger," he agreed. "Dirty little gutter fighter, weren't you?"

It was the "dirty" that got her. Angel felt herself tense. The memory of how Chaya had looked at her the day Bliss was nearly abducted, as though she were something dirty, sliced through her defenses.

"Oh, I was," she assured him before she could stop herself. "A real war-whore. Ask anyone." She spread one hand out as though to encompass the room. "Sold myself to the highest bidder, I've been told. Anything else you need me to agree to, Mr. Cranston, or are we finished now?"

They had better be finished. She could feel herself unraveling, feel the memories of the past as well as the present rising to push against her determination to rein in the impulses that used to see her searching for a bottle of whiskey and a fistfight. And she'd been far too young for either. A child. A child whose mother had left her, deserted her, and forced her to learn to kill.

"How much would it cost a person to convince you to put aside the war-whore and become a daughter for a change?"

Angel felt the breath slam from her lungs, felt an agony so deep, so white-hot, it instantly seared her insides with blistering pain. Her throat tightened until she wondered if she was going to choke on the emotions spilling through her, threatening to break her.

"Good-bye, Mr. Cranston. . . ." She moved for the hall and tried to escape.

"I'll pay it. A hundred thousand? Two?" He rose from the chair, watching her with cool interest, his expression unconcerned, uncaring.

She turned back to him slowly, pain shredding her insides as she faced this too-perceptive, too-cunning little old man. "I held my sister in my arms as she died. Her blood stained my hands, and her screams live in my nightmares. I walked the streets of Baghdad that night," she whispered. "And I cried for my mother. I was a daughter then. Now I'm just the war-whore," she sneered. "And you can't come up with enough money to buy me for anything. Or anyone. What you can do is fucking go to hell and leave me alone before you really piss me off."

She didn't move for the hall again. She turned back to the door and, jerking it open, escaped outside, where the remembered scent of betrayal and blood wasn't nearly so thick, so wretched. Where she could breathe without the need for more than her mother had wanted to give her, more than Duke could give her, tormenting her soul.

Duke stepped into the kitchen slowly, aware of Natches and Chaya behind him, thanking God they'd found a way to convince Bliss to remain downstairs when Natches had seen Timothy and Angel in the kitchen on the security monitor. The fact that the two were involved in a confrontation hadn't been missed by any of them.

"If she doesn't kill you first, I'm going to," Duke warned the older man as he took his seat slowly, his expression marked with grief.

"Piss a woman off and she'll reveal far more than she would otherwise," Timothy said, the low tone emphasized by the lined weariness of his expression. "God." He wiped his hands down his face before he shook his head. A tight, sharp movement, as though he was trying to shake what she'd said from his memories. "I read the report. I saw the hell she lived in. Seeing it in her eyes . . ." He broke off and breathed in deeply. "She doesn't hate." He stared back at Chaya now. "She hurts. And she's terrified of hurting more."

"Timothy, you're a menace," Chaya bit out between clenched teeth, the anger in her expression in no way matching the anger Duke felt roiling through her. "A goddamned menace."

Duke wondered if he should have pushed Angel as hard as he had since bringing her to Natches and Chaya's home. The shadows in her eyes were darker and her expression more solemn than he'd ever seen it. The days spent treading warily around her mother and holding in the anger he knew burned inside her were killing her. Hence the reason he'd tried to push her in Chaya's direction. What Timothy had done was strip her to the bone, though, he realized that evening.

Angel wasn't one to restrain the anger. Other emotions, yes, but the anger she tended to give free rein. It was the only thing men understood, she'd once snapped when Tracker had dared to call her down for it.

So it was more than a little surprising that she'd not just restrained it, but managed to hide it from everyone in the house, except him, after Timothy left.

He knew her. He knew her better than he'd once realized. He knew what the stormy gray of her eyes meant, and the emotions threatening to swamp her when the color softened, lightening to that of a dove's wing.

Today, though, the color was neither that of a storm cloud nor that of a dove's wing. Her eyes were an in-between color that warned him she was hurting inside and had no idea if she was angry over it or not.

Standing in the doorway after dinner, he watched her on the patio as she lifted the bottle of expensive Irish whiskey to her lips and sipped at it. She rarely bothered with a glass and she hadn't drunk enough to do more than relax in over three years.

She'd showered, changed into one of his shirts. Her pretty, tanned legs shimmered beneath the tails of the garment, several buttons still undone, the edges falling away from her legs. The dark gray shirt emphasized her peach-toned flesh and delicate build and clearly showed the bandage on her leg that he had yet to ask her about.

A knife wound, Tracker had told him when he called, demanding to know what she'd done to herself. A bastard determined to kill the little girl he'd abducted had taken exception to Angel's determined efforts to keep him from his goal. Angel's prowess with a knife was exceptional, but she had the girl to worry about and she'd been distracted. His knife had buried in her thigh even as she'd cut his throat.

Tracker had sewn the wound up and he was a damned fine medic, but nowhere near as good as Ethan.

The leg didn't seem to be giving her problems, so he hadn't called Ethan to the house. Yet.

For the past five years, Angel had been a magnet for near-fatal wounds. She'd nearly died more than once and Ethan swore she had a death wish.

She lifted the bottle to her lips and tipped her head back, taking another drink of the whiskey.

His shaft throbbed, so engorged with lust it was pathetic. There was just something about watching Angel enjoy that whiskey that made him hard as hell. Made him want to grab her to him and ride her through the night.

Tonight, the drink was being enjoyed along with one of the thin, fragrant *cigarros* her foster grandfather hand-rolled and doled out with miserly impatience. Sprawled back in the cushioned swing suspended from the crossbeam roof of the enclosed patio, one leg bent, the other stretched out, eyes closed, she gave the appearance of complete immersion in the liquor and tobacco.

He knew her, though. She was strung as tight as Uncle Ray's banjo and ready to explode into action.

"Want to talk about it?" he asked softly.

Leaning against the doorframe, arms crossed over his chest,

he wondered how she managed to keep all those emotions so tightly contained all the time.

Tonight, they were beating at her, though, and he knew it. It was the knowledge that the quieter Angel became, and the more somber her expression, the greater her inner turmoil. Being in the house with her mother, feeling that Chaya hadn't wanted her as a child and didn't want her now as an adult, was breaking something inside her.

And that was killing him as well.

"Nothing to talk about," she mumbled, never shifting position or opening her eyes. "Besides, talking to you just makes me crazy."

"That's why you're doing something you only do when you're upset? Because you're not upset?" He didn't bother to hide the mockery in his tone. "Come on, baby, I know you better."

The tension increased at the statement.

"Yes, you do." Her eyes opened, the gleam of anger unhidden as she focused on him. "Because you spent five years spying on me."

He chuckled at the accusation. "I'm an investigator, that's what I do. But Natches really wasn't too serious about it until you showed up in Somerset again nearly two years ago. I didn't have enough info to give him and I wasn't going to give him fairy tales. Or hurt you worse than I knew you already hurt."

Yeah, he had known. The nightmares the night they'd pulled her from the debris of that hospital had bred the suspicion, but he was just supposed to ensure the team wasn't a threat to the Mackays, not dig into their pasts. And for the first time, he hadn't wanted to dig.

There had been no escaping the need, though. That was why he and Ethan had joined the team, why they'd gathered the information needed to start peeling back the layers of a woman that some of the hardest men Duke knew hesitated to confront.

"I wanted to kill you when I learned you were a Mackay," she whispered before lifting that bottle to her lips again. "And I wanted to kill Cranston this morning."

He didn't reply; he just watched her, knowing better. She hadn't wanted to kill either of them. She'd been hurting too bad at the time and trying too hard to figure out why it hurt.

"You should have known it was coming." He watched her face, saw the knowledge in it, and knew she'd been aware she was living on borrowed time, so to speak. She'd known it was only a matter of time before she'd have to face Chaya and all the baggage that came with it.

"I was always careful." She stared up at the crossbeams over her head for a long moment. "We stayed out of Kentucky and away from the Mackays. We made sure our paths never crossed with Natches and Chaya."

He nodded at that. "And that was damned suspicious. Suspicious enough that when Rowdy first heard how diligent Tracker was in his efforts, he became very curious and asked Natches about it. That was all it took. When he caught you in town that same summer, Natches got real curious."

That was literally all it took. When Natches became real curious, he tended to stick his nose in real deep.

Or Duke's nose, whichever the case may be.

"You couldn't keep hiding, Angel," he reminded her softly as she put out the *cigarro* in the small ashtray on the table beside her. "It was catching up with you, if only emotionally."

He'd become just as ensnared by her, though.

She rose slowly to her feet. "You don't know me as well as

you think you do," she warned him, eyes narrowing on him as he dropped his arms and straightened from his relaxed stance. "You want to believe you do, but you don't."

But he did. He knew her even better than she knew herself.

The challenge in her gaze and in her tone wasn't to be discounted, though. It was a dare, a dark need to pour all that pain and anger, hunger and need into something more than the bottle, the night, and her own wounded heart.

"Don't I?" He grinned, letting her know he'd take that challenge any day. "Baby," he crooned, "I know you so well it terrifies you."

He knew her so well he could feel her pain, and yet she was still just as much a mystery to him as ever. Hell, it terrified him.

Her eyes narrowed. Her nipples hardened beneath the thin cotton of the shirt.

"Nothing and no one terrifies me, Duke," she drawled, the brittle amusement infuriating him as he sensed the need behind it. "Even you know better than that."

Her emotions terrified her. That hungry need that existed in the very depths of her heart and refused to lie still terrified her and he understood why. He knew, because he often faced that demon himself.

"I terrify you," he informed her, feeling her needs, his own tugging at the less-than-secure hold he had on his restraint. "Because I make you want. Because you can't hide that fact from yourself or from me. You want me so bad your body aches with it. Because you're wet and ready to fuck even though you know each time we touch it will make it harder to walk away from me."

And he'd be damned if he'd let her do that.

"No . . ." Fists clenched, teeth grinding together, she fought the truth just as he'd fought it for five long, hungry years.

"Oh yes." And he'd be damned if he'd let her deny it.

One step and he reached her, his fingers gripping her upper arm, pulling her to him as the fingers of his other hand buried in her hair to hold her against him, refusing to let her hide from this at least.

The first time he'd taken her he'd barely had enough control to take her gently. Enough restraint to give her the best of the man he was, rather than the full force of his lust. But now it was the lust that raged through him, hungry and desperate for the taste and feel of her.

He was lost when he wasn't a part of her, wasn't with her. When she hid her emotions and her needs, he realized the void that was left within him.

He'd been like a wounded animal for the eight months he'd been without her. Wounded and hungry . . .

He consumed her kiss now, consumed the heat and hunger, and found she consumed his in turn. Lips and tongues ate at each other, meshed and tangled as their moans escaped and mingled. Her hands burrowed in his hair, clenched at the strands, and held him to her as he lifted her, his lips slanting over hers, taking the kiss deeper, filling his senses with her.

Turning, barely able to remember to be gentle, not to jar her thigh, he fought to restrain himself. He couldn't let go of her, even to lay her back on the bed, to take time to undress, to love her as she deserved. He pushed her against the wall, lifted her until those pretty legs wrapped around his hips, gripping him as mewling little cries escaped her lips.

Groaning into the kiss, his tongue thrusting against hers, he released the tortured length of his erection from his jeans. He was so damned hungry for her he couldn't wait. Grasping the shaft, he tucked the bloated crest between the bare, juice-laden folds of her pussy and swore he felt sweat pop out on his fore-head as the silken inner lips caressed his flesh.

Slick heat surrounded the throbbing crest and sent forks of incredible, blinding pleasure whipping through the ultra-sensitive head, along the engorged shaft, and straight to the taut sac of his balls.

"Ah, fuck!" he snarled, jerking his head back from their kiss as electric waves of sensation began building through his senses.

Thighs tight, a ragged groan left his throat as he began pen-etrating the lushly slick channel awaiting him. A sensual vise locked around his testicles, tightening erotically as he pushed deeper, withdrew, and thrust again. Each lunge dragged a groan from his chest and a cry from Angel's lips.

He tried to ease inside her . . . tried to go slow, to go easy. Until her sweet, hot muscles clamped down on the crest, rippling over it like the most incredible little mouth.

"Oh God . . . Duke . . ." She moved against him, bore down on the thick flesh penetrating her, tightened on it. The feel of her juices spilling from her and traveling along the length of his cock nearly blew his mind. "I need you. . . . I need you so much. . . ."

The words, torn from her, slammed into his head and for a second stole the last thread of control he possessed. He pulled back and slammed his hips forward, buried his full length inside her, and fought the need to pound into her.

Stilling, he held her to him, fighting to drag in enough air to clear his senses and take her like a man instead of an animal with his first fuck.

"Move," she said. Her hips undulated, the fist-tight grip of her sleek inner muscles rippling around his flesh, sucking at the head of his cock.

Duke tightened his hands on her ass, fighting to hold on to his control. Fuck, she was killing him. Pleasure tightened through his body until he swore his mind was going to explode along with his balls.

"Move now," she demanded, her nails rasping against his scalp a second before she pulled his hair. Hard.

His lips slammed down over her hers, he pulled his hips back, slammed forward, and he was a goner. Hot silk tightened on him, rippled and stroked along his cock, and his head exploded with the sensations.

Her leg . . .

Fuck, had to be careful . . .

One hand slid beneath her wounded leg and his control snapped. He was pounding inside her, fucking her like a man possessed.

Hell, he *was* a man possessed.

He'd been possessed by this need for her since she was eighteen and it had only strengthened over the years. Each time he was around her, each time he gained a smile when he wanted a laugh, each time he'd seen the flash of awareness and growing hunger in her eyes.

God help him, but this woman was his weakness and rather than running as far and as fast as possible when he'd realized it, he'd stayed right in the line of fire.

He was possessed by this pleasure.

By the flames burning up his spine, and the woman holding tight to him, crying out his name, her sheath tightening, her breaths gasping, her nails digging into his scalp. Her snug channel clamped down on his dick, stroked along it as he felt the little spasms, the convulsive clench, and the orgasm that raced over her, through her, spilling her slick juices in a fiery rush of liquid heat.

"Fuck. Angel." His release took him by surprise.

Fireworks exploded from his balls up his spine then back again to the torturously hard length of his cock before exploding past his control.

"Sweet baby . . ." The groan was torn from him as he slammed his full length inside her, semen spilling inside the heated, rippling depths of her body as he held to her.

Relishing every powerful ejaculation, every flexing stroke of her sweet sheath, he knew somehow, someway, she'd slipped beneath his shields farther than he'd ever imagined.

She owned a part of him.

No one had ever owned any part of him until now, until Angel.

As the final pulses of his release shot inside her, he knew the fractures she'd somehow found in his defenses had to be repaired.

If they could be repaired.

Turning, all but stumbling inside to the bed, Duke eased her to the mattress, his lips buried in her neck, his cock still buried inside her, still encased by a pleasure he was loath to extract himself from.

Forcing himself back from her was one of the hardest things he'd ever done.

Hell, he'd done no more than release his cock from his pants before taking her. He was still perfectly dressed other than the opening of his jeans and the belt he'd only barely managed to loosen before jerking the metal button free and unzipping the material.

"Fuck, you're gonna kill me." He breathed out roughly as he lay back on the bed beside her.

He'd get up in a minute and fix his clothes. Or finish removing them, which would be a far better idea.

Looking over at her, he wasn't surprised by the feeling of smug satisfaction that filled him.

Angel lay back on the bed, boneless, completely sated. Her hair lay tangled around her face, the vulnerability that she somehow managed to keep hidden from the world softening her face and revealing the delicate femininity normally overshadowed by her incredible will.

"That was different." Breathless, lazy, and incredibly sensual, her voice wrapped around his senses and reminded him that he hadn't nearly had enough of her.

"Is that what you call it? Different?" He snorted, sitting up on the edge of the bed to pull his boots off.

"Want flowers and praise?" The edge of laughter in her voice caused his heart to constrict.

It was rare to hear her so relaxed, replete. Hell, he didn't think he'd ever heard it.

Tossing his boots to the side, he turned back to her, his fingers curving over the flesh above her knee as he prepared to stroke his way up.

The surprised cry and painful flinch of her leg away from him had his gaze going to her in surprise. No less, though, was Angel's.

Hurriedly gripping her below the knee to hold her in place, Duke stared down at the bandage covering the knife wound she'd taken two weeks before. The gauze beneath the waterproof adhesive was stained dark, the entire four-by-four square showing a seepage that would have occurred within only a few hours of her shower.

He knew Angel. She would have changed that bandage the second she dried the water from her skin.

The skin around the covering was red, and when he laid his hand over it, he could feel the added warmth of her flesh.

"What the hell?" He stared up at her, his temper slowly rising at the look of guilt in her gray eyes and the mutinous set of her lips.

"I was going to have you call Ethan tonight anyway," she bit out, glaring at him as though it were his fault. "It wasn't like this until today."

"All day?" Yeah, he knew Angel.

"This morning," she snapped back, jerking into a sitting position as he rose to his feet, reclosed his jeans, and stomped to the dresser where he'd laid the phone.

"Why didn't you say anything then?" Duke turned back to her, barely able to believe she'd gone all day without mentioning the problem. "Ethan could have been here earlier."

The muscle at his jaw jerked, tightening in response to the irritation she could see gleaming in his eyes.

His face was suddenly in hers, almost nose to nose, anger flaring in the mossy green eyes glaring back at her.

"I've been rather busy, Duke." The mutinous look on her face only irritated him more.

She was going to drive him to an early grave, he decided, from sheer worry alone.

"I have a gray hair," he snarled. "I know you're the reason for it."

Lifting her eyes Angel checked the deep black, thick strands of hair. Sure enough, right there on top.

"You're welcome," she assured him, a mocking smile curling her lips. "Give me a minute and I'll give you another."

"I have no doubt," he snapped.

He had his cell phone at his ear and gave a clipped, "She's done it again. Get here."

"Ethan?" she asked as he tossed the phone back to the dresser.

There was something about his expression, the concern in his eyes, that hint of anger, that warmed her, though. That made her feel not so alone.

"Ethan," he assured her, though he didn't sound in the least pleased by that fact. "Hell. Angel, what am I going to do about you?"

She had a feeling it wasn't a rhetorical question, which was too bad, because she really didn't have an answer for him.

TWELVE

Less than an hour later, a quick knock on the door of the suite heralded Ethan's arrival. Without a word, Duke strode from the bedroom only to return moments later with not just his brother in tow but Natches and Chaya as well.

Angel glared at all of them. It was bad enough she had Duke watching her, but he just had to bring Chaya in with him, didn't he?

Ethan stepped inside and unpacked the mobile surgical unit, as Tracker called the heavy, waterproof case he kept loaded with medical supplies.

Duke and his younger brother could be twins they looked so much alike. Tall, powerfully built, with thick black hair. The major difference was in their eye color. Duke's eyes were a deep, dark moss green. Ethan's were a mix of blue and green, the oddly colored orbs shifting in color with his moods or emotions.

"You didn't mention being wounded," Chaya stated, her tone coolly disapproving.

The frown on Chaya's face was meant to be imposing, Angel was sure.

"Didn't I?" She widened her eyes as though surprised with herself. "Now wasn't that so bad of me? Perhaps I'll remember next time."

Natches's brows lowered broodingly at her response while Chaya's brow lifted mockingly.

"Perhaps you will," Chaya drawled, the slow curve of her lips devoid of amusement. "Otherwise, we'll see how well you enjoy dealing with me once you've pissed me off. I wouldn't—" The sudden order came as Angel considered rolling her eyes.

She turned her gaze to where Ethan had knelt beside her, his pack opened at the end of the bed.

Duke stood behind his brother, his arms crossed over his chest, and he just stared at her. He didn't speak, just watched her. That brooding, half-angry expression he wore when displeased with her made her feel highly uncomfortable.

Angel brushed the front of her hair back nervously, wishing she'd braided it after her shower. She scratched at her temple a second later, not because it itched, but because that steady regard of his just made her nervous.

He made her nervous all the damned time.

"Get them out of here," she hissed at Ethan as he reached for her leg. "Or you'll lose that hand before you ever have a chance to touch me."

"Oh for God's sake," Chaya muttered. "Natches, Duke, let's leave the little princess to Ethan's care while I have a word with the two of you."

She could stay pissed, Angel thought as they crossed the room to the patio.

"The wound is still bleeding, princess. What did you do to it?" Ethan asked, turning back to her.

Princess. She should shoot Chaya for that one herself.

"Aspirin." She breathed out heavily. "I've been taking them for a week or so now. They increase the bleeding. The antibiotics should have healed the wound enough, though, that they wouldn't be a problem."

"Well then, let's see what you've done to yourself," he suggested. "Or was done to you. How did it happen?"

"Misjudged a bastard with a knife, I guess." She sighed as he began peeling the adhesive from her leg. "Tracker cleaned it thoroughly before stitching it closed. It should be healing, not getting worse," she admitted.

A low murmur of agreement met her statement as Angel looked to the door Duke, Natches, and Chaya had disappeared through.

"Let's see what's happened then, Shorty," Ethan breathed out, his voice somber despite the nickname he'd given her years ago.

She slid him a resentful look. "Stop with the 'Shorty' stuff, Ethan. I'm going to hurt you if you don't stop with the cute little names."

He snorted at the threat.

Angel caught herself staring toward the door.

She didn't want to look at her leg anyway, she thought dismally as Ethan peeled the bandage away from the skin. She'd looked at it earlier; that had been enough for her.

"Fuck, Angel, are you trying to get Tracker killed?" Ethan's curse was low, his tone amazed as he began checking the wound.

"Duke would skin him for leaving you here alone, if he saw this."

Yeah, it looked pretty bad. The wound itself was becoming reddened rather than the healing pink it should have been by now. The flesh around it was warmer than it should be and she was certain it was infected despite the alcohol she'd been dousing it with and the antibiotics she'd been taking.

"Just fix it and stop with the doomsday crap," she muttered, brushing her hair back again. "And hurry before he comes back in here. I don't want to deal with his attitude."

Duke acted like a damned father with a five-year-old where she was concerned. She didn't need a father. Her biological father hadn't given a damn and she didn't need Duke attempting to take his place.

"He worries about you." Ethan sighed, turning back to the open case at her feet. "He just about drove himself crazy searching for you."

"He was already crazy," she informed him flippantly. "And I doubt he did it because he was worried. He did it to attempt to rack brownie points with those cousins of his. Too bad it was a wasted effort."

"Hmm," he murmured, probing at the stitches and causing her to wince at the sensitivity. "I'm going to have to clean this and replace these stitches."

"Like hell." Her gaze snapped to her leg as she tried to move her thigh from his grip and she got a good look at the reddened flesh.

Yeah, those stitches had torn quite a bit. Enough that the pressure she'd put on her leg and the aspirin had caused it to seep blood for most of the day.

"Just patch it up, and hurry before he gets back in here." She so did not want to fight with Duke. "The stitches will be fine."

"I'll reclean this wound and replace those stitches or call Duke back in here right now and see if he can't convince you." His voice firmed, turning from tolerant and nice to that arrogance she was beginning to associate with Mackays alone.

"I'll kick your ass if you don't hurry and bandage it." She leaned closer and inserted her best "do it now" tone.

Ethan's smile was a little too patronizing to suit her as he glanced back at her from surveying the med kit and lifting several sterilized pouches free.

Needle and thread, several prefilled syringes, and various bandages.

"I said now. . . ." she growled.

"I said Duke," he reminded her and he meant business.

"Did I mention I hate you, too?" she snarled, narrowing her eyes on him. "I was prepared to forgive you for letting him lie to me, but I've just changed my mind."

Duke stepped in from the patio, his gaze going immediately to her leg. A second later he gave a slow shake of his head and his expression tightened, a sure sign he was trying to hide the depth of his anger. And of course, right on his heels were Chaya and Natches.

"She won't let me restitch it, Duke," Ethan complained, obviously hiding a smile. "She's whining like a petulant little five-year-old. Would you do something with her?"

Sliding Ethan a look of promised retribution she pulled her leg to the side again as he reached for it.

"I'll take care of it myself," she gritted out, shooting him a furious glare. "Go away."

Duke shook his head, lifted his hand to pinch the top of his nose, then moved to her.

"Stop being such a little wimp," he berated her as he moved around the bed to the other side of the room. "Let him fix it before I have to hold you down."

Watching him closely as he moved around her, she silently dared him to try anything.

Hold her down, would he? She'd bust his balls.

"I so wouldn't try that if I were you. Trust me, Duke, that would be bad. . . ." Her head jerked around at the sting in her arm, eyes widening in outrage as she watched Ethan pull a syringe back from it.

"You'll feel great once you wake up." He was obviously laughing at her. "Can't believe you fell for that one again, Shorty . . ."

She blinked at him.

"Hate you . . ." She sighed, already feeling the effects of whatever he pushed in her arm. "Gonna neuter you."

Her eyes dipped closed as she felt Duke's arms go around her and lift her from the bed, only to lay her back on the pillows, giving Ethan easy access to her leg.

She stared up at him, those dark green eyes meeting hers so somberly.

"Make her leave," she whispered. "Not while I'm weak . . ."

She couldn't let her mother see her while she was weak.

Duke was aware of Chaya and Natches as they stared at Angel silently, concern marking their expressions before Chaya turned on her heel and left the bedroom.

"She's the same way." Natches sighed heavily, shaking his

head before meeting Duke's gaze. "Find me when Ethan's finished."

Nodding in reply, Duke waited until the door leading to the hall closed behind them before turning back to Ethan.

"She's hurting, and I'm not talking about her leg," Ethan stated as Duke sat on the bed next to Angel and brushed her hair from her forehead.

Ethan was meticulously cleaning the three-inch cut she had in her leg after removing the previous stitches. Tracker had warned Duke about the leg when he called to inform him she was in Somerset and possibly in trouble and he had laughed when Duke promised to kill him.

"I know." Staring down at her unconscious face he tried to feel guilty about the trick he and Ethan had played on her, but both of them were well aware of her squeamishness when it came to stitches as well as needles.

For a woman that risked bullets on a nearly daily basis that aversion surprised him.

Duke restrained a need to smile at the little snort of breath Angel made as she slept. Not a snore, but definitely bordering on it.

Ethan actually chuckled as he began restitching the wound. Taking care of her when she was wounded was a job itself at times. Watching his brother meticulously sew the flesh back together and tie the thread off, Duke wondered how the hell that infection had happened. Angel was too careful, too exact about keeping wounds clean, he thought as Ethan smeared the goop he got from Memmie Mary on the newly stitched flesh.

Their grandmother made the noxious salve for Ethan and stored it until he visited to collect more. For as long as Duke could remember the family had used that salve for every known ill they'd ever faced and Ethan swore by it.

"Being here with Chaya hurts her," Ethan guessed, repacking the case. "She's not going to give in easy."

Yes, it does, Duke agreed silently, and he had no idea how to fix it. He'd spent five years trying to take away Angel's hurt, only to hurt her worse in the end, just as he'd feared he would. And it wasn't about to end. This situation had to be fixed, and like a wound that had healed badly, it would have to be reopened first.

The pain, the loss, the uncertainty Angel felt in keeping her identity hidden only weakened her. Duke was terrified it was going to end up getting her killed.

Applying a large adhesive bandage over the stitches, Ethan made certain each side was securely hugging the skin before he sat back, his gaze returning to meet Duke's.

"She'll sleep for a few hours," his brother predicted. "If she goes a little longer I won't worry. From the shadows under her eyes it's been a while since she's had a good night's rest."

Duke recalled the nightmare she'd had the other night. Years of blood, death, and seeing the worst humanity had to offer weighed too heavily on her young soul.

"Stay here with her," he told his brother, staring down at Angel's sleeping face. "I'll go let Chaya know her little lamb is doing good."

Ethan snorted at that. "Better get back before she wakes. I'm not knocking her out again and she's not hitting me because you're not here. I need to get some blood, though, while she's out. I'll have Doc Marlin run it for me, make sure everything's okay."

"If she wakes, tell her if she hits you I'm going after Tracker and Chance. And they won't enjoy the meetup." And he was known to keep his word, just as he was getting ready to do in another matter.

"I'll be back soon." He sighed, easing from the bed, though he was reluctant to take his eyes from her. "Maybe we'll get lucky and she won't be too mad."

Chaya sat alone in the dark, curled in the over-sized chair, a hand-sewn child's blanket pulled up to her chin. She had made the blanket herself during her first pregnancy. Block by block, thread by thread, sitting in this chair awaiting the birth of her daughter. The child created during a not-so-loving night with a jealous, abusive husband, who she'd eventually ordered away from their home. The whoremongering bastard. She'd known he was cheating on her, known he had a mistress, but by the time she'd thrown him out, she hadn't cared to find out who it was.

After she'd learned she was pregnant, something changed inside her. Her child, despite the conditions of the conception, became her world. She'd never had anyone that belonged to her. Never had anyone to love her unconditionally. Wasn't that a baby? That someone that belonged to her? Someone who would love her unconditionally? And her beautiful Beth had more than completed her. Craig hadn't wanted their child and that had suited her just fine.

And her baby had been such a mini-me. And so smart.

She'd walked more than a month early, had begun talking early. And after watching Chaya working out and practicing with her knife, her two-and-a-half-year-old baby had found her-self a stick and shocked the hell out of her by imitating Chaya's movements with a babyesque lack of grace. She couldn't execute the moves, but she'd shown such talent. So much so that it had become a game. Beth with her stick, then the hard rubber prac-tice knife Chaya had given her.

Weeks after she turned three, Chaya had bought herself a new weapon. She completely dulled the blade of the bone-handled knife passed down from her great-grandmother and gave it to her daughter.

Beth had very solemnly tucked that knife in the pocket Chaya had made in her favorite teddy bear, closed the pouch, then once again picked up the rubber knife Chaya had originally given her, and so sweetly said, "Play, Momma."

"Play, baby," Chaya whispered into the dark, her voice hoarse, strained. . . . "We played."

For six more months Chaya had "played" with her baby. Then Army Intelligence and Timothy Cranston had arrived on her doorstep, and one month later, she'd left her baby with the sister she rarely spoke with but loved. Trusted.

How had she not known her sister had been pregnant, given birth to a little girl only a few months after Chaya had given birth to Beth? A child Craig had fathered.

Jo-Ellen had come to Chaya's home a handful of times to get to know Beth. When Chaya had taken her daughter to her sister's home in Canada, she hadn't gone past the living room. She saw a few toys and assumed Jo bought them for Beth. Chaya had tried every way imaginable to get out of her assignment, but neither her superiors nor Timothy would hear of it. Chaya knew it'd be too dangerous to leave Beth with Craig, so she had left her baby with her sister while she was deployed to Iraq.

"Momma . . . please don't leave me. I'm scared, Momma. . . ."

Chaya's breathing hitched, the tears of the past building once again.

She'd been in the hospital in Iraq recovering from the torture she'd been subjected to when a spy had captured her. If it hadn't been for Natches and Declan, she would have died there. She'd been eager to heal, turn in her report, and leave for Canada with Natches, when she'd learned Beth was being held at the hotel by Craig. It was one of the agents she worked with who had forced her way past the guards at Chaya's door to give her the information.

Chaya had hurriedly dressed and run from the hospital to the agent's car. Nearly half a mile from the hotel they'd been forced to leave the car due to debris in the road. Natches had arrived as she'd begun running for the hotel, fighting to get to her daughter. He'd been there to throw her to the street and cover her as a rogue missile slammed into the building and destroyed it, along with Chaya's heart.

She'd cried for what seemed forever. For twenty years. Every year on Beth's birthday, every Christmas, every anniversary of that fucking explosion, every fucking nightmare . . .

She was barely aware of the broken cries that escaped her lips or the slow rocking motions of her body.

"Why do you have this room, Chaya? It's morbid. A shrine to a child that's not returning. Beth wasn't taken, she wasn't lost or missing, sweetheart. . . . She's dead." Timothy's voice whispered around her, heavy with grief and with regret.

This was Beth's room. The same type and color of carpeting, and every toy, piece of furniture, and article of clothing from Beth's room. As though somehow she'd known. Had she known Beth was alive?

She had to have. Look at the bedroom, the presents from every year, the shrine, as Timothy called it. What was it, if not a knowledge that her baby wasn't dead?

"Oh God . . . Oh God, baby, I'm so sorry. . . ." she whispered into the dark, the control she had always depended upon so thin now she knew it was nonexistent.

How could she have not realized her baby was still alive? How had she not known, even then, that something wasn't right?

She was an interrogator, a profiler. If she'd found this room in a suspect's home, she'd immediately have suspected the child wasn't dead. For twenty years, her baby had lived in a hell Chaya couldn't imagine. Training to kill from age three. Her baby had been forced to stab someone at six to keep from being raped.

Had her baby screamed? Cried? Had she wondered why her momma didn't come for her? Why her momma hadn't come for her and her half sister before her life exploded around her? Had she cried for the momma she'd loved? The momma she had stopped loving for some reason?

And now, hurt, unconscious, her daughter hadn't wanted her with her. She'd wanted her mother to leave. Didn't she know how desperately Chaya wanted to comfort her? How desperate she was to just ease a moment of the pain her daughter was suffering? How badly she wanted to just hold her, to touch her hair, her face, reassure her baby that she was going to be okay?

Instead, she'd left rather than have Angel awaken and know someone besides Duke and Ethan had seen her weak.

As though she couldn't trust her mother enough to allow her to see her when she was weak, unconscious.

A movement at the door had her head lifting, her gaze connecting with her husband's as he walked to her then eased down beside her on the chair. Touching her cheek, his fingers came away damp with her tears.

"I would have come for her, if I'd known," she whispered, trying to hold back her sobs. "I would have come for her."

"And I would have gone with you, baby," he swore, drawing her into his arms. "I would have gone with you."

THIRTEEN

Stepping into the kitchen the next morning after doing an excellent job of pretending Duke didn't exist, Angel faced yet another morning of a full house. Didn't her mother—Chaya—ever get tired of having so many people around her?

The work island with its large stove and small sink also held an array of food in warmers obviously kept on hand for just such emergencies. Scrambled eggs, pico de gallo, bacon, sausage, ham, pancakes, and piles of toast.

Christa, Kelly, and Dawg's sisters and mother were all behind the stove working, their voices a quiet murmur as they filled plates and handed them out or refreshed the warmers. Folding tables and chairs were set up in the huge living room, and the murmur of voices from within the room assured her that most of the men were gathered there.

Peeking inside the living area, she saw Duke standing on the other side of the room talking to Rowdy and Dawg. Catching her look, he shot her a little wink but went back to his conversation rather than joining her.

"There you are." Christa looked up from the fried potatoes she loaded a warmer with. "I thought you'd sleep awhile longer."

Brushing back her fringe of bangs nervously, Angel lowered her hand and tucked both into the front pockets of the camo pants she wore, looking around.

"I slept enough." She shrugged, uncomfortable as Mercedes Mackay turned from where she was unloading the dishwasher and handing off the dishes to one of her daughters to put away.

"This one, she likes to prowl the night like a little cat," Mercedes said and Angel had to restrain a grimace as the other woman smiled back at her warmly. "Did you think I would not remember the young woman that stayed with us that summer? You can change your hair and your eyes, but many things will always remain the same."

And some people were just too damned perceptive, now weren't they?

"Most people don't realize that." She shrugged, hoping Chaya wasn't around to hear this conversation. "Have you seen Bliss?"

She'd promised her sister they'd work on her knife skills.

"She is in her parents' room speaking with them," Mercedes said quietly, her expression somber. "I believe Natches is beginning to get a clue that his young daughter is not going to be as easy to protect and guide as he believed she would be. She is certain she needs to participate in drawing these men who wish her harm out into the open."

Hopefully, she'd listen to her parents, Angel thought.

"She's as stubborn as Natches is," Angel said, not really certain what to say to any of them.

"They butt heads often." Mercedes laughed then, looking to her daughter Zoey. "That I believe is as much a Mackay trait as well as one Chaya possesses."

Angel nodded uncertainly, looked around the kitchen, and felt about as out of place as she imagined she'd ever felt.

"All the girls are as stubborn as their fathers," Christa pointed out with a low laugh. "They have the potential of being more stubborn."

The other women's soft laughter was an agreement as they continued with what they were doing. They worked well together, too, she noticed. It was a comfortable, familiar rhythm between them that spoke of practice and a knowledge of each other that came from working together often.

"Chaya was bragging about your cooking skills this morning." Kelly, Rowdy's wife, smiled back at her from the counter where she was buttering toast and placing it on the stack of bread already browned. "Even Bliss can't boil water. Maybe I won't worry about them starving to death so much with you around."

Angel met her brown gaze in surprise.

They thought she was actually going to be able to stay? Weren't they such an optimistic bunch.

"Bliss needs to learn to cook then." Angel frowned at the knowledge of how Chaya was spoiling the teenager and just how much Bliss chafed at the lack of responsibility. "I knew how to cook certain things at six. A campfire's low enough that height wasn't an issue, and all you have to do is burn your fingers once to learn not to do it again."

She shrugged as everyone seemed to look at her in surprise. Or was that shock? With this group, who the hell knew for sure?

She knew they were grilling her with such friendly warmth that it was impossible to get truly angry.

"Tracker's mother taught you to cook then?" Mercedes asked, turning back to her as she began loading the dishwasher again.

"Hunger taught me to cook." She was ready to find an escape route now. She didn't do interrogations well. "Do you need any help or anything?"

"Yes." Zoey turned from the other side of the far counter, a steaming cup of coffee in hand. "Here's your coffee, pull up a stool, and let us get to know you. That's what we need."

"Zoey, your manners." Mercedes sighed as though it were a recurring chastisement.

Zoey winked back at Angel and placed the coffee on the counter in front of a stool with a nod to indicate Angel should sit.

"Mom even remembered how you took your coffee." Zoey grinned. "Strong, with plenty of sugar and cream."

"Why?" Angel asked, then immediately regretted it. Dammit, they were making her uncomfortable and that never failed to make her defensive. But she couldn't figure out why they wanted to get to know her now when they hadn't given a damn before.

Everyone was staring at her again. Seven pairs of eyes locked on her inquisitively.

"Because it was something we should have done long ago." Mercedes answered the question gently. "Just as you should have come to one of us, at least, with the truth at a less upsetting time. Family, Angel, they can make mistakes just as others can, my dear. None are perfect."

The chastisement was there, she heard it, felt it, but it was done so gently and with such logic that Angel couldn't exactly deny it.

She looked away, her gaze going to the closed shades over the windows then back to the women as they began moving around, finishing breakfast rather than staring at her.

"Come on, Angel, sit with us for a little while. No one's at fault for the lack of communication, but we all want to get to know you. As you've already learned, one person alone can't accomplish that." Kelly glanced up at her from the bacon sizzling on the stove. "And as this situation has reminded us, sometimes we don't always follow our instincts as we should. As we should have when we met you."

She'd given them a chance, plenty of chances. Hadn't she?

"I remember when I first met you." Lyrica turned from the counter behind the stove, a dish towel in hand. "You were there when that van ran me off the road. If you hadn't been, I'd probably be dead. I wish you had let me thank you for that."

Angel glared at the floor a second, trying to figure out what to say. What to do.

Yes, Lyrica had tried to thank her, but Angel had been so upset that day, because Chaya had refused to allow Bliss to go to the marina with the other girls when Angel had come to tell them good-bye, that she'd been unable to process the gratitude Lyrica had shown.

"No thanks were needed." She cleared her throat, looking up. "If we'd known Zoey was in trouble, we would have been here." She focused on the other sister where she stood next to the work island. "We didn't hear about it until it was too late to get here in time to help."

"But you came the minute you heard," Zoey pointed out. "I think Graham said the three of you dropped a job to hurry back. But you'd been here a few weeks before leaving for that job, hadn't you?"

"A few times," she agreed. For five years she'd been there as often as possible.

"Come on, drink your coffee before it gets cold. Breakfast is nearly ready and then it's going to be like feeding time at the zoo." Zoey laughed.

Angel listened to them debate over which of the men could eat the most before the conversation shifted and flowed again. They drew her in without interrogating her, let her listen and draw every piece of information they gave her into her hungry soul.

They called Chaya the keeper of Natches's sanity. He could drive even the steadiest person to the brink of murder if she wasn't there to pull him back. The older he got, the worse he got, they claimed.

Zoey laughed and recounted the fact that she'd been the only one of them to force him to pull back. Lyrica glared at her sister and recounted how Natches had not just hit Graham in the face, but nearly caused her to move from Kentucky entirely.

Eve and Piper, the two oldest sisters, laughed and claimed Dawg as their tormentor during the beginning days of their relationships with their husbands. And through all the upheavals and arguments with the two men, it had always been Chaya that watched their backs and they hadn't known it until recently.

Rowdy was the keeper of their secrets, though. They could go to him, and though he couldn't do anything to pull his male cousins back from whatever schemes they had regarding the girls, he'd always had advice and, in Zoey's case, had actually kept a secret that nearly caused him and Dawg to come to blows.

The Mackay men were as complicated and ever-changing as their wives, it seemed. But they were dedicated to family, to protecting the girls as well as each other.

"I remember when Chaya showed up that summer," Christa said softly as the last of the warmers was filled. She looked over at Angel, her gaze somber with whatever memories filled her. "Dawg told me about this agent they were working with." She almost grinned. "Called her plain. She smoked too much, cursed too often, and she was making Natches erratic. The truth was, Natches was terrifying Dawg because he'd gone so quiet, refusing to discuss whatever torment he was experiencing."

Shock shook Angel. Chaya smoked? Cursed? The mother she'd known had never done either thing.

"She wore frumpy clothes, Dawg claimed, and whatever her problem was, she was going to piss him off. But he was already pissed. And worried. Something about her just set him off, he said." Christa shook her head and leaned against the counter, silent for a moment before continuing. "The next summer she was back, searching for the person or persons behind the theft of the missiles they'd been investigating the year before. Following up." She grinned. "Dawg would sneer the word and go off on her 'follow-up' like it was some kind of immoral act. Because he knew something about her was killing Natches, and he couldn't figure out what." The look she gave Angel was compassionate, understanding. "Then Natches told him how he and Chaya had come together four years before in Iraq and how she'd lost her daughter, and he warned Dawg their relationship hinged on his acceptance of the woman he loved because now they were having a child together. That's when Dawg realized how far he'd been pushing because he didn't know what was wrong or how to fix things for Natches. That's how they are, Angel. All of them, including Chaya. They'll tear themselves apart trying to make sense of things. And Chaya was so torn over you. She sensed more than you would tell anyone. She sensed the deceptions, and your hunger to know her and Bliss, and she couldn't make it fit, couldn't force it to make sense. But all of us saw the conflict inside her. That need to let you close, to let you be a part of her life versus far too many years of hard lessons and the destruction she'd already survived when she'd believed you died in that hotel."

Everyone believed so deeply in Chaya. Duke, the entire Mackay family. Everyone believed and she wanted to hold on to that so desperately that it was a hunger inside her.

But she couldn't discount what she remembered. She couldn't put aside that damned phone call where her father had raged at Chaya to come for her and argued with her when she refused to do so.

She didn't say anything, she couldn't. Pushing back the pain, the anger, the sheer fury that she couldn't make herself accept a different version of the past, she finished her coffee and turned her gaze to Zoey.

"Thank you for the coffee," she said softly. "If you'll excuse me, there's things I need to do now."

Like run away. Escape these women with their certainty that Chaya would never turn her back on her child. Their belief that Angel had to be wrong. And she didn't want to disabuse them of their belief in her mother, she realized. She didn't want them to think harshly of her or Chaya. This was the family Chaya relied on, had lived within for so many years. Their opinion of her, their love for her, mattered to her.

Angel wouldn't threaten it.

She hadn't come there to threaten her mother's life; she'd only wanted to be a part of it. As Angel Calloway, not as Beth Dane, the child she'd lost. She could have survived being on the periphery of her mother's and sister's lives, being a friend that came when needed. She couldn't handle being the child Chaya had lost, though.

She couldn't handle the fact that everyone had a far different memory or opinion of that time when Angel had been Beth and she'd listened to her father raging at her mother on the phone.

Because neither of them had wanted her. He'd had her brought to Iraq as leverage against Chaya when he'd learned she was close to identifying him as the spy in Army Intelligence that was selling troop movements to the enemy. But her mother hadn't wanted to come for her, because of her lover, Natches Mackay.

Fine, she'd been in a hospital rather than in a bed with Natches. But she didn't come and she didn't send anyone to collect her daughter, for whatever reason.

If she'd shown up, if she had just come for her daughter, then Jenny wouldn't have died. Jenny wouldn't have died and Beth wouldn't have had to become Angel and all their lives could have been different.

But none of that had happened.

Now she had to figure out how to ensure Bliss's safety. The fact that everyone knew who she was, and that everyone felt the need to assure her that her mother had never turned away from her wasn't why she was here.

Besides, if that were true, then Jenny wouldn't be dead, Beth wouldn't be Angel, and she wouldn't be sneaking from the house by climbing through the open crossbeams that served as the patio's roof, praying she found someone dumb enough to be where they shouldn't be so she'd have an excuse to expend the rage and the pain.

"That leg is never going to heal if you don't stop overexerting it." Chaya stepped around the corner of the enclosed patio, her tone thoughtful as Angel sent her a disgruntled look.

What was with these damned Mackays anyway? They just couldn't seem to leave well enough alone.

"The leg is fine," she muttered before pursing her lips in irritation. "Why don't you go find Natches? I bet there's something he needs to talk to you about."

Not that she actually thought that was going to work.

"Even Bliss can come up with something better than that." Chaya grinned, moving with Angel as she strode from the patio wall and headed around the side of the house.

"At her age she better be able to come up with something better." Angel swiped at the hair that insisted on escaping her braid and falling over her forehead. "Fortunately, I don't have to. I can just tell you I don't want to talk to you."

Yet she couldn't make herself ensure Chaya did just that by doing as she'd threatened to do with Timothy and letting the bitch out to play. Instead, rather than finding a way to escape, she kept her pace even and kept her mother in her peripheral vision. And she wondered why she was remaining silent rather than ensuring Chaya returned to the house.

No, she didn't wonder why, she amended that thought. She knew why. Because as angry as she was, as much as she wanted to hate her mother, she couldn't. She'd convinced herself she did for years. She'd tried to tell herself nothing mattered but Bliss, but she'd been lying to herself. She didn't need just her sister in her life but her mother as well, and sometimes she hated herself for that need.

"How's your leg feel?" Chaya asked as she walked next to her, her hands pushed into the pockets of her shorts, the short-sleeved white blouse neat and complementing the other woman's tan.

Angel shrugged at the question. "Better. Ethan always manages to fix me."

"So I hear." There was a thread of stress in Chaya's voice, almost worry, that made Angel want to believe she cared.

"Look." Angel stopped and turned to her, unwilling to admit to the nervousness she couldn't push away. "You don't have to pretend when we're alone. Just say whatever it is you want to say and we'll get on with our day."

She couldn't let herself believe that Chaya wanted to be a mother to her at this late date. The time for that had long passed.

"You think I feel as though I have to pretend to be concerned?" she asked rather than doing as Angel suggested. "You're my daughter. . . ."

"Please don't." She couldn't bear it. She couldn't deal with platitudes or lies. She was too hungry, too desperate to believe them. "I'm sorry Duke forced you into dealing with me like this, but I don't need you to start swearing your motherly love and concern for me. It's okay, really."

The frown Chaya leveled on her made her feel like she was three again. It was filled with disappointment and an emotion she simply didn't want to try to decipher.

"Little girl, that mouth of yours is writing checks you can't hope to cover," Chaya warned her, her tone low, almost gentle.

Really? She'd actually said that?

"I'm not three any longer," Angel reminded her. "I haven't been three for a very long time. And trust me, Chaya, I learned a long time ago how to back up every word out of my mouth."

Sort of. She'd learned how to talk nastier and meaner and how to fight with a viciousness that had the power to actually make her feel ashamed of herself now.

"By drinking too much, smoking too often, and trying to

disguise the pain inside by making certain the outside hurt worse?" Chaya asked softly then. "How did that work out for you, Angel? Did it really help?"

That was exactly what she'd been doing, Angel knew. Hurting so bad inside that it actually seemed to fade a little when the outside hurt worse.

Rather than meet the compassion in Chaya's expression, Angel turned away from her and stared into the leafy, twisted vines of the border Natches had somehow convinced to grow around the perimeter of the yard surrounding his home. Better to stare into it than to see concern, or a mother's affection, where it didn't really exist.

"Whether it worked or not doesn't matter anymore," she finally said, wishing she could hide who she had been and the ugly behavior she'd displayed in those days. "And it doesn't change the fact that I don't require you to pretend with me." She turned back to her mother and met her gaze with a cool, unaffected stare. "You should go back to the house. . . ."

"So you can keep hiding? So you keep telling yourself that it's not killing both of us to continue ignoring the anger and pain?" Chaya demanded, and Angel could have sworn the pain in her eyes was genuine and the huskiness in her voice was due to the unshed tears gleaming in her eyes. "Angel, we have to talk about this. I won't let you continue telling yourself that I didn't want you. That I deserted you."

But that was exactly what she had done and Angel couldn't make herself pretend otherwise, no matter how much she wanted to.

"It's okay," Angel promised her, wishing she could rage at her, wishing she could spill all her pain and fury onto this woman's shoulders as she'd once promised herself she would. "I survived. . . ."

"Oh God, Angel . . ." Chaya whispered, her voice thick with emotions Angel simply couldn't deal with, and when Chaya moved as though to embrace her she jumped back, suddenly terrified, certain she'd break and become that three-year-old again. The one that wandered Baghdad's streets crying for her mother.

"Don't," she demanded, strangling on her own words, desperate to escape what she was feeling, what she wanted to believe her mother was feeling.

"Why?" Chaya questioned her softly, her arms dropping to her sides, her expression twisted with pain. "Why, Angel? Are you afraid you can't keep telling yourself I didn't want you when you know differently?"

Angel shook her head, terrified of what she knew she'd end up doing if she wasn't careful.

"No. I'm scared I'll want to believe you even knowing the truth." Remembering every moment of it and hurting worse for the deception. "I'm afraid, Chaya, I'll want the illusion over the truth, and in the end, that will only destroy me. That's what I'm afraid of. Now if you'll excuse me, I'm sure there are things I need to be doing, even if there's nothing you need to be doing."

Turning, she hurried away from the mother and the single tear that began falling down Chaya's cheek. Angel didn't look in her eyes; she couldn't. She wasn't strong enough to resist and she knew it.

What had happened to her in the past years? Once, she would have lashed out at her mother and told her exactly why she knew better than to believe anything other than what she remembered. She would have ripped into her and shredded the lies with the truth and enjoyed doing it. But she couldn't make herself do it now. All she could do was run away.

From the need for a mother who had walked away from her, from the need for a man she knew would never stay and a life she had promised herself she'd never let herself dream of. A life secure in Duke's arms and her mother's life. And how very foolish was that?

FOURTEEN

Being in her mother's home was odd, Angel thought that evening after the house became silent once again, the in-laws and outlaws having all left. Bliss was in her room chatting with her cousins on video, and Natches, Chaya, and Duke were outside.

Moving through the quiet home, checking doors and windows, ensuring everything was secure, she couldn't help but notice the warmth and the feeling of peace that surrounded her, as well as sense that the house was actually a home.

The family room was large with a wide stone fireplace on the outside wall, a flat-screen television on the wall separating the room from the hall. Several wide, comfortable chairs faced the fireplace, while a large leather sectional faced the television. The space was designed to allow for quiet evenings as well as family gatherings, and functioned superbly for both.

In the far corner there was a round coffee table and board

games stacked beneath it, bean bag chairs were scattered around it, and the shelves on the wall displayed pictures of the four girls: Bliss, Annie, Laken, and Erin. The cousins looked enough like each other that they could be sisters.

The room was a family room in every sense. Here, Chaya had found a way to display family pictures and pictures of her daughter in a way that didn't make the room seem overly crowded with them.

Floor-to-ceiling shelves held books of every kind from children's books to mysteries, suspense, and even a collection of teenage fiction in the form of the old Nancy Drew and Hardy Boys mysteries alongside a popular vampire series and a magic series.

This room and the kitchen were the central part of the house and Angel had noticed the first time she went through it that the layout, as well as the furniture, was arranged in a way that allowed for maximum defense in the case of a home invasion. The safe room was accessible to the main bedroom, Bliss's room, kitchen, and living room. And she had no doubt Bliss was well versed in getting her ass to it as quickly as possible.

Moving to the fireplace once again she tipped her head to the side and studied the pictures on the mantel. There were pictures of Declan with Natches in Iraq. The young man had been only eleven. His immigration and adoption papers listed him as twenty-one when he'd come to the United States, but she knew from one of the reports she glimpsed in Duke's file that he was actually only seventeen.

His life as a child mirrored hers in a lot of ways. The son of a U.S. serviceman who returned home and the young Afghani girl he'd married and left behind, Declan hadn't had an easy life.

He'd been orphaned at five and learned to survive in the

harsh desert landscape and within the village where his life had meant so very little to his mother's family. Natches and Chaya's adoption of him and his move to the United States likely saved his life. The older he became the higher the chances that he would have been taken into one of the rebel groups, where he would have eventually died.

These were the pictures she'd tried desperately to ignore the first day Duke had brought her there. Pictures of everyone except Chaya's first child.

Alone now, the house finally cleared of all the Mackay family members save those that lived there, she found herself helplessly drawn to the family portrait on the fireplace mantel. Natches, Declan, Chaya, and Bliss. Her eyes narrowed at the picture hanging on the wall in the background of the photo. She leaned in closer, certain it couldn't be . . .

"That's my sister, Beth."

Angel swung around to see Bliss stepping in from the doorway on the far side of the room leading to the hall. Dressed in shorts and a tank top, her feet bare, her long hair left loose in heavy curls to the middle of her back.

"The girl in the family picture." The teenager walked to her slowly, her emerald eyes solemn as she stared at Angel. "She's my sister. But Mom lost her when she was only three."

Not "she died," but "Mom lost her."

"I see." Angel turned back to the picture, her heart racing sluggishly in her chest at the sight of the inclusion of her picture.

"She used to have Beth's pictures out everywhere, but when I started asking about her more and more, Mom moved them upstairs to Beth's room. Every time she tried to talk about Beth, she cried."

Angel felt herself flinch. "Your father showed me the room."

Bliss blinked in surprise. "Wow, they must really like you, Angel. Mom doesn't let anyone but me and Dad in that room."

"It's a nice room," she said, once again finding herself at a loss for words.

"Mom was married before Dad," Bliss told her. "When she and Dad built the house, she had Beth's room put just the way it was in the house Beth lived in with her. All her clothes and dolls and everything."

Bliss stopped beside her and stared at the picture, her expression a little sad.

"Every year on her birthday Mom buys her a present and every year at Christmas Mom puts a present in her bedroom. Twenty years. Mom still cries every year. . . ." Bliss's voice trailed off and Angel felt as though she'd taken a blow to the chest.

"Why? She died." She wanted to hate the mother that left her to die in that hotel. She didn't want to glimpse a mother that had grieved or felt sorrow for the death.

"Did she?" Bliss asked softly. "She's still alive in Mom's heart. And she's still alive when Mom hides in her room and cries for her."

Angel inhaled slow and deep, careful not to let the teenager see how her words affected her.

"You don't sound jealous," Angel said softly. "Some kids would be."

"Jealous?" Bliss shook her head. "No. I wish she was here, though. Sometimes I need someone to talk to that wouldn't blab to Mom and Dad. My cousins are cool and we keep each other's secrets, but a big sister would understand things they don't. And maybe she would help me make sense of stuff."

Angel glanced over at the teenager, seeing the shadow of that confusion on her face. "Bran?" she asked softly, remembering the young man Bliss had been fascinated with all summer.

Bliss lowered her head and shrugged. "I guess he went back home. Annie heard Uncle Rowdy tell Dad that Bran was packing up to leave. I didn't get to tell him good-bye. And I was sorry."

"Sorry for what?" Angel asked softly, knowing how affected the teenager was by the young man.

"Dad caught me flirting with him last week. Just a little bit . . ." Bliss hurriedly explained as Angel turned to her again. "He wasn't flirting with me at all. We were just talking. And I'm afraid Dad went and talked to Lucas Mayes and told him to keep away from the marina."

Oh yeah, Natches would totally do that.

"Well, your dad's just trying to protect you. I'm sure Bran can understand that. Bran seems like a smart young man, Bliss. But he's still a man."

A man with problems Angel hadn't quite figured out yet and hadn't had any intentions of delving into actually. Until now. It seemed Bliss was a little fonder of him than Angel had first suspected.

"Angel?" Bliss was careful not to look at her, and Angel followed suit, staring up at the pictures again instead.

"Yeah?"

"Why, if what I'm feeling is natural and what I'm supposed to be feeling, because of the birds and bees stuff, does it just happen with one boy, and not all of them? Shouldn't I be boy crazy? As in plural 'boys'?" The confusion in her voice was heartbreaking and it was so like Bliss to overanalyze it.

Angel frowned at the pictures, wondering what she was supposed to say now.

"Times like these," she said softly, "are when I get really angry that my momma left me to be raised by Tracker's parents. Because right now, Bliss, when I would give the world to have the answers for you, all I have is ignorance."

The year she turned fifteen they were in three different countries and conducted six different missions. Angel carried her own weapon and she knew how to use it. She had used it. She'd already killed a man, nearly died, was almost raped, and spent twelve horrific hours locked in a tiny, cramped crawl space beneath a hut some whack job had tracked her to.

She didn't have the answers her sister needed, and God knew she wished she did.

She slid her arm around her sister's shoulders instead and pulled her to her.

"Growing up isn't supposed to be easy, though, from what I understand," she told Bliss. "It's supposed to be filled with uncertainty, and feelings no one else seems to have and all these weird hormones attacking your body and emotions you don't know how to handle suddenly flooding your heart. Just let yourself feel, Bliss, but remember, don't ever forget, that right now, young men are feeling all these things, too. And right now, at your age, it's just a tiny spark compared to the light show you'll find it can truly be once you're older, and your body and emotions are more in sync."

Bliss was silent for so long Angel was certain it was one of those times when the younger girl just tuned out what she didn't want to hear.

"What if I still feel it for the same guy when I'm older?" she asked then.

"When you're older, six years' difference in age isn't a big deal," she told her sister gently, remembering that Duke was six years older than she was. "But right now, if he hadn't tried to gently reject you, then I'd have to kill him. Ya know?"

A snort of laughter erupted from the girl.

"God, you sound just like Mom." She giggled before a disgusted groan tore from her. Both arms went quickly around Angel's neck in a hard, fierce hug. "You would make an awesome big sister, Angel. Because you're the best."

Apparently in good spirits once again, her heartbreak momentarily abated, Bliss released her and almost skipped across the room to return to her bedroom.

"God save me from teenagers," she muttered, shaking her head before turning to the kitchen.

She'd put a soup on for dinner, then go outside and check that boundary line around the yard. She knew there was a trick to getting through the naturally growing fence. She just had to find it.

And she was determined to find it.

It was late before Angel heard Duke enter the bedroom after his shower. Sitting on the patio once again, comfortably curled into the chaise longue, the bottle of whiskey beside her, she enjoyed the last of the *cigarro* she'd begun the night before.

"Wench," he murmured, taking a seat on the lounger at her knees and reaching for the smoke. "I was dying for one of these while dealing with those damned cousins of mine today."

She relinquished it, almost grinning at the gripe in his tone, not to mention the fact that he was shirtless and all that gorgeous muscle was on display for her viewing pleasure. Barefoot, wearing nothing but a towel, and completely unashamed.

"Which cousins?" she asked, letting the man and the night

begin to soothe the ragged edge of emotion that had scraped her nerves raw over the day.

"All of them," he snorted. "Sometimes I think the ones I was raised with are just as damned hardheaded and stubborn as Dawg, Rowdy, and Natches ever were."

And that was saying something.

"Have they found anything new?" she asked.

"Nothing yet. Thankfully, DNA collected from Bliss's hands is due sometime tomorrow, as is that from the two assailants from the safe house." He inhaled the fragrant smoke of the *cigarro*; his eyes narrowed as he seemed to glare at the patio doors before exhaling. "Did you get the picture I sent you earlier of the guy the security cameras picked up across from the safe house? He was watching it the night it was attacked. The way he was hunkered down in that car trying to avoid the cameras . . . There's no way he was unaware of them."

"I didn't recognize him." Laying her head back on the lounger she gazed up through the weaved, ivy-covered hardwood crossbeams that made the roof of the patio.

"I was hoping someone would." He sighed, handing her the tobacco back when she reached for it. "How's Bliss doing today?"

"She's hanging in there," Angel assured him, thinking of the conversation she had with her sister about Bran. "She's incredibly resilient."

She gave him the last of the *cigarro*, watched as he finished it then tapped the fire out in the ashtray she'd placed on the table next to her.

She liked this, she thought. The antibiotic injection Ethan had given her was working. Tonight, she was relaxed, mellow. And she'd missed Duke.

"She's not the only one," he murmured. "I know someone else in the family that's very resilient."

"Yeah, Natches bounces back pretty fast, too," she agreed with a straight face. "Amazes me how well that man adapts to new situations."

Before she could guess his intention, he bent, lifted her, and a second later tossed her over his shoulder.

"Duke Mackay, you're a dead man." She gripped his hard hips as he strode into the bedroom, one arm holding the backs of her thighs as she giggled—good Lord, he had her giggling.

His hand landed lightly against her rear, the material of the shirt all that separated their skin. The little sting and resulting pleasure of the caress wasn't hampered in any way, though. Damn his hide.

"Neanderthal," she gasped when he patted her bare butt before tossing her to the bed.

Coming to her elbows as he whipped the towel from his lean hips, she found herself having to fight to breathe.

Tanned muscle, his chest rising and falling as quick and as hard as her own, the green of his eyes gleaming with carnal intent, wicked and hot.

"Unbutton the shirt," he demanded with a quick upward tilt of his head. "Slow."

Now this was interesting.

Working on the first button she watched his expression, the way his lashes lowered, giving him a sexy, erotically brooding look as a flush tinted his sun-bronzed cheeks.

"I've thought about this all day." The darker, deeper rasp of his voice caused her lower body to clench as pleasure tightened her sex.

"What have you thought about it?" Releasing the buttons slowly, she could feel her sex growing wetter, slicker.

"Watching you unwrap all that soft, silky flesh." The anticipation in his expression was intensely exciting. "You have the softest skin, all flushed and warm like a summer peach."

Heat flushed not just her face but her entire body. She released the final button but left the shirt as it lay against her.

His gaze dropped down her body, sliding along the bare skin between the open edges of the material.

"Just the sweetest, juiciest peach." The sensual tilt of his lips as his gaze came back to hers made him look like a sex god. Hot, powerful, hard. "And I can't imagine anything as sweet and juicy as my own personal peach."

"You really do have a thing for peaches, don't you?" She gave him a devilish grin.

"Spread the shirt open," he demanded. "Let me see my peach."

The playful wickedness gave the intensity a softer edge, the feel of an adventure rather than something to be wary of.

"You're crazy." She grinned, breathless, blood thundering through her veins, heat rushing through her body.

"Naw, I'm so fuckin' horny my dick's like iron," he groaned, one hand stroking the length of the shaft as she parted the edges of the shirt.

"Can I do anything to help?" she asked, running her fingertips from between her breasts to the top of her sex before stroking upward once again.

She'd never done this, teased sexually, but she could definitely see the benefits of it. The absorbed, fascinated look on his face could become addictive. Maybe it *was* addictive. An invisible drug rushing through her system as her fingertips reached her breasts again.

Spreading her fingers she cupped one mound, let them curve over the swollen flesh before rubbing over the nipple with the tip of one finger.

"Son of a bitch." He breathed out, his voice hoarse, guttural with lust.

Feeling his gaze on her, knowing she was pleasing him, making him hungrier for her, Angel became bolder. As he watched, she gripped her nipple, rolled it, and couldn't hold back the moan that escaped her lips as pleasure shot through her senses.

"God, yes," he encouraged her further. "Spread your legs for me. Let me see how juicy you're getting, baby."

The demand had the wet heat spilling harder from her vagina, slickening her, making her sex highly sensitive.

Lifting her knees and pressing her feet into the mattress she spread her thighs, the brush of the AC against her inner flesh a caress all its own.

"Oh hell yeah." He breathed out, the sound roughened and filled with lust. "You're so slick and wet, baby. You just keep petting those pretty breasts while I eat all that sweetness."

Coming up on the bed between her spread legs, he slid his hands beneath her rear, lifted her to him, and sent his tongue licking between the sensitive folds to the engorged bud of her clit.

Angel jerked in his grip, her hips rising to him, her fingers tightening on her nipples, increasing the lash of white-hot sensation tearing through her.

She would never grow used to the explosions of building sensations. Her senses flooded with the drugging sensuality she only felt with Duke. Only his touch could do this to her. Only his hard male groans and the carnality of his lips and tongue consuming her intimate flesh.

Arching, crying out, her entire being was completely possessed with every slow lick through the narrow slit, every lashing caress against her clit and shocking thrust of his tongue inside the aching center.

Writhing beneath the pleasure, her head tossing on the pillow, she had no thought of rushing it or falling into the chaotic grip of the orgasm awaiting her. She didn't want to rush it, didn't want to miss a single second of the ecstasy building and burning inside her. She wanted to hold this to her forever. She needed to memorize every surge of deepening sensation. Every lick, every thrust of his tongue and draw of his hungry mouth.

As the intensity of the pleasure rose, her fingers curled into the thick, heavy strands of his black hair, holding him to her, her hips rising and falling, grinding against his ravenous lips and tongue. Deep pulses of sensation began building in her womb, in her sex. Hard, convulsive spasms that echoed to her clit as his mouth enclosed it, sucked it, his tongue licking, stroking . . .

The explosions shattered her.

One second she was flying on the pleasure, the next she was spiraling through the maelstrom of complete ecstasy she lost herself to. For blinding, rapture-filled seconds she jerked in his grip, her body thrashing against the onslaught of pure ecstasy.

Fuck.

He couldn't wait. If he didn't slip inside the silky vise of her pussy he was going to pump his release onto the sheets instead of the milking heat of her body.

Forcing himself from the lush sweetness he'd found, Duke

rose quickly to his knees, coming over her as he held her beneath him, her gasping cries echoing around him. He positioned the tortured length of his cock between her thighs and thrust into the clenching heat. . . . Ah God.

Releasing her hips he braced his knees in the mattress, fisted his fingers in the blankets next to her, and gave himself to the desperation clawing at his balls. An inch at a time he penetrated the clenching grip of her pussy. Each thrust sent him deeper, increased the pleasure and the tension gripping his balls.

Just another minute. Just another second in time to experience the most exquisite pleasure. To burn in the center of the flame his Angel possessed.

Each thrust was agony and ecstasy. Each second without coming, without spilling himself inside her . . .

She tightened beneath him, hips writhing, a low, breathless wail tearing from her. The feel of her coming around him again, so fucking tight and hot, rippling around his cock, clenching on the throbbing shaft, was too much.

"Fuck . . . Angel . . . Baby . . ." Plunging inside her to the hilt he threw his head back, a throttled groan escaping as each heavy pulse of release shot from the tortured head of his cock.

Agony and ecstasy didn't come close.

Duke knew he'd never find this again, never know anything this perfect, this complete with another woman.

"Oh, baby." He shuddered against her, caught his weight on his elbows, and fought to catch his breath, to find reality once again. "Sweet, sweet Angel."

She shivered beneath him, her hands gripping his shoulders, little cries escaping every few breaths as her flesh still rippled around his.

"Don't let me go. Not yet," she whispered, the plea broken by her heavy breaths.

About the same time he realized that sometimes breathing takes effort.

"Never, baby." Rolling to his side he took her with him, holding her against his heart. "I'll never let you go."

FIFTEEN

Angel woke, surrounded by warmth as she lay against Duke's chest, sprawled across it actually. Her head rested against his heart, one arm flung over his hard abs, a leg thrown over one of his.

She was draped over him like a clinging vine.

And she couldn't quite figure out how she'd managed to do that without becoming aware of it. She was a light sleeper; she woke herself if she shifted from her side to her back when asleep. But she hadn't awakened when Duke had come to bed, nor had she become aware of shifting against him and flowing over him like she wanted to sink right inside him.

A part of him.

She'd never been a part of anyone before, she realized. She'd been so aware of the horror that losing someone could be, at such a young age, that she'd made certain to keep defenses in place so that she could never be hurt like that again. So that if she failed to protect someone she loved again, it wouldn't destroy her as it had when she was three.

Somehow Duke was slipping past any shield she could put up, though. He razed them, tore them aside, and touch by touch, he was beginning to own a part of her. The question was, did she own a part of him as well?

Stroking her hand along his side, she remembered overhearing his conversation with Ethan about Duke checking in with Tracker. She was bothered that he didn't tell her, because Duke had broken a rule he almost considered sacred: lying, even by omission. Not that she shouldn't expect it in some cases. The lives they led required lies and omissions to everyone. Sometimes even to each other.

Each of them had their own safe house, one the others knew nothing about just in case. After all, everyone was breakable under torture, Tracker was prone to say. If they didn't know where it was, then they couldn't tell. He believed in safeguards and backup plans, and extreme wariness.

Yet Tracker had allowed Duke and Ethan into their personal lives. Duke and his brother had met the man and woman everyone believed were not just Tracker's parents but hers and Chance's as well. For the past several years he'd joined them during their two-week vacation in Bermuda.

He'd seen baby pictures. J.T. and Mara had even told Duke of Angel's childhood. They'd raised her in one war-torn area after another as they worked together. Homeschool lessons weren't just reading, writing, and arithmetic but self-defense, shooting, and tracking. They'd recounted the more harrowing events of that life growing up in a world soaked with blood and violence at times.

They had never told anyone else.

They had never trusted anyone else.

Tracker must have known who Duke was, she suddenly realized. He'd known all along that Duke was a Mackay, and if he had known that then he would have known exactly who Duke's parents were. And he hadn't told her.

She was his second-in-command and he'd kept that information from her as though she didn't need to be aware of it. Because if she had been aware of it, then she would have run. She would have done everything possible to avoid him and she wouldn't have been part of the team when they were hired to kill Lyrica Mackay.

Tracker sometimes saw ties, bonds, and potential events in the littlest things, but he would have seen something more than that in Duke. He would have seen the means to do exactly what Tracker and the family had been urging her to do since she'd remembered exactly who her parents were and what had happened when she was three. To go to her mother.

For years she'd suppressed the memories of her mother, Craig, and Jenny. It had been normal for her to wake screaming from nightmares as a child, crying out at someone that they weren't her father. They would never be her father again.

She still didn't remember what happened during the time between the explosion and the day she regained consciousness as Angel Calloway, though.

Nearly a week had passed before Angel awoke, unaware of who she was, where she was, or how she knew that Mara wasn't her momma.

The death of Brutus, the war dog that had led her to J.T., brought back the memories. From her earliest childhood memory of taking her first step to her mother's arms, to the second the missile had slammed into the hotel, exploding around her as she lay beneath the metal desk, aware that Craig hadn't managed to get Jenny there with her.

Things were fuzzy after that, clear in only bits and pieces. One of those bits and pieces was holding Jenny's broken body against her own as her younger sister reached out for a mother who wasn't there.

Now Angel lay there in Duke's arms, her fingers sliding against the fine mat of hair that grew beneath her head, and knew it had never mattered to her that he was the son of the man that sent that missile to destroy her life. She'd known many men and women born to parents who had loved them, raised them with care and laughter, only to retreat to the basements of their lavish mansions where their victims were brutalized.

Kings, despots, dictators, generals, and wannabe leaders. They'd taught their children to be compassionate, strong, honest, because their children were their public face. They were how the world saw them, how they'd deflect suspicion against them.

And more than once it had been those very children who had aided in the apprehension of those parents. She, Tracker, and Chance had helped rescue several of those young people. They'd helped protect others and seen the struggle that eventually created men and women whose sense of purpose and determination were far stronger than any monsters.

Seeing those past examples had given her a unique understanding into Duke and Ethan, but especially Duke, she thought. He was the oldest, the one who bore the weight of his parents' crimes the heaviest because he had been unable to protect his younger brother from their parents' actions.

And now he was trying to protect Angel from them as well.

God love his heart—as Dawg was known to mutter—he was always trying to protect her from something.

A small smile curled at her lips at the thought of that. From the second he'd forced himself down that narrow shaft to join Tracker and Chance after they'd found her, he'd seemed to feel like it was his duty to make certain nothing else happened to her.

Of course, that had been rather extreme, even for her life, she knew. Caught in the memories of her childhood, hysteria taking hold of her, she'd been fighting the rubble and the heavy beam holding her pinned to the cement floor rather than working to be free of the weight.

Twisting, clawing at the rubble, animalistic screams and growls tearing from her chest, she'd lost her mind and Angel wasn't certain, even now, that she would have found herself again if Duke hadn't forced his way to where Tracker and Chance were breaking their backs trying to keep her from being crushed.

It was a battle they'd been losing, too. They couldn't calm her down, couldn't force her to listen to them, to find her sanity and help them free her. Not until Duke's voice had snapped across her senses like a steel-tipped whip. The strong, deep tone, unknown, but ringing with authority, had sliced past the growing horror and given her a second, a small fraction of time to gain a desperate fingerhold on reality.

Just long enough to make her see the predicament she was in and use her head rather than the fear driving her.

He was there. Nothing would happen to her as long as she listened to him, he'd told her with such an undertone of certainty and force that she'd had to believe him. In a calm, steady voice, he'd quickly talked her through describing how she was trapped, then he'd briefly outlined what they were going to do.

They were running out of time, he'd told her, refusing to lie to her. And if she didn't get herself free, then the rubble settling into the basement would take not just her, but her brothers and him and his brother. They were there for her; now she had to make her escape happen.

Keeping her attention on him, he'd counted to three, then he, Tracker, and Chance had forced every shred of strength they had into their backs and legs to shift the beam that tiniest bit needed for Angel to twist her ankle and jerk it free of the smaller rubble the steel beam had held in place.

As she dislocated her ankle beneath the piece of twisted metal to get it free, Ethan had been there to drag her out and he'd kept dragging her through the narrow tunnel they'd used to get to her. A tunnel collapsing around Duke, Tracker, and Chance even as they clawed their way through it after releasing the beam.

How could a woman hate a man that risked not just his life, but the brother he'd always tried to protect as well, to save an eighteen-year-old mercenary with more issues than a long-running tabloid?

Shifting against Duke, she ran her finger along the line of dark curls that ran from his chest to his abs, her gaze caught by the fiercely erect shaft rising along his lower stomach.

"You're awake," she murmured.

"I'm exhausted," he growled. "You've been lying there thinking so hard I swear you wore me out. What the hell's going through that complicated little mind of yours?"

She couldn't stop the little giggle that escaped. He'd always claimed to know when she was thinking too hard. He'd frown at her and tell her to "stop that," she was making him tired just watching.

"How do you always know?" she asked now, her finger playing at the indent of his navel, just above the wide, fiercely throbbing crest.

"That you're thinking too hard?" he questioned. "Hell if I know. But it makes me tired. Find something else to concentrate on," he demanded, lust darkening his voice, deepening it to a sexy baritone that had her creaming.

"Like what?" she asked with affected innocence as she moved against him, watching as her fingertips skirted the head of his cock to stroke the bend of his thigh.

"You really want me to go there?" He grunted, laughter teasing his voice. "You'll blush."

"You don't like it when I blush then?" Yeah, right. She knew better.

"I love it when you blush," he growled. "When you get flustered and don't quite know what to say. Your eyes get darker, that hint of blue gets brighter, and your whole face turns the color of a pretty peach. I told you I was fond of peaches."

She flattened her hand along his thigh and dipped to the inside with her caresses when her attention was snagged by something else.

"Duke?" She sat up, staring at the heavy sac beneath his cock before turning back to him in surprise. "Do you wax?"

She was going to bust a gut laughing. She couldn't help it.

He frowned back at her, the dark green of his eyes gleaming beneath that heavy veil of lashes.

"Fuck no!" he exclaimed. "No one's putting hot wax anywhere near my balls, Angel. You should know better than that."

He wouldn't lie about it, but there wasn't a single curl down there, and she'd seen enough men naked in her line of work to know that portion of their anatomy could rival any woman's when it came to the thick mat of curls they carried there.

"I use that damned girly-assed hair remover." He chuckled then. "Works wonders."

"Why?" She couldn't help but touch him, wondering why she hadn't paid attention before.

A groan rumbled in his chest as she cupped the heavy weight, her fingertips rubbing against the rougher texture of his sac.

"Damn, baby, you're killing me," he groaned, his thighs tensing as she caressed him.

"Tell me why?" She laid her lips against his chest, tongue peeking out to taste his flesh as she began to lay teasing kisses down a slow path lower.

"Why?" He breathed out, his voice rougher now. "Because the drag of my mission pants are hell if I don't. And you know I don't wear briefs."

No, he did not. But she knew Ethan had once stated he didn't either. And she knew Tracker and Chance didn't. They said the briefs could become uncomfortable in the snug pants they wore on missions.

"I like it." She blew a little breath against the head of his cock as she kissed her way closer.

"You don't know a difference," he pointed out, groaning again before he could finish the sentence. "At least, you better not."

She smiled but refused to say. Her fingers played against the rapidly tightening sac and heavy spheres they contained. Cupping, rolling against them, memorizing the feel of them as she kissed her way to his thigh.

"Not a good idea." His fingers suddenly clenched in her hair. "I don't have much control right now, baby."

"Poor baby." Her lashes fluttered at the little sting as she tugged at his hold, moving to her destination despite the pressure against her scalp. "Keep pulling my hair like that and I might lose mine pretty soon."

She loved the feel of his fingers tugging at the strands while they touched. The sting and release, the little pain mixing with the surfeit of pleasure.

"You like that?" He sounded as though he was pushing the words past clenched teeth.

"I do." She gasped at the sharper little sensation that was there then gone as he pulled and released. "Oh God, Duke. I really like it."

She nipped at his thigh as she moved between his legs, needing to pleasure him, to show him the same hunger that he always showed her. A hunger she fought, one that terrified her at times, but one she couldn't keep ignoring.

"Angel, sweetheart," he groaned, the warning in his voice clear as she lowered her head and licked over the slightly ridged flesh of his testicles. "We're going to get critical here. You know I'll get nasty. Especially this morning. Come up here and let me fuck you nice and easy . . ."

A gentle nip to the flesh she was caressing with her tongue had his whole body stiffening. His cock jerked and just as quickly his hard, broad fingers gripped the base firmly.

"Oh, that looks so hot," she whispered, staring up at the sight, letting her lips caress the flesh as she watched him hold the heavy shaft.

His cock was fully engorged, bisected with heavy veins, the flared head darkened to a purplish hue.

The hand still locked in her hair tugged and released, and as she watched, he stroked up the heavy shaft and back down with a firm grip.

"Keep playing, baby," he urged her with silky warning. "I can take the heat if you can."

She could feel the heated, dazed fascination beginning to

overtake her senses. Everything she'd ever read, seen, or been told merging in her mind in her desire to pleasure him, to see if he could indeed take the heat. She knew she couldn't, but she was sure as hell going to try.

"Suck at them," he ordered, his voice hardening as he used the grip on her hair to urge her head lower. "Let me feel it."

She whimpered, lips parting along the side of the tense sac, sucking one of the spheres inside her mouth, her tongue measuring it, lashing against the flesh covering it, then probing with a firm caress.

Repeating the caress to the other side she could feel her juices spilling between her thighs, dampening her folds, preparing her for him.

"That's it, pretty girl," he groaned, his hips lifting in response, his fingers stroking the fierce stalk above her. "That sweet, hot little mouth. Now come up here." He tugged at her hair again. "Suck my cock just a little bit, baby, while you keep driving me crazy there with your fingers."

His hold tightened in her hair, dragging her up his body, her lips trailing, tongue stroking along the iron-hard shaft until she reached the flared, helmet-shaped crest. A tiny pulse of pre-cum beaded at the slit as the head flexed, drawing her tongue first.

She lapped at the bead of moisture, relished the salty man-and-storm essence of it before rolling her tongue over the sensitive crest.

She moaned as he pushed the thick head against her lips, parted them, and slid inside. It was so damned arousing, the way he was holding her, the pull of her hair, the submissive quality of the hold, and the feel that he was taking her mouth.

She swirled her tongue over the wide head, aware of his body tightening further, and the hoarse groan that filled the air.

She could barely breathe for the erotic excitement building inside her as he filled her mouth with the head of his cock and her senses with pleasure.

"That's it, sweetheart," he rasped. "Suck my dick as deep as you can. Deep, Angel. Fuck, you make me crazy."

Duke knew he was losing control. He ground his head into the pillow, fighting to breathe as he watched her, her gaze slitted and staring up at him as he held his cock up to her hot little mouth.

She sucked him in tight drawing motions, her tongue rubbing against the underside, her fingers cupping and playing with his balls in sensual enjoyment. And it was killing him.

Darts of fiery sensation lashed at his cock, his balls. Up his fucking spine. Every part of his body was being assaulted by ghostly lashes of pleasure that were damned discomfiting but too good to stop.

His balls were painfully tight now as she cupped them, her thumb rolling over them, stroking the tight sac with such wicked enjoyment she had him ready to cum from that alone.

The sight of her mouth stretched around his cock as she drew on the sensitive head was like a shot of gasoline to fire. She was going to melt him with her touch. He could feel it coming.

She was loving it, too. She sucked the head of his dick, tongued it. Her cheeks hollowed as she drew on it, and her face flushed that pretty peach pink that drove him insane with lust.

His fingers tightened on the base of the wide shaft, a groan tearing from him.

She was working the head of his cock with such innocent, erotic enjoyment it was killing him.

"That's it, baby," he groaned, watching the pleasure she derived from the little endearments increase the look of sensual enjoyment in her expression. "Fuck, I love your mouth on my dick. So sweet and hot . . ."

Using his grip on her hair he pulled her head back, watching her eyes darken as he held her lips poised at the tip of his cock before pulling her back down, pushing deeper inside the suckling heat of her mouth.

He did it again, watching, feeling any chance he had at maintaining his sanity unraveling with each moan that vibrated around the sensitive head each time he thrust inside her again, taking her mouth as deep as he dared.

"Ah damn, that's good." He could barely breathe. His entire body was strung tight, his scrotum taut, tortured with pleasure as she cupped and caressed it. And he was going to fucking die if he lost her, he thought, because he knew this was something he'd never find again.

She was in too deep, and Angel knew it. Knew it, but couldn't help giving herself to the overwhelming need to pleasure him, to mark his body, his senses, as he'd marked hers.

Each time his groans whispered around her, or his body tightened, each sign of his shaky control only increased her enjoyment. The sight of his body glistening with sweat, his muscles tightening as he fought to hold back, only made her hotter, wilder.

Taking as much of his cock as possible before easing back to suck and tongue the head, she murmured her enjoyment of him. His hand tightened in her hair, the other clenched around the base of his cock to hold back his release.

"Keep teasing me," he warned her. "I lose myself to this, baby, and you might regret it."

Regret it? Oh, she didn't think so. She wanted him to lose himself, wanted to feel him taking his enjoyment, becoming lost in it as she always became lost in his touch.

"Angel, baby." Duke felt sweat trailing down the side of his face, felt the warning tightness at the base of his spine and knew he was quickly losing control.

"Suck it, Angel," he groaned. "Work that hot little mouth on my dick. Fuck. You're killing me."

The suckling pressure increased, her tongue rippled and rolled just beneath the head along the desperately sensitive nerve-laden area, and she took him deeper. So deep he could feel her little moans like fingers rasping over the throbbing head.

Holding her firmly in place with his fingers in her hair, Duke knew he'd already lost control. He'd lost it the second that hot little mouth tightened around his cock.

Holding on to her, watching her, he thrust against the suckling heat, pushing inside, retreating, and feeling the tight heat drawing more firmly, quickening against his flesh.

He'd intended to pull free when he reached that point where it would be impossible to release her. Duke had no idea he'd passed that point the first second he'd watched her lips stretch around his dick.

That point was gone now, there was no retreat, there was no going easier on her. He stared down at her, watching her, as he fucked her mouth, torn between agony and ecstasy as he felt his cock thicken, felt the warning tension of nearing release invading his senses.

Ah fuck.

He was dying in her mouth.

His balls were tight, his release boiling in them. His lips drew back in a snarl, tortured pleasure raking his senses and shredding his sanity.

Angel's hungry little mouth and tongue were destroying him. He'd never expected this, never imagined she could steal into him and shred his control as no other woman had ever done.

"Fuck, baby. Draw back." He barely recognized his own voice. "Angel, damn . . ."

She didn't draw back. She became hungrier, her moans wilder, her wicked, wicked fingers playing his balls as her mouth sucked, her tongue stroked, and she took him with such greedy enjoyment he felt that last edge of reason explode along with his release.

"Fuck. Fuck. Tongue it. Suck it . . ." The first hard blast of his seed tore through him with white-hot rapture. Holding her head with both hands, keeping her in place, he bucked against her mouth, felt the heat of it searing him as each brutal shot of release tore from him in a lightning bolt of such pleasure he swore it would mark his soul.

His head tipped back, eyes closed, but he still saw her face. Saw it flush with added heat, the way her lashes fell to her cheeks, the way she worked to take each shattering pulse of his seed.

Tension racked him. Forked fingers of slamming sensation held him in their grip, ripping along his nerve endings and filling his senses with a pure savage pleasure.

And damn her, it wasn't enough.

The broad head pulsed, throbbed, so damned eager to be buried inside her that even his balls ached.

Pushing her back on the bed he moved between her thighs,

lifting her to him, watching as each inch of flesh disappeared into the lush, hot depths of her pussy.

She was the most pleasure he'd ever known in his life. She was a challenge, a comfort, a constant dare in the face of danger, and a reminder of everything worth fighting for.

Easing inside the snug grip, he came over her, his hand cupping her face, his gaze locked with hers. He had to clench his teeth to keep from saying something totally sappy. Something completely crazy.

Like he couldn't imagine life without her, without this. That he couldn't let her go, he wouldn't let her go.

But he knew Angel. And his ability to speak, to do anything but let the pleasure rush through him, around him, was gone. The second he buried his full length inside her, the second he felt her coming around his flesh, it was over.

He was a man possessed. Moving inside her hard, deep. Thrusting inside her, taking her as though he hadn't already spilled himself in her sweet mouth.

When the explosion shattered his senses again, he didn't fight it, didn't fight any part of it.

He claimed her.

He just hadn't informed her of that yet.

SIXTEEN

Later that day, Angel finished another long trek around the yard surrounding the house. She was pretty certain the twisting, natural border of cleverly woven wisteria and wild grapevines was sprinkled with what appeared to be either dark thorns or sharpened spikes.

Going through any part of it appeared impossible, but the more she studied it, the more she was certain there had to be a way through it.

As much as she hated it, she had to admit she was going to need either Chaya or Natches to explain the puzzle in the natural boundary around the house as well as the strengths and weaknesses of the property.

Should she need to run, with or without Bliss in the event of an attack, or need the best vantage point, then it would be quicker if some of those were pointed out to her. Duke was still learning the property himself and had gone into the forest around the house with Seth and Saul more than an hour before and hadn't yet returned. That left either Natches or Chaya.

Fine, she decided, either/or.

Her leg was beginning to ache again and she wasn't in the mood to play games. If she was going to be here long enough to catch whoever seemed determined to abduct Bliss, then she wasn't going to pussyfoot around where the answers she needed were concerned.

With that in mind she made her way into the house, the sound of the security system's mechanical voice announcing the opening of the kitchen door barely noticed now. It was a strength in the event of an enemy sneaking in, a weakness if the enemy was already in and she needed to slip past it.

She'd use the patio door in the suite to figure that one out later, she decided.

She was nearing the door into the hallway when movement in the family room had her changing direction and striding to the wide doorway between the kitchen and the connecting room. Closing the door behind him Natches was just leaving the office.

"Angel?" His expression was somber, though his bright green eyes were still wild with inner turmoil.

"I need one of you to step outside and answer some questions about the property." She propped one hand on the hilt of her knife where it was strapped to her right thigh, her jaw clenching with the certainty he would probably brush her off.

He almost paused for a moment, something in his expression softening before he shook it off and continued toward her.

"Questions of what kind?" he asked, a small frown brewing on his forehead as he watched her. "Is there a problem?"

"Only if I need to get through that fence you managed to

convince to grow at the property line," she informed him with resigned impatience. "I know how a Mackay's mind works. You have a way to get through the damned thing at any point. I'm just not figuring it out. I need to know the secret."

He paused, tipped his head to the side just a bit, amusement invading his gaze.

"How a Mackay's mind works?" he repeated, curious now. "How does it work?"

"Like a steel trap searching for prey," she fired back instantly. "And that fence is just waiting for me to get my ass caught in it. Admit it."

That gleam in his eye assured her she was right. That fence was a trap just waiting for the unwary.

"You haven't figured it out?" Male satisfaction just covered his face.

Yep, Mackay.

"Listen, puzzles aren't my forte, all right?" She propped her weight to her good leg and arched her brow mockingly. "Need someone small enough to wiggle through a sewer drain? Come find me. You need someone to catch, kill, clean, and cook wild game on a little flame barely big enough to warm your hands? I'm your girl." She shrugged, pointing an index finger back toward herself. "You need someone to help you put a puzzle together, then you better get hold of Tracker or Chance, 'cause I'm just going to confuse you and me both. So, in the interest of not messing my head up any further, could you please bring your intelligent self outside and show me what I need to know?"

He was on the verge of grinning, which was a good thing. She hadn't seen so much as a hint of a grin since they'd arrived and she knew that wasn't like Natches.

"My intelligent self, huh?" he asked with no small amount of male satisfaction.

Jeez, men were just so easy. Even Tracker and Chance fell for that one.

What was it Dawg often said? God bless their hearts?

"Don't let the compliment go to your head," she advised him somberly. "I say that to Duke all the time."

It took him about a second.

He chuckled, shaking his head almost helplessly as he stared back at her.

"I heard you call Duke a slack-jawed moron when the two of you were standing outside earlier. I might have to be offended," he warned her, finally grinning, his green eyes going emerald.

She brushed back her bangs with blithe unconcern. "Yeah, well. We have a complicated relationship maybe."

"Complicated?" His brow arched, that supreme male arrogance that was so much a part of him reigning on his expression. "Is that what you call it?"

"That's my story and I'm sticking to it," she promised with a tight nod. "So what is it? You going to explain this to me or do I have to take my chances and convince Duke to go through it first?"

He snorted at the suggestion.

"Come on then." He chuckled again. "Let me go explain the puzzle to you. But don't feel bad, even Chay didn't see it at first."

Well now, he just had to mention that one, didn't he?

"That was supposed to make me feel better, right?" She shot him a withering look. "It didn't work."

"Sure it did," he drawled as they neared the back door. "You just want me to think you're titanium. I know better."

Really? Oh, he had no idea how wrong he was.

"Good Lord, another know-it-all male," she muttered. "Remind me to keep my ass out of Kentucky when all this is over."

"You'd have to escape first. . . ."

That was what she was afraid of.

Duke watched the exchange, aware of Chaya standing next to him, her hand over her mouth, her breathing choppy as she listened to her husband and her daughter pretending to bicker as they made their way outside.

"That's Angel," he said softly, looking down at her as she walked away from him to the window, peeking around the shade as she followed Natches and Angel as they made their way to the fence.

"She sounded like Bliss," she whispered hoarsely. "She does that when she doesn't know how to respond, or if she has to face something she'd prefer not to face."

Well, he knew where Angel got it from now; he'd wondered about that.

"I bet Natches accuses you of the same thing." He watched her expression, a mother's hunger and pain reflecting clearly on her face.

A tear eased from her eye and slid slowly, unashamedly, down her cheek.

"How do I get her to talk to me?" she whispered, turning back to him. "What do I do, Duke?"

"I'm not allowed to conspire." He sighed heavily, crossing his arms over his chest. "That was a promise I made her years ago."

She stared back at him, eyes narrowed, her expression just a shade calculating, and that look was pure Angel.

"And you always keep your promises, huh?" she asked thoughtfully.

"My word wouldn't be any good if I didn't, now would it?" he asked.

"So if I wanted to know something . . . ?" she mused.

"If I break my promise to her, she'd never forgive me. I promised her I wouldn't conspire with anyone but her, and I won't break that promise."

Chaya nodded slowly. "I understand, Duke. I won't ask you anything then."

"I appreciate that." He nodded. "Now I think I'll go see about that puzzle of Natches's. I think I might have figured it out." Saluting his fingers to his forehead with a grin, he strolled to the door and left the house.

There were things Chaya needed to know if she was going to find a way to get Angel to talk. They had to find common ground before it was too late and Angel walked away from the mother that loved her.

Because if she walked away from Chaya, she'd have to leave Kentucky. And that, Duke simply couldn't allow. He couldn't interfere, but if interference was needed, there was always Tracker. . . .

It was nearly dark before they made it back into the house. Angel washed up quickly, then returned to the kitchen, where she placed the soup she'd made earlier in the day on the stove to warm and hurriedly baked a skillet of cornbread to go with it.

As Chaya and Natches, Bliss, and then Duke made their way

into the kitchen, rich, creamy potato soup bubbled merrily, the buttery, bacony scent of it drifting through the room.

"Is that Ms. Tully's potato soup?" Natches sniffed the room curiously as Angel began ladling the soup into the bowls she'd put out.

"She gave me her recipe when I was staying in the apartment between her and Lyrica," she admitted, a little self-consciously, as Chaya continued to stare at her. "I like to cook."

"Ms. Tully won't even give her sister that recipe," Chaya stated, attempting to smile. "She must have really liked you."

Was it so hard for her to believe someone liked her?

"I guess," she answered faintly, returning to the bowls, trying not to believe that was hope she saw in Chaya's eyes. "Anyway. Everything's finished."

"You're lucky Natches didn't catch you frying the bacon," Chaya teased her—and why she was teasing her Angel couldn't figure out. "He would have eaten it before you had a chance to put it in the soup."

The look Natches sent his wife was decidedly sensual. "Now, baby, you know I love your burned bacon," he murmured.

Chaya blushed. The look was so rife with love and lust Angel thought she might have blushed herself.

Mackay males were dangerous.

"I did most of it earlier while everyone was outside." She cleared her throat. "It's easier to cook when no one else is around."

She'd learned that young.

After handing out the bowls, she quickly ate, then excused herself when Chaya and Bliss insisted on cleaning up. She needed some time away from Natches and Chaya. Some time to think, to figure out how the hell she was going to handle it if she was there much longer.

The longer she stayed around them, the harder it was not to demand answers, to demand explanations.

"She's waited all day for a few minutes to talk to you," Duke said quietly as he entered the bedroom. "This thing between the two of you is going to have to be discussed."

She inhaled slowly. She didn't want to fight with him, not tonight.

"Duke, the best thing you can do is stay out of this 'thing,' as you call it, between Chaya and me," Angel warned him, facing him as she tried to make certain he understood the fact that this had nothing to do with him. "Becoming involved in it any further is only going to drive a wedge deeper between you and me. When this is over, I want at least a chance to figure out for myself what was between us without this situation shadowing it."

"Was?" he questioned, his expression tightening with the anger flickering in his eyes. "You mean what *is* between us."

She had to laugh, she couldn't help herself; the only problem, it wasn't amusement, it was sheer incredulity.

"You really are such a Mackay," she told him wearily. "More so than I ever imagined." And it was actually more of an accusation.

"I actually expected you to figure that out years ago, baby," he assured her, and though she tried to hide it, he could see the pleasure she felt at the endearment.

Ethan called her silly girl names and he'd seen the secret enjoyment she derived from it, but the endearments filled her with emotion, with pleasure.

"I should have." The slightest tremble of her voice spoiled her mocking tone as he pulled her into his thighs, the hard wedge of his cock pressing against her lower belly through his clothes and her sleep shirt. "Dammit, Duke, this won't solve anything."

"Except your fear? Your certainty nothing lasts forever?" He smiled down at her chidingly. "Or are you just too scared to fight for it?"

"Maybe I just don't believe in fairy tales." But she wanted to. That hunger filled her voice, darkened the soft gray of her eyes.

Pushing his fingers through her hair, he tugged her head back, loving the silken feel of the soft waves and that little flush of pleasure that filled her face as the tugging motion created a sensation he knew she loved. For years he'd dreamed of how damned good it would be to touch her, take her.

With the other hand, he began to slowly unbutton the shirt she'd borrowed from him.

He had to have her again. Now. The explosive pleasure of hours before hadn't nearly sated his need for her. It had only burrowed deeper inside his balls, made him thicker, harder than ever before. He had to touch her, taste the sweetness of his need, and feel her taking her pleasure of him as well.

"Duke, this is insane. You know it is," she whispered as he pushed the shirt from her shoulders, leaving her warm and bare against him.

"Insane? Oh, baby, I've been insane for you for years. This is just going to make it better."

Maybe.

Hell no, it would only make his hunger for her higher, hotter.

Tugging her head back again, he covered her lips in the kiss he hungered for. One of those deep primal kisses that shredded his restraint and left him lost in the taste of her, the feel of her.

She was every fantasy a man could possibly have of a woman.

The taste of her exploded through his senses. Like the taste of fabled ambrosia, she drugged his senses and filled his soul.

A shudder raced through her as his lips moved over hers, his tongue stroking against hers, his body hardening, lust whipping between them, fiery and mind-numbing. Her fingers pushed into his hair, clenched and pulled, as desperate as he was to deepen the kiss, to burn hotter, higher in the sensations erupting between them.

Fuck, she'd been worth waiting for, worth giving her the cold, lonely months after she'd run from him.

He felt things he only felt with her, needed things she alone had ever made him need.

Emotions she fought, refused to acknowledge. But just as she couldn't fight the pleasure, she'd realize she couldn't fight the emotions either. She was beginning to realize they went hand in hand.

Tearing his lips from hers, they went to her neck, as both of them fought his clothes, his boots. It took forever to undress, to release the engorged, painfully sensitive length of his cock. The broad head pulsed, throbbed, so damned eager to be buried inside her that even his balls ached.

He swore he'd go slow and easy. Swore he'd show her he could be patient and teasing. Son of a bitch, he didn't know if he was going to make it.

Naked now, his head lifted from her neck only long enough to get her laid out on the bed.

"Duke . . ." She moaned his name, her gray eyes slitted and staring back at him with dazed need. "We're both crazy."

"Not yet." He was getting ready to get crazy, though.

Coming over her, he locked his gaze on her tight, hard nipples. Candy pink and tempting.

"Oh God, Duke. Please . . ." She arched, shuddering as he

sucked one of those sweet nipples into his mouth, drawing on it, loving it.

Damn. Damn. Nothing mattered but more of her.

Angel felt pure, unexplainable sensation begin exploding through her in rapid-fire succession with each strong draw of Duke's mouth. Heat surrounded her nipple, raking blasts of pleasure erupted in her womb, spasms of reaction clenching her lower belly. His teeth raked against the tender tip, his mouth enclosed it again, drew on it, his tongue rasping it with delicious heat.

Oh God, she wasn't going to survive this.

How was she supposed to hold any part of her heart from him when he kept destroying her with such pleasure?

Then his hand stroked her thighs, between them, and her nails dug into the hard flesh of his back as she felt his finger part the saturated folds he found there, press against her entrance, then thrust full length inside her.

Sensation exploded through her. It shot to her bloodstream, clenched her responsive womb, and rippled through the snug flesh surrounding his finger.

"Fuck, you make me wild for you, Angel." His finger retreated as he moved, his shoulders parting her thighs further.

"Duke . . ." She cried his name as his head bent, his tongue sliding through the slick, sensitive folds with delicious pleasure. "So good . . . Oh God, Duke, that's so good."

It was exquisite. It was so damned good. Her hips lifted and a cry escaped her despite her determination to hold it back. What he did to her should be illegal. She bet it was illegal. Somewhere. But not here and now and not as far as Duke was concerned. Not as far as his wicked, hungry tongue and his tormenting fingers and lips were concerned.

Duke hadn't even realized how much he needed her, the

sweet taste of her and the feel of her going wild beneath him. Her knees lifted, her pretty legs parting farther as he ran his tongue around her hard little clit and tried to throttle the desperate groans in his throat as she arched against his mouth.

Her fingers were in his hair, clenching, kneading like a cat as he buried his tongue in the heated center of her body, desperate for more of her.

She arched into him again, twisting against the stroke of his tongue against her clit, then crying out as he drew it between his lips for a heated kiss and lash of his tongue. "Oh yes . . . like that . . . more like that."

"Like this, baby?" Her clit throbbed as he held it between his lips a second later, then rolled his tongue against it.

Fuck, he was dying for her. Not just dying with the need to satisfy the throbbing in his cock, but the needs wrapping around his heart, clenching it as the pleasure, the hunger for every part of her rose with the same vicious demand as the lust pounding in his balls.

She was his. She didn't want to acknowledge it, she wasn't ready to accept it, but she was his.

"Duke . . . please . . ." she gasped beneath him as he lapped at her, his tongue parting her bare folds, licking every slick, wet curve of her inner lips, as he moved lower. Finding the snug entrance again, he rimmed it with quick licks, flickering over it as her hips jerked and a shudder raced through her.

She was stealing inside him with her innocence and her need and, God help him, he was defenseless against her.

"I could eat you for hours," he groaned. "Keep my mouth right here and just taste you, feel you coming apart for me." His tongue rolled around her clit again, pulling another of those helpless cries from her.

Before she had a chance to realize his intent, he was pushing two fingers inside her, feeling the snug muscles tighten further, bearing down on his fingers, and clenching desperately on the invasion.

"So sweet and tight," he groaned against her clit. "Feel how tight you are, baby. How hot and sweet."

He stroked her inner flesh with slow, languorous rubbing motions, feeling each convulsive clench of her pussy around his fingers.

"Duke, please!" she cried out. "Please, let me come. Now . . . please . . ."

Angel was certain she couldn't possibly survive the sensations building inside her or the storm she could feel waiting to fracture inside her.

The deep, internal spasms clenching her pussy around his fingers only built the sensations higher. They did nothing to ease the pleasure spiraling out of control.

She could feel perspiration glazing her body, the heat building inside her, not in the least cooled by her body's response to it or the AC running on the other side of the room.

"Duke, please!" she gasped, shuddering as the stroke of his tongue around her clit became firmer, hungrier.

A second later he sucked her clit between his lips, drawing on it as his finger began moving, fucking into her with quick strokes that shattered her senses, exploding through her in a rush of ecstasy so intense she lost herself within it.

Before she could recover, before the blaze of sensation could ease, he was on his knees, his cock pushing inside her, parting the clenched, rippling tissue still gripped by waves of pleasure.

"Oh fuck . . . Angel . . ." he groaned, pushing inside her, an inch at a time, stretching her, separating her flesh with such lashes, a pleasure-pain she knew she couldn't survive. "That's it . . . so fucking tight . . . sweet hot pussy's so tight . . ."

She bucked beneath him, driving him deeper only to catch her breath on a shattered cry as he plunged fully inside her. And he didn't stop. She would die if he stopped, die if it eased before she reached the pinnacle he was pushing her to.

A guttural groan tore from him as the pace became faster, harder. Pounding inside her relentlessly, he fucked her like a man possessed, like he knew she was possessed. And she knew it would destroy her. There was no way to survive.

Each hard plunging stroke shafting inside her pushed her closer. Lashing, white-hot arcs of sensation slammed through her, pierced her womb, her clit. . . . Her pussy clamped down on the iron-hard erection shuttling inside it with a driving rhythm and in one blinding second, she shattered.

The sensations exploding through her senses were chaos. They ripped through her body, her heart, and she swore they dug into her soul as a hoarse wail met the kiss he slammed over her lips.

Driving her through the explosive orgasm, he thrust inside her, deep, lodged in to the hilt then filled her with hard, heated blasts of his own release. Each pulse of semen sent a shudder through his powerful body and deepened his kiss, deepened the fracture he made in the shields protecting her from caring too deeply, too much. He was destroying her and he didn't even know it. Taking hold of her, owning a part of her she knew she'd never regain again.

SEVENTEEN

She was going to drive him to an early grave, Duke decided as he found her outside the house later that evening crouched by the natural barrier between the yard and the woods. She'd been out there half a dozen times throughout the day, pacing the back of the yard, checking the vines for openings, staring into the forest surrounding the house.

She'd acted damned strange when she'd stepped back outside more than half an hour ago. The tension he'd felt gripping her, the feeling that her mind was moving too hard and too fast, had him following her when he couldn't reconcile the reason for the sudden alertness.

"What the hell are you doing out here?"

She was kneeling on one knee, her head tilted to one side, a frown on her face as she stared at a depression in the dirt.

"Be quiet," she muttered.

He watched curiously as she stood and turned in the direction of Declan on watch, then turned again until she would have been facing Harley.

At the point where she stood, both men would have had a clear bead on her.

"I don't feel it." She shook her head quickly. "It's not there."

"What?" Duke could feel the hair standing on the back of his neck.

Her head jerked around to him, eyes widening as something akin to panic flashed in her face.

"Inside," she suddenly snapped, then turned and ran as though she didn't have stitches in that damned thigh.

He followed her, though. Across the yard and into the back door of the house.

"Bliss! Chaya!" She screamed their names, fear, an edge of panic echoing in her voice as she slid around the kitchen table and raced into the hall. "Chaya . . . ! Oh God . . ." She threw open Bliss's bedroom door.

"Angel, what did you feel out there?" He grabbed her, twisted her around. "What?"

"Angel." Chaya stepped from the bedroom, Bliss behind her, her weapon held close to her thigh as she stood protectively in front of her younger child. "What's wrong?"

"Angel?" Natches was armed as well as he rushed into the house through the garage entrance. "What's going on?"

"Declan and Harley—where are they?" she demanded. "They always sight me when I go outside the border. They didn't do it when I was just out and there's a boot print with unfamiliar tread in a perfect sighting position for both men. Someone was drawing their attention, and now I can't feel them out there."

"Bliss, safe room." Chaya hit the digital pad and pushed her daughter into the secured room.

They didn't question her reaction or the sense of danger suddenly pushing at her mind.

"Go with her." Angel grabbed her mother's shoulders, suddenly terrified for her. "We'll check it out. You stay with her."

"Bliss, close that door," Chaya snapped, though her gaze stayed locked with Angel's.

A second later the steel door hissed closed.

"Do you think I'd trade my safety for yours?" Chaya demanded caustically. "Or knowingly allow you to face danger alone? Not this time, girl. Not ever again if I can help it."

Damn her. Now wasn't the time for this argument.

"I won't forgive you if you die before I have a chance to tell you exactly how mad I am at you," Angel snarled in her mother's face as something settled into place inside her.

What it was she'd have to define later, not now. But she knew the time was coming to settle the years between them, and she wasn't lying. She wouldn't forgive Chaya if anything happened to her before they did that.

Chaya narrowed her eyes on her. "You think you're the only one that's mad? Don't think I don't have a few things to say to you as well, so you damned well better make certain you're in shape to hear them."

"Help will be here in minutes," Natches informed them, the ice in his voice, in his eyes, pure death. "Duke, you and Angel go after Harley, we'll go for Declan. Use your suite entrance. Chaya and I will go through the office."

"If someone took out Harley and Declan, they'll know you'll go for your son, Natches," Duke pointed out. "They'll be waiting for you."

Natches froze, his gaze swinging to Angel, and in his eyes Angel saw a confidence, a flash of certainty in whatever he saw in her that she hadn't expected. "No doubt both of them will be a trap," Natches assured him. "Go in with your eyes open. When Dawg and Rowdy arrive with the others, they'll split up and come in hard, so be watching for them."

If Declan and Harley had been taken out, then the men coming for Bliss were better than Angel had believed possible.

"You be careful, girl." Chaya pointed her finger at Angel imperatively, her brown eyes fierce. "Don't you dare let anything happen to you either."

"Girl?" she scoffed. She was getting rather tired of the "girl" title. "Same to ya, Mrs. Mackay," she muttered, turning back to Duke. "Let's go."

The weapons they needed were waiting in the bedroom. It took only seconds to clip the holster to her good thigh and shove a clip in the military-grade rifle she'd just cleaned and checked before she followed Duke out the French doors at the side of the suite that morning. Using the natural cover Natches had planted in the yard, she and Duke hurried to the hidden break Natches had shown her the day before that led to Harley's position above the house.

The path to the sniper's position held natural evergreens, fallen trees, and dips and creases in the upward slant of the property that provided the perfect cover to move to the heavily branched pine Harley was supposed to be positioned in. As they headed in, the sound of sirens could be heard coming closer, racing to the house.

Using hand signals Duke directed her to a route that would take them above and behind Harley's tree. Moving quick and silent, the soft-soled boots she wore made no sound, her lighter weight making it easier for her to move silently as they hurried to the young man's location.

She'd been through here several times, familiarizing herself with the mountain, and she'd returned often—unless she felt those sights tracking her. She hadn't seen the sheltered paths then, hadn't connected the very intricate puzzle Natches had created within the forested rise of the mountain behind the house.

They didn't speak, but used hand signals when communication was needed. Sound carried far better than the unwary realized and caused a chain reaction that anyone experienced in reading those signs could use.

Signs such as the birds usually twittering in the trees were quiet as they neared Harley's position. It was as though the wildlife had paused, waiting to see what the humans were going to do.

Once they had the tree in sight, she knew why.

Harley was crumpled at the base of the pine, still and silent. Blood marred the side of his face and his arm, but it was impossible to see if he was alive or dead as they crouched behind the dubious protection of several fallen logs.

The sound of sirens abruptly stopped. Help was at the house. Bliss would be safe. Declan's perch was closer to the house, ensuring that help would reach Chaya and Natches first.

Duke indicated he'd head in and check Harley while she took a watch position.

Moving in to cover him, the assault rifle she carried held ready, she let her gaze move upward, let her instincts have free rein. A hunter could always tell when they were being hunted, and she could feel that sensation. But whoever hunted them hadn't yet managed to get a bead on either of them. Finger next to the trigger, she nodded back at Duke slowly and watched him ease in to check Harley's pulse. As he neared the sniper, her gaze was caught by the faintest gleam of brilliant blue almost unnoticeable behind the veil of his lashes and the sense of slowly readied tension in a body she'd been certain was completely relaxed, maybe dead.

Her fist jerked up, a move Duke caught from the corner of his eyes. He became still, his gaze roving though his head didn't move.

In a single gesture, she indicated the younger man was conscious and prepared to explode into action. Harley was about Angel's age, twenty-three or twenty-four at the most. Incredibly skilled but not likely to possess the finer points of patience and control that an additional five to eight years of training would give him. That or a lifetime of survival, such as Angel had endured.

She didn't know what Duke said to the younger man, his lips did little more than tighten, but Harley's blue eyes opened, blinked, then a frown grimaced his face. A second later, Duke snagged the rifle Harley eased from beneath him and slung it over his shoulder before gripping the younger man under the shoulders and pulling him to his feet. Taking most of the boy's weight himself, Duke moved as quickly as possible, made his way to Angel, then with a nod in her direction, moved past her.

She had no more than eased into the sheltered dip of the path when a shot exploded through the forest. Immediately Duke went into a defensive position as Angel froze. Fear exploded inside her as she gestured in the direction Natches and Chaya had taken with the flat of her hand.

The sound ricocheted through Angel's soul.

"No . . . Momma . . ." Soft, torn, and filled with fear, even as she directed Duke to continue along the path.

"Forget me," Harley snapped. "Get to Natches and Chaya. . . ."

"Shut the fuck up!" Angel snapped as Duke began moving faster.

Staying close, her rifle up and ready, she moved backward, following the soft sound of footsteps while keeping her eyes moving, watching the terrain behind them. She could feel the threat. That sensation of a shooter searching for a mark. He was out there, higher, but not buried in one of the trees. Probably above them where the grade of the mountain became steeper.

That was where she would be, she knew. A tree would take time to extricate from safely. But a nest on the side of the hill, likely close to one of the faint trails, would be an excellent vantage point.

She kept her gaze there, searching, waiting for a sign.

"Chaya . . ." Harley gasped. "Is she with Natches?"

"If he doesn't shut the fuck up, I'll shoot him," Angel muttered. "Sound carries, asshole."

Duke was doing everything he could to shoulder the younger man's weight, keep him moving, and keep him quiet. He was making damned good time, too, but Angel would almost bet someone had been or still was watching for them at some point.

As they began to clear the heavy pines, she moved quickly ahead. Staying low, she positioned herself at the best vantage point, turned, and kept a careful eye behind and around Duke. They weren't much farther from the main entrance into the backyard. Once past the natural shield around the yard, they'd be a hell of a lot safer.

Then they could drop the big-mouth sniper and head to Chaya.

Oh God, she had to be okay. She had to be. . . .

Bliss needed her mother.

Chaya had to be okay.

"Moving behind." Rowdy's voice reached her as movement behind her to her right had her grimacing in irritation.

They didn't need more traffic in the area right now. Lifting a hand, she gave them a signal to stay back.

"Clear," Rowdy spoke, moving quickly past her even as she gave the signal to stay back.

Shock raced through her.

He had ignored her?

And he wasn't alone.

Two of Dawg's brothers-in-law rushed past her, heading for Duke.

The second Rowdy called the word and the men began rushing to Duke's position, she felt it. The sudden attention focused on them, watching them.

She slid her finger closer to the trigger of the assault rifle, remained in place, knowing Duke had better by God remember to watch her rather than listen to Rowdy's opinion of "clear."

Was he doing that, though?

She didn't dare give her position away to whoever she could feel out there, searching for a target. She would have the only chance of . . .

There . . .

It wasn't a flash, a gleam, or anything so easy. It was like the foliage itself, positioned with the only straight view to this particular entrance, took a deep breath.

She didn't think, she fired.

Rolling quickly to her knees behind a nearby log, she continued firing, laying cover for the men to get to safety. Ignoring the sudden sharp pain in her leg, she kept firing. The camouflaged figure moved as she kept her shots precise.

Pop. Pop. Pop.

She didn't spray the area with gunfire, she forced him to move. Distance shooting wasn't her strong suit. She made a better spotter than a shooter, but she knew how to compensate.

Her target jerked, went down, then a breath later, rolled.

"Go. Go." On her feet, she quickly followed, bringing up the rear as she ran backward, until she cleared the heavy growth of thick branches and foliage that would provide a barrier to return fire.

"Move. Move," someone snapped behind her.

Once in the clear herself, she turned quickly and moved for the house.

They'd be inside whether wounded or not. From her periphery she caught sight of Chaya and Natches with Declan. The younger man was pretty much carrying himself, though with a pronounced limp as Natches covered them with that rifle he was known for.

"Ethan's inside," she heard someone snap. "Get her inside. She's bleeding."

Her? She stopped, her gaze searching for Chaya, the only other "her."

A flash of movement at her side had her rounding, finger on the trigger of the Glock that cleared her holster and stopped only inches from the surprised face of Army Intelligence officer Major Graham Brock.

His dark gray eyes went to the barrel of the gun even as his arms were held carefully out from his sides.

"My bad," he said calmly as she stared back at him. "You're bleeding, Angel. It's dripping from your fingers; your shirt's wet with it. You're wounded."

She was aware, distantly, of the fact that she stood in the kitchen now. Shades were closed, the room was thick with male tension, and too many eyes were on her.

Her blood dripped from her wrist, three beads of scarlet dropping in slow motion to the tile floor at her feet.

She dropped her arm as she swung to where Duke stood next to Natches, Chaya, and Bliss.

"Mad skills," Bliss breathed out, her green eyes shining with excitement as her mother watched her, her face pale, grief and something else shining in her eyes.

It wasn't her sister, her praise or pride, or anything else that held Angel's attention. It was the pure raw fury that exploded in her mind as she stared at Duke.

He'd broken rank on her. Rather than waiting for her "all clear," he'd taken someone else's. Someone that hadn't been out there with him, that hadn't kept his back covered coming in. Rather than waiting for her signal to proceed, he'd taken Rowdy's instead.

"I'm kicking your fucking ass," she yelled as she flew at him, nearly shaking, her finger poised in his surprised face as Chaya, Natches, and Bliss stepped back hurriedly. "Go fight with Rowdy and his merry band of fucking assholes next time. You'll die with them, too, but at least it won't be on my watch."

Her gaze swept around, her look encompassing the room of government agents and former soldiers.

Current morons was what they were.

"You're all dead men." She sneered. "That sniper could have taken you out before you ever made it to Declan and Harley. And he could have taken this dumbass with you." She flicked her fingers at Duke. "Now get the hell out of my way. You caused me to bust my damned stitches when all you had to do was give me a damned minute." She had no idea what she'd done to her shoulder. She felt like stomping in fury. "I hate men! I hate all of you! Son of a bitch, I need an intelligent woman to fight with, not a bunch of damned testosterone."

She pushed through the wall of surprised, offended males and rushed for the door to the suite.

"Send Ethan to me when he's done. If his ass is still alive, that is," she ordered as she pushed into the suite and slammed the door behind her. "Assholes."

Silence filled the kitchen as all eyes turned from Angel's retreating back and the men filling the room gazed at each other in shock.

"You know," Natches drawled into the silence, "I'm pretty sure I want to be Angel when I grow up."

Duke could only shake his head. "You'd have to be alive first."

"Hey, Chaya and I didn't fuck up," he all but crowed. "We dumped the body in the garage, Seth and Saul are collecting the one Angel took out, and no one was shooting at us. So I get to grow up"—he chuckled—"when I get around to it."

Everyone looked at him with various expressions of doubt. Natches grow up? That wasn't going to happen anytime soon and all of them were aware of it.

"Son of a bitch, she made my drill sergeant look like the tooth fairy," Graham grunted, his expression hardening. "But she's right. Every one of us could have died out there if she hadn't known what she was doing. We ignored her. I won't make that mistake again."

"Yeah." Bliss looked a little too smug. "For an older sister, she's cool as hell, huh?"

The teenager turned and strolled from the room, puffed up with pride as she left the adults in shock.

Angel could feel the outrage and anger burning

through her, but beneath it, crawling insidiously through her mind, was pure terror.

Duke could have died.

Because he hadn't waited for her.

He hadn't trusted her.

Easing the drab green T-shirt over her head, she barely held back a moan at the pain that shot through her arm. Blood and pus were seeping beneath the bandage on her thigh, the wound there busted open, the stitches ripped past flesh. She'd felt the break the second she'd begun firing.

Her arm had slammed into something as she rolled to the dubious cover of those logs, then knocked into the sharp point of one log sticking out from beneath. And what the fuck was wrong with her leg?

It was screaming.

She wanted to scream.

Quickly removing her pants she stared at the heavy dark stain on the pad and the blood oozing from beneath the adhesive. And that blood looked odd, just as the stain on the pad did.

Grabbing the long shirt she'd taken from Duke, she pulled it on over the thin black tank top and boy shorts she wore, buttoned a few buttons, and sat on the cushioned hope chest at the bottom of the bed.

How had her leg become infected again? And so quickly. Ethan was certain the problem had cleared up, but as she stared at the gauze beneath the adhesive she knew it was infection. She could see the faint redness now where it hadn't been the night before. The advanced tenderness, the throb just beneath the flesh.

And it was possibly worse than it had been the first time.

That was why she felt so crappy, she thought dismally. She'd awakened with a faint headache, that off-kilter feeling. She should have known she was running a fever. She knew the signs, but everything was so crazy emotionally that she hadn't stopped to think.

"There you are!" Ethan rushed into the bedroom, the case he carried gripped in his hand as Duke moved behind him carrying another smaller case.

"Declan and Harley?" She frowned as he tossed the case on the bed, the sound of the metal locks being released behind her.

"They can wait," he announced. "I was already on my way here when the sirens raced by. I had Doc Marlin send off a swab of the discharge from that leg for testing the other day. He just called about an hour or so ago. I would've been here sooner, but I had to stop by the hospital."

She lifted her hand to her head, the words drowning into each other as she felt herself sway.

"Angel, baby . . ." Duke was kneeling beside her, his hands on the buttons of the shirt. "Let's get this off, then we're going to get you on the bed so Ethan can do what he does best."

"Fix me?" She frowned.

That was Ethan's favorite saying. That was what he did best, fix Angel and keep her on her feet.

"Nothing needs fixed, sweetheart." He eased the shirt from her shoulders, bracing her weight as he did.

She couldn't hold herself up.

She felt odd . . . disconnected.

"Duke." She tried to reach for him, but missed him somehow. "Duke, what's wrong with me?"

"Adrenaline rush added to the infection, Angel. You were already weak and running low, now you're crashing. You remember the crash, right?" Ethan sounded so reasonable.

"Come on, let's get you in the bed."

Someone else was speaking; she could hear them. Something about a blanket under her . . . A woman's voice . . . A memory, a need she'd never been able to conquer.

"Momma?" She grimaced. Fear tore through her. She couldn't seem to hold on to the memory that she didn't have a momma. "Duke. What the fuck's wrong with me?"

She stared up at him, feeling the prick of something in her arm and rolling her head to Ethan.

"It's okay, little sister," he promised. "We got this, right?"

They had what?

What did they have?

"Allergy to penicillin when she was a baby . . . Be careful of the antibiotic. . . ." She heard the voice again, soft, soothing. That voice she always searched for when she had been sick as a child.

She stared at Duke where he sat next to her, one hand brushing her hair back.

She could still hear that woman's voice advising Ethan on antibiotics and it was scaring the shit out of her.

She licked her suddenly dry lips, watching Duke desperately.

"Am I hallucinating?" she whispered, feeling whatever drug Ethan had pushed into her system taking hold of her. "I keep hearing her."

"Hearing who, baby?" His gaze flicked to Ethan then back to her. "Who do you hear?"

"I keep hearing Momma." Were those tears she felt in her eyes, one rolling down her cheek? "I hear her. . . ."

She had to close her eyes, just for a minute. They were so heavy. But when she opened them again, she knew she was dreaming.

"I'm here, BeeBee," her mother whispered as she wiped the moisture from Angel's cheek. "I'm right here."

Why was she there?

Why . . . ?

Ethan and his damned drugs.

Her eyes drifted closed again, that darkness she couldn't stop or control easing over her.

It was a dream. Just a dream . . .

Standing at the side of the room, Chaya watched as Ethan hung the IV he'd attached to Angel's arm on the metal pole Duke had hastily screwed together and attached to the headboard of the bed.

He'd cut the stitches free on her leg, cleaned the wound, packed it with an antibiotic he'd picked up from the hospital, covered it with that noxious-smelling salve Memmie Mary made, then secured gauze over it rather than a bandage. The arm he did the same to, just to be safe, he'd stated, though the puncture from a sharp branch couldn't possibly cause the same reaction as the chemical that had been on that knife. That chemical was the cause of the infection, but the penicillin he'd used because the severity of the wound had been deemed minimal didn't work well with Angel's system.

It wasn't just the wounds that had Chaya fighting her tears, though. It was his comment that the leg was going to have a hell of a scar to add to her collection. When Ethan finished she moved closer to her daughter, gazed down at her smaller, more delicate body, and felt her breath hitch.

The tank top had ridden up just enough to reveal the scar on her side from a bullet she'd taken the year before. Duke had shown her the scar higher up where Angel had taken another knife. A knife had pierced her lung a few years prior, and that scar, too, showed clearly on her other side.

There were small scars, a few larger, on both legs. She'd taken a bullet in her right arm at some point, and there was a scar from a knife just beneath her jaw that looked at least a decade old.

"She has more war wounds than you do," she whispered, lifting her head to gaze at Natches where he remained next to the patio doors with Dawg and Rowdy.

"Let me pull the sheet over her and he can come over with you," Duke murmured, dragging the fabric over Angel's tanned legs to above her waist. "She doesn't like anyone seeing those scars."

"Badges of courage," Chaya whispered as Natches came behind her, his hands settling on her shoulders before he pulled her against his chest.

"The chemical on that knife is a habit that gang uses. We weren't aware of it until Doc Marlin called." Ethan breathed out roughly. "When the tests came back he asked where it happened. When I told him he pulled the information for me while I was on my way to him. The infection comes on slow and unless it's treated correctly will keep coming back, stronger than before. He's pretty sure this will clear it up, though."

"She should be in a hospital," Chaya whispered.

"We take her to a hospital and she'll slice and dice every one of us when she comes out," Ethan grunted. "We tried that once in Texas. The rescue of a little girl being held by cartel members there. She has a pretty little scar on her head where a bullet winged her, scared Duke to hell and back. He forced Tracker to call the paramedics. When she woke, she disappeared on all of us for months and swore she'd kill us the next time we put her in one of those germ labs, as she called them."

"Can I stay with her for a while?" Chaya turned her gaze to Duke. "I know the others wanted you with them when they went over the information they've pulled in. Bliss and I could stay with her."

She needed to stay with her. She needed, at least this one time, to comfort the baby that had been taken from her. To cry over her. To tell her how very much she loved her without the suspicion and pain that filled Angel's gaze at any other time.

She saw the indecision in Duke's face, his need to be with her as well.

"You can leave the door between the suite and the kitchen open. When she wakes"—she swallowed tightly—"she'll be defensive again and won't want me with her. I need this, Duke. And so does Bliss."

His lips tightened, but he finally gave a brief nod of his head.

"She gets pissed, you take the blame," he grunted. "She gets damned prickly over things that happen when Ethan has to knock her out."

Wrapping her arms around herself, Chaya looked down at her daughter then back to Duke.

"Why knock her out? He could have just given her something for the pain." As many scars as that child had she couldn't be pain-phobic.

"Pain meds alone make her dopey, then she gets phobic," Ethan stated, checking Angel's blood pressure on the other arm. "She completely freaked out on me once, thought she was a kid again, trapped in that hotel. We had to hold her down and all of us swore we never would again."

The memory was obviously one that neither Duke nor Ethan were comfortable with.

"I'll be right outside the door," Duke told her. "You need me or Ethan, send Bliss."

Chaya nodded. When Natches released her to follow Duke and Ethan from the room, she sat on the side of the bed, touched her daughter's still hand, and wiped away another tear.

God help her. How could she possibly fix this?

EIGHTEEN

Chaya glanced at the doorway as Duke entered the bedroom on the tail end of the ridiculous story she'd been telling Angel. One she used to make up for her daughter all those years ago.

Binny's Adventures in BeeBee's World.

"Binny was her teddy bear," she told Duke, seeing his thoughtful expression. "God, she loved that damned bear. Dragged it everywhere. He would get so filthy." She laughed softly. "I finally became desperate to keep from washing him so often. I sewed straps to his back and shoulders so she could carry him like a backpack. The damned thing was almost bigger than her." She grinned. "Then she had to have a pocket in his tummy so she could store her treasures, as she called them."

A heavy frown came over his face. Stepping to the dresser on the other side of the room and the canvas pack left there, he opened it and, a second later, drew out the worn, droopy-eared teddy bear her baby had so loved.

Chaya covered her lips with her fingers to hold back her sobs, aware of Bliss watching in interest from where she lay on the bed next to Angel.

Red straps, because red had been her favorite color, and a red gingham bandana tied around his neck were faded from time and obvious love.

Accepting the plump little bear with shaking hands, Chaya caressed its face, the bright black plastic eyes, a worn area next to his ear.

Lifting his finger to his lips to keep his secret, he gave Angel a look filled with such love Chaya knew that she'd never have to worry about him breaking her baby's heart.

"I just wanted to check on her," he said softly. "We're still working in the kitchen."

"She's resting easy," Chaya promised him. "The fever's gone, her blood pressure's normal, and her color looks normal. She's going to be fine, Duke."

He nodded. "Of course she will. She knows I won't be happy with her otherwise." Leaning to her he brushed his lips over her forehead, then placed his lips at her ear and whispered something to her.

Surprisingly, Angel's fingers moved, just a little, as though searching. When Duke's fingers covered them, she stilled and seemed to settle back into sleep.

Straightening, he lifted her fingers, brushed his lips against her palm, then placed her hand on the bed once again with no sign of self-consciousness or embarrassment.

"We've been through this before, ain't we, baby?" he said softly, his expression gentler when he looked at Angel. "But we're going to try to make sure it doesn't happen again, huh?" It sounded as though the words were well worn, as though he'd said them many times before.

Holding the bear to her heart, Chaya had to force back the tears, the sobs. If she didn't stop crying Bliss was going to start crying with her, and that Chaya couldn't bear.

"Come get me if she wakes?" he asked, not for the first time. Each time he checked on her he made the same request.

"You know I will," Chaya promised him. "We're just talking, aren't we, little baby?" She let her fingers curl over Angel's, her thumb brushing over the faint scars on her knuckles. "We had a little talk about those bar fights she gets into earlier. We don't want Bliss to think it's okay to do the same, right?"

The look Duke gave her was highly suspicious. Bliss was going to be a handful and they knew it.

"Hey, little baby." Chaya leaned closer. "I have a friend that wanted a moment of your time." Placing the bear against Angel's hip she lifted her daughter's hand to the bear's legs and let it rest there. "Binny's here, BeeBee. Aren't you going to say hello?"

Duke waited a moment, then turned and left the bedroom. As the door to the suite was opened Chaya watched as Angel's fingers curled against the bear's fur, rubbed, then settled once again.

"If you had been able to tell me about her, I would know about Binny, Momma," Bliss said then. "Then I could have told you how Angel showed me her teddy bear that her momma gave her, and how much she loved it."

"Oh, Bliss," she whispered, so many regrets lying inside her heart. "Every time I tried, all I could do was cry for what I had lost, and the sister taken from you. If I had known . . ."

"Tell me about her now, Mom." Bliss rested her head on the pillow next to Angel's.

Her girls. Her babies.

"Tell you about her." She smiled, the memories rushing in. "Oh, Bliss, what a little imp she was. . . ."

Laughter.

It was light, floating just out of touch and filled with happiness.

"What did she do, Mom?" The teenager's giggles made Angel want to laugh, too, but she wasn't certain what was so funny.

"She propped her hands on her hips and got that look you get when you and your dad go head to head, and she informed me point-blank that three was not too young for school. She was plenty old enough and I just wanted to be mean and keep her home forever just because I loved her so much."

The laughter whispered across her, the images that began to float through her mind warming her. Memories she hadn't let herself think of in so long.

She had wanted to go to school so bad. She could already read. And she knew her letters and her numbers. That meant three was old enough. . . .

"Then she smiled and said that was just fine and threw her arms around my neck, kissed my cheek, and ran back to her toys. She never failed to surprise me with the things she would say or do." Her mother sounded so soft, so loving.

"I think she still surprises you," Bliss said softly. "She told me once when I asked her about her mother that she lost her momma. And she looked away. Talking about it hurt her. Like talking about her hurt you."

How had Bliss known that? Angel wondered. She thought she'd been so very careful.

"How did you know she was your sister?" Chaya asked as Angel felt a feathery caress over the top of her head.

"The knife," Bliss said softly. "She was cutting a pizza box with the knife and it turned just right. It was like the word on the blade just jumped out at me. It was the same knife in the pictures. I knew who she was right then."

Angel drifted closer to the surface, desperate to be a part of the laughter and warmth she could feel around her now.

She liked this, though. They weren't watching what they said; they were talking and including her. She liked that very much.

"Every time I saw her, I could feel her hiding from me, lying to me," Chaya said then, her voice low, but so gentle. "When she tried to tell me who she was, I couldn't speak. I thought it wasn't possible. She couldn't be Beth, but I wanted her to be. I wanted it so bad I couldn't speak for the need. And I was just too damned blind to see the truth." That soft caress to her brow was light, but it sank inside her.

"She told me once that when she was really little, she heard her dad arguing on the phone with her mom. That her dad was really mad and wanted her mom to come pick her up, but she wouldn't. She thinks you didn't want her, Mom." She was going to have to be careful what she told Bliss in the future. The girl told her mother everything, it seemed.

"That's not what happened, Bliss. She was supposed to be in Canada with my sister. I had no idea she was in Iraq or even with Craig until one of my agents rushed to the hospital with the news." Why did Chaya sound so sincere? So sincere that Angel couldn't make herself disbelieve her. "My agent had to fight the guards to get to me that day in the hospital. When she told me Craig had my baby in that old hotel, I went crazy!" Her mother's voice hitched. "I died with her that day. For years, Bliss, I was a ghost, running from myself, from your father, from the knowledge I'd failed her. . . ."

"Don't cry, Momma. We have her now," Bliss whispered. "She's here with us and we'll make her understand. She'll know you tried. And she still loves you so much. And you just know Dad is going to adopt her. Before you know it, she'll be fighting with him just like I do."

"And how do you know that, sprite?" Love whispered through Chaya's voice, warmed Angel, pulled her closer to wakefulness.

"She told me so," Bliss revealed. "She said there were three people in the world that she loved above all things. A man on her team, a sister that didn't know her, and her mother. Now who do you think she was talking about?"

Jeez Marie. What the hell? Couldn't that girl keep a damned secret at all? Someone gag her already. . . .

"Shhh." She tried to shush her sister before she completely spilled every word Angel had ever told her. "Shhh."

For a moment, silence filled the room. She didn't want that. She wanted them to talk, to remember again.

"Uh-oh." Bliss giggled. "I'm in trouble now."

Not in trouble, Angel thought. Never in trouble. But she might have to explain the sister rules to her baby sister.

"Angel, are you awake, little baby?" her momma whispered softly, her fingers against her forehead. "Wake up for Momma now."

She didn't want to wake up, not yet. She wanted to hold this to her for just a little while longer. Just for a bit, so she could pull the warmth around her, inside her.

She realized, though, the wounds that had once been so torn

inside her soul weren't as ragged anymore. She wasn't as cold as she'd once been. Duke was there, she thought, content with that knowledge. And he'd slowly been drawing the edges of those wounds closer together.

"She was going to leave and never come back the day those guys tried to take me," Bliss said, her voice soft, so soft Angel had to strain to hear her. "I could hear it when she came to tell me good-bye. That was why I was so angry with you that night."

Angel knew she'd tried so hard to keep Bliss from knowing that. She hadn't wanted her sister to miss her, just remember her; that was all.

"We'll find a way to get her to stay." Her mother sounded so fierce, so determined. "I don't know why Craig brought her to Iraq, or why he murdered my sister, but I'll find a way to make her believe me. I never would have left her with that bastard. . . . I never would have left Jenny with him either." Her voice hitched again. "Oh, Bliss, I would have saved that baby if I could have. Both of them. I never would have let them be separated if I had known. . . ."

But hadn't she known?

Angel had heard Craig on the phone. He told Angel and Jenny when he hung up that Chaya was a bitch. She thought no one wanted her, not even her momma.

Had he lied to her? Had he just wanted to hurt her? She had screamed at him to take her and Jenny to her momma, over and over again.

"Sweet baby," Chaya whispered, brushing a kiss over her brow. "No matter what happens when you wake, take this with you. I always loved you. And I would have loved Jenny more than you know. You have always been my sweet little heart. . . ."

She drifted closer, forced her eyes open, and stared up at her momma's face. Damp with tears, her brown eyes soft and filled with love.

"Momma . . ." She sighed, fighting to hold her eyes open, to hold this vision as long as possible.

"Hey, imp." Her mother smiled gently, softly. "There you are. It's about time you woke up."

"So mad at you," she told her mother, but the sound wasn't angry, just sad.

"So mad at you, too," her momma assured her with that loving fierceness she'd used when Angel was little. "Get better and we'll yell at each other."

Get better.

She had to get better. She had to get off her ass and make sure Bliss was safe.

"Bliss." It was so hard to stay awake. Just for another minute. She had to stay awake another minute. Feel this feeling for just a little while longer.

"Bliss is fine, Angel," Chaya promised, the gentleness in her voice, the sound only a mother has, filling it.

Angel gripped her mother's fingers, fought to hold her eyes open just a little longer.

"Momma . . ." She stared up at Chaya; she had to tell her.

"I'm here, baby," Chaya promised. "Just sleep. Everything's fine."

"I love you," she whispered. "Always loved you."

"I always loved you, Angel. Always . . ."

The words drifted away as she slipped into sleep once again. There were dreams, as there always were. That parade of figures from her childhood and bits and pieces of things she knew she needed to remember but never did.

She'd remember eventually, though; she could feel it. And when she did, the past would be over. . . .

Angel was still weak, shaky the next morning when Duke helped her to the kitchen, and more than a little put out. Hell, she was pissed off. She wouldn't speak to Ethan for keeping her under for so long, and when he came at her with the syringe loaded with antibiotics, she threatened to skin him if it knocked her out again.

"Sure you feel up to this?" Duke asked her as Bliss placed a cup of coffee, heavy with sugar and cream, in front of her.

She thanked Bliss softly, then shot Duke a disgusted look.

"Stop babying me, Duke," she muttered. "You're embarrassing me already. I need to see the pictures you have."

Dawg and Rowdy were both smirking, but for once Natches wasn't.

"Sorry, badass," Duke drawled, his lips quirking in a grin. "I'll just slink away in shame now."

"Yeah, you do that," she told him, shooting him a disgruntled look as she lifted the coffee and sipped at it gratefully, aware of Bliss standing behind her in case she needed anything else.

"Seth and Saul hit the area where the sniper was located above you and found the body. You got your man," Natches said, and winked at her. "I knew you would."

"Lucky is more like it," she griped. "I'm not much of a shooter. Duke could tell you that. But I'm a damned good watcher."

"Well, you were a damned good shooter when it counted," he assured her. "The DNA came in and we have pictures of that one as well as information on the two dead men that hit the safe house." He looked behind Angel. "Bliss, honey, you shouldn't be here."

Angel stared at Natches in surprise and disappointment. Bliss shouldn't be there? It was her life that was being threatened; she needed to know what was going on. Didn't she?

"Natches," Chaya said softly behind him. "You can't protect her from this at this point. We discussed it, remember?"

Natches's lips tightened and he rubbed at the back of his neck in irritation, but didn't say anything more on the subject.

"You're sure you remember the men from the cabin?" he asked, pulling the photos he'd turned over in front of him. It had been months ago when Angel had tracked the young man Bliss was interested in to a secluded fishing hole several miles from the marina. She'd seen the cabin and the men outside it, but hadn't paid much attention to them. The same cabin the August twins had learned the dead men had been staying at.

"I have a very good memory," Angel answered him, a little stiffly.

"Duke said you saw a blue van parked behind the cabin. What exactly were you doing there?"

She glanced at Chaya as she stood behind him before returning her gaze to Natches.

"I thought Chaya was the interrogator," she pointed out mildly, a bit irritated with the questions.

Amusement gleamed in his eyes then, a teasing gleam she had a feeling he was helpless against. "I taught her everything she knows."

For a second, his wife stared at the back of his head in disbelief.

"Oh, good grief," Chaya muttered then with a roll of her eyes. "Have you lost your mind?"

"Probably, but that doesn't change the question." He cleared his throat, obviously holding back a grin.

Angel shrugged. "Getting the lay of the land. I was hiking and sightseeing."

Silence met her answer.

"Angel." Chaya said her name softly, the expression on her face knowing and demanding at the same time.

Angel looked over at where Bliss was moving into the living room at the urging of Annie and Laken.

"I feel sorry for Bliss." She sighed. "She'll never be able to hide anything from the two of you."

It was so sad; sometimes a girl needed to have her secrets until she could figure things out on her own. Having a mother that could just look at you and know you were lying would simply suck.

"I was following Bran because I'd noticed Bliss was interested in him. He hadn't said or done anything." She shot Natches a silencing look. "I don't even think he was aware she was flirting with him. She's very subtle."

"But something about him bothered you?" Chaya asked.

"Maybe. I don't know." She frowned. "He was with two other young men about his age and passed by the cabin. They continued on to a part of the lake I hadn't known went back that far and settled down to fish, so I turned around and headed back to the marina. That's when I saw the blue van parked behind it. Then after Bliss was nearly abducted, I recognized it as possibly the same van in the video footage from the marina's security cameras. When I returned the day Bliss was nearly abducted, the van was gone, though, and the cabin was empty."

The explanation didn't sit well with Natches.

"So rather than alerting anyone else, you just went and

checked it all out yourself?" he demanded, glaring at her, his expression filled with disapproval.

Her brow lifted. "Considering the fact that several hours before that you threatened to kill me?" Her lips pursed in consideration. "Yep, that was exactly what I did: went and checked it out all on my little lonesome."

He stared back at her, those emerald eyes darkening to almost a jungle green as his expression tightened with arrogant reproach.

"You knew better than that," he finally snorted. "If I was going to shoot your ass, I wouldn't warn you first."

She wondered how the hell she was supposed to have known that.

"Now see, that's just rude," she stated, as though offended over his inconsideration. "I wouldn't mind a bit warning you first. It makes the playing field even, so to speak."

She really hoped he remembered her warning where messing with food she was preparing was concerned.

He rubbed at his neck again before turning and throwing Chaya a look that had her smiling serenely.

"Let me see the pictures already," Angel demanded, holding out her hand. "Before I get too tired to recognize anyone."

Turning the pictures over, he handed them to her, his gaze hardening as she took them.

Laying the photographs in front of her, she recognized the first one instantly.

"That's the one whose DNA Bliss managed to get when he grabbed her," Natches told her quietly.

"He was at the lake several times when I was there with the girls. I'd remember those ice-blue eyes and that scar on his face anywhere." She drew a slanted line down the man's cheek.

Laying that picture aside she went to the next one.

"The one I killed at the safe house," Natches said as she stared down at the handsome face.

"Oh!" she said, startled. "He was at the lake with Bliss's friend Bran!" She tapped a finger against the pretty boy who had kept ensuring his thick dark hair was lying just right.

"The next one is the one you shot," Natches said softly as she laid that one aside.

"I haven't seen him around her." But she'd seen him somewhere. It was odd for her to see a picture and not immediately place the face. Her memory was too damned good for that. "I've seen him before, though," she said, frowning. "He must have looked different somehow, different hair color or something."

Brown hair, brown eyes. He didn't look quite thirty, but he looked hard and mean. His eyes were cold and unemotional.

Where had she seen him?

She laid the picture aside.

"That's the one I took out in the woods," Natches pointed out needlessly.

An older man, black hair with a touch of gray at the temples.

"The two I can place," she told him. "But this one." She tapped the picture of the man that seemed so familiar. "He must have been trying to disguise his looks. I'll remember where I saw him. Who he is. It will just take a minute."

She rubbed at her temple, weariness dragging at her again as she fought to remember where she'd seen the younger man.

"Come on, you need to rest a little more." Rising to his feet Duke just lifted her in his arms rather than helping her to her feet. "She's still tired, Natches." His voice hardened, that "don't fuck with me" tone she always hated whenever he turned it on her. "Anything else she remembers, I'll let you know. She's going back to bed."

"You're so bossy," she accused him, but spoiled it when she yawned.

"I knew it was too early to let you up," he growled, laying her back on the bed.

"Don't fuss, Duke." She sighed. "God, I hate being so weak."

Fists clenching as she rolled to her side, she fought the feeling of exhaustion. "I want to kill that bastard that shoved that knife in my leg all over again."

Once wasn't enough. He deserved to die over and over again for whatever he'd dipped that blade in before using it on her.

"Don't fuss, she says," he grunted, pulling the wingback chair closer and sitting down heavily. "You scared the life out of me, Angel, do you know that? And you've spent two days practically unconscious, waking up to go to the bathroom only. I have gray hair."

She glanced at his thick black hair and couldn't help but grin. "It will look very good on you, I promise. Very distinguished."

He frowned back at her and she couldn't help but giggle.

"You're a freak." He shook his head at her. "You're always laughing at me."

No, she always loved him.

She had. She'd fought it, she'd denied it, she'd tried to tell herself it wasn't love, but she'd always known better. And realizing that wasn't easy for her.

"I'm really tired, Duke," she whispered.

How many more emotions was she going to dredge up to deal with? What was next, anyway? Realizing she loved spinach when she really hated the stuff?

"Like hell. You stubborn little minx." Before she realized his intent he moved her over in the bed and slid in beside her, pulling her into his arms. "Getting scared, are you, baby?"

Fists pressed against his chest, the thin material of her T-shirt and cotton pants doing very little to protect her from the warmth of his body, she tried to tell herself he didn't know near as much as he thought he did.

"I don't get scared, remember?" She scowled up at him. "I'm tougher than that."

She was a wuss. A bona fide, card-carrying, bring-out-the-bitch wuss. And she didn't care a bit to admit it.

To herself.

"Tougher than that, are you?" he asked, rolling her to her back and coming over her.

And he was so incredibly gentle, taking care to make certain he didn't hurt her.

He always had been, she remembered. Whether she was wounded or not, Duke had always been instinctively gentle with her. And he'd always found a reason to touch her.

Why hadn't she realized this before?

She couldn't blame it on the wound; she'd had a hell of a lot worse. This one had been easy compared to many of the others.

"I'm definitely tougher than that," she assured him, though she didn't sound in the least bit tough and she knew it.

She wasn't acting tough either as her hands slid beneath the shirt he wore to touch the warmth of his skin, to feel the rasp of chest hair against her palms and feel his heart beat beneath her fingers.

Could she go back to fighting and take the chance on never feeling this again, never touching him, never being held by him?

Tracker was prone to say that "dead" meant no regrets, but she didn't think even death would keep her from regretting the loss.

"I love you, Angel."

She froze.

She couldn't have heard that. It wasn't possible. Just because she loved didn't mean she was lucky enough to be loved; she'd always known that.

"Angel?" Gripping the side of her face he tipped her head back, staring into her eyes, the dark green of his gaze a little amused, his expression . . .

"Do you think this guy is going to be easy to catch?" She sounded breathless.

Her heart was racing so fast, so hard she could barely talk. And what was that damned shakiness in her voice? She was making a fool of herself. She knew she was.

"Angel, I love you," he repeated.

She watched his lips form the words, heard them, knew she wasn't imagining it.

"Why?" She couldn't help the confusion that pulled a frown to her brow, that left her feeling a little lost, a whole lot scared.

"Because you make me laugh when no one else can. Because as tough as you are, your heart is soft. Because everything inside me screams that you're mine." He grinned down at her with such male confidence it should have had her ready to argue just for the hell of it.

She wasn't arguing. She felt as though she were melting on the inside.

"I know you love me, Angel," he told her then, brushing her hair back from her face, never once seeming to doubt his own certainty. "Just as you've known I love you."

"I do love you." The words whispered past her lips. "I do. But Duke"—her voice was shaking, all the fear she felt filling it—"what if something, or someone, takes you from me? What will I do? Don't you understand? Losing that love, losing you . . ."

Her hands gripped his wrists and she fought just to breathe. "What would I do?"

"Baby, all I can promise you is that I won't walk away." He laid his forehead against hers, still holding her gaze. "I won't stop loving you. I won't willingly leave you. That's all either of us can give the other. But if I knew I had only a day, I'd want to spend that day loving you and being loved by you."

"A man shouldn't be able to say something so damned corny and still be so fucking sexy. It's unnatural, Duke." But she could feel emotion swamping her, stealing any sting from the words.

"Sweet Angel." His lips lowered to hers. "Trust me. I got this."

She couldn't help but laugh. And she couldn't help but hold him to her, to return his kiss, to share what she couldn't hide any longer from him or from herself. And trust that fate loved this Mackay as much as she seemed to love the others, and would allow Angel to hold him, to love him, for a long, long time.

NINETEEN

The next morning, Angel knew she was stronger, refreshed. She actually felt better than she'd ever felt before she'd taken that knife to her thigh.

She definitely felt good enough to want to fix breakfast.

She was starved.

Duke was already up and moving around. She could smell coffee coming from the suite's kitchenette, the sound of his voice a low, deep murmur as he spoke, then Ethan's reply. She couldn't hear what they were saying, but the sound was familiar and comforting. It should be, she thought, amused; she'd been hearing it for years whenever she managed to take another wound.

Duke was right, she was lucky to be alive at this point.

And it didn't make sense either, because she knew she was damned good in the field. Hell, it was all she'd been doing for twenty years; she should be good at it. But for as long as she could remember, her luck had sucked in the field. From being found by a stray guard in a hut in Guatemala at six and nearly getting her throat cut before Tracker had arrived, to any number of other debacles. Life threatening, but debacles all the same.

Duke seemed to believe the problems began with that hospital falling in on her. How very wrong he was, unfortunately.

Knowing Ethan would insist on checking the wound, she didn't bother checking it herself. She quickly showered, then put on just the long shirt she'd worn the night before over her tank top and boy shorts.

She'd never been able to tolerate thongs or the lacy pretty stuff under the standard mission gear clothes. Plain old black cotton with no chance of riding between the cheeks of her ass. Maybe, though, if she stopped fighting, she could buy some pretty lacy stuff.

She could watch all that hungry lust fill Duke's eyes and fly apart in pleasure as he showed her how much he appreciated it.

A little smile tipped her lips at that thought when she stepped into the kitchenette to find Duke and Ethan at the table, a tablet between them as they scrolled through pictures.

"Updates?" She nodded to the tablet as she stepped past them to the coffeepot.

"Doogan and the boys have been busy," Duke stated. "Alex actually found some information on the guys who attacked the safe house."

Carrying her cup of coffee, she sat down in the chair next to Duke as he flipped the tablet to face her.

Her brows lifted in surprise. "Grecia Davinov?" She almost blinked in shock. "The Russian billionaire. We worked for him one time years ago when his family was being threatened. Why would he target us? Besides, kidnapping's not Grecia's thing, and there's no way he could have known who I am to Bliss."

"This"—Duke flipped to the next picture—"is one of the men Saul took out at the safe house. Grecia's brother, Rastor Davinov. Former Russian Special Forces and expert marksman. The other was a known associate of Rastor's, a small-time Russian mobster that works out of Moscow."

Duke showed her the next picture. "Our snipers were Rastor's sons, Ilya and Gregor Davinov, also Russian Special Forces. They're all rumored to speak excellent English and were actually high-level emissaries for Grecia's Russian business at one time." Ilya matched the DNA under Bliss's nails from her near abduction; Gregor was the one Natches killed outside the house. Duke flipped to the younger man Angel had been trying to remember for the past two nights. "We suspect this is Grecia's estranged son, Viktor. Which explains why you might have remembered him. His looks have changed a bit since you were with Davinov's security detail."

Maybe. She remembered the old photos she'd seen of Davinov's son, but as Duke said, his looks had changed quite a bit. No matter what, the man in the photo was definitely one of the dead men out in the garage.

"My original question," she reminded him. "Why come after Bliss if the reason they're here is to kill me? And why try to kill me to begin with? We weren't the only security personnel Grecia Davinov has used over the years."

As she spoke Ethan pulled his chair over with a quiet, "Leg, please."

"Well, I didn't say we had all the answers, baby. I said we identified them. I called Tracker earlier. He's calling some of his contacts close to Davinov's organization. We should know something soon."

He had called Tracker? Oh Lord.

"Did you spill your spineless guts about my leg?" she snapped, then her eyes widened in horror at the knowing look on his face and Ethan's snicker as he cleaned the salve from the fresh stitches to apply more. "You told him?" Outrage filled her voice. "You knew I didn't want him to know. God—" She tightened her lips against the rest of the curse. "We are going to discuss this habit you have of telling everyone my damned secrets, Duke. We really are."

Ethan's chuckle just pissed her off more.

Jerking her head around she gave him a killing look. "Slap a Band-Aid on it already, Chuckles. I have things to do. And I don't want to hear your comic relief crap either." She pointed a finger back at him imperiously.

He wisely kept anything he was about to say to himself. Damned good thing, too, she thought, directing another furious look in Duke's direction.

"Come on, Angel," he chided her gently. "Tracker and Chance would have tried to hurt me for keeping it from them."

As she stared at him, she knew instantly that he hadn't just told Tracker in the last few hours or since learning the identities of the Davinovs.

"Oh my God, you called while I was out of it, didn't you?" Pure amazed disbelief filled her. "Why, Duke? Why would you do that?"

If Tracker knew, then J.T. and Mara knew. And Mara would have called Duke herself. . . .

"Because he had a right to know." His expression got that too-arrogant, too-damned-sure-of-himself look on his face that she absolutely hated. That look that assured her she was screwed.

The whole damned family would know at this point.

It had been four days since her collapse, and knowing Duke as she did, she knew he would have called them that first night. Sweet baby Jesus, it was a wonder the entire damned family hadn't arrived yesterday. She could actually expect them at any time now.

"J.T. and Mara will show up with him and Chance." She came to her feet, suddenly uncertain, wary.

Brushing at the front of her hair nervously, she had an overwhelming urge to bite her nails. Mara and Chaya in the same area? Chaya had already stated her opinion of Mara, and it hadn't been kind.

"They will just show up, unannounced," she groaned. The thought of it scared her spitless.

Who are your "parents" to have allowed you to live this life? You didn't have parents, you had commanders . . .

Your parents should be shot . . . were some of the nicer comments.

She did not need her mother and the woman that had tried to mother her coming together.

"Angel, it's not that bad." He actually had the nerve to laugh. Complete with real, genuine amusement, he laughed right in her face.

"You are a damned menace." She forced the words past clenched teeth as she pointed a finger back at him. "You can deal with them when J.T. and Mara show up. I'll leave."

That would solve it right there. Just wouldn't hang out for that little get-together. She was smarter than that.

"You can't just leave." He shook his head, grinning up at her as though there was nothing at all to worry about.

Well, there was plenty to worry about.

"You make me crazy!" She felt like pulling her own hair out, that was how insane he was, how impossible to deal with. "I'm going to go fix breakfast. You better pray they don't show up before I'm finished."

She might have to shoot someone.

Jeez, she couldn't believe he'd done this to her. She knew he was smarter than that.

At least she'd thought he was—that was what she got for thinking, wasn't it?

Stalking from the suite she was all set to expend her anger on breakfast when she entered the kitchen and came to a hard, horrified stop.

It wasn't anything so merciful as J.T. and Mara.

Bliss stood at the kitchen table, one hand covering her mouth, silent tears rolling down her devastated face to drip onto the pictures spread out before her.

Confusion filled Angel. Bliss hadn't actually seen the men that had died, and those weren't corpse pictures. Why was she crying as though her world had just shattered?

Angel stepped around the table, but she doubted her sister saw her, or even knew she was there.

"Bliss . . . sweetie?" Gripping the girl's shoulders she turned her to face her, the fear hardening to ice inside her at the realization that something was horribly wrong. "Bliss." She firmed her voice, terrified that her sister had yet to acknowledge her.

"Angel?" Duke stepped in the doorway, Ethan behind him, their gazes concerned.

"Find Mom and Natches. Now," she demanded, barely glancing at them.

Bliss's face lifted, her green eyes still overflowing with tears.

"You called . . . her . . . Mom." Her voice hiccupped with strangled sobs, the sound of it so hoarse and filled with pain that Angel wondered how long her sister had been standing there alone.

"Yeah? I'm sure she'll forgive one lapse, right?" she asked gently. "Are you hurt, honey?" She ran her hands down Bliss's arms and let her gaze go over the girl quickly for any obvious injuries.

Bliss swallowed as though trying to push back the sobs she refused to allow free. "Can your heart break"—she breathed in raggedly—"at fifteen?"

If it could break at three, then it could break at fifteen.

"I think it can break at any age. Who broke your heart, honey?" Because she'd kill them painfully. Make them beg to die.

Bliss turned away and Angel felt her heart sink to her stomach, where it lay like a heavy weight filled with dread, when her sister pulled two pictures from those spread out over the table.

Viktor and Rastor Davinov. "That's . . ." A sob nearly broke free from the teenager. "That's Bran's brother." She pointed to Viktor Davinov. "And that's his uncle." She pointed at Rastor. Tears fell harder from her eyes and a shudder raced through her body. "Bran's the guy at the marina," she clarified, though Angel knew who Bran was. "The one I told you about."

Angel nodded, remained calm, kept the killing rage that began to burn inside her carefully contained.

"When he smiled, Angel, I felt it in my heart," Bliss whispered. "Why would I do that? Just for him? Why, when he wants to hurt me?"

Angel had to admit it didn't sound like the young man she'd followed that day along with his friends to their favorite fishing hole.

"We're not sure Bran's even a part of this." She pushed the

long, silky black curls from her sister's face. "We don't assume, we get proof. Remember that, Bliss. We don't get angry . . ."

"We get even." Those Mackay green eyes flashed in pure vengeance.

"No, baby, we get smart," she said gently, desperate to ease her sister's pain. "I'll fix this, Bliss. I promise."

And her baby sister tried to smile as though to ease Angel's worry for her.

"Now you sound like a Mackay," Bliss whispered.

That sad little smile that shaped her sister's lips was killing Angel.

"Close proximity to Duke. It's contagious." She brushed Bliss's hair back again, those silent tears breaking her heart.

"And no cure . . ." Those little half sobs in her voice sliced at Angel's soul.

Catching her attention from the hall entrance Duke quickly indicated that Natches and Chaya were coming in. Good thing he'd warned her. The back door slammed open and Angel barely had time to get out of Natches's way.

"Daddy . . ." Bliss cried out, sobbing the second Natches picked her up in his arms as though she were still five and strode quickly to the living room, where he sat on the couch with her.

Chaya settled in beside them facing her daughter, her arm around Bliss, her head on Natches's shoulder as he bent his head over his daughter and rocked her gently as she sobbed.

Angel stepped to the doorway and found her throat tight, her chest aching at the sight. Bliss was where she needed to be, and the thankfulness Angel felt that her baby sister would never know the life Angel had filled her. But there was that demon spark of envy as well.

She'd never known that. A father's love, his caring. She hadn't known what it felt like to sense a measure of security, or something right in her life, until Duke. But still, it wasn't the same as a parent's love. Of being fifteen and brokenhearted and having a father hold her.

She turned away from the sight of them and moved to the refrigerator for the ingredients for breakfast. She was aware of Duke and Ethan there, armed with coffee, their voices low as they stood near the back door talking.

She doubted much of the food would be eaten, but she needed fuel, and she knew Duke and Ethan did as well. If there was information to be gained on why the Davinov family was in Somerset, then Tracker would find it, and he'd contact Duke as soon as he had it.

She wasn't waiting on Tracker, though. She knew the boy, Brannigan. She'd made certain to check him out when she'd seen how strong Bliss had taken an interest in him.

At twenty-one, he was too old to be hanging around a fifteen-year-old kid. It hadn't taken Angel long to learn that Bran was staying at Lucas Mayes's place. Lucas Mayes was a retired Navy SEAL and was now Zoey's landlord. Angel was sure she could find Bran there and ask him about the others she'd seen at the fishing hole.

He would often stop at the marina for gas and drinks, always with his fishing gear in tow. And when he was there, he never flirted with the cute girl behind the register. He was patient and polite with Bliss, but then paid for whatever he purchased and left quickly.

Bliss talked to him nervously, excitedly, but too shy to flirt. A greeting, a comment about the weather or what he'd caught that day. It had been interesting watching Bliss try to hide her attraction to the boy.

Brannigan seemed like a good boy, but as Angel peeled and cut potatoes, fried bacon, and put on biscuits, information, relationships, and resemblances flowed through her mind. She was pouring the eggs into a hot skillet to scramble when Bran's maturing features finally slid into focus with a kid she'd seen long ago.

Nickolai, Grecia Davinov's youngest son.

She'd seen him once when she was in Russia. He would have been about fourteen. The strength of his features hadn't been apparent then. The height he'd attain nowhere in sight. But it was the same boy, she was sure of it.

What in the hell was Grecia Davinov's heir doing playing lake bum in Kentucky? Why was he calling himself Brannigan?

Putting the food out on the counter, she made her own plate, fixed her coffee, and moved to the table, where Ethan and Duke joined her, their own plates filled.

Fuel. Food was fuel, she reminded herself. She needed the energy even more than she had before to recover from the infection, but she also had a job to do today.

She was going after that kid and bringing him back here. She was going to find out what the hell was going on and waiting didn't seem like a good idea.

She ate mechanically, speaking only when she had to. When she finished and placed her dishes in the dishwasher, she waited for Ethan and Duke to do the same before meeting Duke's gaze with a look she knew he couldn't mistake.

Her mind was set. Softly, she told him she was going to track down the youngest Davinov and refusing to accompany her wouldn't stop her. When he finally nodded she felt something loosen inside her soul. She'd expected him to refuse, to count all the reasons why it wasn't a good idea.

Instead, it seemed Ethan was determined to be the naysayer of the group.

"Hell no," he hissed, glaring at her, disbelief twisting his features before he turned to Duke. "Dammit, her leg isn't ready for that kind of stress."

Duke's expression didn't change nor did the ready tension that had gathered in his body.

"Then be ready to fix it," he suggested. "Call Saul and Seth into the house. We'll be out of here as soon as we're ready."

"Oh, I really don't think so," Chaya drawled from behind her, causing Angel to grit her teeth at the sheer lousy timing her mother displayed.

"So you can instead?" Turning slowly Angel faced her, seeing in her mother's face the same resolve she felt herself.

Chaya stood, apparently relaxed, though Angel could sense the tension in the other woman's body.

Chaya shook her head. "Saul and Seth can go after the boy," she stated. Her voice was low but it didn't change the demand she was making of Angel.

"I know the boy, they don't," she argued. "I can find him faster."

"You're not the only one that knows him," Chaya informed her, weariness flitting over her features as she glanced over at the living room doorway. "I know him as well. Trust me, after losing one child, I made certain there wasn't a part of Bliss's life or anyone in it that I didn't know."

"But you didn't know he was a Russian billionaire's son," Angel pointed out. "And you don't know anything about the family; I do."

"No." Chaya stared back at her with icy eyes. "I will not have that between you and Bliss if anything happens to Bran. I will not have Bliss stare at you, or me, with the look in her eyes that you had in yours that first time I saw you at Graham Brock's."

Angel blinked back at her in surprise.

"How did I look at you?" she exclaimed, her hands going to her hips in frustration. "Like we were meeting for the first time?"

The look her mother gave her was both chiding and filled with mockery.

"Ever heard the expression 'don't try to bullshit a bullshitter'?" Chaya drawled, tilting her head to the side curiously as she spoke. "Well, honey, don't try to snow an interrogator. You're lousy at it, BeeBee."

"Oh for God's sake," she muttered at the nickname, shooting her mother a warning glare.

"BeeBee?" That pure, unholy amusement in Ethan's voice had her glaring back at Chaya again in irritation.

"Thank you so much, *Mother*," she ground out between clenched teeth as Ethan poked her in the back with a whispered, "Buzzz."

The look Chaya shot Duke's brother instantly filled with heavy, disapproving suspicion.

"Duke." The snap in her voice had even Angel looking at her in surprise. "Please tell me you and your brother don't practice the same wild ways my husband and his cousins used to practice. Because I wouldn't be happy. I'd be very unhappy over that."

Wild ways?

Angel blinked back at her mother as the meaning of her statement sank in.

"What?" she hissed, horrified. "With both of them?" She glanced between Ethan's shock and Duke's dark scowl. "That is so nasty. . . . Motherfu—" She bit the word off as Chaya leveled a sudden frown on her. "I'm gonna be sick," she muttered. "That is just sick."

She backed closer to the door of the suite, needing to escape, staring at her mother as though she had never seen the woman before. To compare Duke and Ethan to the deviants her husband and his cousins had been in their youth was criminal.

"That's like accusing me of sleeping with my brother." She was certain she was going to throw up.

"Well, that wasn't unheard of in the family," Dawg announced from the doorway. "Though, not in our generation."

Rowdy was behind him, the long suffering look on his face a clue that Dawg was just as crazy as Chaya.

"I need a drink," she whispered faintly.

"It's only eight in the morning," Chaya reminded her. "You'll have to wait awhile."

Only eight? It felt like she'd been up all day. Wasn't that what mattered?

"Its five o'clock somewhere." Angel backed out of the kitchen and through the open doorway into the suite, still staring at the Mackays in disbelief. "This place is insane. I swear to God . . . insane."

"Duke didn't give you deets on the family history?" Dawg laughed as she felt like finding a hole to crawl into. "That was remiss of you, Duke."

"Not much on family history, I guess." Duke didn't look any happier than she did at the moment.

Angel glared at Dawg. His sense of humor was completely tacky this morning.

"Oh, I know the family history," she assured them. "All of it. I just can't believe she'd think . . ." She swallowed again. "I really think I'm gonna be sick."

Duke managed to hold his laughter in until the door slammed behind Angel, drowning out her outrage.

"Very good," he complimented Chaya with a tilt of his head in true admiration. "You never would have talked her out of going after that kid. At least you've delayed her for a while."

Talking Angel out of anything when she had that look on her face was impossible.

"With her leg in that shape?" She stared at the door Angel had gone through, shaking her head in disbelief before pushing her fingers through her hair and breathing out wearily. "You keep her here. I'll fill Dawg and Rowdy in and they can tell Saul and Seth what's going on. The twins can take care of collecting Bran and my stubborn daughter can keep her rear in place and let that leg rest."

She was good; Duke had to give her credit. She'd picked something that immediately shocked Angel and distracted her for a moment. But that didn't mean it would keep her from going after the Davinov boy before Seth and Saul could leave.

"I think your plan worked," he told her with a nod. "Ethan, you can update me after they leave."

His brother nodded as Chaya went to the table and stared at the pictures, her expression hardening. She wanted to exact vengeance herself, Duke knew. She was sending the twins rather than heading out herself with Natches so that if there were any problems, Bliss wouldn't blame any of them. As much as she needed to hurt someone for Bliss's pain, she didn't want that between her and her youngest daughter. Or between Bliss and her sister.

Drawing her attention, Dawg nodded toward the living room,

where Natches still held Bliss, their low voices reaching into the kitchen.

"She okay?" he asked softly.

"She will be," Chaya answered, looking up from the pictures. "As soon as Saul and Seth find the Davinov boy. He's staying with—"

"Lucas Mayes." Dawg nodded. "The twins are coming now. We'll join them and get him here fast."

Chaya stared into the living room a long moment, her expression as hard as granite, her brown eyes burning with anger and pain.

"Hurry, Dawg," she finally told him, her gaze worried now. "I don't have a good feeling about this. I don't have a good feeling at all."

He and Rowdy stared at her for a long moment, and Duke had seen that expression too many times to mistake it. It was the knowledge a soldier has that the shit was going to hit the fan, and when it did, it might not be pretty.

It was the same feeling Duke had felt himself since first hearing of the attempted abduction.

"Got it." Dawg nodded. "We'll go now. Call us if you need us."

The door closed behind the two men as they left, leaving Duke, Ethan, and Chaya alone in the kitchen.

"Make sure Angel stays," she told Duke, a hint of fear resonating in her voice. "Don't let me lose her again, Duke. I couldn't live with losing her twice. . . ."

TWENTY

Duke knew Angel.

If there was anyone in the world that he knew better than he knew his brother, then it was his wild, fierce lover.

Stepping into the bedroom he found her next to her duffel bag, tightening the tactical belt to her snug camo mission pants. The army green T-shirt she wore was tucked into the pants, and over that she wore a camo vest.

Hell, he was hard. Harder. His cock hardened even further, thickened more, throbbed in desperation, and there was no way in hell he could have her right now. The effect she had on him might be an addiction.

Her Glock was strapped to her bad thigh, just below the stitches, though she'd threaded the support strap behind the holster and attached it to the belt to relieve any stress to her leg. On her left thigh she wore the sheathed, bone-handled knife that he knew Chaya had left her when she was three. And no doubt there was a smaller knife tucked into each boot and two four-inch throwing knives in small sheaths tucked between her T-shirt and pants.

The woman was hell with a knife, just like her mother. Laying within easy reach on the dresser was her preferred assault rifle. The shorter stock and barrel made it perfect for her smaller frame.

"You should weapon up," she warned him. "You and Ethan both. If I remember correctly, Rastor Davinov had a team of Russian Special Forces members that worked for him when he was given the Davinov properties and businesses in Russia. There were five of them, not counting Rastor and his sons, Ilya and Gregor. If Ilya's still alive, they'll follow him to complete Rastor's objective. Whatever that may be."

"You think the boy's involved?" he asked.

"I saw him once in passing. Grecia kept Nickolai out of the public light pretty much. He's Grecia's only male heir after he disowned Viktor. What he's doing in Somerset with Lucas Mayes, I have no clue." She lifted the assault rifle from the dresser, inserted a loaded magazine, and chambered it as she spoke.

Watching her push several more loaded clips into the pockets of the mission pants positioned on the outside of each leg, he frowned at the information she'd given him.

"And you think Rastor's remaining men will still try to take Bliss? What would be the point?" It didn't make sense to him that they'd keep coming after their commander was killed.

"What was the point to begin with?" she asked him, now fully armed. "Whatever it was, he was still coming after Bliss even after he realized I was here. And he knew who I was, there's no doubt of it considering the order to kill me before they took Bliss. When we were protecting Grecia, it was just after he married his French wife and they moved to Paris for the summer. I remember he and his brother were at odds at the time because Grecia was transferring businesses to France. He wanted to leave Russia. Now his son is here with an American SEAL he's calling uncle, and his Russian family members are trying to kidnap a kid the boy is known to talk to?" She stared back at him, her expression confident now, knowing. "This isn't about me or the Mackays. Grecia's been hiding his heir from his eldest son and the family he left in Russia for some reason. And someone's afraid Bliss knows something. That's why she was targeted. And that's why the rest of those soldiers won't stop until the mission is finished. It's not just the son and uncle. Grecia had four other brothers who lost heavily financially when Grecia left. No doubt they all want revenge. And they'd know me as well as my reputation."

That made far more sense than a former client suddenly targeting Angel.

A mistake, Duke thought. If they had killed Angel, the force that would have come after them, from Russia to hell and back, would give the most fearless heart nightmares.

"Did you profile the Davinovs before Tracker took the job?" Duke narrowed his eyes on her.

Tracker often had her profile certain jobs that he got a feeling about. That feeling that it could be more than he was being told.

"Of course." She blinked back at him. "I profiled Grecia Davinov and his children, as well as Rastor. Gregor and Ilya not so much, but considering it's been four days since we killed two of their shooters as well as Rastor and Viktor, then I'm surprised Ilya hasn't already attacked. We're resting on borrowed time, though. They'll make their move soon. If it were me, personally, I would have struck yesterday."

If there was anything that the Army and his cousin Natches,

a hell of a Marine commander, had taught him, it was that no one lived long as a soldier if they didn't develop certain instincts. Instincts that led a man to follow a certain commander or not to.

Angel was Tracker's second-in-command as well as their profiler when needed. She didn't have military training, per se, but she'd been training nearly her entire life. She'd learned in the face of overwhelming odds how to survive and how to size up people quickly on limited information.

They stepped into the small kitchenette, where Ethan still waited.

"Weapon up," he ordered. "I'll be out as soon as I've done the same. Warn Natches and Chaya we need to get ready, just in case."

Nodding quickly, Ethan turned and left the room while Duke returned to the bedroom and began changing into mission clothes.

"You've got it bad, don't you?" he asked, referring to that feeling that would take over her, that sense of danger on the horizon.

"From the second I saw Bliss crying in the kitchen," she admitted. "But I've been restless since I saw the pictures the other night. Now it's like I can feel their breath bearing down on my neck."

After putting on the matching camo mission pants, he pulled the drab green T-shirt over his head only to meet her knowing look.

"What's the family's ETA?" she asked as he tucked the shirt into the pants.

"Midnight," he admitted. "Tracker was picking up J.T. and Mara after meeting with a contact and they were flying straight out to Hickley's Farm. Chaya knows they're coming. She and Mara spent several hours on video chat while you were unconscious."

She cocked her hip and propped a hand on it, her expression going from knowing to irate.

"You know, I'm getting tired of everyone believing they can manipulate me without my knowledge of it. Or hide details I might think are important," she warned him.

Now that sounded ominous enough.

Sitting down he pulled a boot on and laced it quickly.

"I'll make note of that," he promised, pushing his foot into the second boot.

Damn her, she could make his heart melt in his chest at the most fucking inopportune times.

Like right now.

"You know I love you, right, Angel?" He wondered how the hell he'd managed to wait so long before he claimed her.

"Yeah, well." She cleared her throat and brushed back that little fringe of bangs that just fell right back in place. "I love you, too. But I'm still going to end up hurting you if you don't stop conniving against me, Duke. It's very disconcerting."

There was no time to kiss her. If he started, he'd never stop.

"No more conniving," he agreed. Lowering his lashes, he shot her a look of sensual promise. "Unless it involves that very pretty little body. How's that?"

She blushed, brushed back that fringe of hair again before turning and heading quickly out of the bedroom. Seconds later he heard the door between the suite and the kitchen open then close, and he knew she was back in the main part of the house.

Running his hands over his face and blowing out a silent breath, he stared around the room. Like Angel, he could feel that tension at the back of his neck, like a breath of dread bearing down on him.

Hunter's instinct, Tracker called it.

His uncle Ray called it a prey's instinct.

In this case, he was more apt to call it as he saw it. Prey. That was what he was beginning to feel Angel had become, along with Bliss. They were the prey, and he'd be damned if he was going to allow it to continue, and he knew his Angel. Being prey just wasn't in her nature. Soon, she'd become the hunter, and the thought of that . . .

He snorted in amusement, shaking his head.

Hell, this hard-on was going to kill him.

Stepping back into the kitchen, Angel saw Natches putting two plates and silverware in the dishwasher. His and Chaya's, she assumed, because Bliss was picking at the food on the plate sitting in front of her.

"Breakfast was wonderful, Angel," Natches told her, his expression, his voice solemn as he glanced at Bliss.

"Yes it was," Chaya agreed from where she stood at the door. "And Natches was happy not to have to worry about it."

The weariness and heartache in her mother's face was painful to see.

"Chaya does good. Don't let her fool you," Natches drawled then, the look he shot his wife one of love and concern while the comment had Bliss's head jerking around to stare at him momentarily, as though he were crazy.

"Really?" Angel questioned innocently. "Because I seem to remember her deciding to fix me breakfast one morning." She watched the little wince that passed over Chaya's face. "My favorite. Pancakes."

At that, Chaya turned to her quickly with a warning look.

Angel smirked. "Before I got breakfast that morning I had to listen to one of the fire crew beg her for a date no less than three times before he'd take no for an answer."

Natches gave his wife a long, thoughtful look. "Why was the fire department there, sweetheart?"

Angel tucked her hands in her back pockets and waited for Chaya's answer, affecting a look of pristine innocence when her mother threw her a disgruntled look.

"Natches, you know how sensitive security systems used to be." She rolled her eyes as though it were silly. "Burn something the least bit and it would go off. And if you didn't get to the keypad fast enough the program contacted the fire department." She shrugged negligently.

Angel nearly gaped at the gross understatement.

"The curtains were burning," she reminded her mother. "And they were far enough away from the stove that I still have trouble figuring that one out."

Why did she want to laugh? Why did that look of narrow-eyed warning her mother shot her have laughter bubbling in her throat?

"You were three, BeeBee," Chaya pointed out tolerantly before turning back to Natches. "You know kids remember things far differently than the actual events."

Angel was about to choke on her amazement now. Chaya said that so innocently, so sincerely.

"Hmm, no, but maybe you'll explain it to me later," Natches suggested as Duke stepped into the kitchen from the suite at the same time Ethan entered from the hall.

"Declan and Harley will be ready if they're needed," Ethan told her.

"Two other cousins from the other side of the mountain, Jacob and Jonah, are on overwatch. We'll join them," Natches stated, collecting his assault rifle, one similar to Angel's, from the counter behind him. "If they do come and they get past us, then get to that safe room with Bliss until help arrives."

Angel arched her brow and noticed Chaya's lips twitch.

"I mean it, Chay," Natches growled. "Don't take chances."

"Yes, Natches. You're still sexy when you get all He-Man," she assured him as though it were a question. "Get your ass in trouble out there and you sleep on the couch, though."

His eyes narrowed back at his wife.

"You're in trouble," he muttered, pointing his back at her with arrogant certainty. "Trouble."

"According to you, I *am* trouble." That smile of complacency and sensual awareness that curled her mother's lips was highly uncomfortable to see, Angel realized, looking away as Natches pulled his wife to him for a quick kiss.

"Disgusting, huh?" Bliss sighed, shaking her head. "You'd think those two are still on their honeymoon."

"Completely disgusting." Duke laughed, swung Angel around, and stole a quick kiss, then tapped her ass as he strode past her.

"Buzzz," Ethan hissed as he followed, obviously finding immeasurable enjoyment in the nickname.

"You know I'll end up hurting him," she informed Bliss, who'd obviously heard it, if the small tug of a grin at her lips was any indication.

"I think it's cute," Bliss decided. "Like an older brother. Only nicer than mine."

"I thought Declan was nice." He'd always been nice to her anyway.

Bliss shrugged.

"He calls me Sister Mary Bliss," she said, her expression uneasy as she pushed the fork through cold scrambled eggs. "He said Dad has already ordered my habit and chosen the convent."

The too-serious and far-too-responsible Declan?

"Who knew he could joke?" Angel was impressed. She wouldn't have expected Declan to do so.

"I don't think he's joking." The uneasiness in Bliss's voice and expression wasn't for effect either. "I keep finding searches for convents on the computer after Dad's finished using it."

Natches was going to end up getting his ass in trouble where his daughter was concerned if he wasn't careful.

"Let me guess, it just started since he realized you were interested in boys?" Angel snorted. "Go figure. Of course you found the searches. He wanted you to find them. I've watched so many fathers we've protected play those games with their kids." She gave a dismissive wave of her hand at the idea of it.

It never failed to amaze her the games those fathers had played with their daughters.

"Really?" The fear had eased some from Bliss's face, but the curiosity that filled it now had Angel instantly realizing she could be stepping into something she didn't want to step into. At least not yet.

"The convent trick." Angel cleared her throat. "There's so many different ways of playing that one, I could write a book."

Yeah, that cover was lame as hell, she admitted.

"Uh-huh." The knowing look on the teenager's face assured Angel she hadn't pulled that one off. "That book's going to be really boring, Angel."

"Eh, I'll fill it in with Mackay machinations. It'll definitely sell then." That was bestseller material there.

Picking up her fork once again, Bliss continued to play with the cold, now-unappetizing food on her plate. And Angel couldn't ignore that tingle just beneath her neck any longer.

Glancing at Chaya, she saw the way her mother stayed focused on the property behind the house as though searching for something.

Moving to the window next to Bliss she looked between the slat and the wall. The sun-dappled yard looked peaceful, serene.

Which didn't explain the chill crawling up her spine.

"Angel?" Bliss asked softly.

"Yeah, Bliss?" She searched the boundary line and as much of the shaded forest as she could see.

Davinov's men, all Russian Special Forces, would be damned good. Not that she and the team hadn't gone against them before; they had. They'd moved several individuals out of Russia with the Davinov organization hot on their tails. But that didn't mean they could be taken for granted.

"Why did you wait so long to find us?" Bliss asked, her voice low. "Why didn't you let us know who you were, that you were alive, sooner?"

The question had a wave of emotion straining at the mental gates she placed on them, had to place on them whenever she worked. But there were those that slipped free, that leaked past her guard and filled her mind.

Why hadn't she come forward? It was more than just believing her mother had deserted her. As much as that had tormented her, memories of how much her mother had loved her before that trip to Iraq had tormented her more.

"I was fifteen before I remembered," she told her sister. "And it took several years just to process what I was remembering, to accept the memories and make sense of them." She was still trying to make sense of so much. "Maybe one day, when this is over, you and I will talk," she assured her. "When both of us can think and make sense of what we have to say to one another."

She remembered how she'd felt when she remembered.

Shame. Fear. Anger.

Those first memories had been of her time in that hotel and Craig's phone conversation. A conversation her mother swore had never taken place. That anger had followed her until she was trapped in the hospital at eighteen.

What she'd felt after that still confused her. She'd been at a bar several weeks later, the trash mouth she had running like it usually did, when something had awakened inside her.

Shame.

Pure, painful shame.

She had drunk far more whiskey than normal, was quickly becoming drunk enough that Tracker would have to carry her out of the bar. And Duke and Ethan had been there. Duke had been glaring at Tracker, Tracker staring into his drink.

And she'd just been finished.

Finished with the person she was, finished with so many things that didn't make sense.

Evidently she'd been finished with living, too, because after that, the near-fatal injuries had begun. One per year. Keeping her out of the fighting, keeping her sidelined in logistics and planning only.

Maybe Duke had been right. Maybe she'd been desperate to get out of that life and find more time to grow hungrier for the family she knew she had in Kentucky.

Whatever the reasons, the hunger had grown after that, and she'd found it impossible to stay away for long.

The tightening at the back of her neck was driving her crazy.

If she were there with her team and the safe room wasn't set up to call everyone but the Air National Guard, then she would have already shoved Chaya and Bliss inside it and gone hunting.

Because they were out there.

Reaching to her ear, she gave a tap to the earbud communication device she wore and waited for the return tap from Ethan and Duke.

Nothing. Which didn't mean they weren't capable; it could just mean they were waiting, watching, and unwilling to move enough to tap the device.

Or it could mean they were tracking a problem.

Careful to keep the move from Bliss, she slid the assault rifle to her chest, her finger moving close to the trigger.

"Bliss, stay low and get in the hall. Now," Angel ordered her, keeping her voice low.

Bliss didn't argue or demand explanations. She slid from the chair to the floor and quickly crawled to the hall.

"Chaya, join her." She could feel it now, that veil of complete emotionlessness. The hardening of the shields around her soul, the determination to kill rather than be killed or have those she was protecting killed.

"You join her." Chaya's tone was identical.

There was no way she was going to be able to convince her mother to get in that safe room.

"If they hit, once Bliss is secure, get to my room," Chaya told her. "We have a reasonably safe exit from the house."

Angel's finger slid to the trigger.

The walls were secured against most incoming gunfire, but not the windows. They'd try to shock with taking the windows out first, then they'd come through the door. If they'd been watching the house as she suspected then they knew the kitchen was the central gathering point of the house.

"Pull back to the hall," Angel told her. "Once they hit, it's going to be hard and fast. I can't pull Ethan or Duke up on the comms. We have to be as close as possible. Go."

Angel kept her eyes on the sunlit beauty outside them, feeling the waves of ugly maliciousness coming their way. They weren't just after Bliss now; they were after vengeance.

Staying low, Chaya moved across the kitchen, heading for the hall. Once she passed behind her, Angel went to the floor and quickly crawled past the window.

She'd just come to her feet when it came, and it didn't start with gunfire.

"Go!" she screamed as the grenade tore through the window and shades first.

She threw herself across the room, taking Chaya down and dragging her into the hall a second before it exploded.

They were both on their feet, grabbed Bliss, and within a heartbeat had her at the safe room. Chaya hit the palm pad and they waited what seemed forever for the door to pop open.

Angel pushed Bliss inside, and just as she went to pull back felt the force of the shove at her back that sent her toppling inside the room with her sister.

"No. No." Scrambling to her feet she found herself staring at the steel door as it locked in place, securing her with Bliss, leaving her mother out there, alone. "Damn you, no!" The scream was one of anguish as she threw herself at the door, her fists hitting it, knees weakening as she realized how easily she'd let herself be fooled by her mother.

"I didn't see that coming." Bliss sounded as shocked as Angel did. "I should have. I really should have, Angel. But I didn't see that coming."

Angel should have seen it coming, too. She was sloppy. She'd been too confident, too concerned with protecting Bliss.

She closed her eyes and slid to the floor, allowing the rifle to rest against the carpet as she leaned against the door.

She'd failed. . . .

She was only barely aware of Dawg's voice coming through the communications setup on the wall or Bliss's quick responses. The teenager wasn't crying, but her voice was strained and hoarse with fear. Dawg was assuring they were coming. Just minutes away. Just minutes away . . .

And Angel was locked in a room with no exit until others arrived. Her mother was out there, possibly alone, facing only God knew what without backup. And Duke was out there. He hadn't answered her tap. He'd be expecting her to cover his ass and she wouldn't be in place.

She'd failed both of them. . . .

TWENTY-ONE

Chaya could hear the back door shattering as she slid into her bedroom and locked the heavy door carefully. The wooden look of the steel door wasn't as heavy as the one on the safe room, but it would give her a minute.

She could hear gunfire outside, shouted voices, both English and Russian, and her only thought was to reach Natches.

He should have been at the house before the attack. He and Duke were supposed to pull back to the house if they saw a threat. And they hadn't pulled back. There hadn't been so much as a warning that anything was coming before that damned grenade was launched into the kitchen.

Running across the bedroom she paused only long enough to check outside the window for a threat before throwing the shade open and unlocking it. She was pushing the lower frame up when the first thump against the door reached her.

The door was stronger than most, but it would only take a few good hard kicks to bust past the reinforced doorframe. Natches had built the house for security, but not for a sustained force.

Another crash against the door and she heard the warning crack of the doorframe. She didn't hesitate.

She jumped through the window, throwing herself to the ground before rolling and coming to her feet.

The blast that sounded stopped her in her tracks and sent her stumbling back a step or two rather than pushing off into a run.

She felt the bullet slam into her chest in a distant, hazy sort of way.

There was no pain.

She'd always imagined there would be pain, an agony unlike anything she'd known. Instead, it was just a rather distant ache as all the strength seemed to flow out of her body.

She looked down, saw the quickly spreading scarlet stain on the front of her once pristine white shirt as she felt her knees hit the dirt.

Slow motion.

How completely cliché, but everything was moving in slow motion.

Lifting her eyes she stared across the yard to the tall, dark-haired male that stood just inside the natural fence. Ice-blue eyes stared at her with hatred, a deep scar cutting across his cheek, the gun in his hand pointing to her head, his finger on the trigger. It wasn't enough to shoot her in the heart, she guessed; he was going to put a bullet in her brain as well.

She'd never imagined she'd die like this.

The shot that echoed through her senses didn't even cause her to flinch as she waited for the blow. Instead, she watched as the side of his head just exploded. Blood, flesh, and brain matter flew in all directions as the body was thrown backward.

"Natches . . ." She whispered his name, the weakness that swept through her legs now spreading through her body as she felt herself swaying on her knees. "Natches . . ."

Her talisman. Her soul.

She didn't want to leave him. She wasn't ready to leave him. Life with him was always filled with so much laughter and un-expected adventure. And they'd promised each other they'd live to be old enough to torture their great grandchildren.

She was breaking her promise.

She didn't want to leave Bliss or Angel.

She'd only just found her baby. . . .

She could hear more gunfire, hear Natches screaming her name, his voice broken, his arms catching her as she began to topple to the ground.

She stared up at him as he laid her back gently, horror, stark, agonizing pain contorting his face as tears began to fall from emerald eyes.

"No! No! Don't you do this to me!" he screamed, his face enraged, his eyes like green fire. "Don't you leave me. Don't you dare."

She lifted her hand to touch the tears falling from his eyes. They were so hot, and she was so cold.

"I love you . . . so much. . . ." she whispered, fighting to breathe.

It hurt now. Oh God, it hurt so bad now.

Something pushed against her chest, someone. But she couldn't look away from her wild man, the man that held the very depths of her soul.

"I'm sorry," he sobbed, touching her face, his fingers so warm and filled with life. "Oh God . . . I'm so sorry, baby. I'm so sorry."

Agony lanced her chest as hard hands held her down, forced her to stay to the ground when she would have heaved up from the agony.

"Angel . . ." she gasped. "Don't let her blame herself . . . please. . . ."

Her daughter, both her daughters, they'd blame themselves.

"Bliss . . . make her talk . . . don't let her hide. . . ." There were so many things she needed to tell him about Bliss.

He had to stop with the convent crap. He had to start listening to their daughter. He had to let her grow up.

There was so much he needed to know, and there was no time.

"No, by God, I won't do that for you," he snarled down at her. "You're giving up. You will not give up on me. If you die, Chaya Mackay, I'll follow you. They'll bury me in that fucking box beside you. Right beside you where I belong."

Panic. Disbelief.

Pain struck at her chest again, nearly stealing her breath forever before she forced it back into her heaving lungs.

"No . . . Bliss . . ." she tried to protest. He couldn't leave Bliss, too.

And Angel would need him.

Declan . . .

"You're giving up on her for both of us." Fury filled his face. "Live or die, you make the choice."

"Bliss . . . Angel . . ." she gasped, fighting for air, fighting to breathe as she felt a strange, painless lassitude begin to steal over her.

"Make the choice. . . ." He wouldn't relent; she knew he wouldn't. He would die with her and she wouldn't be able to stop him.

"Momma . . ." Angel seemed to just drop to her knees beside Natches, her eyes wide, so filled with horror, with guilt and shame.

No . . . God, no . . .

"I'm so sorry," Angel whispered, her face white, and for the first time, Chaya saw herself. "Oh God, Momma, please . . . I'm so sorry. . . . Don't leave me now. . . . Please don't leave me now."

So long ago, when Chaya was young and too damned dumb to walk away from the military, she had been Angel. So determined, so filled with a wild rage and fury because so much had been taken away from her. She'd lost her baby, forced herself to walk away from Natches, and all she'd had was the fight.

Her daughter looked just like her at that age, too. The shape of her eyes, the arch of her brow, the curve of her chin. So stubborn and so determined. Her mini-me. Her baby.

"I'm so sorry," Angel whispered again.

Bliss was screaming in the background, hysterical, her voice broken, begging her.

Chaya felt the tears that escaped her eyes, felt the weakness growing in her body.

"No . . ." Not yet. She couldn't go yet.

She gasped for air, but there wasn't enough. She fought to breathe, but it was so cold now, and she couldn't make her body obey, couldn't make it work.

Not yet. Oh God, not yet . . .

She couldn't make herself breathe, but she didn't feel like she was suffocating. She felt like she was drifting. Just drifting.

She wanted to cry out in fear, but everything was so distant, so hazy. She wanted to hold on, she really did. For Natches, for her daughters.

Darkness rolled over her, waves of it, stealing her will, taking her, just taking her away.

Terror washed over her and for a moment, a single heartbreaking moment, she mourned everything she was losing.

She was just . . . gone.

Four hours later
Lexington, Kentucky

Angel stood still, silent. Her back rested against the white wall of the hospital waiting room, her gaze focused on the identical wall across from her. She looked as devastated as he felt, Natches reflected, watching her. Her face stark white, her eyes like storm clouds rolling over the mountains. And she just stood there. In the hours since the chopper Doogan had ordered had deposited them on the hospital roof, just minutes after Life Flight had turned Chaya over to the surgeons and they'd been shown to the waiting room, Angel hadn't moved.

"Mom's going to be fine," Bliss said, not for the first time from where she sat next to him, her head on his chest as he held her against him. "I know she is, Dad."

But he didn't know it. For once, he couldn't look into the future and know for a fact that when the sun rose in the morning, she'd be there with him, if nothing else, somewhere in the world.

Breathing. Living.

There was this cold, aching hole in his heart where his wife had resided since the day he'd pulled her from certain death all those years ago. Even after she'd disappeared on him for five cold, lonely years, he'd felt her there, holding him back from the brink of the dark, murderous fury he knew would have eventually ensnared him.

And now, he couldn't feel her there.

He couldn't have imagined ever feeling this alone in his life. Even as a boy suffering beneath his father's abuses, he hadn't felt so adrift in the world.

He tightened his arms around Bliss, wondering how the hell he could go on if he lost his heart. If death stole her from him, how could he bear it? How could he go on for his daughter and still function?

He didn't think he could. Not even for the child he knew would depend on him.

"Dad? You need coffee or anything?" Declan asked from the seat next to him.

Declan. He'd been a half-wild kid born of an American serviceman and Afghani mother killed a few years after his birth. Orphaned, he'd been watching half-starved goats when he'd seen a helicopter land in a small Taliban encampment where a pretty blonde had been carried, kicking and screaming, into a stone building. He'd immediately used the radio a soldier at one of the bases had given him and sent out an SOS. Natches had been only a few miles away, and he'd been curious.

"Dad?" Declan's voice firmed when Natches didn't answer him.

He shook his head. He didn't want coffee. He wanted Chaya to hang on, to live. If nothing else, for him.

"You made me live when I lost Beth, and for a while I think I hated you for that. . . ." Her words drifted through his mind, the memory of her brown eyes filled with so much love and with so much loss as they lay together in his bed, wrapped around each other, warming each other.

"I loved you. I love you forever, Chay." He stared into her eyes, giving her the only thing he had, himself.

A hint of confusion touched her expression. *"You whispered that in my dreams."*

"I whispered that into the darkness." He sighed as he held her to his heart. *"No matter where it found me. I sent it to you a thousand times a day. God, Chaya, every breath I took was a thought of you. . . ."*

"Mom's going to be okay," Bliss repeated. "You'll see, Dad."

Her voice was hoarse from her screams that morning. She'd fought Dawg like a wild thing, screaming for her mother, for him. And Natches hadn't been able to comfort her, just as he hadn't been able to keep Chaya with him.

"Come on, Sister Mary Bliss." Declan rose to his feet, his voice gentle as he teased her. "Let's go get a donut and a soda."

Declan had a weakness for donuts and sodas. Keeping that boy's teeth from rotting out had been a full-time job when he first came to them, Natches remembered. Chaya had fussed at the boy, took him to the dentist, and when they'd put braces on him she'd sympathized and fussed some more.

She had made him her son. She had mothered him, loved him, and when he asked her why, she'd told him it was because he was her son. Did she need any other reason?

And that night, she'd cried for the daughter she'd lost.

"I'll be back, Dad," Bliss promised, pushing from his hold and getting to her feet.

"Bliss." He caught her hand when she would have walked away and left him.

"Yeah, Daddy?" Her eyes, so like his, but her strong, independent spirit was so like her mother's.

"I would never send you away from me," he told her, suddenly desperate that she understand that. "You know that, don't you? I couldn't do that to myself, or to you and your mother. Tell me you know that."

A tear slipped down her cheek. "I know that, Daddy," she whispered, her gaze moving to where Angel stood so still, so silent. And so alone. Suddenly Bliss threw her arms around his neck in a tight hug. "I don't care if I'm fifty, Daddy, I still want you to pick me up and rock me when I hurt. Promise me you will."

He had to close his eyes, swamped with emotion, uncertain how to hold it back. "I promise, baby." He kissed her brow gently. "I promise."

Pulling away from him, she glanced at her sister again then rushed off with Declan, wiping the tears from her cheeks.

"Who held my baby when she cried?" Chaya sobbed in his arms, Duke's file scattered on the floor where she'd thrown it in rage before he'd caught her to him. "Who rocked my baby, Natches?"

His head jerked up, certain he heard her, heard her whisper, her pain drifting around him.

He shook his head at the illusion and looked over at Angel again.

Duke had pushed her into the helicopter with him, Bliss, and Declan even as she reached for him, cried out for him. He'd promised to be there for her as quick as he could and told her to wait for him, as though he expected her to run off as she had before when she had to face the loss of someone she loved. Or something.

He'd reported that Tracker had told him that Angel had disappeared for a week when she was fifteen after the war dog that led her to their hut the night of the explosion died. No one could find her, and when she'd come back to the farm they owned, she refused to tell anyone where she had been.

Leaning forward, elbows propped on his knees, Natches wiped his hands down his face and stared at her again.

Like a sentinel standing there, staring straight ahead, waiting for a blow.

Until Duke, he doubted anyone had held Angel. He doubted she let anyone hold her, even as a child. And he doubted anyone had insisted on doing so.

"Who rocked my baby, Natches?" Chaya's sobs echoed inside him.

If by some cruel twist of fate he lost the woman that held his soul, then when he met her again in the afterlife, he wanted her to know someone had cared enough about her child to rock her.

Getting to his feet, he didn't question the impulse that had him striding to her or the instinct that assured him this was something that not just Angel needed, but something Chaya needed as well. And maybe it was something he needed.

Don't leave me. . . . Don't leave me. . . . Please, Momma, don't leave me. . . .

The words were a chant in Angel's head, a prayer she couldn't keep from repeating. They were the same words she'd sobbed when her mother left her with her aunt the day she left.

She stared at the wall across from her, but the nightmare

image of her mother's eyes closing, the feeling that she was drifting away, was all she could see, all she could feel.

Where was Duke? She'd promised to wait for him, but she didn't know if she could. The pain and coiling rage was tightening inside her, threatening to explode, and she couldn't do that here. She couldn't be weak. Not in front of so many people.

But what would she do when she couldn't wait any longer? Would she finally just disappear inside herself where it would never hurt again? She'd done that after she'd lost Jenny, and again after Brutus, J.T.'s war dog, had died. Until the summer she turned eighteen, she'd just been hollow inside, trapped within herself. Until she'd been locked in the dark, trapped in that hospital basement, her screams echoing around her, memories pummeling her.

Memories were pummeling her now as well, raking through her soul with merciless claws.

Craig dying, blood easing from the corners of his lips. He said he was sorry for bringing her there, sorry about Jenny and Aunt Jo. But it didn't matter that he was sorry because her momma never came to get her. If he hadn't ever brought her to Iraq, he probably would've killed her momma. Because of his secrets. Because he'd lied. Either way, her momma would be dead and it would be all her fault.

She stared at the wall harder. If she concentrated hard enough, if she didn't let herself feel too much, then the well of emotions threatening to boil over might ease for just a minute, just long enough for Duke to get to her.

As she focused on a single blemish in the wall, it disappeared, replaced by the bloodstained camo T-shirt Natches wore.

"Angel?" Natches demanded her attention, his voice soft. "Look at me."

She forced herself to look up, to stare miserably back at the man that should hate her. She'd failed. She hadn't protected her mother. She didn't want to face him, to have him ask her why she hadn't been smarter, why she hadn't kept this from happening.

"Bliss lets me hold her when she cries," he told her then. "That's what dads do, you know?"

Confusion made it impossible to understand why he'd say that to her. Was it a taunt? Was this her punishment?

"Come on, baby girl. It's okay to cry." His arms surrounded her; his hoarse voice broke her. "It's okay to cry right here. That's what Dad is for. We can just cry together."

Shudders tore through her, pulling a ragged cry from her lips.

She was only barely aware of the fact that he picked her up as he had picked Bliss up. Cradling her like she was five as he sat down, one hand pressing her head to his chest, his head lowering over hers, his other arm wrapped around her, holding her on his lap.

Like a father would hold his child.

Like Angel had never been held, never been comforted.

And his shoulders jerked; a tear fell to her arm. His tears.

And she broke.

Sobs tore from her. Twenty years of grief, loss, hope, and pain filled the desperate cries as her arms wrapped around his neck and she cried as he held her. Rocked her. That child that had forgotten how to cry, the father that would have been, and all the fear that they were losing the woman that meant so much to both of them. Mother. Wife.

And neither of them knew how they'd bear it. They didn't know if they could bear it.

Dawg had to turn away, the tears that ran down his cheeks glimpsed only by the wife he pulled to him.

The cousin he'd once believed would never know how to be a father was surprising him again. The natural instinct Natches had with his daughter, Bliss, had made Dawg kick himself for that thought for years. But this, seeing Natches accept the child that hadn't come from his blood but had become a child in his heart, was staggering, humbling.

Pulling a semblance of control around him, he turned back to them and strode to the chair next to his cousin. He gripped Natches's shoulder and patted Angel's knee, not really certain how to comfort either of them, as Christa sat next to him, always close, the strength he hadn't realized kept him going until he'd seen Chaya clinging to life.

Rowdy sat on the other side. Ray, Rowdy's dad, the man that took wild-assed heathen nephews to his heart so long ago, crouched in front of Natches, bad knees and all, tears running unashamedly down his lined face.

They comforted them the only way they knew how. They were there, close, willing to help them stand if they needed it. If the worst happened, Angel was still family, just as she was before. She was Chaya and Natches's daughter and that would never change.

Chaya stared at the scene her sister had drawn her to. There, with his cousins and his uncle surrounding him, Bliss with her head on his knee, Angel cradled in his arms, the man she loved held on to the children that were so much a part of her.

Angel isn't alone any longer now, she thought. And as Duke rushed into the room then moved more slowly to where Angel sobbed on Natches's shoulder, his hand reached out, settled on her shoulder, and he just stood there with her.

He loved her so much. She hadn't realized how much that Mackay loved her daughter, but she should have. She'd told Natches once, when Duke was barely fourteen, how much he reminded her of Natches.

Her Bethany, her BeeBee, and now her Angel, was finally home. She didn't have to worry about either of her girls; they were both grounded with family.

"They're grounded by you," her sister said softly from where she stood next to her. "Have you seen what you needed now?"

Chaya nodded slowly. She had. She had needed to know her babies were safe, that they were okay.

"It's time to go then. Come on, Chay. Stop being a wuss," Jo-Ellen chided her gently.

"Stop being so bossy," Chaya ordered. "We were never close enough for that."

"We weren't," her sister agreed. "But our babies were, Chay. Our babies were."

Exhausted from the tears and emotion, Angel sat against Duke later, wrapped in his warmth as Natches and Bliss sat on the other side of her. Her gaze flicked to the clock on the wall. It had been so long since her mother had gone into surgery. So many hours without word. Could a body actually sustain that long?

"The doctor's coming out," Doogan announced from the waiting room entrance.

Natches was on his feet instantly, one hand enfolding Bliss's, the other catching Angel's wrist and pulling her to her feet.

"Wait." She tugged on the hold. She didn't know if she could do this.

"We face this together," Natches told her, his voice hardening. "As a family."

Family.

With Duke on one side, a father she had no idea how to deal with on the other, and dozens of other Mackays, in-laws and outlaws, surrounding them, they met the surgeon and Ethan at the door.

Their faces were exhausted. Ethan looked haggard.

"Natches." The surgeon stepped to him, his blue eyes weary. "Before I begin, she made it through surgery. She's in ICU for now, but we're optimistic. She's alive. We work from there."

She was alive.

That was all that mattered. She was alive.

TWENTY-TWO

Two days later

Angel woke in Duke's arms, the warmth and strength that surrounded her sinking all the way to her soul.

She was content, she realized.

No, she was more than content; she was happy. She was fully happy, something she'd never known before, something she'd never imagined she'd have a chance to know.

Would she have known this without Duke?

She wouldn't have, she didn't believe. She would have died in a no-name country and she would have never known what could have been or how happy she could be.

"You think too hard, baby," he drawled, his voice sleep-drowsy and sexy. "I should spank you for waking me."

She smiled at the threat. "Keep threatening to spank me, Duke, and I'm going to end up spanking you."

He chuckled. "Hmm, I go first."

Rolling to his side, those gorgeous too-thick lashes opened

just enough to allow a glimpse of mossy green eyes and male hunger.

"I'll be happy to spank you first," she assured him, twining her arms around his neck as his head lowered, his lips brushing against hers as laughter rumbled in his chest.

"I doubt that's going to happen, darlin'," he assured her. "At least not without a hell of a lot of convincing. For a hell of a long time," he tacked on.

She smiled against his lips.

"Marry me, Angel."

Her eyes jerked open in shock.

Pulling his arm from beneath his pillow, he picked up her hand and slid the most beautiful diamond she'd ever seen over her finger.

"I'm tired of carrying it around," he told her. "I told Uncle Charlie I was marrying you three years ago and he gave me his mother's engagement ring for you. Marry me, Angel."

Marry him? Wake up with him every morning? Lie down beside him every night?

"Really? You're serious?" She was almost too scared to believe, to accept that it could be real.

"Honey, I'm so serious my dick's hard," he groaned, with feeling even.

He sounded so serious it took a minute to really grasp what he'd said.

She couldn't help but laugh.

Staring up at him, seeing the complete sincerity in his face, she erupted again.

"You freak," she gasped. "Your dick is always hard."

"Just for you," he assured her with a mocking frown. "And I'm so serious, it's harder."

To prove his point he slid between her legs, the broad head meeting the slick flesh between her thighs.

"And you're wet," he groaned. "Slick and hot. Say yes so we can celebrate."

And she wanted to say yes. She wanted to say yes so bad she could barely stand it.

"I can't," she moaned, pleasure racing through her. "I can't say yes yet."

"What?" He stilled, staring down at her in surprise. "Why? Of course you can."

"No. Not yet." She almost laughed again at his expression of offended male pride. "You have to ask my father for my hand first." Now didn't that statement sound strange as hell.

He blinked once. "You mean J.T., right?"

"Duke." She pouted. "Dad would be so disappointed." It was all she could do not to laugh at him again.

"I'm going to have erectile dysfunction," he whispered. "I know I am."

Angel rolled her eyes. "You already have erectile dysfunction. You're always erect. That has to be some kind of dysfunction."

"You are a cruel woman," he informed her piteously.

But he was moving against her, pushing inside her.

Angel's breath caught. Heat began sizzling over her body, the blood racing hard and fast through her veins as he took her by slow degrees. Forging inside her, retreating, impaling her further, he stole her senses as he'd already stolen her heart.

"Oh, baby," he whispered against her lips, his breathing growing heavier, his muscles tightening as he worked the heavy length of his cock inside her. "You feel so good. So perfect."

Vocal and expressive, the words sent a glow of added pleasure, like a ribbon wrapping around her soul, warming every part of her.

Each slow thrust was the ultimate caress, stroking over flesh more sensitive than ever and rushing through her senses faster than ever before.

"I love you." Her arms tightened around him, her hips moving beneath his, lifting closer.

Those strong, powerful thrusts quickened, pushing her closer to the edge of ecstasy.

She could feel the static fingers of sensation racing through her. They tightened with each deep penetration, each stroke of heat and pleasure. Her hands tightened at his shoulders, nails pricking his flesh. Her neck arched for the heated, desperate kisses he spread down it.

Sensation upon sensation until she felt herself coming apart beneath him, felt her soul flying, colliding with his and exploding in showers of rich, vivid emotion.

In that moment Angel knew she was home. Right here in Duke's arms.

She was home.

Arriving at the hospital several hours later, she and Duke stepped into the waiting room to find J.T., Mara, Tracker, and Chance talking with Natches. The Calloways had shown up in Somerset at midnight the night Chaya had been shot, then headed straight for Lexington and, like Angel and Duke, they hadn't left the hospital until late the night before.

Moving to them Angel hugged J.T. and Mara, then the foster brothers she'd fought with for so long. Turning to Natches, she saw his gaze drop to her hand and that little flash of disappointment in his gaze before he could hide it.

"You're just in time," he told her. "She regained consciousness about an hour or so ago while I was with her. They're letting the three of us in to see her in about thirty minutes."

She couldn't speak. Angel felt her throat close with emotion, and fought to simply breathe.

"She's going to pull through this," he promised, pulling her in for a hug. "We're going to get her through it."

She nodded against his shoulder, holding tight.

"And she'll want to see that ring," he told her softly.

"I haven't said yes yet," she admitted, pulling back to look up at him with a smile. "I told him he had to ask my father first. So be gentle."

He grunted at the request, but that shadow of disappointment was gone and the kiss he pressed to her forehead reminded her more eloquently than words that this man had accepted her as his own.

Behind her Duke was muttering something about fathers, but he didn't sound too put out.

"You say something, Duke?" Natches asked, narrowing his eyes as Angel stepped back.

This is bullshit, Duke thought in frustration, until he glimpsed that little flash of vulnerability in Angel's gaze.

Well, hell.

He rubbed at the back of his neck. If this was what she needed, then he guessed he could do it. Couldn't be any worse than when he'd asked Tracker. Right?

The hell it couldn't. But it was for Angel.

"Natches." He cleared his throat. "Could we talk for a minute?" He even asked politely.

Natches stared at him for a few long seconds before turning to Angel and Bliss. "Why don't the two of you go over there with Kelly and Christa?" he suggested. "Let me and Duke talk for a minute."

Angel shot him an encouraging smile, then moved away with her sister, though she did look back just as Dawg and Rowdy moved in and hid him from her gaze. The smiles on their faces could best be described as evil.

Duke drew in a hard breath.

"I asked Tracker two years ago, but Angel reminded me this morning that she has a father now," he told Natches, putting on his best manners. "I apologize for forgetting that, but I'd like your permission to marry your daughter."

He expected the normal Mackay hard time, but all three men went completely solemn instead.

Natches cleared his throat and blinked quickly. Hell, if that bastard started crying, Duke swore he was going to knock his ass out before he made a fool of both of them.

"I've not had a chance to get to know her yet," Natches said, inhaling roughly. "I was hoping for a chance to do that."

Okay, it wasn't "no" exactly.

"She wants to wait until her mother's stronger." He nodded, remembering their conversation after their shower. "And I know she wants a wedding. That takes a while to plan, I've been told. Besides, once we marry we're moving to the farm. Maybe raise a few cows. A few babies." All parents wanted grandkids. Right?

"She won't be fighting again?" That was definitely an edge of hope in Natches's voice.

"No, sir," he stated emphatically. "And that's a promise from her. She stops fighting and I give her a home and babies. Sounded like a deal to me."

A grin edged Natches's lips as Rowdy and Dawg both looked at their younger cousin and gave a slight nod.

"A year," Natches demanded. "A year and she stays at our home. Chaya needs time with her, Duke. Let her have a year."

"As long as I can stay with her," he demanded. "You don't want to separate us, Natches. She tends to get into trouble."

Amusement gleamed in Natches's gaze as Rowdy and Dawg grimaced at the statement.

"So J.T., Mara, and Tracker have been telling us." Natches rubbed at the back of his neck while sneaking a look at his new daughter before turning back to Duke. "If she's anything like her mother, then keeping her out of trouble is going to be a full-time job."

"One I look forward to," Duke assured him, watching as his fiancée showed off her new ring, her face flushed with pleasure.

Hell, she made his dick so damned hard.

The curtains were pulled around the small cubicle, the dimly lit area meant to be comforting, Angel was certain. Machines hummed and beeped and the sight of her mother on the narrow hospital bed, attached to those machines, stole her breath.

She appeared to be asleep.

Her once vibrant will had disguised the delicacy of her build somehow, because she now looked frail, fragile, as she lay beneath the hospital sheet.

Her once golden brown hair looked darker, her face pale

beneath the light, dark shadows giving her eyes a bruised appearance.

Angel approached the bed slowly, lips trembling, fighting not to cry as relief poured through her at the sight of her mother's chest rising and falling slowly. Her hand lifted from her side as though to touch Chaya's, then fell back in place, her fingers trembling.

She was only barely aware of Natches moving to the opposite side of the bed, his hand clasping his wife's as it lay at her side.

"Hey, baby, you awake?" he asked, his voice rough, low. "I brought someone to see you." Reaching out with his other hand he pushed back the hair that fell over her brow, his fingers lingering to stroke down the side of her face.

"She's sleeping. Leave her alone," Angel whispered, glaring at Natches. "Let her sleep already."

His lips quirked into a grin. "Know how Duke is always telling you to stop thinking so hard?" he asked. "It's because sometimes, those around you can actually feel the gears rolling in your head. I can feel the gears rolling in her head. Don't you? She's there. It just takes her a minute, that's all."

That sense she sometimes got of certain people, Angel realized. She could stare at them and sometimes she knew before they opened their lips if it would be the truth or a lie.

It never failed that if she concentrated hard enough, others around her could sense her tension as well, though. Like Duke. Sometimes Tracker and Chance could as well.

"She does that, too?" she whispered, staring back at him, suddenly inordinately pleased that she shared that with her mother.

"It's what makes her such an intuitive interrogator," he told her, stroking Chaya's arm. "She said that about you once. That she could look at you and feel you thinking. Feel the gears rolling in your head and the lies ready to spill from your lips." He grinned back at her. "It made her crazy, too."

"I should have told her sooner." She'd never forgive herself for that. "I should have come to her when I first remembered, but she wouldn't have liked me then, Natches. Even I didn't like me."

She cursed worse than a sailor on leave, drank too much, smoked too often. Even Tracker and Chance hadn't known what to do with her or about her.

"She would have loved you first, straightened you out second," he assured her. "She does that, you know? She has a way of convincing those she loves to love her back, and to want nothing more than to please her."

"That was all I wanted when I was little." She could hear her laughter drifting through her head, her mother's love, even when she messed up, and her determination to find a way to do better.

"You were her light when I met her." Natches's voice was reverent. "While she was in the hospital in Iraq, we made plans for me to come to Canada to meet you. Then she learned she'd lost you, and she lost herself, too. She never let you go, Angel. In her heart, you were always alive."

Chaya's eyes lifted slowly, blinked, then focused in on Angel as she stood by the bed.

Angel stared down at her mother, wishing she knew what the other woman was thinking, feeling. Pain clouded her mother's brown eyes and drew a slight furrow to her brow. She looked groggy, and Angel knew why.

"I hate those drugs when Ethan pumps them in me," she told her mother softly. "Makes me feel all wacky. Like I don't know if I'm really real or not."

Her mother's face softened, though the drowsiness remained.

Angel licked her dry lips, fighting her tears and the complete horror she felt that she'd nearly lost the mother she hadn't even had a chance to get to know.

"Hey, Mom." Bliss moved in closer to her father. "I told Dad you were going to wake up. Now don't try to talk to me, or I'll fuss at you." Her youngest daughter grinned mischievously. "You just lie there and let us spread the love for a while."

Emotion filled Chaya's face, her eyes. Her fingers moved against Natches's as he gripped them and brought them to his lips.

They drifted down again, that drowsiness pulling her back, Angel knew all too well.

"You should tell her about Duke asking you to let him marry Angel, Dad," Bliss suggested playfully. "I thought he was so cute."

He had been cute, Angel admitted silently.

Dropping her hand from the bed rail to her side, the feel of the knife still strapped to her thigh drew her attention.

She didn't know what to do, what to say. She could feel herself trembling, her chest tightening, and she couldn't make sense of the chaos battling inside her.

Her mother's eyes opened again, slowly, her gaze finding Angel.

"You were so little," Chaya whispered, tears glittering in her eyes as Angel felt panic building inside her.

No. Her mother couldn't cry.

"She still looks pretty short to me, babe," Natches said, his voice soft as Angel fought to speak around the lump in her throat. "No more than a li'l bit."

A little bit. It was something she'd heard him call Bliss and her cousins more than once. It was a term of affection. One she hadn't expected, but one she held to her.

"You made me cookies. It was the only thing you could cook without burning the house down." That was one of her favorite memories, though it was more knowledge than memory. "Peanut butter. Bliss says they're her favorite, too."

Chaya's face softened further, the hand nearest Angel lifting weakly, reaching out.

"Momma." Trembling, Angel reached for her hand, forgetting about the knife she held in a death grip until it was in her way.

Taking her mother's hand, she wrapped it around the sheathed blade.

"You gave me the knife, remember?" she said as surprise registered on her mother's face. "You sewed the pocket on my teddy bear so I could hide it there."

Chaya's lips trembled and a tear eased from the corner of one eye.

"No. No, please don't cry." Angel was shaking, trembling so hard her voice shook with it now. "Please don't cry. I'm good. It's kept me safe, just as you said it would. It's yours again now."

Emotion was swamping her. Years of holding everything back and now, to be confronted with a lifetime of dreams, of hopes, and of fears. It was too much.

"Yours." Chaya pushed the knife back into her hand. "Always meant to be yours." Her breathing was ragged.

Angel looked up at Natches worriedly. This couldn't be good for her mother. Too much emotion. And if her momma started crying, then it would hurt her chest.

"I should let you rest. . . ." It was too soon for this. It couldn't be good for her mother's recovery.

Chaya's fingers tightened on hers. Not a lot, but enough to jerk the emotional bonds tighter and hold her in place.

"Had to protect you." Sorrow glittered in her mother's too bright eyes. "You wouldn't hide. . . . Had to keep you safe. . . ."

Tracker had once said Angel didn't know the meaning of the word "hide," let alone "caution" or "defeat."

"I understand," she assured her mother. "I hate it. I'll yell over it later. But I understand."

Chaya's fingers clenched and unclenched weakly against Angel's before she looked at her husband and youngest daughter.

"Keep them safe. . . ." she breathed. "For me."

Pure love filled his face and burned in his fierce emerald eyes. Even after sixteen years of marriage and what had to be a fiery relationship considering the type of man he was, he wore his heart on his sleeve when it came to his wife.

"That's a two-person job, Chay," he said gently. "And she's not used to having a dad yet, so you better get better so we have a hope of keeping the two of them out of trouble."

Worry shadowed Chaya's expression, a weak moan passing her dry lips. "Natches, please . . ."

"Get better, Chay." His voice firmed, his expression tightening with pure challenge. "I can't do it alone. And she's your daughter, honey. Just imagine how stubborn she is." The imperceptible wink he gave his wife softened the determination in his expression, but only marginally.

"You need to rest," Angel told her again, worried about the paleness of her face, the trembling of her lips. "I'll come back later. I promise."

Angel eased her hand from her mother's, then leaned closer and kissed her brow.

"Angel." Chaya breathed out her name, love filling her weak voice. "My baby. I love you. I have always loved you."

Another tear eased from her mother's eyes and ran slowly down her cheek.

"I always knew that." Angel nodded, realizing that the knowledge of that love had always sustained her. "And I've always loved you. Always."

She rushed from the room to Duke as he stood outside the door. And he was waiting for her, his arms enfolding her, his strength and his warmth sinking into her.

"Come on, you two," Bliss announced as she pushed through the door. "I'm hungry. Can we please find some food? I'm a teenager. I need energy."

Angel couldn't help but laugh. Pulling her sister close for a hug, she knew finally she had hope.

No, not finally. She'd always had hope; it had just taken Duke to remind her of that, and to give her a reason to reach out for it. For her dreams.

Natches turned his gaze back to Chaya's, her hand still clasped in his, his battle to hold back his tears hard fought.

There hadn't been many times in his life when he'd actually cried since he was too young to remember. He'd shed tears with Chaya the day she watched that hotel explode with her daughter inside. Holding her, rocking her, loving her, those tears had fallen.

The birth of their daughter. God, he'd had to go hide that night when he'd actually lost the battle with the silent sobs that had welled from inside him.

And when he'd held Chaya, her blood staining the grass in their backyard, certain he was going to lose her, his sobs hadn't been quiet. They'd torn from his soul, shook his body, and spilled as unashamed as a child's.

Now, watching the tears dampen her face, her eyes filled with so much hope, he found himself close to losing the battle again.

"Remember the first time you met her, you said she had too many secrets and too much pain?" he asked her as he dried her tears with his free hand. "And I agreed, and said she reminded me of someone else who once watched the world the same way?"

Her lips trembled and more tears fell. "I was cruel to her. . . ."

"You were scared. And you knew she was hiding things from you that were far too important to remain hidden. Logic said it wasn't possible, but you knew, inside, and you weren't going to tolerate her silence."

"My baby . . ." Her breathing hitched on a smothered sob. "She's too stubborn."

He snickered at her, causing her to frown, causing a bit of fire to burn in her pretty brown eyes.

"She's your daughter." His brow arched. "You couldn't deny it if you wanted to. And from what Duke says, she might be a little better with that knife than you are now."

"Trying to piss me off . . ." she accused him with a little sigh.

"I succeeded." He flashed her a grin, the one he knew she secretly loved, though she often chided him for it.

"I love you . . . so much. . . . " Her words caught him off guard. "With all my soul . . ."

Hell, there went that fucking tear.

Sniffing, he turned his head, wiped it away discreetly, then turned back to her. And she knew. The knowledge of what he'd done was there in her soft brown eyes, in the love that filled her pale face.

"You're my soul," he told her simply. "All that I am is in you, Chaya. Without you . . ." He inhaled sharply. "Fuck!"

"Bad word," she murmured, her eyes drifting closed, but her lips were soft with the beginning of a smile. "My naughty dream . . ."

She drifted away, the weakness, the pain medication slipping past that incredible will she possessed.

She should be dead.

How many times had Doc Marlin and the surgeon, Ben Hart, repeated that phrase?

Ben had been amazed she'd even made it to Lexington, let alone through the first hour of surgery, swearing that if it hadn't been for Ethan's quick thinking, she would have been gone before Life Flight made it to the house.

They'd lost her on the table twice, but each time, she'd come back, struggling to remain, too damned stubborn to give up, and he thanked God for that.

Still holding her hand he laid his forehead against it and let the tears that wouldn't stay contained free.

He wouldn't be able to go on without her, and he knew it.

If he had to, he'd try, for Bliss's sake, but he wouldn't be able to bear it for long. Life without her wouldn't be worth living.

"Shh . . ." The soft sound had a smile touching his lips, despite the emotion pouring through him.

Lifting his head, he wasn't ashamed for her to see the tears. There was no part of him she didn't know about, nothing inside him that she wasn't aware of.

Her eyes were barely open. She was more asleep than awake.

"I'm okay," she slurred. "I promise, wild man. I'm okay. . . ."

Then her lashes drifted closed again, her breathing deepened, and he knew she'd slipped into the healing sleep she needed.

She'd kick his ass later for ordering the doctor to increase the pain medication. But he couldn't bear the pain in her eyes, the knowledge that he hadn't protected her. That he'd let some bastard sneak up and knife him, causing him to be too late to keep her from taking that bullet.

The stitches at his side were barely felt. The knife had missed anything vital, but he'd bled like a stuck pig and been so damned weak he'd stumbled to the house rather than running as he'd fought to do.

Touching her cheek gently he let the tears fall, unashamed and filled with every hope and prayer he could come up with to send to the heavens.

"And I love you, my heart," he murmured. "More than words could ever say, I love you."

EPILOGUE

It was nearly a week later before Chaya came out of ICU. She was still weak but progressing nicely, the doctors promised them. They expected a full recovery, though the scar her mother would carry just beneath her heart, where the bullet had pierced her body, would forever be a reminder of how close she'd come to dying, and they were still uncertain why.

Leaving her mother's hospital room with Duke and Natches, Angel was making a mental note to ask Tracker about that when her foster brother, along with Dawg and Rowdy, stepped from the waiting room to meet them.

"Problems?" Natches asked, moving alongside her as Duke's hand tightened at her hip.

It was enough to make her want to roll her eyes. She had a feeling it was a problem she'd be dealing with as long as there was a Mackay around, though. They were far too protective at times.

"Not sure," Dawg drawled, his expression brooding. "We have company, though."

He turned back to the private waiting room and they followed him in, stopping when the small family awaiting them turned to face them.

"Grecia, look how pretty she has become," Solange Davinov exclaimed as Angel's eyes widened at the sight of the delicate Frenchwoman Grecia had married and left his home country for. "I told you she would be a beauty, did I not?"

Solange was the beauty. At five foot six, fine boned, and dressed in dark blue silk slacks and a gray silk blouse paired with gray heels, she looked cool and sophisticated. Her shoulder-length strawberry blond hair was twisted into a graceful chignon, her wide gray eyes set in delicate, graceful features.

Beside her, tall and regal, Grecia Davinov watched them with a heavy expression, his dark brown gaze direct. He stood head and shoulders above his wife, his thick dark blond hair still cut to an almost-military length, displaying his still-handsome features. With them were Solange's daughter from her first marriage and the young man Bliss was so enamored of, Nickolai Brannigan Davinov.

"She is even more lovely now than ever," Grecia agreed, his expression approving as it went over her. "I am only sorry that we must see her again in such circumstances." He turned to Natches. "Mr. Mackay, I wish there was some way to show the depth of my regret for your wife's injuries. Had I even suspected this would happen, I would have never sent Bran to stay with my good friend Lucas. I would have found another way to ensure his safety, I assure you."

"It would be nice to know exactly why it happened." Natches's tone wasn't exactly friendly.

Grecia sighed heavily.

"Is Mrs. Mackay recovering?" Bran asked, his looks promising to mature to closely resemble those of his father, though his height was nearly there already.

His eyes were a deep hazel brown, gleaming with hints of green as he stared at Natches despite the hard look Natches shot him.

"She's recovering," he answered the younger man. "No thanks to any of you." He turned back to the father. "Want to explain to me what the hell happened?"

"It was my fault, Mr. Mackay." Bran stepped forward, his shoulders back, his jaw clenched. "When Viktor found me at the marina we argued in the parking lot. He thought I should return to Russia with him and force Father to reinstate him into the family. We were arguing in Russian, but Bliss heard us." He pushed his fingers through his longer blond hair in frustration, a grimace twisting his expression. "When I assured him she didn't speak Russian and that she would tell no one of our meeting, he . . ." Bran frowned, his jaw working for a moment. "Bliss is a good kid." He stared back at Natches somberly. "A nice girl. But Viktor thought there was more when there wasn't." He grimaced again, his lips thinning for a moment. "He tried to kidnap her, thinking he could force me to do as he wanted. When my uncle and cousin were killed at the house where they thought she'd been taken, he didn't care if she could be used against me or not. For him and Ilya, it became vengeance then."

Bran was clearly more than a little upset over what had happened. Guilt filled his face, his dark eyes.

"If we had known this was happening, we would have come at once," Grecia assured Natches gravely. "But when Bran told Lucas that Viktor had found him, Lucas took him away for a while until we could decide our best course of action. Lucas only heard of the problems with my family when your wife . . ." He swallowed tightly, anger and regret twisting his features. "When your wife was shot."

Solange touched her husband's arm gently, her saddened expression as sincere as Grecia's and Bran's anger.

"I am very sorry, Mr. Mackay," Bran said, taking the heaviest portion of responsibility onto his own shoulders. "And I would hope you would tell Bliss how very sorry I am that this has happened to your family. She was kind to me when I had no friends. And I appreciate that sincerely."

Angel turned to Natches when he didn't speak. He was staring at Bran, his features hard, his expression revealing very little. The young man didn't flinch beneath his gaze, but there was no doubt he was distinctly uncomfortable and felt responsible for the pain his older brother had caused.

Taking his eyes from Bran, Natches turned to Grecia. "Thank you for coming here, Mr. Davinov," he said quietly. "And thank you for letting us know why we suddenly had Russians targeting our family."

Solange's gaze met Angel's then, worry filling the gray depths as the tension began growing between the two men.

"I am glad, Angel, you have found your parents once again," she stated, her sincerity and the pain she felt evident in her expression as well as her voice. "I can see now where you inherited much of your strength and daring, yes? Your poppa has an overabundance, does he not?"

Angel snorted at that but couldn't help but feel a bit of pride that the other woman believed Natches was actually her father.

"They call it balls around here." She shot Natches then Duke a teasing look.

"Yes, we call it such as well, but I do so like remaining polite when my attempt to make amends for the wrongs of others is ignored. Do you not find it a balm to your pride when you do so?" she asked, clearly hurt that Natches had remained so cool in the face of their apologies.

"It's not the actions of others that keep him silent," she sighed, restraining a spurt of amusement. "It's the fear his daughter's actually become a teenager. It terrifies him."

Solange flicked him a suddenly understanding look before glancing at her stepson. "Ah, I see. Yes, we have this problem as well with my Aleda, do we not, Grecia?"

Her daughter frowned at her as a flush brightened her pretty features.

"Often," Grecia sighed. "I warned her there are many convents in Paris."

Natches seemed to perk up at the comment.

"Think it would work?" he asked the other man.

Grecia shook his head, a long-suffering look of frustration crossing his face. "I fear it would not. She assures me even convents can burn to the ground."

Solange's smile was gentle, though still heavy with sadness. "We have much in common, Mr. Mackay, and, I would daresay, much we need to speak of to repair the damage caused. Let us do so as friends, yes?"

Natches gave a heavy sigh before leveling a hard look on Bran. "Don't flirt with my daughter."

Bran merely stared back at him, his expression becoming chillingly polite despite the heavy frown that began to crease Natches's brow.

"Is he deaf?" he growled then.

"He is a young man." Grecia shrugged as though that explained it all. "He does not take orders well."

"I have a rifle." Natches bared his teeth. "And I know how to use it."

Bran turned to his father. "I will be leaving now, Father," he stated clearly. "I'll wait in the limo."

He walked away, as proud and as arrogant as any Mackay had ever been.

"Dammit," Natches muttered, watching him leave. "Knew I should have checked out those convents for real. . . ."

Photo © Jenna Underwood

Lora Leigh is the #1 *New York Times* bestselling author of the Nauti series and the Breed novels. Visit her online at loraleigh.com, facebook.com/loraleighauthor, and twitter.com/LoraLeigh_1.